FIC   OLDHA
Oldham, Nick, 1956-
Critical threat /
          R0023473418

D0092882

NOV   2007

CRITICAL THREAT

CRITICAL THREAT

Nick Oldham

This first world edition published in Great Britain 2007 by
SEVERN HOUSE PUBLISHERS LTD of
9–15 High Street, Sutton, Surrey SM1 1DF.
This first world edition published in the USA 2008 by
SEVERN HOUSE PUBLISHERS INC of
595 Madison Avenue, New York, N.Y. 10022.
This first trade paperback edition published 2008 by
SEVERN HOUSE PUBLISHERS, London and New York.

Copyright © 2007 by Nick Oldham.

All rights reserved.
The moral right of the author has been asserted.

British Library Cataloguing in Publication Data

Oldham, Nick, 1956-
    Critical threat
    1. Christie, Henry (Fictitious character) - Fiction
    2. Police - England - Blackpool - Fiction 3. Murder -
    Investigation - Fiction 4. Terrorism - Prevention - Fiction
    5. Detective and mystery stories
    I. Title
    823.9'14[F]

    ISBN-13: 978-0-7278-6550-2   (cased)

Except where actual historical events and characters are being
described for the storyline of this novel, all situations in this
publication are fictitious and any resemblance to living persons
is purely coincidental.

All Severn House titles are printed on acid-free paper.

Typeset by Palimpsest Book Production Ltd.,
Grangemouth, Stirlingshire, Scotland.
Printed and bound in Great Britain by
MPG Books Ltd., Bodmin, Cornwall.

To my father, Edward Vincent Oldham.

R0023473418

One

As Sabera walked along that evening she made the fatal mistake of thinking that she was a free woman.

She was on Victoria Street in Westminster with her new friend Aysha, walking away from Parliament Square, feeling more alive and exhilarated than she'd felt in the last four years. Her life had become so stultifying, as though the pillow of a lifestyle that had been imposed on her by duty and expectation was smothering her. It had been a life of restriction, small-mindedness and fear – and she had been treated like a dog. That was not what she had signed up to, not what she had been promised; an existence of subservience instead of equality and of deep fear and loathing for a man who saw himself, and all other men, as masters. He thought nothing of maltreating her and assaulting her and believed it his right to rape her. Which he had done. Twice.

In the end she had broken out of the shackles.

It had taken extreme courage and careful planning on her part to make that break – in the aftermath of the second rape – knowing that once she walked through the door there could never, ever be any hope of a pleasant return.

For weeks following her departure, she had lived in constant, gut-wrenching terror, causing her to lose most of her hair and more than two stones in weight, to become a bag of bones. She hardly dared to venture out, and then only briefly with trusted friends and always watching, expecting the worst, her heart missing a beat at every unexplained shadow or knock at the door. This, despite having run 250 miles from her hometown to one of the biggest cities in the world where, it was claimed, a person could lose themselves for ever.

Paradoxically, the urge to return and face the consequences had been quite strong in her in those first few weeks of high tension. But she fought it, as she knew she must. That would have been what everybody would have expected – her to come snivelling home, throwing herself on her husband's mercy, but Sabera knew he was a man without such a trait. Her life would not have been worth living and the abuse she would have suffered would have been ten times worse . . . add to that the shame the rest of her family and community would have heaped on her . . . she could not have survived such a move.

So she held out, knowing it was the right thing to do. The worst of it was not being able to see her immediate family, mother, father, sister, grandfather, but she did contact them by phone occasionally, ensuring the number she called from was disguised and never telling them where she was. She knew her husband would intimidate and threaten them and they would easily cave in and spill all they knew. If they knew nothing, they could say nothing.

Now it was six months down the line.

There had been one close shave, never to be repeated, an incident that was a steep learning curve but which she had survived intact. But even that unpleasant experience was far from her mind whilst strolling in the pleasant evening sunshine past the rear of New Scotland Yard, swinging her handbag as though she didn't have a care in the world.

The weight she had lost had now returned, and been redistributed in all the right places. She was dressed in a tight, thigh-hugging knee-length skirt – which did retain some of her in-bred and conditioned modesty, and a lovely cream and gold silk blouse which, whilst it did not accentuate her generous bosom, did not hide it either; four-inch heels on smart black suede ankle boots and meticulously applied make-up completed her stunning appearance.

Sabera knew she was strikingly beautiful and was now not afraid to show it to the world, to allow others to look at and admire her without her feeling ashamed or as if she was doing something wrong.

It was as if the world she'd once inhabited was nothing more than a bad, if recurring, nightmare, a world of subservience and near slavery.

No more.

She hadn't gone to university and medical school for all those years to train as a GP suddenly to be informed by her

domineering, violent husband that she could no longer practise medicine simply because he said so. It displeased him.
Her place was behind a veil in the home, caring for him and
their children-to-be. Fortunately she hadn't managed to
conceive; a relief to her, a source of anger for him.

Now, with the help of friends she had made at university
who had also become doctors, she had established herself as
a locum for several health centres in the Earl's Court area of
London. She also ran a weekly support group for abused Asian
women. She was happy to be earning good money, doing
something worthwhile, and feeling truly alive for the first time
in years.

She also had a boyfriend who she was on her way to meet,
along with other friends, at a smart Spanish restaurant on the
ground floor of a shopping mall opposite Westminster
Cathedral.

They hadn't made love yet, despite his urges to do so and
her own feelings deep inside. It was still something she was
wrestling with – being a Muslim, still being married and all
the ramifications that came with adultery. However, she knew
that giving herself completely to this gentle man was something that would happen. They had kissed and lightly caressed
and her whole being had been set on fire by his touch. She
knew that the step over the edge into the abyss of total inti-
macy would be taken soon. Maybe tonight.

She shivered excitedly at the prospect of him on top of her
– or, heavens above, her on top of him. A smile, broad and
mischievous, broke across her face, her thoughts causing her
to miss the last few words her friend had said to her.

'What? Sorry . . . my mind drifted,' she said, giggling.

'I said, there they are.' Aysha pointed to a group of people
seated at the tables on the fenced-off concourse outside the
restaurant. Aysha stopped and gripped Sabera's arm, halting
her. She smiled conspiratorially. 'I think I know where your
mind went,' she said knowingly. The two women looked
into each other's eyes. 'I know you have your doubts, so
make sure this is what you want,' Aysha cautioned, aware
of everything Sabera had gone through to reach this point
in her life.

'Thanks – I will.' They hugged quickly and carried on
walking into the mall.

'He is a bit of a dish, though,' Aysha whispered naughtily out of the corner of her mouth.

'Hands off, he's mine,' Sabera hissed.

They reached the restaurant to the warm greetings of their friends.

Sabera's eyes – deep brown, long-lashed – were only for the handsome, dark-skinned man by the name of Sanjay Khan, a GP at one of the health centres where Sabera was locum. They had known each other since medical school. Sabera's body went limp as Sanjay guided her to the vacant chair he'd saved beside him and whispered words into her ear which made her gasp; simple words no man had ever said to her before: 'You are beautiful.'

Eddie Daley could hardly have been said to be a great, or even adequate, private investigator. His self-produced business card, made at a machine in a motorway service area, advertised him as a retired Lancashire Constabulary detective, which was true, but the other words thereon which insinuated he was honest, loyal and had integrity, were certainly not.

He'd been a sleazy cop, always on the tightrope, before being hounded out of the force following the collapse of a Crown Court trial during which his corruption had been exposed. He had been lucky to keep his pension intact and frozen after twenty-five years of less than honourable service.

Now, at the age of fifty-three, waiting for his pension which he couldn't get his hands on until he was fifty-five, he scraped a living as a sleazy PI, specializing in divorce and surveillance. He got his kicks following people round and then screwing up their lives; or, as he termed it, 'Getting them what they effin'-well deserve.'

Being twice divorced himself, hung out to dry by two ex-wives who still hovered like vultures around his thin assets, also waiting to pounce on his pension, Daley was bitter and twisted and knew what he was talking about. By doing the job he did, he was taking a kind of perverted revenge on his wives, both of whom had humiliated him with their affairs, then gone for his cash.

He didn't usually get involved with Asians because he thought they were far too complicated. He much preferred good old-fashioned English working-class infidelity – cheap hotels and the back seats of cars – because it was usually pretty straightforward. Asians were bad news – having played a significant part in his downfall in the cops – and more often than not they sorted out their own dirty washing, anyway. He did not get much business from that side of the community, so he'd been surprised to be approached for a job and he had taken it only because he saw it was one he could stretch out and milk; and because, having warned the client that it would take time and money – £250 per day plus travel, accommodation and any other reasonable expenses (a figure he had pulled out of the ether and hoped he'd kept a straight face) – the client did not flinch.

On the face of it, it was a fairly simple job: locate and trace.

'We had a very big argument and I said things I wish I hadn't,' the client blubbered through tears which Daley was certain were false. But it was a good act. 'She left me. I am devastated and deeply saddened.' Although he had a hankie to mop his cheeks, Daley wasn't convinced by the display.

'If an adult doesn't want to be found or doesn't want to return home, it's their choice,' Daley explained to the man who had introduced himself as Mansur Rashid. 'And anyway, I thought you lot had inner lines of communication, a bit like a black grape vine?'

A slight shadow crossed Rashid's eyes when Daley had said 'you lot' – but it was gone in a flash. 'I've tried to find her, but there are millions of Asians in this country and no, we do not have a "black grapevine" as you suggest. I have been searching for her for six months and you are my last hope.' He looked forlornly at Daley, his saviour.

'Finding folk is my bread and butter,' Daley said. 'I do it well. But, y'know' – his head shook – 'this one would mean me getting my hands dirty with Asians – no offence intended, mate.' He pulled himself up sharply with a cough of embarrassment. He'd had numerous courses on race relations whilst in the police and none of the learning had ever gone in, even at the time. 'So it'd be quite a hard thing for me, being white an' all that, but I'm sure I could do it.' It was at that point he'd invented his new daily rate, fully expecting Rashid to back off and scuttle away.

He didn't. Rashid simply said, 'I want my wife back. I want to restart our marriage.'

'I'll need a thousand up front – and there's lots of questions I'll need to ask you about your wife.'

'That is fine.' Rashid pulled a buff envelope out of his inner jacket pocket and from it eased out a thick wedge of bank notes, making Eddie Daley's eyes pop open. Rashid counted out the money in twenties.

Daley counted also, his lips moving almost soundlessly – 'Twenty . . . forty . . . sixty . . .' – until Rashid raised his head and pushed the neat pile across the table, sliding the envelope back into his jacket. Instinctively Daley's hand slapped down on the money and virtually snatched it from under Rashid's nose before he had a chance to change his mind.

Daley walked slowly past the Spanish restaurant, inhaling the aroma of garlic, seeing someone tucking into a plateful of seafood paella, both of which made his stomach turn. Personally, he couldn't abide continental food. He was a pie and chips kind of guy – as evidenced by his increasingly rounded figure – and garlic in particular made him want to vomit. Still, each to their own, he thought.

The place was heaving, inside and out, even so early in the evening. Daley noticed that most of the customers – well, a fair few of them – had a swarthy look about them. Not many pasty white English folks digging into greasy, olive oil-laden dishes, he thought proudly.

He passed within a few feet of his target. She, and her companions, did not even glance in his direction. Which was good, how it should be. A follower should simply blend into the background.

Daley's piggy eyes lingered for a few moments on Sabera, but not too long. He'd been tailing her for a few days and liked what he saw. A real dusky maiden with long, lustrous black hair, dark brown, shining eyes and a beautiful face attached to a slender, well-proportioned body by a smooth, long neck. He could understand why Rashid wanted her back. Daley imagined she would be considered to be a bit of a trophy wife within the Asian community. At the same time he could see why she wouldn't want to come back to boring Blackburn, stick a veil over her head and hide her face for the rest of her life.

From what Daley had seen, she had a much freer, more enjoyable life here in London.

He shrugged mentally as he passed the restaurant, took his eyes off Sabera and veered across the concourse to an Italian restaurant at which he could sit outside and keep tabs on her. It wasn't his problem, he thought, as he settled his bulk into a metallic-backed chair and ordered a straight coffee – none of that frothy shit – and a brandy. His job was to find her and report back, even though, strangely for him, he felt a little uncomfortable in doing so.

Something to do with Rashid. Something seedy about the guy.

Still, not his problem. It was husband and wife business. He just had his job to do, sod any other issues.

His drinks arrived. The coffee was an Americano and he winced at its strength, but it tasted good, had a real kick, especially with four sachets of brown sugar tipped into it. Just what he needed to get himself going after such an arduous assignment.

He chuckled. As if!

He took out the crumpled photo of Sabera that Rashid had given him, flattened out the creases and looked at it. He'd been working on the case for five days, which meant he'd earned an extra £250 plus expenses on top of the grand up front. He'd get at least another day out of it because he intended to let it drag on past midnight. On top of that he intended to claim a success fee for finding her – say, £200? He was sure Rashid would be able to afford that.

Five days of hard graft. Digging, travelling, overnight stops, questioning people, making diligent enquiries. Eating expensive – English – meals.

At least, that is what he would be telling Mr Rashid, and producing all the receipts if necessary, even if he had to forge them on his computer.

Truth was, Daley had found Sabera on the second day without actually setting foot out of Blackburn.

So easy. Telephone, combined with the Internet. Wonderful tools for an investigator.

By simply using the information furnished by Rashid, doing a bit of lateral thinking, digging through a few archives, trying to put himself in Sabera's shoes – she was ambitious, a doctor, had friends from university and med school; that and going off the odd snippet of gossip Rashid had related, mainly that

Sabera had always wanted to live in London, Daley had locked on to her.

It was the medical thing that was the main drive, that and that she would probably be using her unmarried name of Ismat. Countless hours of trawling through Internet sites for doctors' surgeries and health centres was where Daley began and ended his search.

It had been hellishly boring, sitting at the computer with a beer in one hand and his lady friend either perched on a knee or occasionally kneeling in front of him.

He worked from a variety of search engines, knowing it would only be a matter of time before he struck pay dirt and found Mrs Rashid, née Ismat, the wayward little minx that she was. It was unlikely that she was a practice partner, but Daley guessed that she could probably find work fairly easily as a locum, and quite a few websites he visited even named the locum doctors who were associated with surgeries, often providing photos and little pen pictures of them too. There were also websites of agencies that represented locums doing much the same.

Daley eventually found Sabera on the website of a health centre in Earl's Court, London. She was using her maiden name, as suspected, and her photograph and a few sketchy details about her qualifications were posted on the site, too.

If she had been trying to cover her tracks, she hadn't done the best of jobs. But that was par for the course for most runaways. Somewhere along the line they usually had to put their heads above the parapet, usually when they felt it was safe enough, or they got sloppy. That was when they got spotted. On the whole, people didn't know how to cover their tracks, and the electronic world, in which every contact left a trace, meant it was particularly hard to stay hidden when people like Daley – who was by no means a web wizard – were after them. Nor did people realize they were being followed – it just wasn't human nature to look over the shoulder – and nor did they realize they were being photographed, even when the guy with the camera was within spitting distance.

Daley fished out his small but powerful state-of-the-art digital camera and switched it on. He was sitting perhaps fifty feet from Sabera and the zoom picked her out a treat, with her head tossed back, sexily revealing the full length of her desirable neck, her hair shimmering like in some sort of shampoo advert on TV, a wonderful, happy smile on her face.

'That's gonna get wiped off, soon,' Daley mumbled as he fiddled with his camera. His job was made easier because a man in another group of people at the restaurant was taking photos of his mates. 'Always hide in plain sight,' the PI said to himself as his two snaps and their accompanying flashes simply became part of the background, drawing no attention to him, even though he was sitting alone.

He examined the results on the display, using the zoom to really focus in sharply on Sabera's face and neck, even down to the unusual pendant on the chain around her long neck. Two good shots. Definitely her. Job done. Seventeen hundred quid in the back pocket – tax-free, of course.

Turning over the photograph Rashid had given him, Daley fished out his mobile phone and called the number scribbled on the back.

There was a bank of flashes from digital cameras, but they meant nothing to Sabera. Her world was focused entirely on Sanjay, with occasional input to the rest of the group just for the sake of sociability. Their eyes constantly locked; they often touched – just a brush of excitement, nothing too obvious, but enough to send shockwaves through each other's body and ensuring that Sabera inhaled deep, shuddering breaths.

They ate sparingly, picking at the numerous plates of tapas on the table without interest, and sipping their drinks occasionally. Two hours passed as if they were only seconds and then the meal was over. The party started to break up until only Sabera and Sanjay remained.

'Well,' he smiled, 'here we are.' She thought he was the most handsome, charming man she had ever met. She was reminded of a young, but darker version of Elvis Presley, without the sneer, just a shy smile. She had found herself opening up to him like no one else before and she felt so comfortable in his presence it was just a little bit unnerving.

'Just the two of us,' he said.

'It's been wonderful.'

'Yes, but I wish it had just been us, no one else.'

'Me too.'

'Maybe next time?'

Sabera put her glass to her lips, eyes playing thoughtfully on him.

'Would you come back to my place for coffee?' he asked hesitantly, raising a hand, palm outwards. 'Nothing more than that, I promise. You can call a taxi from there, or I could walk you home. It's not too far to yours from there.' He shrugged.

'A coffee and nothing more?' she asked suggestively, arching her dark eyebrows and flashing her eyes at him, knowing that she wanted more than that, much more. This would be the night. 'How about a walk first?'

'That would be good. Allow all that food we've eaten to digest.'

They laughed. Both had eaten like sparrows.

Leaving the restaurant and turning left on to Victoria Street, they walked slowly towards Westminster Abbey and the Houses of Parliament, crossing Westminster Bridge and turning down by the London Eye on the south bank of the Thames. Their arms were interlinked and their bodies continually bumped together gently. They did not speak much, just enjoyed the leisurely stroll, the pleasant evening . . . being together.

'You smell amazing,' Sanjay told her, almost conversationally. 'Intoxicating.' They were re-crossing the Thames on the footbridge leading on to Northumberland Avenue and were about halfway across.

Sabera stopped and squeezed Sanjay's arm, pulling him round to face her, blood coursing through her veins, suddenly feeling weak and light-headed, her legs hardly able to keep her upright. The cocktail of emotions she was experiencing was incredibly powerful.

'Hold me,' she gasped. 'Kiss me.'

In the end, Sanjay had almost to keep her from falling over following the kiss. Their lips devoured each other, tongues flashing and tasting each other's teeth and mouths. Never had Sabera been kissed like this – never had a man had his tongue in her mouth, for one thing. In fact, Sanjay was the only man, apart from her husband, she had ever kissed and there was no comparison between the two. Her husband's mouth had always been hard, cold and closed. It had been like kissing a desktop and his kisses had only ever been a prelude to equally cold and hard sexual intercourse, sometimes rape.

But Sanjay knew how to kiss. He knew how to hold her

tight, where to put his hands. She could feel his hardness through the clothing against her belly and she knew she wanted him more desperately than anything, ever.

Their lips parted slowly.

'I'm a married woman,' she whispered.

'I know.'

'This is a big step for me. It has to be right.'

'It is right,' he assured her.

They turned and walked on, unaware of the bulky man fifty metres behind them, camera in hand, watching their every move.

Since leaving her husband, Sabera had kept in irregular touch with various members of her family, making short phone calls, always withholding her number, telling them she was OK, don't worry, she would be fine. She never allowed herself to get into any lengthy conversations with them for fear of her resolve weakening.

But there had been one almost terrible mistake.

Her sister Najma. Sabera had actually kept in touch with her on a more regular basis than with the others. Sometimes the calls were quite long. She trusted Najma implicitly. They had grown up almost inseparable, Sabera being slightly older, and because of this Sabera had allowed herself to be cajoled into having a meeting with her sister. Just so that Najma could see truly that she was all right, so they could hug each other, have a few tears, then part.

The meeting was to take place on a motorway service area – southbound – near to where the M6 joined the M1, south of Birmingham. Najma had made a solemn promise she would tell no one of the meeting, come alone and make sure she was not followed.

It was planned to take place at noon, giving both women the time to travel from opposite ends of the country.

As it was in the very early days after leaving her husband, Sabera was more suspicious and careful than she later became when she thought everything was fine. She drove up the motorway to the junction above the services, circled the round-about, then came back down and parked on the outer edge of the services car park one hour before she was due to meet Najma. And she was in a hire car. She made sure she had a good view of the entry slip road, the car park itself and the entrance to the shops and cafés.

It wasn't that she mistrusted her sister – she didn't – it was more that she feared the deviousness and influence of her husband.

Better safe than sorry.

As it was she was right to be wary. She had only just parked up and settled low in her seat when Najma drove in to the car park in her Nissan Micra, which Sabera recognized instantly, and pulled up near to the shops. Sabera's relief at seeing Najma arrive alone was almost palpable, the pleasure of seeing her overwhelming . . . her hand moved to the door handle and she was about to open it, when something made her hesitate, stay back in the car and sink down low behind the steering wheel. Maybe it was because Najma had never arrived on time for anything, let alone fifty minutes early. A punctual Najma was not the sister Sabera knew, so she waited.

Najma got out of the Nissan and stood by it, looking nervously around and back towards the slip road, checking her watch.

A feeling of dread coursed through Sabera as she observed her sister. Why was she waiting there? They had arranged to meet in the café.

Less than five minutes later a battered Transit van trundled off the motorway and drew into a vacant parking space near to Najma's car. Now Sabera's heart plummeted and caught up with her dread as her husband stepped down from the passenger seat and stretched himself like an overweight lion. Two of his brothers also got out.

The idea that Najma had betrayed her made Sabera want to be sick.

She sank even lower as she watched the four people. Najma and Sabera's husband were having a discussion. He laid his hands on her shoulders and seemed to be speaking soothingly to her whilst she nodded in response to his words.

Sabera sat there stunned as all four of them then entered the services, her husband's hand at the small of Najma's back.

She wanted to believe that Najma was acting under duress, but from what she had witnessed, that was not the case. She gave them a minute, then, eyes blurred with tears, drove off, heading south, lesson learned.

Trust no one.

Since that day Sabera had never spoken to her sister. It wasn't that she totally blamed her, but it meant that any face-to-face contact with any of her family was fraught with danger.

At 2 a.m., Sabera lay awake in Sanjay's flat – in Sanjay's bed – thinking about the incident at the motorway services and how she had felt, whilst fingering the wonderful necklace Sanjay had presented her with earlier that night, a total, incredible surprise. It had been devastating to be let down by Najma and to never speak to her again had been horrible but necessary, even though Sabera desperately wanted to ask her why.

A period of great self-doubt and depression had followed, but Sabera had stuck to her guns because she knew that despite the massive personal cost to herself and her family, she could never return nor let them discover her whereabouts.

And now here she was, having made probably the next biggest step in her life . . . to allow a man back into it.

She sighed and turned her head slowly, brushing her hair out of her face, and looked at Sanjay asleep beside her, his face illuminated by the low-wattage bedside lamp.

It had been more wonderful than she could have imagined – and to be honest, she had feared the worst, a rerun of her husband. But it had been nothing like. She had never experienced anything remotely close to it. That was how it should be all the time. Tender. Loving. Slow-fast-slow, sometimes almost out of control from both sides, but always – always – with love, passion and respect.

And, when he urged her to straddle him, she had done so shyly at first, but finished writhing in ecstasy, her head thrown back whilst they both came together, and she knew it would be all right.

So that's what an orgasm is, she'd thought, smiling to herself as she sank down, exhausted, on to Sanjay's chest. I want more.

She rolled over to face him and laid a warm hand on his chest, touching his nipples with her fingertips. He mumbled something and stirred. She ran her hand across his flat stomach and touched him timidly, feeling him grow. Something else she had never done in her life – taken hold of a man in such a way. With her husband it would have been unseemly and sluttish, even in the early days of her marriage.

From that moment, as Sanjay awoke fully, their lovemaking clicked up a gear to frantic – and fantastic – but this time with Sanjay on top, Sabera's hands stretched above her head whilst he gently held her wrists and moved and wriggled inside her in a way she had never thought possible, touching nerve endings she never thought she had. She rose, once more, to an amazing climax, Sanjay following shortly after, then, spent, his weight crushed down on her.

They lay in each other's arms, sweating, panting, hearts beating, hands touching, caressing, until everything subsided and they fell asleep.

It is estimated that the time of least resistance of the human being is around four in the morning, the time when the metabolism is at its slowest. Which is the exact time that the door to Sanjay's flat was smashed from its hinges by two men bearing sledgehammers. Shattered by the first few blows, the flimsy door virtually disintegrated into splinters and a third man rushed through the newly created opening. It was only a tiny, one-bedroomed flat, and this man entered that room within seconds.

Both occupants, Sabera and Sanjay, woken from their deep sleep, were confused, stunned and frightened, unable to offer any form of resistance.

The lead intruder lunged at Sabera, grabbed a fistful of her hair and hauled her naked out of the bed and threw her face down on the floor. With speed and skill he twisted her arms behind her, knelt down on her spine between her shoulder blades and bound her tiny wrists with parcel tape, which he tore with his teeth. He flicked her over and ran tape right around her face, covering her mouth, preventing any noise.

At the same time, the two others manhandled a dopey and submissive Sanjay, dragged him across the room, and threw him into a wicker rocking chair, to which he was fastened and gagged by more parcel tape.

To secure and gag both of them took less than a minute.

A large, curved knife appeared in the hand of one of the men standing by Sanjay.

He moved behind the wicker chair, yanked back Sanjay's head and held the knife at his throat.

The other men removed the quilt from its cover, then laid the empty cover on the floor and lifted up the now struggling, squirming Sabera and dropped her on to it, rolling her easily in it and binding it with more tape.

Her terrified lover watched in wide-eyed horror from his ringside seat. His eyes rose and looked into those of the man behind him with a knife resting across his exposed throat.

The two men easily lifted the bundle that was Sabera and carried her out of the bedroom between them as though she was a roll of carpet.

The third man stayed with his knife at Sanjay's throat, saying nothing. The incredibly sharp blade began to cut Sanjay's tender skin. Then the two other men returned, accompanied by another who stood directly in front of Sanjay. At first Sanjay could not look at him, jerking his head away, but the man touched his chin and rotated Sanjay's face back.

Instinctively Sanjay knew he was looking into the eyes of Sabera's husband.

Sabera lay bound and gagged, trussed up in the duvet cover. She remained unmoving, trying now to stay calm and concentrate on her breathing, which was proving extremely difficult through the parcel tape wrapped tightly around her face. Her mouth was clamped shut by it and she could just about inhale through one nostril. Even that was not easy as the duvet cover prevented a free flow of air.

Then she started to cry when she thought about Sanjay and what might have happened to him. If he had been harmed, and she was sure he would have been – because it was the way things were – then it was all her fault for recklessly involving him in her stupid, ill-conceived life.

Sobs wracked her body, but it was as difficult to cry as it was to breathe.

And now here she was tied up in the boot of a car, travelling quickly on straight roads – motorways. Had to be. M1 out of London, then on to the M6, heading to the northwest.

Back home.

She began to cry for herself.

Two

Henry Christie had not been having a good time of things recently. Having been harassed and threatened by his boss, Detective Chief Superintendent Dave Anger, over what should have been a long-buried personal matter (Henry had slept with Anger's wife when she hadn't been his wife many years before), Henry had handed the guy's head on a plate, metaphorically speaking, to the chief constable. The side dish had included secretly taken video footage of Anger trashing Henry's trusty Mondeo with a metal bar.

But the organization he worked for – Lancashire Constabulary – had done its usual job of dithering, stalling, 'umming' and 'ahhing' and doing nothing, which it often did in such touchy circumstances. So by default of its inaction, the victim ended up suffering whilst the perpetrator was allowed to carry on, business as usual, and the organization tried to brush the whole sorry mess under the chief's carpet in order not to lose face. Henry thought that there must have been a lot of such bumps under that carpet that no one seemed to have the bottle to stamp on.

What surprised him the most was his own pathetic naivety. He had actually believed that something would be done, that the firm would grasp the nettle, show that it wasn't afraid to address such matters and the offender would get his just desserts and find himself demoted or transferred or fined or prosecuted or jobless even . . . whatever . . . and that the innocent party – in this case, Henry James Christie – would be allowed to continue operating as a senior investigating officer on the Force Major Incident Team knowing that the wheels of justice were grinding away.

Wrong.

Eventually, when nothing happened, when no one from Professional Standards contacted him, when no one from Human

Resources offered him a shoulder to cry on, he took to his local and at the bar had a series of good, long bourbons until he ended up cackling with hysterical laughter at himself and had to be asked to leave because he was frightening the other customers.

Six months down the line, the offending chief superintendent was still at the helm of FMIT in his cushy headquarters office with a nice, leafy view of the sports field, whilst Henry was still on the team sitting in his satellite office ('office' being a euphemism for 'cubby hole') at Blackpool Central Police Station finding his position completely untenable.

He should have known they would close ranks. They always did at that level, rather like the three musketeers – or was it the ten masons? It was made known to him, with some subtlety, via informal inter-force chat lines and bog gossip, that he would not be getting a decent job anywhere again and that it was actually poor Dave Anger who was the victim of a spiteful, unprofessional, unbalanced inspector who was at best unreliable and at worst a dangerous liability who used force resources – unauthorized – to further his ridiculous claims. But these were only whispers, of course. Nothing on paper, zero said to his face. They were a powerful bunch, the chief supers, especially when threatened.

And then came the news that completely floored Henry, making him immediately request an interview with the chief constable – something that proved almost as tough as getting an audience with the Pope.

'Why do you want to see him?' the chief's staff officer had barked down Henry's mobile phone in response to the email request Henry had sent. Henry knew that the staff officer was a filter for all emails to the chief and that he would try to block anything he could. The chief was a busy man and liked to avoid as much work as possible.

'Personal,' Henry said shortly. He had no time for this newly-appointed little jerk of a chief inspector, a jobsworth who had far greater career prospects than Henry had ever had. 'Why?'

'He needs to know.'

'I expect he'll have an inkling.'

'An inkling isn't good enough.'

'I'll tell him when I see him . . . as I recall, I'm not obliged to put it on paper if it's a personal matter.'

'You haven't even put it on paper.'

'Print out the email,' Henry suggested.

'I mean a typed, signed request on form G43,' the chief inspector qualified, getting shirty.

'I'll have it to you in ten minutes.'

'Eh? And how will you achieve that?' said the chief inspector, now a little flustered.

'Ways 'n' means,' Henry said, and thumbed the end-call button on his phone. 'Ways 'n' means,' he said to himself grimly.

The staff officer, whose name was Laker, had obviously expected Henry to be in his office in Blackpool. He was actually at the headquarters training centre on a two-day Race and Diversity course for middle managers, having a mid-morning coffee break in the main dining room. He swigged down his bitter, machine-brewed latte and rose from the circle of other course participants gathered glumly around the table and strutted out to the student resource room next to the training centre reception. He sat down at a free computer and logged in to the system. He opened a word document and bashed out a short, pithy request, hammering the keyboard with his bitten fingertips, hoping that his frustration would pass itself from key to letter. He then printed it off, signed it, logged out.

As he left reception, he passed his shell-shocked classmates trooping back for the next session about transsexuals in the workplace and how to manage them. He could not even be bothered to ask one of them to apologize to the trainer on his behalf for his non-appearance.

He wended his way across the grounds, through the leafy trees and down by the side of the former student accommodation block which had been converted into offices to house the headquarters section of FMIT some years before.

He knew that Detective Chief Superintendent Anger was still sitting pretty in his first-floor office, and it made him shiver, propelling him into a short power-walk across the path that dissected the sports pitches outside headquarters and led directly to its front door. The automatic sliding doors opened and he passed through something resembling an air lock on a space ship into the foyer where he haughtily ignored the receptionist and bore left to the stairs, which doglegged up to the first floor. A man on a mission. He swiped his cardkey through the machine and he was granted access on to the corridor off which all the chief officers had their hidey-holes. It was the only wide corridor in the building, the only one in which it was possible to pass shoulder to shoulder with someone without having to stand aside and let them pass. The only carpeted one that did not creak. Even those thoughts drew a snarl of contempt on Henry's face. As much as he despised it in himself, he could not stop himself from growing more bitter all the time.

He did not even bother to knock on the door which led into the office housing the chief constable's and the deputy chief constable's bag carriers, as the staff officers were mockingly known, and admin support. He just opened it, breezed in, and without acknowledging anyone else in the room, focused on his target and strode across to Chief Inspector Andy Laker. New to both job and rank he looked a little shocked into Henry's glaring eyes as though he was just a probationer faced with one of the many dinosaurs in the force.

'Henry,' Laker said with a shaky swallow and a rise and fall of the Adam's apple. He quickly pulled himself together. 'I thought you were in—'

'Blackpool? Nah.' Henry smiled falsely. He handed his hastily concocted report to Laker, suddenly aware that two lines of text – one and a half lines to be exact – seemed woefully inadequate.

Laker glanced at it with an expression of resignation, then looked wickedly up at Henry. 'I didn't know your surname was Christ.' There was a degree of malicious pleasure in his tone.

'What?' Henry heard a muffled guffaw from the staff behind him. He snatched the report back. He had indeed written 'Christ' instead of 'Christie' in his angry eagerness to get it done. Typing was not one of his strong points at the best of times, being a two-fingered thumper. He stole a quick glance at the others in the office – two secretaries and an inspector who was the deputy chief's staff officer. They had been watching Henry's antics, but their eyes dropped with alacrity as he looked round at them with madman eyes. They were all suddenly glued to the work on their desks, not a sign of a snigger on any of their faces.

Henry's attention returned to his report. 'Typo,' he said,

sniffing, found a pen on Laker's desk and added the missing letters of his name as neatly as possible.

'Thought you might be getting ideas above your station,' Laker commented as he took the amended report back between his finger and thumb and dropped it into his in-tray. 'See what I can do.'

'Sooner rather than later.'

'It'll be processed,' Laker said with a shrug and Henry knew he had to back off. Pursuing the pen-pushing idiot too far would result in the request finding its way to the bottom of the pile – again and again.

'Thanks.' Henry swallowed and turned to leave just as the door to the chief constable's office opened and the man himself appeared with one of the divisional commanders, the chief superintendent in charge of Blackburn division, their meeting having ended. They were having a bit of a chuckle at something, then shook hands. The divisional commander bade the office a grand goodbye, then left.

'Right, good,' said the chief. He turned, saw Henry – but looked right through him – and without saying a further word retreated into his cosy office, closing the door.

Henry's nostrils flared. It was almost as though the guy didn't know him. Twisting to Laker, he said, 'Can I see him now?'

Laker shook his head, his supercilious eyes half shut, a slight grin on his lips. 'Appointments.'

Suddenly the chief's door reopened and the tubby incumbent poked his head out, bellowing across at Laker, who winced, 'What's next? Completely forgotten.'

'Erm . . .' Laker consulted his computer, tapping on the keyboard to bring up the chief's electronic diary. Henry's eyes zoomed in on the screen and even before Laker had seen it, Henry said, 'It says "office", sir,' over his shoulder. 'Next appointment half an hour.'

'Right, ta.'

'Henry,' Laker growled warningly under his breath, sensing the next move.

'So could I possibly bob in and have a quick word? Sir? If that's not too presumptuous?'

He was unimpressed.

'Downright bloody cheeky, not presumptuous,' the chief

constable corrected Henry, pointing him to the low leather sofa in his office with a flick of the finger. 'This'd better be quick. I don't do unannounced visits. Sit.'

The sofa was just comfortable enough. Not too soft so as to let someone sink into it, but just enough to lull them into a false sense of security. Henry sat, but didn't lean back. Instead, his elbows were dug into his knees, his fingers loosely interlocked in front of him.

The chief sat on the arm of the leather chair opposite: management body language for 'You're not staying long, mate.' A large, beech-framed, glass-topped coffee table divided the two men.

'Well?'

There was a slight hesitation as Henry gathered together his thoughts, staring at the carpet. He hadn't actually expected to be sitting across from the chief constable so PDQ and he didn't want to blow it through lack of preparation. He pursed his lips and looked up.

Robert Fanshaw-Bayley – known as FB – was the chief constable of Lancashire Constabulary. FB was an affectionate term used by the people he hadn't yet wronged. 'That 'effin' bastard' was a phrase often bandied about by those leaving his company less than pleased with the result, ensuring that FB also stood for something not very nice. He had been a career detective who had risen surely through the ranks within Lancashire, clinching the helm of the organization following a short stint out of force.

He and Henry went back a long way and they had always maintained a less than healthy relationship, biased in favour of FB, who used Henry's skills, often ruthlessly, to achieve results, then discarded him when it suited. Henry had once believed that FB quite liked him and he definitely had some good things to thank him for, but that belief had just been another example of Henry's naivety. Since the incident with Dave Anger, when Henry had expected FB to be ruthless, the chief constable had actually dropped Henry like a handful of hot cat shit.

FB waited.

'I just want to know what's happening, that's all.'

'How do you mean?'

'With me and Anger, of course,' he said irritably. 'I'm still

holed up as a temp DCI in FMIT and he's still the department head. He's still running the show like nothing's happened
and I'm sat there with my thumb up my ring piece. My life
is a bloody misery and I've done nowt to deserve it, except
stand up to a bully. The only thing that's kept me sane is the
Trent trial.'

'Well, you know' – the chief twisted his head as though
his neck was hurting, but Henry recognized it as a monstrous
nervous tic – 'these things move slowly.'

'Boss – I'm the victim in all this and I'm the one on the
ropes here. The guy who harassed me, damaged my car, is
still my boss and now I'm starting to pick up the vibes that
I'm the baddie in all this and that no one wants to know me.'

'Henry – I feel like flicking your fat, blubbering bottom lip
and making you go, blub, blub, blub like a babykins.' FB's
face hardened. 'You've got a whiney voice and you feel sorry
for yourself – snap out of it!'

Henry bridled. Heat ran up his spine. He sat bolt upright.
'I have the right to know what's happening. No one has been
in contact with me, no one at all. You and me go back one
hell of a long way and I deserve something from you at least.'
Henry's mouth tightened. 'Have the divvy commanders rallied
round him, the other chief supers? Am I screwed career-
wise?'

FB shuffled uncomfortably, pulling at his collar, which was
tight fitting around his plump neck. 'The divisional
commanders are a pretty influential lobby.'

Henry shook his head in disgust. He sat back, unable to
conceal his cynicism. 'And is it true about the footage I got
of him trashing my car?'

FB's body language began to leak like a drain, reinforcing
Henry's position even more. 'Is what true?' he croaked.

'Unexplainably gone AWOL.'

FB looked away.

'It bloody has, hasn't it?' Henry had only ear-wagged a
rumour that the film he'd managed to obtain of Dave Anger
merrily smashing his Mondeo to pieces had gone walkabout.
There had been nothing confirmed about it – until now.

'I'm afraid it has.'

'Oh dear.' Henry sighed.

'These things happen.'

Henry slumped back on to the sofa, his face angled towards the ceiling. 'Was anybody going to tell me officially?'

'At an appropriate moment, of course, yes.'

'I take it the mobile phone records are still intact?' He was now referring to the phone company records of the text messages that Anger had sent him, mostly of a threatening nature.

'They are.'

'Well, that's something.' Henry chewed the inside of his cheek noisily for a while as though chewing the cud. 'This ain't going anywhere, is it?'

'Probably not,' FB said, pouting.

'And what's happened to my extra pip?' He touched his shoulder. Now he was talking about the promotion to the substantive rank of chief inspector FB had promised him, which had never materialized. At the moment Henry was still temporary in the rank, which meant it could be taken away from him in the blink of an eye.

FB remained silent, cogitating, doing what chief constables do best – as little as possible. He stood up and thoughtfully paced the large office, pausing at the window to gaze blankly across the sports pitches that Henry had hurried across a few minutes earlier. He turned.

'What exactly do you want out of this?'

'It's not about wanting something. It's about principles. About seeing justice done,' he spouted grandly. 'A bit of belief that the organization actually does what it says in all those highfalutin policies about equal opportunities and fairness and all that – y'know, the drivel that's being rammed down my throat across at the training centre right now. How can I be expected to "walk the talk"' – Henry twitched the first two fingers of both hands to represent speech marks – 'when I don't have any faith in the firm itself?'

FB blinked theatrically, then looked at Henry as if he were dumb. 'Fine words, noted . . . now what do you want out of all this?'

'Anger to be dealt with. Him to suffer, not me.'

'And in the real world?'

The words permeated into Henry's noggin. He held up his hands in submission. 'It's quite obvious you don't want the stink this would cause, making the organization look bad.'

'Thing is,' FB explained, 'other than his minor problems with you, Dave Anger is the best head of FMIT yet. He's respected and liked by the divvy commanders and his clear-up rate is excellent. Everyone who works for him likes him . . . but then again, not every one of them has screwed his wife.'

'It was a drunken one-night stand over twenty-five years ago and she wasn't even his wife then,' Henry bleated. 'They weren't even going out with each other.'

'I know, I know . . . I just didn't expect the kind of back-lash that came with all this, OK?'

'All right,' Henry said, taking in the reality of the situation and the invertebrate in front of him, 'what do I want? Substantive DCI . . . somewhere other than FMIT, say Major Crime . . . otherwise I'll be knocking on the doors of the federation's solicitors with my tale of woe and I'll drag this whole thing through an employment tribunal, the press and maybe the court. The local rag loves dishing the dirt on us.'

'Henry,' the chief declared, 'I always knew you were a cunt.'

'And I always knew you were one, too. Sir.'

They came out of the office, all smiles and handshakes for the benefit of the chief's entourage.

'How's the trial progressing?' FB asked. 'I know it constantly makes the papers, but I only get a chance to glance.'

'They've had a break this week . . . the final summing-up begins next Monday. Hopefully verdicts by the end of the week. Looks good, though.'

The trial at Preston Crown Court of Louis Vernon Trent had been going on for six weeks and Henry had been present every single day. Trent stood charged with the murder of several young children and a police officer, amongst many other serious matters. The trial had attracted massive media attention across the world. Henry had been involved in Trent's arrest and had spent the bulk of his time leading up to the trial ensuring that the complex case was watertight – and the proof was now in the pudding. As difficult and challenging as it had been putting the case together, Henry was convinced Trent would be spending the rest of his misery-causing life behind bars, unless he escaped, something he had a knack for.

'Good stuff, but he really deserves to be hung,' FB said, patting Henry on the shoulder and opening the door which led out into the corridor, ushering him out with an 'I'll let you know about things, but don't harass me for a while, OK?' Just before he closed the door, Henry caught sight of the new deputy chief constable, Angela Cranlow, emerging from her office. It was the first time he had ever seen her in the flesh and he was quite taken aback, but didn't get much chance for a lengthy appraisal as FB's hand in the middle of his back propelled him out like a drunk being ejected from a bar into an alley.

He exhaled and rubbed his face, turned and walked towards the stairs as his mind tumbled over what had just taken place in FB's office. He was only vaguely aware of the door reopening behind him and the quick approach of footsteps – then a hand on the shoulder.

It was Chief Inspector Andy Laker – bag carrier extraordinaire.

'Henry,' he growled low, 'don't you ever do anything like that to me again. I can see why you're a pariah. You are a loose cannon and you need putting out to grass.'

With disdain, Henry peeled Laker's fingers off his shoulder and flicked them away. 'Fuck off,' he said, proud of his well thought out retort. 'And another thing' – Henry turned and stepped menacingly towards Laker, making the smaller man step nervously back – 'don't mix your metaphors. It doesn't suit you.'

With that, he spun away, leaving the staff officer speechless in the corridor, his mouth popping like a grounded fish.

Henry could not quite face going back to the classroom and being bombarded with race and diversity, particularly as the theme of the day was gender issues, including transsexuals, transvestites . . . trans-everything, most of which just made him angry. The race stuff had been quite interesting, all about Islam and religion, but men becoming women, or wearing women's clothing other than in a pantomime? It made his blood boil. It was like most things these days. He felt like he had become an angry old man and it didn't feel good.

Instead he meandered down to the HQ canteen and was just in time to rescue two sausages and wrap them in bread before breakfast time ended. Then, with a strong coffee he found a table in the corner of the room, and sat, observed and pondered as the food and drink calmed his soul.

* * *

With the dubious expectation that he was about to meet and
be treated to the tale of woe of a man who had undergone a
sex change operation and been discriminated against as a result
– boohoo, Henry thought – he made his way back to the
training centre with a heavy heart, wondering in a very un-
PC way where they managed to unearth such people who were
happy to be wheeled out in front of a class of cynical cops
to face a barrage of nooky questions. He guessed a nice, fat
daily rate helped to grease the wheels.

The footpath across the sports pitch carried on through the
pleasantly wooded grounds of the centre, past the FMIT block,
which he had no intention of visiting. Even his training course
had more allure than that.

As he rounded the corner of the block, he ran into Dave
Anger emerging from the front door, pulling on his jacket.
They almost collided face to face, but managed to stop a foot
apart.

Henry's heartbeat moved up a pace.

'Henry,' Anger said. At least the guy looked as rough as a
dead badger, with dark circles under his eyes, his skin a deathly
pallor, his lips drawn and scrawny.

'Dave.' Henry didn't bother with a 'sir' or anything
approaching respect. 'I've just been to see the chief.'

'I know – that's where I'm going now.'

'To discuss yours truly?'

'Don't think you're that important, pal,' he said. 'Maybe
we'll get round to you if we need a laugh.'

'Funny about those tapes going missing,' Henry said.

Anger's eyes narrowed behind his small round glasses.
'Nothing to do with me,' he said with a twitch of his shoulders which looked like someone had just walked over his grave.

'Course not.'

'Anyway – excuse me.'

'Certainly.'

Anger grimaced a tight smile and eased past Henry on the
narrow path.

'By the way,' Henry couldn't resist calling. Anger's shoulders drooped visibly. He turned, a hateful expression on his
face.

'What? You want to rub it in? How good she was?'

Henry crinkled his nose. 'Nah . . . I don't even remember

it . . . is that worse?' he asked, although he was fibbing. One could hardly forget having sex with a randy young police-woman on the bonnet of the commandant's car at the regional training centre. Not an experience easily erased from the mind. 'No, it's not about that.'

'What then?'

'D'you think I'd be daft enough not to have a copy of the tape?' With a smirk of triumph, Henry continued his journey back to the classroom, hoping Anger would stew, even though it was a lie. He didn't have a copy.

The graphic details of the sex change operation – including a toe-curling PowerPoint presentation – made Henry squirm and cross his legs like most of the other guys in the room. The ladies seemed to be revelling in the male discomfort, whilst the speaker, the one who had undergone the op, was very blasé about the whole thing.

When the lunch break came, Henry knew there was no way he could ever eat anything after watching such a gruesome spectacle, so he decided on a stroll around the grounds.

He mulled over whether his career as a detective was truly over as he walked past the slimy duck pond in the direction of the huge building which housed the firing range. The deal he had hatched with the chief was that if Henry quietly let the Dave Anger 'thing' drop, there would be an extra pip on the way and a transfer. That latter bit needed to be worked out, as most of the chief inspector roles within force were filled. FB said he couldn't promise a detective role immedi-ately and left it at that. Still, Henry thought philosophically, two years more on a chief inspector's wage before retirement; maybe he could hack it anywhere they put him and then do a runner with the enhanced pension and substantial lump sum he would receive.

Walking past the rear of the training admin building, Henry bumped into an old colleague of his, a guy called Bill Robbins, a PC who was a firearms instructor. Bill had about the same length of service as Henry and they had worked as constables together in the early eighties. Bill was a cool, laid-back sort of bloke who played a mean bass guitar in a rock band in his spare time, a gift Henry envied. He was also a brilliant shot.

However, today he looked out of sorts.

After a bit of mutual back-slapping, they both commented on how miserable each other looked – 'you look like you've seen your arse' being the exact phrase Henry used to describe just how morose Bill was looking.

'I can't believe it,' he moaned. 'I work here training all the time and now they also want us to go out on bloody shifts, like we don't have a day job! They wring every last drop out of you these days . . .' He shook his head in disgust. 'You look like you've seen my arse, too.'

'Is it that one with a big black hole in it?'

They chuckled, then Bill looked slyly at Henry. 'How do you fancy a bit of a blast, shake some cobwebs off?'

It was totally against procedure, but what the hell. Henry fancied living dangerously for once.

He had a pair of ear defenders around his neck, a pair of protective goggles covering his eyes.

Similarly attired and standing next to him, Bill held up the weapon for Henry to see. He recognized it instantly. 'Smith and Wesson, .44 Magnum,' he gasped. 'Hell.'

'The very one,' Bill said. 'Handed in at the recent firearms amnesty and strangely enough, no criminal history to it.'

'Aren't you supposed to destroy stuff that's handed in?'

Bill smiled conspiratorially. 'Always keep the cream of the crop – for educational purposes only, of course . . . and to play with.'

He handed the revolver to Henry with the cylinder open and empty. Henry took the heavy beast into a sweaty palm, feeling the weight pull his hand down. All thoughts of FB, Dave Anger and other associated things were suddenly banished from his mind. That is what handling a gun does – purges everything.

It was a wonderful piece of equipment, substantial, black and dangerous looking.

'It came with two hundred rounds of Magnum ammunition. I've tested it already,' Bill said. 'It's wick.'

'OK.'

'Want a go?'

'Yeah, I could do with the release.'

Bill gave him two speed loaders, six thick, chunky bullets in each, which looked capable of taking down brick walls.

They turned to face down the firing range, which was fifty metres long.

'How about a walk through? Keep it simple, but fun?'

The range lights dimmed to recreate conditions a firearms officer might have to face in a building in real life. Right at the end of the range, fifty metres away, were four targets turned facing him, the classic combat target of the charging armed man with the rings centring on his body mass. Ten metres in front of him, jutting out of the right-hand edge of the range, was a waist-high mock brick wall made of hardboard; ten metres further, on the opposite side, was another wall; then ten metres further a stack of old car tyres and an old fridge.

Henry stood ready at the fifty-metre mark, jacket off, ear defenders in place, safety goggles secure, feet shoulder width apart, the heavy weapon held in his right hand, left hand clamped underneath it for support, the muzzle pointing downwards to a point about three feet in front of him. Six bullets had been loaded. The tip of his right forefinger rested on the trigger.

He was suddenly extremely nervous. His mouth had dried up, his legs gone slightly weak with excitement. He had given up breathing.

Bill, positioned a pace behind Henry, placed a hand on Henry's shoulder. 'Be ready for the recoil,' he warned. Henry nodded, focused on what lay ahead. 'Are you ready to shoot?'

'Yes.' He was a hundred per cent aware of how his body was feeling.

In his hand Bill held the remote control, no larger than a TV remote, which controlled everything in the range from the movement of the targets to the lighting, to background music if necessary.

There was an interminable pause – probably no more than two seconds although it seemed for ever – giving Henry the chance to scan the range ahead and take in the obstacles.

Bill pressed a button on the remote and all four targets spun out of sight.

Henry swallowed nothing.

'As discussed?' Bill asked – because as against procedure as this little foray might have been, he had gone through a thorough, rigorous pre-shoot safety briefing with Henry.

'Yes.'

Another pause, then, 'Watch and shoot.'

Bill patted Henry on the back and he started to walk slowly forwards, revolver still pointing towards the floor.

Three metres down, one of the targets spun to face him.

Henry reacted. He stopped, adopted the classic combat stance, bouncing down on his knees, bringing up the gun at the same time and double-tapped – bam! bam! The gun recoiled wildly as the powerful bullets exploded out of the muzzle. The noise in the confined space, in spite of the earmuffs, was incredible.

The target spun away, having shown for two seconds.

Henry knew he had missed at this distance.

A bead of sweat trickled down his temple. He lowered the gun, gritted his teeth and walked on, two rounds discharged, ensuring he remembered how many he had fired. It was easy to forget in the heat of the moment.

Two different targets spun to face him. Henry took them in and was surprised to see that one of them was a woman holding a baby; the other was the gunman. He dropped into the combat stance and double-tapped the correct target, again knowing he had missed.

Four gone, two left.

The targets clattered out of sight.

Henry walked another two metres and a single target appeared, into which he drilled his remaining bullets, now having got some measure of the recoil of the huge gun. Before the target disappeared, Henry dropped to one knee behind one of the walls and transferred the gun into his left hand, whilst at the same time flicking open the cylinder and ejecting the spent cartridges on to the floor behind him with an exaggerated flick of his hand. He fumbled in his pocket and found the speedloader, slotting the bullets into their new homes, then stood up, ready again – just as two targets reappeared, both wielding firearms.

He reacted instantly, a double-tap for each of them, and was feeling pretty good at the result.

Four bullets gone, two remaining . . . he walked on, heart pulsating, sweat dripping, adrenaline gushing . . . ready to shoot again.

*   *   *

'And I am a transsexual,' the person at the front of the class-room announced proudly, bringing an inner groan from Henry, who began to wonder how much more of this he could stand as his eyes flickered to the transvestite sitting next to the trans-sexual. It was becoming a freak show and he could sense a creeping feeling of despair in the room from all the other delegates. And there was another session to go after this.

He could still feel the kick-back of the big revolver in his hands, smell the cordite in his nostrils, and half-wished he had the Magnum in his possession to see how well he could double-tap live targets. I'd give them a head start, he thought sportingly, then hunt them ruthlessly down.

He twitched as his mobile phone vibrated in his pocket. He sneaked it out and glanced at the newly arrived text message asking him to contact the force incident manager regarding a murder which had just been reported. He didn't want to jump for joy that some poor unfortunate person had been killed, but at least it got him out of this purgatory, because if he stayed there was every chance there would be a gender-bender-related murder.

Three

Six months later

As much as Henry Christie had been assured at the 3 a.m. briefing that his task, his responsibility, during the oper-ation – codenamed 'Enid' – was probably the one with the least chance of risk associated with it, he could not help but feel just a little bit excited.

It had been stressed that his role was peripheral to the main operation and, more subtly, that he was there only to make up numbers; it was just that they needed someone of his rank to help out and because chief inspectors were thin on the ground for various reasons; the corporate barrel had been scraped and Henry had been found lurking in a crack like an ugly germ.

Obviously that had not been said out loud at the briefing, but Henry knew this to be the case. He had been called in because no one more suitable – preferable – was available and they needed someone of his rank to hang the blame on should something in his corner of the op go tits up. The 'no blame culture' that had been bandied about a few years before was now a dead duck, floating feet up in the water. Today's climate of fear and failure in policing definitely needed scape-goats, hence Henry's presence. If it all went well, then he wouldn't even get mentioned in dispatches. It was one of the things that came with being someone who was considered too hot to handle, someone who nobody even wanted to be near enough to cattle-prod away.

But for once, Henry couldn't care less, because for the first time in an eon, he was feeling enthusiastic.

It came not from the minor role, but from the feeling that had made being a cop so worthwhile throughout his long, often tortuous career. Here he was, sitting in a scruffy, battered police personnel carrier, kitted up to the eyeballs in protec-tive equipment like a Jedi knight, in the dead of night, amongst a feral gang of Support Unit officers who belched, swore, farted, laughed and joked, and didn't give a rat's scrotum whether or not Henry was a chief inspector, because they knew they were good, the best. They knew their job and as soon as they stepped out of their van, they would leave the childishness and inappropriate behaviour behind and become cold, ruthless and professional whilst performing their allo-cated task. He'd once been on Support Unit and had been just the same.

It was 4 a.m. now. An east Lancashire dawn was just around the corner. The streets of Accrington were damp and silent and a dozen hairy-arsed bobbies were raring to go on the word of command.

What could be better than this?

Henry was back at the razor sharp end after months of lying fallow. A wonderful sensation. Out playing with the lads 'n' lasses (there were two female officers in the back of the van and the rather butch sergeant next to him), just waiting for the nod via his earpiece. It was something he didn't do enough of these days, rarely getting the chance to grubby-up his hands with day-to-day policing.

The buzz was incredible.

Just sitting in the front of the van on the bench seat with the sergeant squeezed between him and the driver. Biding time. When every other non-crim soul was tucked up in bed asleep, he was out on the streets.

He was even in uniform, wearing his public order overalls – which, if he was honest, he'd had to cram himself into, steel toe-capped boots and a flat uniform cap with the chequered band. The chief inspector's model, of course, with a bit more padding for the brain than the plebs of lower rank were issued with. However, no matter what sort of police cap he wore, he always thought he looked more like a bus conductor because, for the sake of comfort, he always wore it tipped on the back of his head.

Here they were, waiting for the signal, all systems go.

Despite the air of flatulence, Henry could not mask his smile. In the next few minutes, a collection of size eleven boots and heavy metal, double-handed door openers would combine as his team for the night 'front-and-backed' a terraced house and then, as the doors flew off their hinges, they would pour in like wolves. Around the division, half a dozen similar raids were being choreographed concurrently, one of them being a fully armed incursion.

Terrorism was in the neighbourhood and this was the police response to it.

Henry's smile became grim. How the world had changed, he thought sadly, wondering what would greet his team as they roared into the target address. His smile changed again, this time becoming twisted and sardonic, when he realized that if his one and only fleeting experience with the Security Services was anything to go by – and it seemed that most of the intel for Operation Enid (who the hell chose that name?) had come from MI6 – Henry's raid could go one of a number of ways. Either it could be spot on as promised, or it could be completely the wrong address, or, worst case scenario, they'd barge into a highly dangerous terrorist cell hiding out in a booby-trapped house and get themselves either blown up, or shot to bits.

'Excuse me, boss,' the sergeant next to him said, interrupting his thoughts, 'but are you OK?'

'Yeah, yeah, why?'

'It's just you had a bit of a strange look on your face, that's all.'

'I'm fine.' Henry folded his arms, tilted his head back and tried to relax. There was no point in fretting about anything now. What would be would be. He closed his eyes and took in a deep breath through flared nostrils, exhaling slowly and thought, with more than a trace of bitterness, that whilst he was excited to be involved in Operation Enid, the reality was he would have much preferred attending the scene of some grisly murder or other. That was what he really loved doing. He truly believed he had found his niche as a senior investigating officer after years of bouncing around in various detective roles, but other people had other ideas. Obviously.

He was as sure as he could be that he had investigated his last murder.

And that irked him personally, because the key word was 'investigated', not 'solved'. He hadn't come anywhere near solving it, hadn't even started investigating it properly.

He uttered a snort of contempt without meaning to, which he covered up with a cough when he opened his eyes and squinted at the sergeant, who was still giving him curious looks.

'Sure you're OK, boss?'

'Yep, yep, fine.'

She regarded Henry as if he were strange.

The uncontrollable snort had been uttered as he had thought about that last murder six months earlier and how things had changed for him in the intervening time . . .

When he had discourteously flounced from the Race and Diversity training course, he had been eager to get to the scene of the murder, even though he had only the sketchiest of details. Because he believed he had been sidelined and given only dross to do, he was desperate to grab this one by the throat and make it his. He knew he had to get in there quick, take charge and stomp his identity on to the front of the policy book. If he dallied he knew there was the probability of some more favoured detective being handed the job by Dave Anger. He needed to ensure a fait accompli.

He had traded in his trusty Ford Mondeo after Dave Anger

had trashed it and bought an almost new Rover 75, which was slotted into a tight space at the far end of the training centre car park. He rushed across the tarmac in a very ungentlemanly fashion, before manoeuvring it out of its spot and speeding out of the headquarters complex, slowing only for the road humps on the drive.

He arrived at the scene within half an hour, having managed to elicit more information en route: a burned body had been found on the edge of a piece of woodland not far from the Kirkham exit of the M55, junction 4. That was really all he needed to prepare himself. The rest he would discover on arrival.

Sitting, eyes shut, in the personnel carrier, Henry could still visualize the body.

He'd had a bit of a run of bodies that had been set alight. There had been the low-life Manchester drug dealer whose charred remains had been found just inside the Lancashire border; then, unconnected, the sad remains of a young girl in the back of a car in Fleetwood which had been torched when her abductors panicked. That had been the work of Louis Vernon Trent, who Henry had hunted down and who now languished in prison serving life following the successful Crown Court trial.

Now this one.

Henry had got results on the first two, but as he looked at what was left of his hat-trick, he had one of those queasy sensations that experienced investigators are prone to, telling him this was not going to be an easy one. No quick glory here, he thought. A hat-trick, maybe, but third time unlucky, too.

At least he could not fault the initial response of the uniformed officers. It had been done by the book. Nothing at all wrong in that. The first cops to arrive had actually done a great job.

As ever, priority had been given to identifying the crime scene itself. In this case it was far wider than just the area immediately around the body. Following directions given, Henry found the entrance to a farm track off the A583, about halfway between junction 4 and the small town of Kirkham. And it was from this entrance that the scene was protected. A few police cars were parked on the main road, including a

Scientific Support van. Several white-suited people were hanging about as well as officers in uniform and a guy with a broken shotgun over his arm and a spaniel. Henry pulled in a hundred metres away and walked the rest on foot.

A man broke from the huddle and approached him. It was Rik Dean, a detective sergeant based in Blackpool, and well known to Henry. Rik was one of the good guys and Henry, seeing his potential several years ago, had assisted him to get on CID initially, but his promotion to DS was entirely Rik's own doing. He was an excellent thief taker and was also proving to be an excellent supervisor, even if he did have an eye for the ladies which sometimes got him into warm water.

'Henry – glad it's you.'

They shook hands. 'What we got, pal?'

Rik turned away from the road and looked across the fields. He pointed. 'This track – it's narrow, wide enough for one vehicle at most – leads up to those woods.' His finger was aimed at what was basically nothing more than a copse in a hollow in the middle of a field, maybe two hundred metres from the road. '"Staining Woods", they're called. The track here leads to the edge of the trees and the body was discovered ten, fifteen feet inside the perimeter of the trees.'

'Discovered by?'

'Local guy hunting foxes on the land – with permission,' Rik added quickly. 'Literally stumbled over the body in his wellies. That's him.' He indicated the man with the shotgun and dog Henry had already noticed.

'The body?'

Rik shrugged. 'Burned to a crisp, almost to the point of breaking up, particularly the legs and arms. Looks like the local wildlife have been having a barbecue.'

'Male, female?'

'Hard to say, other than the body's about five-six, slim, so fair guess is female. No other distinguishing features at the moment.'

'Been here how long?' Henry asked, aware he had constructed the question rather like that strange little creature in the Star Wars films.

'Not too long. Day or so, probably.'

'OK, let's have a nosey.'

The lane, and the fields ten metres either side of it, had

been cordoned off to preserve any evidence as this was the most likely route the person who had dumped the body would have taken. This meant that Henry – once attired in the obligatory white suit and wellingtons provided by the CSI guys – had to approach by a very circuitous route, through hedges, over dykes and across fields, before even getting to the immediate scene itself.

All this Henry approved of, though one of the things he decided to do as he tramped across a boggy patch was to widen the scene even more.

As Rik had said, the body was lying inside the woodland, in a small depression in the earth.

A tape had been slung from tree to tree around this part of the scene, preventing unauthorized access. A miserable looking PC with a clipboard ensured all details of people coming and going were recorded. A crime scene investigator was down near the body, photographing and videoing busily.

Henry didn't want to get too close because the fewer who went up to it, the better. Once he was convinced that all the evidence that could be collected had been, then he'd have a closer look. He just wanted to become familiar with the scene, start drawing hypotheses, then pull back and allow the specialists and scientists to get on with their tasks.

'From what we can gather from the guy who found her, the body had been lying face down in that hollow,' Rik explained. 'He's apparently been chasing a fox on foot with the dog – who's called Pepper, by the way. The fox has nipped into the woods and the guy's run after it. The dog, by all accounts, just leapt across the body, while he tripped over it at a fair whack. He's gone flying, dislodged the body, his shotgun's gone spinning out of his hands, and he's ended up on the ground face to face with a screaming skull. Scared the living crap out of him.'

'Is he a suspect?'

Rik shook his head. 'Nah . . . but he's going to be interviewed properly shortly.'

'Good – and the fox?'

'Not yet managed to trace it,' Rik said with a straight face, 'but I've already got a team on it.'

Henry put his hands on his hips and surveyed the scene, turning away from the woodland and looking back towards

the road, which was the main 'A' road connecting Blackpool
to Preston.

'Not a lot of cover,' he mused. 'Lots of passing traffic. But
not many houses, either. You'd think a body on fire, anything
on fire, would be noticed.'

'Ahh – one thing I forgot to mention,' Rik said sheepishly.
'I was going to get round to it.'

Henry turned on him. 'Go on.'

'From the initial CSI inspection, it looks as though the body
wasn't actually set on fire here. There's no evidence of burned
ground. Looks like the murder took place elsewhere and the
body was dumped here after.'

'OK . . .' He raised his face to the sky. Clouds scudded in
from the east. The wind had an Irish Sea chill to it. 'We need
to get as much as possible from the scene, so let's convene a
scene conference now, then get the show on the road.'

Henry yawned and tapped his earpiece. Very little had been
transmitted on it for the last few minutes and he wondered if
something had gone wrong somewhere with the operation.
Not that it was his problem. If it had to be chopped, as sometimes happened, he would just shrug and make his way home,
slide in next to Kate and get up when he felt the urge, maybe
not even bother turning in for work, have a day off, doss. It
was something you could afford to do if you were super-
numerary and nothing would fall apart even if you never even
bothered showing up.

He checked his watch. The time had rolled on to 4.11
a.m. Already eleven minutes behind schedule. Well, there
was a surprise. He rested his skull on the headrest, wafted
away a particularly vicious fart, and allowed his mind to
drift again . . .

The public mortuary at Blackpool Victoria Hospital reeked of
smoke and burned flesh. Henry stood by a stainless steel
dissecting slab, a surgical mask wrapped around his face, and
looked down at the charred . . . thing . . . on the table that had
once been, as he now knew, an adult female. He was wearing
a surgical gown, too, hoping it would keep the tang of death
off his clothes, though he knew it wouldn't be a hundred per
cent successful. He would need a shower and his suit would

probably need dry-cleaning before it could be worn again.
And the aroma would linger in his nasal passages. Next to
him stood Rik Dean.

'Done.'

The Home Office pathologist stood on the other side of the
table, removing gloves and mask, revealing the face underneath.

Keira O'Connell was the locum pathologist standing in for
the currently absent Professor Baines, a man Henry knew well.
He had been initially disappointed that Baines wasn't available. Apparently he was away on an international conference
for pathologists in the Bahamas, concentrating on forensic
dentistry, which was one of Baines's big interests. Henry had
to admit, though, that the temporary replacement was much
better looking, even with her blonde hair scraped severely
back off her face into a tight ponytail. Her face was round
and sweet, yet her eyes, which Henry had studied over her
facemask, were steel-cold grey and deeply intelligent.

O'Connell leaned on the table and inspected her handiwork
as her assistant busied himself doing a tidy-up. It had been a
nasty and gruesome task, extremely smelly, terribly unpleasant.
Henry – the 'new man' who even did the ironing at home –
despite his recent diversity training found himself hard pressed
not to comment that this wasn't the sort of job a woman should
be doing. He refrained, mainly because he suspected that she
would have stabbed him with a scalpel, and also because she
had done a terrific examination which Henry had watched
with a mixture of distaste and awe.

On the work bench behind her was an array of test tubes,
plastic bags, swabs and trays containing specimens taken from
the body which would require laboratory examination down
at the forensic science lab.

'Summary,' the pathologist said in the staccato way in which
she spoke. Her words were spoken clearly both for Henry
and Rik's sake and for the audio/video recording that had
been made of the post-mortem. 'Female, aged between
twenty-five and forty. Difficult to ascertain the ethnic origin
at this time due to the extensive damage caused by the fire
which I would grade as fifth degree. She was set on fire
whilst naked as there appear to be no traces of clothing on
her. However, the fire was not the cause of death. She was

set alight after death as the burns on the body show no signs of vital reaction.'

O'Connell turned away from the cadaver, which lay split open from neck to lower stomach. She stepped to the steel draining board on which the organs from the corpse had been laid out and examined. The display reminded Henry of a butcher's shop he'd once seen on holiday in Tunisia.

She picked up the lungs and inspected them like a big, floppy book. Henry was always amazed at how large lungs were.

'The lungs were filled with water, indicating the victim had inhaled water. They are wet and heavy, very pale and distended. No sign of any lung disease.'

'So the victim was drowned?' Rik asked.

'Yes.' Next she picked up the fist-sized chunk of muscle that was the heart. 'Good, healthy heart, too.' Then she moved to the brain which had been sliced open like a country loaf. 'Severe bruising of the brain, causing much internal bleeding, indicating a frenzied attack with a heavy, blunt instrument.' Next came the liver, slimy and difficult to hold. 'Liver healthy.'

O'Connell glanced at the two detectives. 'All in all, this woman was very healthy before she died. I would say she looked after herself well.'

She placed her hands on her hips and blew out, then turned. 'The trachea had been constricted, indicating an attempt at strangulation, but neither the strangulation nor the beating killed her – it was drowning.' She regarded Henry and pursed her lips, raised her eyebrows and tilted her head. 'All in all, this woman has been subjected to prolonged and severe torture. She has been beaten and half-strangled and her head has been held under water until she died. She was then set on fire. Brutal, nasty.'

'You can tell all this?' Rik said.

She blinked and frowned at his stupidity. 'And more . . . I'm a pathologist, so, death, as it says in some book or other, is my beat.'

'As it is mine,' Henry said.

'Touché.' She smiled pleasantly. 'You don't know who she is yet?'

'No,' Henry admitted. 'No leads as yet. Gonna be a toughie, I reckon, unless we get lucky in the next few hours.'

'Lucky?' O'Connell said cheekily. 'Why not get professional instead?'

'They go together hand in hand. One begets the other.'

She did not look convinced and she was acting as though she did not have much time for Henry, or perhaps she was just being professional.

'You want an opinion?' she asked.

'On me, or the deceased?' He raised a flirty eyebrow.

'The deceased,' she said and Henry saw her hiding a smile.

'Always welcome.'

'It will be difficult to establish the ethnic origin, but there is a gold filling in one of her back teeth which could be helpful if you get the gold analysed. I say that because I actually think we are dealing with a woman of Asian origin here from what I can see of what is left of the bone structure in the face. A facial reconstruction could prove worthwhile.'

'Asian?' Henry said, surprised.

'And if I'm right, you could be dealing with an honour killing.'

Henry's heart sank a few centimetres in his chest. 'An honour killing? Bugger.'

'Just a gut feeling . . . I could be wrong, though.'

'But I'd guess that's not usually the case?'

This time O'Connell did not hide the smile. 'No, not usually . . . now, if you'll excuse me, the job's not over until the paperwork's done, if you know what I mean? I think you've probably got enough to progress your investigation. I'll let you have the report and a copy of the DVD of the PM by tomorrow afternoon.'

Henry took the hint and started removing his mask as he and Rik walked towards the door. 'Thanks, Doctor O'Connell . . .'

'Professor, actually,' she corrected him.

'Thanks, Doctor Professor,' he said. He stopped and looked at her. She shot him a look of amused contempt before returning to the organs. He and Rik went into the office next to the mortuary to hang up their masks and gowns.

'You shameless flirt,' Rik chided Henry.

'Ah, but that's all I do now,' Henry said, his mind pondering what the next stage of the investigation would be. He was thinking about his 'fast-track menu': the list of things to do that included a combination of investigative actions which, according to the *Murder Investigation Manual* (which Henry could almost recite), 'are likely to establish important facts, preserve evidence or lead to the early resolution of the investigation'. He needed to sit down somewhere quietly and jot stuff down in an exercise book which would hopefully get his grey matter on the road to solving the age-old problem of any murder investigation which the manual simplistically states as 'who killed the victim?' and the simple problem-solving formula of 'why + when + where + how = who?'

Dead simple, and all made a bit easier if the victim is identified, although that should not in itself stall the investigation.

Henry had decided there would be a murder squad briefing at 8 a.m. the following morning at Kirkham police station, from where he would run the investigation, that being the nearest decent-sized cop shop to the scene. After that, at 10 a.m. there would be a press briefing – and then the work would really begin. He sent Rik off to start making some phone calls to get a squad together.

The mortuary office was quiet, so he decided to use this facility for a quick brainstorm. Henry had a pen and exercise book in his jacket pocket, which he spread open on the desk, and began blatting down his battle plan.

He was enjoying the process. Mind-mapping, flow-charting, jotting down single words to spark ideas, all designed to foster the thought process. It was a stage of the investigation he loved; those few moments when it was all his; the time before everyone else and their dogs stuck their noses into the pie; the stage when it was all pure and untainted. He felt a bit like a kid at school with a colouring book and crayons, writing with one hand, the other hand curled around to stop anyone else looking at his work.

It was engrossing work, too, and thirty-odd minutes later, he was sitting there staring into space seeking to get some inspiration from the wall in front of him.

There was a noise as the door opened behind him. This brought him back to reality. He twisted in the chair, half hoping to see Professor O'Connell – purely for professional reasons, of course – but caught his breath and sat bolt upright when he saw who it was . . .

*   *   *

Henry grunted and jumped out of his skin. He had dropped off to sleep, his chin bouncing down on to his chest, and had woken with a start and a shake of the head.

A ripple of giggles came from the back of the van as he sucked back the dribble from the corner of his mouth with a slurp. He looked sideways at the sergeant.

'You might be mistaken for thinking I dropped off then,' he said.

'No probs, boss, we all need power naps occasionally.' She yawned and stretched in the confined space. 'Is this going to happen or not?' She peered at her digital watch. 'We should've gone in twenty minutes ago,' which made Henry realize he'd actually been zonked-out for at least ten.

His eyes drooped with fatigue. 'Dunno,' he said, which was not the most earth-shatteringly incisive thing to say, but was about all he could muster at that time of day as he found himself suddenly very knackered. His brain was becoming spongy, starting to shut down.

In the personnel carrier the tittle-tattle had also waned as tiredness drew a veil over everyone. Which was not good, he thought; raiding a house with a possible terrorist connection should be carried out by officers who were on the ball, not ones who were dim-witted and sloth-like because they had become fatigued from waiting around. That bred mistakes.

He inhaled and exhaled deeply in the hope of getting some fresh oxygen into his bloodstream.

Dawn was creeping in more quickly. Soon it would be a gallop. The sky was starting to turn a pale grey; spots of rain clicked on the windscreen.

Unable to help it, and assisted by the slightly hypnotic effect of the rain, Henry's heavy eyelids slid slowly closed even though he fought it valiantly . . .

It wasn't Keira O'Connell entering the office. It was the bluff, angry figure of Detective Chief Superintendent Dave Anger and his sidekick, a DI called Carradine who had been seconded to FMIT recently and who, Henry knew, was the man that Anger wished to replace Henry with. All three of them went back a long way, but it was Anger and the DI who were best mates.

Behind them trotted a helpless Rik Dean, making tiny

gestures to Henry with his hands and shoulders, which said,
'Sorry.' He looked pained.

Anger barged in, Carradine by his shoulder like a parrot.

'Almost pulled a fast one there, Henry,' was Anger's opening
gambit.

Henry swung the desk chair round, instantaneously on the
defensive. 'What do you mean?'

'How did you get this job?' Anger demanded.

'What job?'

'This murder!'

'I was called out to it – it is on my patch, after all.' He was
responsible for covering Blackpool Division, on which the
body had been found.

'Well, you shouldn't have been.'

'Not my problem.'

'You've been relieved of the job.'

The chair flew backwards on its casters as Henry shot to
his feet. 'What?'

'You heard. DI Carradine is taking it on, so you can hand
over everything to him.'

'*What?*' Henry was flabbergasted.

'But there is some good news in it for you,' Anger smirked.
Henry waited, not daring to open his mouth lest what came
out of it totally destroyed his career. 'You've been transferred
off FMIT as of today,' Anger said, and let the words hang
there for effect. Henry's mouth dropped open with a little
bubble of spit on his lips. 'Yeah – transferred on to Special
Projects at HQ.' Anger smiled winningly. 'Hadn't you heard?
No? I'm surprised FB hasn't called you.'

Admittedly Henry knew he had a series of missed calls on
his mobile which he had been studiously avoiding. One of
them could have been FB.

'But then again, why would he call you? It's usually your
divisional commander or department head who gives you that
sort of news these days.' Anger's smile turned into a snarl.
'Unfortunately, the transfer comes with a promotion to chief
inspector, which completely mystifies me.' He shook his head
and looked as though this news was enough to make him
vomit. 'So you can get lost.' The smile returned – venomously.
'DI Carradine is now temporary DCI and despite the fact that
I said you'd never make chief inspector as long as I've got a

hole where the sun don't shine, I'm a happy man. You know what I think of you, so I won't go over old ground.' He gave Henry a little wave.

Henry was tempted to knock the beam off Carradine's face as he crossed the room, and was glad to see the DI cringe back slightly as he came within striking distance. Obviously Henry's body language was pumping out 'beware' vibes. However, he did nothing nor said anything, but pushed past the three of them, getting a muted 'Sorry, mate' from Rik, and stalked into the corridor. He had only gone a few yards when Anger called, 'Henry.' He stopped abruptly and revolved slowly as Anger strolled up to him, a half-smile on his twisted lips.

'You don't seriously think you'd have won, do you?' he said derisively. 'I'm part of a gang, you know.' His eyebrows arched. 'You, on the other hand, are just a minion, a nobody, nothing.'

'Whatever,' Henry said.

'So let's let bygones be bygones, eh? There'll be no need for us to cross paths any more. Let's keep it that way, shall we?'

'I don't think so.'

Anger's face froze. 'I'll fuckin' crush you, Henry,' he said almost conversationally, 'if you don't let this go. I promise you.'

'Your little army going to do your bidding?'

'I will destroy you if I have to.'

'Oh, stop talking like Lex Luther. What you need,' Henry said, 'is an anger management course.' It was something he'd been longing to say to the DCS, but when it came out it sounded limp and pointless under the circumstances.

'I haven't heard that one before,' Anger said mirthlessly.

Even so, Henry made himself laugh as he turned and set off down the corridor again, head held high, feeling the pierce of Anger's blazing eyes burning like lasers between his shoulder blades.

Outside in the car park it was cold and dark and all he wanted to do was scream at the moon.

Instead, he went and sat in his car, engine idling, heater blowing, churning it all over, wondering how best to progress. He wasn't certain how long he sat there, but it was a good length of time – long enough for him to watch Anger, Carradine and Rik leave after, Henry guessed, their briefing from the pathologist.

A knock on the driver's window made him jump. In his reverie, Keira O'Connell had somehow approached his car without him seeing her. She had tapped on the glass. He opened the window and she bent down to speak.

'I noticed you sitting there.'

'Yep.'

'I can't believe you drive a Rover 75,' she mocked him. 'Bit stereotypical, isn't it?'

'I used to be Mondeo man before this.'

There was beat of silence.

'I believe you've been replaced.'

With a sigh, he nodded.

'That was short lived.'

'I'm afraid if I open my mouth I'll say something I'll regret and shock you. I'm presently biting my tongue so hard it might bleed.'

'If you fancy a bit of a diatribe, I'm a good listener and I'm parched, too.'

'Well, I'm not sure what one of those is, but I could do with letting off steam and I know just the thing for dryness – the Fox and Grapes just round the corner.'

Henry spent an hour in the company of the professor in the pub. During that time he selfishly overpowered her with an unrelenting barrage of his tales of woe and frustration. It was a tirade not designed to woo or even remotely impress a woman. All thoughts along those lines had been banished by his contretemps with Dave Anger anyway. Once again, Henry was furious with everyone and anything and Professor O'Connell sat opposite him like a patient sponge, soaking in everything he chucked at her with a wry smile and an occasional 'Oh, no' delivered at an appropriate moment. Even if she wasn't interested, she gave the appearance of being so – at least for a while.

It was only when her eyes glazed over and she took a surreptitious peek at her watch that Henry realized she was probably bored rigid and he had missed an opportunity, should he have wished it to be one. He had broken the cardinal sin of seduction, or so he'd read in one of the tabloids recently: 'Get them to talk about themselves, get them to laugh, and you're on to a sure thing.'

Henry – so self-obsessed and selfish – had done neither. When she politely thanked him for the drink, then got up and walked – again, politely – out of his life, he kicked himself.

Losing my touch, he thought as he finished his pint, sidled back to the bar and ordered another Stella with a Jack Daniel's chaser. He returned to his seat and found it had been snaffled, so mumbling and pulling his face, he squeezed himself into a corner with a chest-high shelf. He sipped his drinks, stone-faced and brooding, and even the thought of the substantive promotion did not appease him, though he had achieved the goal of pension enhancement.

'Special Projects,' he mused glumly. 'What the hell does that mean?' To the best of his knowledge it was a rag-tag bunch of individuals no one else wanted who were tasked to run projects no one wanted to touch.

Henry knew the writing had been on the wall for some time. Now it was confirmed: his career as a detective was over.

'Fuck 'em,' he said out loud, drawing looks of apprehension from other customers, several of whom made space for a bloke who was obviously deranged, a prime example of the social mistake that was 'care in the community'.

Special Projects wasn't so bad for anyone who enjoyed sloshing around in the 'corporate pool' – that sad bunch of people who had been shelved by the force. He was given a refurbished office in one corner of an otherwise open-plan office on the top floor of headquarters with no windows and lots of artificial light. From his enclave he could observe his new team. They consisted of a mixed bag who had, for various reasons (none positive), been thrown together after having been batted round from department to department and were generally, and often unfairly, referred to as 'the sick, lame, lazy and loony'.

He tried not to compare them to the characters in *One Flew Over the Cuckoo's Nest*, because he felt tarred with the same brush.

Their work consisted of steering various projects from

conception to completion – mostly tedious, unsexy ones, all
about as dry as birdseed – as well as quality assuring operational orders.

As far as Henry was concerned, there was one saving grace:
being a headquarters 'shiny-arsed bastard', he made sure his
name was on as many call-out rotas for weekends as possible,
which meant he could still keep in touch with the real world
of policing and detectives.

Which was how he had ended up sitting in an increasingly
stuffy personnel carrier at an unearthly hour in Accrington,
waiting to raid a property which might, or might not, have
some loose connection with terrorism.

He had received the phone call at 8 p.m. the previous
evening. Knowing he was on the rota for that weekend, he
had not drunk anything for almost forty-eight hours and was
experiencing some dithery withdrawal symptoms as he sat
down with Kate to watch the typical mind-numbing Sunday
evening TV fare. That she was on her third glass of Blossom
Hill red, and it looked like the bottle was going to be demolished and she was showing signs of becoming frisky, did not
help matters. But he knew it would be the next evening before
he could even think about having a drink. Sex, on the other
hand, was a possibility.

In truth, the call-out was not totally unexpected. There had
been rumours of a big Special Branch op, but as Henry was
no longer part of the inner sanctum, that's how they remained
to him – just rumours.

The SB detective superintendent had telephoned to turn him
out. The tone of the man's voice made it clear to Henry that
he was only making up numbers. 'Someone's gone sick,
someone else is unobtainable and you're the only one left, so
you'll have to do,' the guy might as well have said.

But what the hell? It ensured he did not have to sit through
a double helping of *Coronation Street* followed by some
Sunday evening romantic drama that would have made him
want to commit suicide.

An hour later he was at Blackburn Police Station, ill-fitting
uniform, overalls and all, watching an SB briefing and trying
to work out who the shady figures were lurking in the background. Spooks, he realized. MI5, MI6: the taskmasters of
the Special Branch. When they cracked the whip, SB jumped.

Henry listened hard and critically and as much as it kicked his already bruised ego, he was glad he had been given a nothing job in the scheme of things.

'*Control to Echo Echo Two-Zero,*' the earpiece burst to life, making Henry jump awake. The call sign of his team.

'Receiving.' Everyone in the van stiffened with anticipation.

'*Green light, I repeat, green light. Understood?*'

'Understood – responding.' Henry turned to the Support Unit team. 'OK, folks, show's on the road.'

Four

There was never an easy way to approach a target address, particularly with a gang of cops kitted out like storm troopers. Sneaking up wasn't really an option and so it had been declared at the briefing that the way in which every property would be hit was through 'shock and awe and professionalism'. Henry had shuddered at the phrase, not only because it probably meant that somewhere amongst the lurking spooks were Americans; but it also meant fast and furious and hope to hell you were piling into the correct address. As everyone was repeatedly assured that the intel was spot on, there would be no problem on that score unless, it was insinuated, thick bobbies misread door numbers. Henry, who felt he was sitting alone in the naughty thinkers corner, remained to be convinced about anything and the look on his face probably said it all.

But that did not mean he wasn't enjoying himself and wouldn't do his best.

The personnel carrier moved off without any undue haste and cruised as quietly as the 3.5 litre diesel engine would allow towards the street on which their target house was situated. It was a terraced house in a row on a steep incline, typical of Accrington. Two-up, two-down, bathroom and toilet upstairs and an extension at the rear which housed the kitchen. The front door opened directly on to the street one side and into the lounge the other. It was the sort of house that had been built over a hundred years earlier for the mill workers in the town and was familiar in style to the millions of viewers glued each week to *Coronation Street*. Unlike *Corrie*, though, the white families were long gone and most of the inhabitants of these houses were of Pakistani or Bangladeshi origin.

At the top of the street, the personnel carrier halted to allow three officers to de-bus and jog as silently as their noisy kit would permit, crouched low, to the back of the target house, six houses along. Their job was to cover the back, wait until the front door got caved in, then enter through the kitchen door, which would be opened for them. They were also expected to grab anyone who bolted from the house.

Not that anyone was actually expected to be there. This was supposed to be an empty property in which, the briefing had informed them, it was suspected that illegal meetings had been held by would-be terrorists and extremists to plan their campaigns. It was possible that traces of explosives might be found, maybe other weapons and DNA traces, but no – definitely no – living creatures. It was the task of Henry's team on that grey, drizzling Accrington dawn to enter, secure it and keep it secure until the arrival of a specially-briefed forensic team. They had been told to touch nothing once inside.

'That should be easy enough for you,' the SB superintendent had said to Henry. His name was Greek and he added, 'Shouldn't it?'

Henry had ground his teeth, even though he thought that ten bobbies, a driver and a sergeant was perhaps overkill just to secure an empty property. That query had been greeted by a sneer and a 'Better safe than sorry' quip. But, judging by the huge number of officers taking part in the operation as a whole, it was apparent that the police were out to make a statement of intent that day.

'*We're in position,*' Henry's earpiece crackled – the message coming from one of the officers in the back alley. That meant they were waiting at the backdoor. Henry nodded to the driver, who slammed his right foot down to the metal and set off down the street, unintentionally kangarooing the van and drawing an unrelenting barrage of laughter, complaints and insults from the people in the back as they lurched in their seats.

Another smooth policing operation, Henry thought wryly, as he discarded his flat cap and squeezed his head into a blue riot helmet, squishing his face up, as required by the Health & Safety risk assessment. It hurt his ears as he forced it down over his skull, making him suspect that the size of his head had also expanded in line with his body.

Fortunately the journey was over quickly. They stopped outside number twelve. Henry shouted, 'Go!' whilst dropping out of the carrier at the same time, closely followed by the sergeant. Henry stood to one side as the well-trained and regimented team descended on the front door. He glanced at the house, only ever having seen photographs of it in the operational order. He took in the door and windows, saw curtains drawn upstairs and down, no lights visible.

The two leading officers brandished sledgehammers, the one behind them wielding a one-man door-opener which was basically a heavy tube of iron with a flattened end and handles used as a mini battering ram. Behind these three officers came the remaining four, all in a disciplined line. Their job, once the door had been battered down, was to tear into the house. Two would go for the stairs and two would go for the ground floor, with their remaining colleagues piling in behind them, just to ensure the house was unoccupied as promised.

They crossed the pavement in two strides. They were then at the front door, which they attacked without mercy but with great accuracy, their movements practised and choreographed by months of training and other 'live' entries, mainly into drug dealers' houses.

For a few moments it was sweet to watch.

The sledgehammers swung at the door hinges at the right-hand side of the door, one high, one low. Henry marvelled at the precision and the fact that the officers didn't smash each other's heads in; at the same time, the third officer swung the door-opener at the mortise lock. All three implements whammed simultaneously into the flimsy-looking door.

Henry braced himself, expecting the door to burst off its hinges, readying himself to follow the sergeant in. He'd seen it happen dozens of satisfying times.

Except in this case.

The door remained intact. Didn't even shudder in its casing. From the blows it received, it should have been halfway down the living room, and Henry realized immediately that it must have been reinforced, otherwise it would have been on its way to matchstick city.

Undaunted, the officers raised and aimed their battering tools again.

'*Movement, rear door,*' came a shout into Henry's earpiece from one of the constables around the back.

A horrible, nauseous dread coursed through Henry, and a feeling of panic.

'Not good,' he breathed to himself as the sledgehammers reconnected with the door – and still it held. 'Situation report,' he said into the mouthpiece of his PR, which was attached to his helmet.

'*Rear kitchen door opening . . . one male at the door . . . Asian,*' the officer said. '*Pistol in hand – armed!*'

Henry whacked the sergeant's shoulder. She turned and looked at him, her face a mask of consternation.

'I thought this was supposed to be an empty house,' she shouted.

Henry did not have time to get into discussion. He yelled, 'Tell 'em to stop' – he pointed at the officers by the door – 'stay here and watch the door and don't try to go in. I'm going round.'

She nodded and turned to yell some orders.

Henry ran up the road, hearing the word, '*Shit!*' come through the earpiece from the officer at the backdoor.

His kit was extremely heavy, topped by the riot helmet, and he felt like he was running in slow motion. He skidded at the gable end of the terrace, then into the cobbled back alley, high brick walls either side of him and a paved drainage channel running down the centre. The three officers who had gone to the rear of the house were standing in the alley, looking through the door into the yard of number twelve, their arms raised defensively. Henry hurried towards them.

They glanced round worriedly, their faces squeezed tight by their helmets, their visors in the 'up' position. He stopped in his tracks behind them.

There was a dark-skinned Asian youth in the yard, pointing a handgun at the cops. He was dressed in T-shirt, jeans and trainers. Henry put him around the twenty mark. He was small, thin, with a droopy moustache and, young as he was, the old adage came into play when facing anyone armed with a weapon – he became a 'sir'.

There was another youth behind him who Henry could not see properly.

'Out, out,' the first youth ordered the police, gesturing with the dangerous end of the gun, which looked heavy and of a high calibre. 'Back, back,' he motioned.

The officers took reluctant steps backwards.

'I will not hesitate to use this weapon,' the youth said, now framed in the backyard door, the second youth still obscured behind him.

'OK, OK, that's fine,' Henry said over the shoulders of his officers, using soothing hand signals to attempt to calm down any sudden urge to pull the trigger. His team members continued to shuffle backwards and round him and he quickly found himself with no one standing between him and the gun-toting youth. Suddenly he was very isolated and vulnerable. He was wearing the regulation stab vest which might have given him some protection from a knife attack around his vital organs; he was under no illusion that a slug from the pistol now aimed at his chest would travel through the fabric and tear his heart and lungs to bits.

'We are prepared to die.'

'I know, I know,' Henry said, finding it hard to speak. 'But no one has to die, no one.'

'I am prepared to take others with me,' the youth warned, not having taken in Henry's words.

'That doesn't have to be the case.'

Henry saw the lad's eyes were wild and staring, that he could not remain still, always jumpy and jittery, dancing on the balls of his feet, the gun shaking dangerously in his hand, his finger wrapped, then unwrapped, and dithering around the trigger. 'Come on, put the gun down.'

The youth sneered and stepped out of the doorway into the alley, giving Henry an uninterrupted view of his companion in the yard behind him.

It was a sight that made him freeze.

The second youth looked much the same as the first, same age, height and facial hair and was similarly attired – jeans,

T-shirt, trainers – but there was one exception. Maybe a dozen blocks the size and thickness of large chocolate bars were strapped across his chest and waist and he was holding something that looked like a stubby pencil in his right hand. Henry knew instantly what he was looking at.

A suicide bomber.

In a backstreet in Accrington.

The first youth saw Henry's expression change – and he smiled.

'Yes,' his head nodded, his eyes wide.

Behind him, the explosive-clad youth held up his right hand, showing Henry the plunger switch and the wire running from it, around his back. He had a wild glare in his eyes.

'Get back, everyone,' Henry shouted over his shoulder. 'He's got a bomb.'

They did not need telling twice and very rapidly Henry was truly on his own in the alley facing two people who didn't care about dying or taking others with them, and there was nowhere for him to go.

The first youth waved the gun at him, holding it parallel to the ground like some hip-hop gangster in a music video. Henry half expected him to start rapping, though with the youth's ethnic background, he was more likely to spout Bangra.

Henry was thinking fast.

It looked like these two had been disturbed in acts of preparation, meaning there could be others in the house, equally well armed. The whole street could end up being detonated if things went badly.

Neither youth was over five-six in height; both were as skinny as pipe cleaners, no muscle, no weight on them. Unarmed, Henry would have had a go at both, but just at that moment in time the scales were somewhat weighted in their favour.

'There's police officers at the front of the house, us here and more on the way,' Henry said. 'This is going nowhere,' he added, hoping they would believe him.

The big Adam's apple in the skinny throat of the gun-toting youth rose and fell. The gun dithered in his hand, his finger curling and curling again around the trigger. His head rocked and weaved. Sweat rolled down his face. He knew the implications of what he was doing, looked determined to go through with it.

'Don't do this,' Henry said. 'Nothing is worth this.'

'You ignorant fool,' the lad almost spat. He twisted his head and spoke over his shoulder, keeping one eye on Henry. 'Has there been time?' he asked the second youth.

'Yes, brother.'

His head spun forward. 'It is time.'

He raised the gun, pulling it upright. It was aimed at the centre of Henry's chest and he knew he would not survive this. He braced himself and in his mind he kind of knew he should be telepathically letting Kate know he loved her, tell her to look after the kids – ha! They weren't kids any longer. They were now exceptionally beautiful young women, hounded by slavering boys. Yes, a section of his mind knew that this is what should be happening – but the biggest part was shutting everything down, knowing he would be able to watch the bullet leave the end of the muzzle in slow motion, see it fly majestically across the gap like a CGI in a movie and enter his chest, then probably leave through his back whilst making a hole as big as a saucer.

Every muscle in his body tightened, from the stretched sinews in his neck to his calves.

'Are you ready, brother?' the youth shouted.

'Yes . . .' The explosive-bound youth raised his right hand, his thumb hovering over the button. Then he looked quickly down at the wire and Henry caught the movement of his eyes and saw what he had seen. 'Omar!' the lad gasped.

'What?' Omar responded impatiently, brow furrowed. He twisted his head to glance, his eyes momentarily off Henry . . . at which point, Henry knew he had to act. He had a nanosecond to do so and he pitched himself at the lad, going in low under the gun with a rugby tackle, driving his right shoulder low and hard into the lad's midriff, flattening him and at the same time grabbing the lad's wrist. He landed on top of him, completely taking him by surprise, slamming the gun hand down on to the hard ground with as much force as he could. The gun clattered out of his grasp. Immediately Henry reared up and delivered the hardest punch he could find, smacking him on the jaw just below his left temple, knocking him senseless. As a blow it hurt Henry's knuckles a lot, but there was the satisfying feel of dislocation and breakage in the young man's face.

Henry had to keep moving. He dived for the gun, scooped

it up and rolled up on to one knee, coming up with it poised and aimed at the second youth, who was desperately fiddling with the wire from the switch.

'Stop!' Henry yelled. 'Or I'll fire.'

The lad dropped the switch on the ground and looked pathetically at Henry, now every inch the immature, scared teenager. He raised his hands, a defiant expression on his face.

Henry climbed to his feet, breathing heavily, his nostrils flaring, knowing he had just cheated a terrible death.

Both lads were quickly pinned down, their wrists cuffed behind their backs, a burly cop standing astride each, baton extended and ready for use.

The one who'd had the gun – Omar – was trussed up in the alley, his face a swelling mess from the punch Henry had laid on him. The other was in the yard, his explosive vest having been carefully peeled from him. They were being kept separate and two vans were on the way to collect the prisoners.

The situation had been radioed in and other assistance was also on the way. The house had yet to be entered and although Henry had been ordered to keep it secure, he was itching to go inside, now that his blood was flowing.

He was not convinced the two lads had been in there by themselves, tooling up for some atrocity or other; they were far too young and inexperienced for that. A team had been disturbed and Henry thought there was a good chance others were still inside, although there had been no signs of movement.

The front door was still intact and Henry intended to leave it that way, three cops guarding it. The rest of his team, with the personnel carrier, were in the back alley and the kitchen door was invitingly open.

'I'm going in,' he told the sergeant.

She regarded him anxiously. 'Is that wise?'

'Probably not – but what the hell? This was supposed to have been a nothing job.'

'We've been told to hang fire, wait until a firearms team has arrived, wait until the circus arrives.' She was toeing the party line, but Henry could see she, too, was raring to get in.

'I used to be part of the circus,' he said. 'You coming?'

'Absolutely,' she said enthusiastically. 'We really do need to check.'

'But carefully,' he warned her. 'Any sign of a gun, we run, any sign of a booby trap, we try not to step on it, OK?'

'OK.'

Henry's stab vest had been replaced by a bullet-proof one from the equipment in the carrier.

The sergeant briefed two of her men to stay by the kitchen door, the rest to come in behind her and the chief inspector. Henry poked his head around the door and looked into the kitchen.

'Police!' he shouted, though he was pretty sure that if anyone was in there, they had a good idea that the law had arrived. He stepped into the empty room, still dithering from his close-run encounter, but not even starting to think it through. It was just like any other kitchen in this neck of the woods: fitted, fairly modern, functional, large enough for all the mod cons, a small table and four chairs . . . and on top of the table, three half-drunk mugs of tea, three plates with the remnants of a curry on them, half-eaten naan breads.

'The three bears,' he said to the sergeant.

She nodded.

Even with a cursory glance, Henry could see there was no one else in the kitchen, unless they were in the fridge. 'Room clear,' he said, then moved across to the inner kitchen door to the threshold of the next room, which was a cheaply furnished lounge: tatty settee, two battered armchairs and a TV. No carpet on the floor, just bare boards, the wallpaper peeling.

Henry ushered a couple of officers in ahead of him and they did a quick search behind the furniture. 'Clear,' one said.

There was a road atlas of the UK and a London *A–Z* on the settee, together with an exercise book, pens and scraps of paper. Two rucksacks leaned against the wall. Henry was tempted to look, but held back because he was pushing his luck by disobeying the instruction he'd received not to enter the property.

'Touch nothing,' he said forcefully, and walked slowly across the room to the open door leading to the next room, the front lounge. He looked in and saw there was no furniture in here at all and could say with reasonable certainty that no one was in it. A wooden, open-plan staircase ran up directly opposite the front door.

He went across the threadbare carpet to the front door, which, as he suspected, had been reinforced. This had been done by an extra skin of hardwood and numerous bolts. But that wasn't the only thing that caught his eye. The wires leading down from the edge of the door into a small plastic lunchbox made him gasp.

'Christ!' the sergeant breathed behind him. 'A booby trap . . . if we had managed to put the door in . . .' Her thoughts were left unexpressed, although her instructions to the officers behind were as clear as day.

Henry exhaled, not even aware he'd been holding his breath, then turned to the stairs, peering cautiously up through the treads. 'Starting to get shaky,' he said.

'I'm sweating like a horse,' she said.

'Too much detail,' he said, grinning. 'We need to be very careful here.'

'I like the obvious statement,' she came back.

Giving the front door as wide a berth as possible, they eased themselves up the stairs without incident, stepping on to a tiny landing from which the back and front bedrooms and the toilet could be accessed. Henry took his time looking round, thoughtful. 'Front bedroom, back bedroom, loo,' he said, pointing at the closed doors. 'Agreed?'

'Yep.'

He raised his eyes and saw a loft hatch.

'So,' he said hoarsely, 'if there was a third or fourth person, where have they gone?' he speculated. 'And if you were a member of a terrorist cell preparing to commit a crime, using a terraced house as a base, what would be a prerequisite?'

The sergeant looked at him, uncertain. 'Dunno what you're getting at.'

'What would you need just in case the cops came calling to break up the party?'

'Ahh – an escape route.'

'Bob on,' he said, 'but why didn't they all use it, if there is one?'

She shrugged.

Henry said, 'I thought it was a good question and I reckon

I know the answer and somehow I don't think it would be the wisest course of action to go barging into any of these rooms through these doors, just in case.'

'What? Just in case number three's behind?'

'No – in case these are booby trapped, because if there is a third person – and I'd bet my newly enhanced pension on it – he'll have gone now across the rafters.' He pointed up to the loft access flap. 'And any terrorist worth their salt will have probably left a calling card behind the doors and that flap . . . so this is where we stop . . .'

'Boss!' came an urgent shout from one of the officers downstairs, interrupting Henry's audible thought process.

'What?' he responded doubtfully, hoping he wasn't going to hear that the two prisoners had escaped, or they'd managed to take cyanide pills. He stepped back down the stairs.

'There's a bit of a kafuffle out back – one of the neighbours says he's just had a nasty experience. Someone's just dropped into his house from the attic.'

'OK, be with you in a sec.' To the sergeant, he said, 'Before we even turn one of those door knobs, we get our act together. We don't want blowing to smithereens, or anywhere else for that matter. And this little contraption by the front door' – he pointed down stairs at the lunchbox – 'needs paying some respect.'

'I'll sort it,' she said, businesslike.

Two police vans arrived as Henry emerged into the alley behind the officer who had called him about the neighbour. The alley was now alive with people gawping at the police activity and probably had not been this busy since the last cotton mill closed down.

He was introduced to an elderly Asian man called Ali Iqbal who had clearly just risen from his slumbers, was unshaven and a little confused and still dressed in what looked like very loose fitting pyjamas. He was a gnarled gent, probably in his seventies, and was chewing something sweet smelling.

Henry shook his hand. 'I'm Chief Inspector Christie. I believe you've had an unwelcome guest this morning?'

Although Iqbal's ethnic origin may well have differed significantly from Henry's, his Lancashire accent was even broader.

'I'll bloody say,' Iqbal said angrily. 'I were asleep in t' front room an' I heard this noise in t' loft. I thawt it were burds or summat. I turns over in bed – me wife's nexta me, by the way, snorin' her fat 'ead off – an' I looks up an' t' bloody loft door's opening. This guy appears, drops down, an' before I can say boo to a goose, he's gone, done a runner.'

'Must've been scary,' Henry empathized, realizing time was of the essence. 'Which is your house?'

'End one – down there,' Iqbal pointed.

'Right.' Henry's mind raced. 'Would you recognize him again?'

'Oh, aye, cheeky little get!'

'And can you describe him?'

'For definite.'

'And would you be prepared to jump into a police car with me and have a scout round, see if we can spot him?'

'Course I would . . . you think he's connected wi' this?' He gestured to the police activity.

Henry just gave him a knowing look, then turned to the officer who had brought him out to meet Iqbal. 'We need a car. I'll drive. Mr Iqbal can jump into the front seat, and you get in the back. We'll have a drive around to see if we can spot our interloper. You can get a description and circulate it for patrols.' Henry saw the female sergeant come into the back alley. 'Everything OK?'

She gave him a thumbs up.

Henry told the drivers of the vans who had come to pick up the prisoners to take them both to Leyland Police Station, which was about fifteen miles away, because it was the only station in the county properly equipped to deal with terror suspects. During its time it had seen quite a few come through its doors.

He then commandeered the first patrol car that turned up, hoiked out the driver and set off with Iqbal and the Support Unit officer to do a quick search of the surrounding streets. About twenty minutes had passed since the raid had kicked off and Henry knew that the realistic chances of bagging the third member of the team were pretty remote, because if there was an escape route prepared through the lofts of the terrace, then there would be a vehicle waiting somewhere too. But, he reasoned, you had to be in it to win it and if there was the possibility of striking lucky, then he was prepared to have a go.

Iqbal was a good witness. He had got a fairly lengthy look at the mystery man and, it transpired, had even jumped out of bed to challenge him and been pushed out of the way by the man as he ran out of the bedroom.

'I woulda gone after him, but me pyjama bottoms fell down,' he explained. He went on to describe him in good detail, including his clothes.

It had been a long time since Henry had cruised the mean streets of Accrington in a police car; a long time since he had driven a witness around, too, searching for an offender. It was always a heart-pounding time.

Henry was now fully awake, the complete antithesis of the dopey-eyed old man he'd been half an hour before.

Much had happened in that short space of time, which was why he liked sharp-end policing so much. One minute you can be half-asleep; the next tackling gun-toting, explosive-clad kids. As he drove, he had time to reflect for a moment or two.

Which was when the backlash struck him full-on and he was forced to take a few steadying breaths whilst he gave thanks that he wasn't in the queue to meet his Maker, maybe alongside two young and foolish Asian boys, to see whether he was going to be allocated heaven or hell. That is if the ultimate 'Maker' was the same for everyone.

He drove down on to Blackburn Road, then turned towards the town centre. A few citizens were knocking about now, the town slowly stretching and yawning into life.

Iqbal's description of the man was circulated by the constable, though Henry knew that at five in the morning, the area would hardly be flooded with uniforms. In fact he recalled that at the briefing he had been told that there were only three officers on duty in Accrington after 4 a.m. – and he had snaffled one car for him and two vans for the prisoners, which meant, frustratingly, there was no one else to assist with the search until the reinforcements arrived.

He settled behind the wheel of the Astra and drove through the drizzle, whilst thinking about Operation Enid, the highly suspect intelligence they'd had to swallow, and putting officers in unnecessary danger. He smiled grimly, anticipating the carefully chosen words he would later be machine-gunning at Detective Superintendent Greek, the SB boss.

When he did it, he hoped that a few of the spooks would be in earshot too.

He drove up to the railway station, saw no one fitting the description, then did a slow tour of the town. Mr Iqbal did not spot the intruder. Henry decided to call it off and get back to the scene.

They had circled the town centre and were on Blackburn Road, an ASDA superstore on their right and a new-ish complex of retail outlets, car dealers and a cinema. The traffic lights outside ASDA were on red. Henry pulled into the nearside lane, signalling (to no one in particular) his intention to turn left. He checked his mirror and actually saw there was a car behind, a BMW, approaching slowly in the offside lane, obviously going straight on towards the M65, about two miles ahead.

The lights turned green.

Henry selected first and – the habit of a lifetime drilled into him by a succession of police driving courses – before moving checked his mirror and noticed that the BMW, instead of setting off, had stopped completely some twenty metres behind.

'What's this guy up to?' Henry said, his eyes still in the mirror.

The PC in the back looked over his shoulder. Mr Iqbal had a look, too.

Suddenly the BMW did a spectacular reverse U-turn, the whole car rocking, tyres squealing, even on the damp tarmac, and shot off back towards the town.

Henry fumbled with his gear and tried to execute the same manoeuvre, which he succeeded in doing with much less panache than whoever was driving the BMW. As he did this, the PC in the back radioed in.

In the seat next to Henry, Mr Iqbal grabbed the elbow rest on his door with both hands and said, 'Fuckin' hell!'

'Just hold tight, you'll be OK, I'm a safe driver.' He rammed his foot on to the accelerator, flicked on the blues, and pushed the Astra hard, making the underpowered engine scream in protest. It did, however, respond well and he was still in sight of the BMW when he reached the roundabout underneath the old railway viaduct where several roads converged just on the edge of town. The driver of the BMW switched off the lights on the German car as he gunned the vehicle up the steep incline that was Milnshaw Lane and, without even the hint of a pause, did a left on to Whalley Road, also quite a steep hill, and sped out of town.

Henry was a skilled driver. He had done all the courses and more, and on top of that he'd had many car chases – even survived them – but even he had a shiver of dread when he too pulled out of Milnshaw Lane and caused a law abiding member of the public, tootling along in his Nissan, minding his own business, to brake hard, swerve, mount the kerb and just miss a lamp post.

'I'll say sorry later,' Henry promised.

In the seat behind him, the PC had started a running commentary: 'Now on Whalley Road in the direction of Clayton-le-Moors; speeds in excess of fifty and accelerating . . . didn't get the registration number . . . yeah, blue BMW . . .'

Mr Iqbal, even in the greyness of dawn, had clearly lost his colour, his face having drained of blood. 'Fuckin' hell!' he said again.

The Astra's engine was ear-splittingly loud, but Henry did not let up on it. He pushed it to its limits and as he shot a red light at the junction of Queens Road – on the corner, by the hospital – he was travelling at sixty, which was fast for the conditions in this built-up area. The BMW had dipped out of sight beyond a slight rise. Henry knew the road ahead was fairly straight, though it was narrow for a main road, and because of the time of day and the lack of other traffic, the BMW had the capacity to leave the Astra standing.

'*Just had a report of a stolen BMW from Accrington town centre in the last ten minutes,*' the comms operator said from the control room at Blackburn, which covered this area. He gave details and asked if this could be the one they were chasing.

'Affirmative,' the PC replied as he sat back and, intelligently, put a seat belt on.

'*Present location?*' comms asked.

'Whalley Road heading towards Clayton . . . just passing the Fraser Eagle Stadium' – Accrington Stanley's football ground – 'but we've lost sight of the car.'

Henry was grimly undeterred. It was unlikely now that he would catch the BMW, but he always liked to go the extra mile and though he reduced speed, much to Mr Iqbal's obvious relief, he decided to go as far as Clayton-le-Moors, then turn back. It was the thought that the BMW could be being driven by the third member of a terrorist cell that made him want to keep looking. Whilst he might be wrong on that score, he hated coincidence.

'*All patrols,*' came the now urgent voice of the radio operator, '*treble-nine just received from a driver on Whalley Road, Clayton-le-Moors . . . reporting a BMW has just collided with two parked cars and flipped over on to its roof, just after the junction with Burnley Road . . . will give further details . . .*'

'We're one minute away,' the PC shouted up. 'Sounds like our man.'

'Thank you, God,' Henry intoned and, once more, stuck his right foot down, bringing a further expletive from Mr Iqbal, who sank down into his seat and gripped his seat belt with two hands.

The BMW driver had run the red light at the Burnley Road junction, but had been unlucky in that at that precise moment another car was legitimately crossing its bows to the green light. It had been travelling at about eighty mph and with the avoiding swerve on the greasy road, the driver had lost control. The BMW had fish-tailed out of the junction, crashed into one car parked on the left-hand side of the road, catapulted across to one on the opposite side and had then been flipped on to its roof, careering dramatically down the road, sparks flying until it pounded into another car, bounced off it and came to a crunching stop, spinning like a top on its roof and blocking the road in both directions, just on the Accrington side of a canal bridge.

Henry stopped in the middle of the road twenty metres short of the BMW, flicked on all the Astra's emergency lights. He and the constable bundled out of the car and trotted to the scene, the constable – efficient as ever – radioing through that they were off at the scene. Iqbal stayed in the Astra, still clutching the seat belt.

The BMW had stopped spinning at ninety degrees to the road. It was a scrunched up mess. The roof was battered down, had damage all around it. Henry thought the driver would have been lucky to survive this in one piece as he reached the car and bent to peer inside, expecting blood and brains and broken bits of body everywhere.

'Shit!' he breathed.

The car was empty.

Henry stood up, looking around, and worked out how the car had arrived at its current location, amazed that, following such a crash, the driver had managed to crawl out and leg it.

'Where the . . .?' he started to say.

'What, boss?' the constable said, then took a look. 'Christ, he's got out!'

'He's gone down there,' came a voice, which made both officers look up to a bedroom window of a roadside terraced house. It was a middle-aged woman, clutching a dressing gown around her bosom, leaning out and pointing. 'Canal,' she added helpfully.

Henry gave her the thumbs-up. 'I'll have a quick look-see and if I don't spot him, we'll get a dog handler down here. You look after the scene.' Without waiting for a response, the charged-up Henry Christie trotted to the canal bridge, then cut down a steep set of steps which led on to the canal towpath. It was the Leeds–Liverpool canal, meandering through the once heavily industrialized towns of East Lancashire. As he reached the towpath, he seemed to immediately enter a more serene world, even though he was only a matter of metres away from a main road and maybe a couple of hundred from the M65 motorway.

In the fast clearing dawn light, and even the misty rain, the canal looked wonderful, very peaceful. Two moorhens squawked off as his heavy boots landed, flapping away and launching themselves into the reeds on the opposite bank.

He stopped, listened to the silence, the sound of traffic merely a vague drone.

To his right was the canal bridge, over which the main road ran, and to his left the canal threaded its way towards Accrington. He walked in this direction for a few metres.

There was no sign of anyone.

He tutted as he realized this was definitely a job for a dog. If he started to search by himself, he would either cock things up for the dog or just waste his time. With reluctance he decided to take a step back and let the experts get on with their jobs when they arrived. And anyway, the search would need armed backup if the suspect was indeed one of the terrorists.

He took one last look and his eyes caught something in the darkness under the arch of the bridge. A shape on the floor in the shadow. The hairs on his neck prickled. He did not move, but allowed his eyes to adjust properly.

It was the shape of a body. Someone trying to hide?

His steps were slow and quiet until he was sure what he was seeing, then he did not hesitate, but ran and crouched down beside the body of a male lying face down, spread-eagled, in a dirty puddle of blood and rainwater.

Five

9 a.m.: Henry Christie, feeling grimy and dishevelled, still dressed in the overalls and boots he had worn all night, sat glumly on a chair in the office occupied by the chief constable's staff officer and other associated staff. He was leaning forwards, elbows on knees, staring blankly at the floor, trying to keep his grit-filled eyes open. He stifled a big yawn, which took some doing and almost broke his jaw, sat up and rubbed his weary face, taking in a deep, slow breath. His eyes flickered around the room. All the desks were occupied: two secretaries, the deputy chief constable's staff officer and Chief Inspector Laker, the chief's bag-carrier, last seen by Henry several months before when Henry had been demanding to have an audience with FB. He was pretty sure Laker had not forgiven him for that day, but to be honest, he didn't give a monkey's something.

He swallowed. God, his throat was dry. He smiled in the direction of the chief's secretary, a young lady by the name of Erica, in an effort to catch her eye. She was engrossed in word processing. Henry coughed. 'Excuse me, any chance of a cup of coffee?' As there was a kettle, milk and a jar of

instant coffee on a table behind her, Henry assumed there was
every chance.

'Yes, certainly.' She saved her work, smiled at him in a sad
way, and spun around in her chair.

Henry noticed Laker looking at him, a scowl of disapproval
on his mush. He said, 'Been up all night – operational stuff,
y'know?'

'So I've heard,' said the bagman.

Henry stiffened. 'What's that supposed to mean?'

'You'll find out soon enough.' Laker refocused on his
computer. A surge of trepidation rushed through Henry.

The kettle boiled.

'Here we go.' Erica handed him a cup of coffee, the colour
of which reminded Henry of the tidal water in the Wyre
Estuary, a sort of murky red-brown.

'Thanks.' He sipped it. Laker's little off-the-cuff remark
had just knocked him off kilter for some reason. He had been
summoned to the chief's office following the less than smooth
raid in Accrington, he assumed for a pat on the back, but
Laker's jibe had made him think differently – or was Laker
just being a bastard, wanting to wind Henry up? If that was
the case, it had worked.

The coffee tasted as bad as it looked and Henry winced,
but managed to transform it into a smile for Erica.

Yes, Laker's remark made Henry wonder, but not for very
long because the chief constable's door opened and FB beckoned Henry in.

There was a polished oak conference table in the centre of
the chief's office and every seat round it, bar one, was taken.
The table itself was an untidy mess of paper cups, mineral-
water bottles, catering flasks of coffee and tea and lots of
documents.

There was silence as Henry was ushered by FB to the vacant
space at the far end of the table. He sat, uncomfortably aware
of the looks, and nodded to the assembled dignitaries, several
of whom he knew; others he didn't and had never seen before.
He wasn't over the moon to see Dave Anger's cruel face
amongst them.

'Ladies and gentlemen,' FB said with the same breath he
exhaled as he settled his rump back into his chair, 'may I

introduce Chief Inspector Henry Christie . . .' Henry did note
that FB hadn't used the term 'detective' on the front of the
introduction. 'And just for his benefit, could we go round the
table as a matter of courtesy? I'm Bob Fanshaw-Bayley, chief
constable of Lancashire Constabulary,' he announced, then
looked to his right.

'Dave Anger, FMIT commander . . . I think you know me.'
He gave Henry a slitty sideways look.

Next along said, 'Percy Greek, detective superintendent,
Lancashire Special Branch.' He gave Henry much the same
sort of look as Anger had.

'Mary Dearden, Security Services.'

'John Threlfall, Security Services.'

Henry had spotted those two skulking around at the briefing
and had rightly tagged them instantly as spooks. They were
both young, mid-twenties, and looked wet behind the ears, as
though they'd come straight out of Oxbridge and gone into
MI5 or 6 to protect the country without having even seen the
place.

Next along was Detective Superintendent Jerry Carruthers
from the Metropolitan Anti-Terrorist Branch. Henry knew him
by sight, having seen him on TV following the 7/7 atrocities
in the capital, but had never met him. Carruthers had also
been at the briefing.

'I'm Angela Cranlow, deputy chief constable, Lancashire,'
the next person said. She was fairly recently appointed and
as Henry had previously noted – when FB had been pushing
him out into the corridor following his unannounced gate-
crash a few months earlier – she did not look anything like
the stereotypical high ranking woman cop. In her mid-forties,
with soft features, quiet voice, but with an air of cool authority
and, Henry guessed, a trim figure under that unflattering
uniform. Based on what he had heard, he had nothing but
respect for her. She had done her time on the streets, been a
detective at several levels, seen some tough times and was
nobody's fool.

'Martin Beckham, Home Office,' said the last person, a
bespectacled, middle-aged man in a nice suit who looked like
he might have walked to work over Westminster Bridge every
morning at eight, then back home for seven in some leafy
south London suburb. He nodded at Henry.

Without a doubt, Henry knew that these were probably some of the main players in the planning and execution of Operation Enid. They all looked weary, as though they'd been up all night.

'Thanks everyone,' FB said. 'As you know, I've asked Henry to come in for two reasons . . . firstly,' he cleared his throat, 'for him to tell us firsthand what transpired a few hours earlier in Accrington; then for us to bring him up to speed, as a matter of courtesy, with some aspects of today's operation that were, by necessity, not dealt with at the briefing.' FB looked squarely at Henry. 'That OK with you, Henry?'

'Mm-yeah,' he stretched out the word hesitantly, 'so long as it's all right for me to chuck in some personal observations, as well.'

FB shrugged. 'Don't see why not.' One or two people shifted uncomfortably.

'OK . . . I assume you know the task allocated to my team of officers, but in case you don't, as part of the wider operation, the results of which I don't know anything about yet, other than what I heard on Radio Lancashire, we were to enter and secure an empty terraced house in Accrington which was believed to have been used as some sort of meeting place for suspected terrorists . . . that's about the long and short of it . . . a "nothing" job, really, and that's what we did . . . except the intelligence was wrong and the place wasn't empty.' Henry's eyes caught those of Dearden and Threlfall, the MI5/6 bods. Their eyes, however, would not meet his.

'We followed instructions and found ourselves faced with one young man armed with a pistol and another packed to the ribs with high explosive.' As he talked, he felt himself begin to tremble slightly, reliving the incident and realizing again how close he and others had come to being murdered by fanatics. 'I need a drink, if that's OK?'

He had left his horrible coffee outside.

'Help yourself,' FB said.

He found a clean polystyrene cup and poured a black coffee from one of the flasks, which he took neat. It was almost stone cold and tasted like River Wyre mud this time. When would he get a decent brew? he wondered, despairing. He put the cup on the table, noticing his fingers were trembling.

'Henry?' It was FB again, almost looking concerned. Almost.

'Well, big do's and little do's, the two young men were disarmed, shall we say, and arrested. We then discovered there was evidence of a third person in the house which we partially searched, but found no one. And the front door was booby trapped, but no other devices were found. A neighbour came and told us that someone'd dropped through his loft hatch and done a runner. Seems that the lofts in the row of terraced houses are separated by breeze block walls which, it transpires, had all had holes knocked into them big enough for someone to slide through and the third person from the house used this as a pre-prepared means of escape. As the neighbour had seen him, we decided to do a street search to see if we could spot him—'

'By "we", don't you mean "I"?' Dave Anger interjected.

Henry looked quizzically at him, shrugged and said, 'Whatever . . . but we ended up chasing a stolen BMW which crashed, severely injuring the occupant.'

'And who was the occupant? The missing terrorist?' Anger asked.

Henry licked his lips. 'Unlikely . . . he was a local car thief, name of Spencer Crawford, a fourteen-year-old . . . he's in intensive care now, but not likely to prove,' he added, meaning there was a good chance the lad would live. He rubbed his tired eyes, which squelched, and shook his head.

'So let me get this straight – you left the scene of a major incident, which you should have stayed on site to manage, and went gallivanting around town in some half-baked search which resulted in a Starsky and Hutch car chase and a near fatality which had nothing to do with the task you were given?' Dave Anger had spoken these words and they rose in fury as he reached the end of them. He threw down his pen and looked away from Henry in disgust.

Most people at the table had their eyes averted, FB and the deputy chief being exceptions.

Henry sat back and closed his eyes, the combination of tiredness and the bollocking making him feel faint. He fought a wicked battle inside himself to remain calm, then reopened his eyes.

'The only half-baked thing here is Operation Enid,' he

rejoined. 'It seems to have been based on sketchy intelligence and poor planning.' FB opened his mouth to speak, but Henry, having none of this, said, 'Let me finish, boss . . . I won't say anything I shouldn't . . . at least that's how it appears, particularly, as the radio reported that only two arrests were made from what, six raids? I presume those arrests were the ones I made . . .'

'And what the hell made you tackle two heavily armed terrorists?' Anger demanded.

'I saw that the wire connecting the switch to the detonator had come free and the lad with the gun had been distracted by it,' Henry explained. 'But, what I'm saying is that officers were put in danger as a result of poor intelligence, which I won't even ask where it came from. More work should have been done, more surveillance to ensure that unarmed officers were actually going to raid an empty house, not a bloody bomb factory!'

'You have no conception of the complexity and scope of the work that went in to this operation, Chief Inspector,' Threlfall, the Security Service guy piped up with a round, plummy, authoritative voice.

Henry held up a hand. 'No, I think I do . . . do not patronize me.'

'Henry!' FB shot warningly.

Henry shrugged a submissive gesture. 'I'll back off, but only after I've said one more thing.' He thought he heard a collective groan from around the table, but he was on a roll. 'Which is . . . because it all went awry' – here he refrained from saying "shit-shaped" – 'it became a very fast-moving incident and yes, I made a judgement call in the way I dealt with it.'

'So you're saying your judgement shouldn't be challenged?' Anger asked. 'Your judgement which has been, at the very least, suspect in the past.'

'I'm not saying it shouldn't be challenged—' Henry's mouth was still open when Anger cut him off.

'In that case, I'll challenge it.'

'OK, OK, OK, enough's enough,' FB barged in through the crap with a chopping motion of his hand. 'End of, OK?' He shot Anger a cold stare. 'Let's save it for the formal debrief.'

'All I'm saying is that if he'd done his job right and stayed

at the scene and directed it all from there instead of swan-
ning off, we might have had a result on the third guy, but no,
he had to take it all on himself and now one of the world's
most wanted terrorists has escaped . . .' Anger's mouth snapped
shut.

'Enough!' FB said again.

'Cop in-fighting,' Threlfall the spook chuckled.

'Sooo professional,' his female colleague added. They both
shook their heads pityingly.

FB glared at them, but the smirks stayed on their faces.
'Let's pull all this back, please . . . Henry, despite the, er, questions, you did a brave thing earlier.'

'Lucky, if you ask me,' Anger said under his breath. 'And
stupid.'

'I'll have that, brave and lucky, they go together hand in
glove,' Henry said, raising his chin. 'Maybe stupid, too.'

'Well, whatever . . . by all accounts you put your life on the
line and two terror suspects have been apprehended. So well
done,' FB said.

'Thanks.' It was a pretty muted word. 'What do we know
about these guys . . . kids?' Henry asked, looking at the SB
and spook contingent.

'Not much yet,' Detective Superintendent Greek – known
behind his back as Prince Philip – spoke out. 'They're being
taken to London for questioning by the Anti-Terrorist
Branch.'

'What's your take on the thing, Henry?' the deputy chief
asked. She smiled pleasantly at him, a bright twinkle in her
eye.

'What do you mean, ma'am?' he asked, getting, as usual,
a perverted kick from calling a woman 'ma'am'. It was probably a domination thing and Henry was glad, for an instant,
to let his mind wander to an imagined scene of debauchery
behind her office door, involving him, her and maybe chocolate sauce. Her look hinted she might have had the same
thought lines . . . or was he beginning to hallucinate?

'Your feeling about it,' Threlfall said. 'Say, about this third
person, perhaps?'

'I don't know anything about the third person,' he said,
dragging his dirty mind back from somewhere it should not
have strayed to, back to the more mundane matter of global

terrorism. Fleetingly, he thought that maybe he didn't have the right mindset to be a serious high-ranking officer. Here he was in the middle of a serious debate finding himself thinking about sex. Would he ever mature? 'But there is one thing,' he said, visualizing the incident in the back alley, 'confirmed by the slip Mr Anger just made about a wanted terrorist escaping.'

Anger blanched. 'Eh?'

'Which is?' Threlfall asked, leaning towards him with interest.

'When we hit the front door, why didn't all three of them pile up into the loft? That front door had been reinforced and it would've taken us a fair bit of time to smash it down – time enough for them all to go, maybe. But it would have been a bit like the three stooges all climbing up there and racing through the rafters.' Henry applied his mind to this. 'I think the two who were arrested were ensuring that the third one got away. That's it,' he declared, 'they were protecting him and were quite prepared to kill and die to ensure he escaped, which means . . .' It all dawned on him.

But Threlfall finished up for him. 'It means they were the pawns and he was a player . . . well thought out, Chief Inspector.' The spook regarded him warily through half-lidded eyes.

'I astound myself sometimes.'

The deputy grinned and looked down at her writing pad.

'Who is he?' Henry asked bluntly.

'That's not something you need to know,' Threlfall said. 'In fact, a decision has been made this morning that no mention will be made to the media of the suspected third person because we do not want speculation or scare-mongering.'

'How do you mean?'

'They could reach the same conclusion as yourself which could cause fear amongst the public . . .'

'If it became known that we let him go, you mean?' Henry said.

Threlfall looked at him with a pained expression. 'We are simply going to say that two terror suspects have been arrested and keep it low key.'

'How do you know who it was who escaped?'

'One of our experts has already looked at the suicide

bomb the lad was wearing . . . and he believes it's one built
by the man we are after. We also have fast-track DNA
analysis equipment available, which proves he was in the
house, too.'

'So this whole operation was directed at catching this guy?'
Henry asked. 'In which case, why was this not outlined clearly
at the briefing?'

'Ahh,' Threlfall said. 'It was, actually,' he went on hesitantly, 'but only separately to the firearms team who were
raiding the house in which we thought he was.'

'But not to the rest of us,' Henry spluttered. 'Talk about
bloody pawns!' Henry realized he was now in a world of spin
and lies, which was always the case with the security services and shady government departments. He despised them
and his expression probably said it all.

Ignoring Henry's last words, the man called Beckham,
who had said he was from the Home Office, opened his
mouth for the first time. 'What I am about to say to you
goes no further than these four walls. Yes, you're right, he
was our prime target and our groundwork prior to the imple-
mentation of this operation may have been slightly flawed,
but the overall intelligence driving it wasn't. We have a
terrorist of the highest calibre operating in Britain and it
remains a priority to apprehend him. As you know, the
American Secretary of State is visiting the north of England
next week and the fact that this man is still at large is a big
worry for us, as Condoleezza Rice is near the top of any
middle-eastern terrorists' assassination list. However, there
is an ongoing operation up and running aimed at capturing
this man, which is all you need to know. As regards what
happened today, it suits us to keep this man's details and
the fact he was even in this region as secret and you are
officially gagged, Chief Inspector. If you utter a word of
this, then the bureaucratic force of the law and government
will land smack-bang on your head. This also applies to all
the individuals in the team that raided that house. They will
be spoken to separately.

'I cannot give you details of this man, but I will tell you
he is highly dangerous, he has been behind many atrocities across the world, and his presence in this county is
worrying. We missed a chance to bag him, but that's how

it goes sometimes. At least we have some trophies to display to the community and the world, thanks to your heroism this morning, Henry.'

'I suppose the cheque's in the post?'

Henry was given the elbow and he rose from the conference table, nodding at FB, catching Angela Cranlow's eye, and giving the rest of the group a general gesture of goodbye. No one showed him out, not that he expected such courtesy, and he emerged tired, but relatively unscathed from the pit of fire, with the exception of Dave Anger's remarks, into the bag-carriers' office. All four members of staff were at their desks, including Henry's best friend, Chief Inspector Laker.

Henry smiled at him, then swung out into the hushed corridor outside, where he leaned against a wall and breathed deeply.

'Ah, dear,' he said to no one and suddenly felt quite shaky and ravenously hungry. It was just after ten, meaning breakfast was still being served down in the dining room. He headed downstairs, his nose following the aroma of bacon.

The dining room was reasonably busy, but there were still plenty of seats and tables vacant. Being self-service, Henry heaped too much of everything on a plate, grabbed a coffee from the machine, paid, and steered a careful course to a free table in the far corner of the room. Because he was feeling unsociable, he sat with his back to everyone and faced a window overlooking the car park. After a few moments' precise preparation of cutlery, plate, mug and napkin, he tucked into the huge meal which he knew would go a long way to shutting down his arteries, but would also cheer him up.

He scoffed it quickly, finishing off with a self-made toasted crispy bacon sandwich that he folded into his mouth. It tasted tremendous. He washed it down with coffee, then got a refill, and returned to his chair to watch the world of Lancashire Constabulary go by. A huge horsebox drove by, a four-wheel drive BMW traffic car purred past towards wireless workshops, and an array of less impressive police vehicles also passed his window.

His head shook involuntarily as he thought through the last few hours of his life, once again realizing how lucky he was to be sitting here eating a meal which would probably kill him anyway. Still, it was better than a bullet, or being picked up piece by piece. Perhaps it was safer in Special Projects, and he thought he would settle there now, carve a comfortable niche out for himself up on the top floor and hibernate until retirement.

'Umph,' he uttered without knowing, not really liking that prospect. Sitting in an office just wasn't him, but his options were becoming increasingly limited.

Dave Anger sat down opposite him. Henry had not seen him enter the dining room.

The two men regarded each other.

'I don't want you thinking that just because you were involved in today's job that you will be doing any further work concerning it.'

'God forbid. I know when I'm frozen out. I was just planning a dry flower arrangement for my desk in Special Projects.'

'Good . . . I didn't think it was clearly stated upstairs. You have no further involvement, OK?'

Henry eyed him with disdain. His breakfast was a mere memory. There was an unpleasant taste in his mouth now. He picked up his coffee, stood up and walked across to the far side of the room to a vacant table, having no wish to get involved with Anger. When he sat down, he saw that Anger had already left. He hunched over his mug and stared at the coffee, then yawned.

'My, that's a big one,' a female voice said from behind. Henry clammed up and turned quickly. It was Angela Cranlow, the deputy chief, mug of tea in hand, bacon barm in the other. 'Mind if I join you, Henry?'

'Be my guest,' he said, flustered, and half-raised himself out of his seat.

'Don't get up, duck.' She plonked herself down, discarding the food and drink for a moment as she unbuttoned her tunic and eased it off, throwing it across another seat, then removed her chequered cravat and unbuttoned her shirt collar. 'Phew – been a long one already.'

'Yes, ma'am,' he agreed.

She bit into the barm, speaking as she ate. 'Hate all that secret squirrel stuff, don't you? MI5, Special Branch . . . I prefer just good, honest, local coppering.'

'Comes with the rank, I guess.'

'Yeah, politics and all that stuff does. Doesn't mean to say I like it, though.'

She was perhaps two feet away from Henry and he allowed his eyes to quickly take her in. With neatly bobbed light auburn hair and a nice, round face, she was very pretty. There were some lines etched in the corners of her eyes betraying her age in a little way, but her skin was soft and lightly tanned. Henry noticed she wasn't wearing a wedding ring.

DCC Cranlow had moved across the Pennines from West Yorkshire, having been promoted to the position after an intense selection procedure in which she fought off some tough competition. Even though there had been a fair amount of coverage about her in the force newspaper, Henry did not know a great deal about her, other than her operational background, which he was impressed with.

'I'm sorry I haven't been able to come up and see you in Special Projects, yet,' she apologized.

'Why would you?'

'Oh, you might not know – the chief officer portfolios have recently been shuffled around and I've got you . . . in my portfolio, that is, amongst other things, of course.'

'Oh, right. I didn't know.' Chief officer portfolios were shuffled like cards, constantly changing.

'So I'm your new line manager, sort of . . . and I intend to come and see you and your team soon.'

'That would be good,' he said.

'Anyway, I just want you to know you did a good job today, Henry, and I'm very pleased, as is the chief.'

'Believe it or not.'

'No, he is,' she defended FB.

'Me and him go way back when,' Henry said.

'I know – I've had a look at your personal file.'

'Interesting reading?' Henry said, feeling uncomfortable.

'Yes, it is . . . quite a history.'

'I try to put myself about a bit.'

'If it's any consolation, Henry, I think Dave Anger has got away with murder and you've been shabbily treated. I'm aware of all the problems there.'

'I don't know,' he said pensively. 'I got that extra pip, bit more on the pension, nice office, cushy job, nine to five . . .'

'It's not about that, though, is it?'

'You tell me, ma'am.'

She smiled sweetly. 'You're a detective, a jack. It's in your blood. You should be on FMIT or Major Crime or be a divisional DCI, or maybe NCIS. But not Special Projects!'

'I'm getting acronym overload.'

'But it's true, isn't it? You shouldn't be getting shiny pants, not really. I want someone in Special Projects who wants to be in Special Projects . . .'

'But no one wants to be in there, they get chucked there cos there's nowhere else to shove them.'

'I want to change that.'

'Ahh,' Henry said, thinking he realized where she was going. 'You don't want me in there, do you? Anger doesn't want me on FMIT. None of the chief supers want me. Makes me kinda stuffed, doesn't it?'

She reared back with a chortle. 'Wrong end of the stick, Henry. Know your problem? Paranoia.' She dipped her face so that her eyes looked up at him in a rather seductive manner, which sent a rattle through him. 'I do want you, actually . . . but that's another story . . . but I don't want you in Special Projects. Round pegs, round holes is my philosophy.' She bit into her butty, wiped a dribble of butter off her chin with her forefinger which she pushed into her mouth and sucked clean.

Henry swallowed, wondering what the hell was happening here. Was she giving him a come-on? Was she toying with him? Or was he, as usual, living in a fantasy world?

Just in case, he kept his lips tightly closed. The worst thing he could do now was to make a flirty remark to a pretty deputy chief constable because he'd misread the signals. That would truly curtail his career.

She gave a half-grin which he found extremely alluring and it was all he could do not to say anything stupid.

'What I mean is . . . I'll see what I can do for you . . . I want the people who work for me to be totally committed, not cruising, not put somewhere because that's the only place there is. I do have some clout as a DCC, even if I am a woman . . . so I'll look out for you, if that's OK.'

'I get your drift,' he said with relief. His dithering hand picked up his mug and he took a swig of coffee.

Six

One week later

The man was dead – that was for sure. The almost perfectly formed circular bullet hole about the diameter of a five-pence piece just above the bridge of his nose was a good clue. The additional fact that the bullet had then somersaulted through his cranium like a mad circus acrobat on speed, then exited spectacularly out of the back, taking with it a mush of skull and brain, splattering it all over the wall, was a further, even more conclusive clue.

Even a no-good detective could have deduced that, in all probability, and ruling out suicide, this man had been murdered.

Whilst a very rusty Henry Christie was painfully aware of his limitations – and strengths – as an investigator, he knew he was a few rungs above 'no-good'.

He was confident he would quickly pull together a few known facts, mesh them loosely with a fairly bog standard hypothesis, and come to some early conclusions. All good, routine stuff, which could easily kick-start a murder investigation and get detectives knocking on, or kicking down, a few doors sooner rather than later. Although Henry knew his resources would be severely limited on this one, he had a strip of confidence in him about it which boded well.

He checked his watch, 02:35, mentally logging the time because his arrival at the scene was crucially important. He had known some seemingly rock-solid cases dither at subsequent court hearings just because a sloppy SIO couldn't remember what time he'd arrived at the crime scene. Evidentially it didn't usually matter that much, but an uncertain SIO gave a good defence lawyer something to chew on and spit out: if the SIO couldn't recall exactly the time, what

did it say about the rest of the evidence, hm? It was one of
those simple things easily overlooked in the vortex of a murder
inquiry. And Henry, who knew he'd be under the microscope
on this one, as ever, wasn't about to make mistakes by forget-
ting the bread and butter.

The call-out had come at 1.15 a.m.

Henry had been at home with his ex-wife, Kate, and the
evening had ended on a high note.

Both daughters were out with friends and boyfriends, leaving
the parents to their own devices for a change. They had sat
through a triple dose of soap operas with Henry whining his
way through them, annoying Kate by constantly asking about
plotlines and characters and grunting angrily at the ridiculous
things they did. 'Why the hell don't they just go to another
pub?' was one of his gripes. 'That way they wouldn't keep
meeting people they didn't like, would they?'

'Dear, it's drama,' Kate had said irritably. 'If they did that,
there wouldn't be anything to watch, would there?'

However, when *Crimewatch UK* came on at nine, he called
for hush, sat glued to the screen and refused to speak because
this was 'his' programme. It didn't seem to matter he had
spoiled her viewing.

Actually, *Crimewatch* wasn't something he watched regu-
larly. He found it made him angry at the bad things people
could do to each other through either passion, perversion or
profit, and even though he had been steel-hardened over the
years, some of the reconstructions made him queasy and
furious at the same time, particularly those in which lone
women or old people were the targets.

However, Henry had a vested interest in that evening's
edition of the show because he'd heard that Dave Anger
was taking a starring role to make an appeal about the
unsolved murder of a female whose body had been burned
to a crisp in the countryside near Blackpool – Henry's last
job as an SIO, the one Dave Anger had gleefully snatched
from under his nose and handed to DI Carradine, one of
his sycophants.

And they hadn't solved it. Ha! Six months down the line
and they hadn't got anywhere and as much as Henry liked
justice to be done, he did have a smug look on his face as he

watched Anger make an appeal for information to the great British public.

'Your expression is extremely irritating,' Kate informed him, sipping from a recently poured glass of Blossom Hill red, her favourite.

'It's one of superiority . . . now if you don't mind, I'm listening.'

There wasn't a reconstruction of the crime as such because there wasn't much to reconstruct, but the crime scene itself was shown and a few theories were put forward, but it was all clutching at straws in the vain hope that someone, somewhere might have spotted something.

'Be lucky to get anything,' Henry said gruffly. 'Should've kept me on it . . . their loss,' he finished with a sneer.

Kate muttered something disparaging and Henry shot her a look.

Back in the studio they cut to Dave Anger, sweating profusely under the hot lights.

'Look at the twat,' Henry had muttered, getting a punch on the arm. There were actually some things of interest which could help to identify the victim, Henry had to grudgingly admit.

First there was an unusual pendant on a twisted gold chain which had been found on the victim's body. 'No it wasn't,' Henry said, puzzled, wondering where it had appeared from. If anyone watching knew the victim, they might have seen it dangling around her neck. Henry generously upped his estimate of the number of calls they might receive – from zero to two – and was still mystified where the jewellery had appeared from. It definitely had not been on the woman's body.

Next along was a facial reconstruction, a bust of the dead woman's head and shoulders on a plinth, which Anger revealed with a flourish. Constructed by some whizzo scientist at a university, it was of a woman of Asian descent, who, in life, had probably been a stunner.

'Maybe they'll get a few more calls,' Henry conceded.

The final piece of information that Anger revealed was that the bones of the dead woman had been geologically examined and from their mineral content it had been established that she had been brought up in Blackburn, Lancashire. It was a stunning piece of analytical wizardry carried out by another university, which had the presenters cooing appreciatively and which, Henry had to acknowledge, was a huge step forward in the investigation. A clincher, maybe.

His expression altered to one of jealousy. 'Bastards!'

Three superb bits of evidence. A piece of unusual jewellery, a face and a place.

On the phone lines behind Anger, Henry spotted a cluster of high-ranking Lancashire detectives wearing headsets, ready to answer calls – something they studiously avoided in the real world. He guessed they'd all trooped to London with first-class train tickets and knew that once the phone lines had closed, they'd all probably be hitting Spearmint Rhino, consuming much beer and curry . . . and the idea consumed him, ate him up. It was his job. Snatched away. His face tightened enviously. He should be down there getting shit-faced, not them.

'Whatever you do, don't stand up and sing "It Shoulda Been Me",' Kate chided.

As the programme drew to a close, the cool presenter warmly told viewers not to worry too much about crime because statistics showed that most people never became victims.

'Tell that to the bloody victims,' Henry yelled at the box.

He could have necked a beer, but was not drinking that night because this was another on-call week, and he had to satisfy himself with flavoured water whilst Kate worked her way through the wine, muttering, 'Someone has to do it,' following one of Henry's scathing glances.

As the show's signature tune faded, Kate said bluntly, 'Are we going to bed then, or what?'

Instinctively Henry's eyes moved to the clock on the mantelpiece. 'It's only ten.'

'So?'

Henry looked at her. The wine had flushed her cheeks, made them rosy, moistened her wide eyes, dilated her pupils. 'OK,' he said, not needing much persuasion. It wasn't often they had the house to themselves, so the chance to indulge in a bout of noisy lovemaking was a rare treat, whether he was on-call or not. There was nothing in the rules about denying yourself sex, just alcohol. And Henry knew from past experience that it only took a drop of booze inside Kate to turn her from a sometimes hesitant lover into an unleashed tigress . . . something not to be missed. With that thought uppermost in his mind, Henry was upstairs with her moments later, tearing off clothing with abandon.

It was wonderful, tender, hard, loving, coming to a head-board-crashing finale half an hour later, both of them exhausted by the exertion. Kate rolled off him and quickly drifted into a gentle, purring slumber. He lay awake, deciding whether or not to go for a pee.

He was dreaming about Dave Anger and the reconstructed head of a murdered woman when the phone by the bed rang at one fifteen. The dream evaporated immediately as he fumbled to answer it, muttering a thick 'Henry Christie' without any enthusiasm.

'Henry, it's Angela Cranlow.'

He sat upright, quickly clearing his mussed brain. 'Hello ma'am.' It was more than a surprise to get a phone call from anyone of such rank at any time of day, let alone in the early hours. 'What can I do for you?'

'Said I'd look out for you, didn't I?' Before he could answer, she said, 'Fancy dealing with a murder?'

'Yeah, course.' All vestiges of the shackles of sleep were shaken off. He swung his legs out of bed, turned on the touch light – three taps to the brightest setting – and reached for the pad and pen on the cabinet.

'There's a shooting just come in from Blackburn . . . details pretty sketchy at the moment . . . as I'm on county cover, I've asked to be informed of all serious crimes before anyone else, then I can decide who deals . . . and also because every detective and his sidekick are in London doing *Crimewatch*, I can wangle this one for you – if you're interested, that is?'

'Yeah, absolutely.' Henry stood up, naked, and gave a salute to the new deputy chief constable. 'Ma'am.'

'Call the force incident manager for details.' She hung up without another word.

Henry traipsed groggily along the M55, slicing across Lancashire, then cut down on to the M6 and on to the M65 towards the sprawling former mill town of Blackburn. He exited at junction 4 on to the A666 – the Devil's Road – past

Ewood Park, home of Blackburn Rovers. He was a couch-fan
of the Rovers, watching their fortunes with interest, but it had
been a long time since he had ever willingly gone to see them
perform. Half a mile on the town centre side of the ground,
he turned right, cutting his way up through a series of terraced
streets past Blackburn Royal Infirmary towards the Fishmoor
council estate, which clung precariously to the harsh moorland above Blackburn.

He was experienced and well travelled enough to have
visited Fishmoor on many occasions during his career. It was
a sprawling sixties/seventies monstrosity of an estate and like
many of that era probably looked spiffing on the plans, but
the reality of living in a place that was a haven for the wrong-
doer was much less fun. It was an estate that had had a whole
bunch of trouble, mainly based around drugs, 'acquisitive'
crime and intimidation by gangs of wild youths who kept
whole communities in lockdown with their ruthless tactics. It
was a busy place for cops and since the advent of the Crime
and Disorder Act, also for the local authority and other agencies now obliged by law to get involved in things they had
previously avoided.

Henry found the address easily – a grotty office over a Spar
shop on the edge of the estate. He remembered the row of
shops from years ago when he had done a spell on Support
Unit in the mid-eighties. As part of a mobile, go-anywhere,
crack heads/kick shins team, he had spent many a head-banging
weekend in the vicinity in the days when he'd thought it great
sport to go around winding people up, then arresting them
just for the hell of it with a bunch of like-minded knuckle-
heads. The row of shops had been a magnet for badly behaved
juveniles and there had been regular police operations to
combat it and, Henry thought as he pulled up, probably still
were.

His only surprise as he drew to a halt in the Rover 75 was
that the shops were still standing, still trading. It was often
the fate of such businesses to end up firstly trading behind
steel bars and mesh, then for the owners to call it a day because
they couldn't stand the heat of the local kids making their
lives hell. Only the strong survived.

He parked a good way down the road and spent a few
moments savouring the police activity, which, despite the time

of day, had already attracted a gaggle of onlookers, mostly kids. Mind you, he thought, four marked cars, one section van, an unmarked car – which he immediately categorized as that of the night duty detective – and a little white van marked 'Scientific Support' were bound to attract the public at any time of day.

The climb out of the car was a little stiff, but he stretched, adjusted his tie, then approached the mayhem, his mind already back in. SIO mode, even though he was no longer one.

The zoot-suited night duty detective had obviously been keeping an eye out for Henry and strode up to him as though he wanted to cut him off at the pass.

'Morning, boss,' said the DC. His name was Hall.

'Trevor,' Henry said, a shiver making his spine judder when a blast of cold air from the moors swirled around him. Henry had known Hall for a long time. He was a career DC who kept his nose just above water, was competent, but hardly a Poirot. In fact he was a blueprint for many of the older detective constables in the county. Henry liked such people, in a way. They were reliable, knew their jobs, had a regular number of arrests, knew a lot of people, often had good informants, but didn't break any pots. 'What've we got?'

Hall shivered too. No doubt he had been dragged out of a warm CID office. But he smiled. 'I was glad when I heard it was you turning out. A blast from the past, a rave from the grave, you might say . . . someone you know well – *knew* well, I should say.'

Henry's paper suit was about two sizes too big for him, but at least the elasticated paper shoes fitted reasonably tightly over his shoes. He climbed the dingy, poorly lit steps behind Trevor Hall, and on the landing followed him down a short, uncarpeted hallway to an open door that led to the crime scene.

'Unfortunately there's only one way to get in and out of the scene,' Hall said over his shoulder, 'but so far there's only been me, you, CSI and the PC who found the guy, plus the witness, who've been to the scene. It was pretty quickly secured.'

One of the problems with a murder scene inside premises was often the ingress and egress, meaning that valuable evidence could potentially be lost because of an army of size elevens tramping back and forth along the route probably also used by the offender. Hall's rundown of the people who had already been to it was discouraging, but inevitable. Henry decided that once he'd had a quick look, no one else would be allowed up until all the scientific work had been done.

Henry was irritated by Hall for keeping him in the dark regarding the identity of the deceased, but allowed him his little charade because he seemed to be getting some amusement from it and he did brief Henry on everything else with a fairly succinct narrative before they entered the premises . . .

'Treble-nine came in about half past midnight to Blackburn comms. Hysterical female by the name of Jackie Kippax . . . yeah? Jackie Kippax?' Hall seemed to expect Henry to know the name, but at that moment in time with a brain still slightly dulled by sex and sleep, it meant nothing to him. 'Hm, OK . . . so hysterical female calls, a double-crewed car attends and finds her down at the phone box there' – he pointed to the box down the road – 'which, surprisingly, worked . . . anyway, they speak to her, get some sort of story. One stays with her and the other, with trepidation, goes up into the flat over the Spar shop here and finds the dead body, who had been shot through the head. I'm already en route and get here about ten minutes later, speak to the woman, still hysterical, and get her carted off to the nick to be looked after – emotionally and evidentially – and then I lumber up to the scene and lo and behold, I'm pretty sure there's a murderer on the loose.'

'Unless it's the hysterical woman.'

'Unless it's her, which I doubt. She, by the way, is the dead man's common-law wife, Jackie Kippax?' Hall raised his eyebrows.

'Means nothing.' Henry shook his head.

'It will,' Hall said confidently.

Henry remained to be convinced, but gave a shrug, then walked across to the Scientific Support van and helped himself to a paper suit and shoes, introduced himself to the young copper who had been detailed to note the comings and goings to the crime scene. He told the young lad not to let anyone else in until further instructed. He'd then followed Hall into the property, through the ground-floor door adjacent to the front door of the Spar shop.

As he'd entered the premises behind Hall, Henry had checked to see if there was any sign of forced entry at the front door and seen nothing to suggest it; no splintering of wood either on the door or its frame . . .

Hall stepped into the room which was the crime scene ahead of Henry, then took a sideways step to the left to give the senior officer an unrestricted view.

Henry placed his feet on the threshold but did not move into the room, just stood and let his eyes wander.

'It's the dead guy's office,' Hall explained. 'He's a private investigator.'

It was sparsely furnished: one desk with a black swivel chair behind it and a chair on the other side of it, one of those uncomfortable plastic ones found the world over. He could see a pair of feet sticking out from behind the desk, trainers on. Behind the desk was a wall and on it Henry could see the mess and blood that had once been the innards of the dead man's head. His eyes lingered on that for a few seconds.

And that was about it.

No other furniture, just a calendar on the wall; nothing on the desk either, other than a pen and an old-fashioned telephone.

A blank canvas. Something Henry was grateful for. Cluttered rooms were a nightmare. At least with an empty one it was generally pretty easy to work out what might be missing or what might be extra, two things that could be crucial to any investigation. And already, Henry was thinking that there was something missing that should be there, but he didn't know what.

So the dead man was lying on the floor on the far side of the desk.

Henry's eyes narrowed as he started to put the pieces together, even though he hadn't yet got a clue what the picture looked like.

He glanced at Hall, who was looking enquiringly at him.

'I like to take my time, think about things,' Henry said. 'Only one chance at a pure crime scene before everyone gets their mits on it.'

'Yeah, I know.'

'What are your thoughts so far, Trevor?'

With a meditative pout, he said, 'Just practicalities at the moment, boss.' He munched his words. 'Front door not forced, which could mean one of several things. Either the offender had a key or was allowed in, unless the door was actually open. It's a Yale lock, so if it was closed, whoever comes in either needs a key or has to be let in. My first thought is that he knew his killer and met him here.' Hall shrugged.

'You could be right,' Henry agreed. He rubbed his face and looked around the room again. Nothing particularly caught his eye, but he did have that uneasy feeling again that something was missing from the whole set-up.

Working on the assumption that the killer would have walked from the door straight to the desk, a matter of six feet, and may have left some evidence on that journey, Henry and Hall avoided this route and edged their way around the perimeter of the room, sticking close to the walls until they arrived at the wall behind the desk, the one splattered with blood, brains and cranium, behind the body.

The swivel chair had been upended, and was lying on its side like some strange, stranded sea creature and the body also lay on its side at an angle to the desk, almost in the recovery position, one knee drawn up, arms pointing forwards. But there would be no recovery from this position.

Henry swallowed as he slowly bent his knees and settled on his haunches, inspecting the back of the man's head. He could not yet see the face properly. He blinked as he thought of the damage the bullet must have done, spinning through the guy's brain.

'Recognize him yet?' Hall asked hopefully.

'Not from this angle.' He pushed himself up. Because of the position of the body, they could go no further in this direction without actually stepping over it, which would have resulted in lost evidence as they would have been forced to step in blood. For Henry to see the man's face, he had to edge back around the room and come in from the other side. He told Hall to backtrack to the door, where they both paused.

'So the killer – or killers – possibly known to the deceased, comes up the stairs after having been invited in, comes down the hall, maybe with the deceased. Perhaps the deceased is already sitting at his desk, waiting for the killer, or he plonks himself behind the desk after entering the room with the killer, who he has just let in. Whichever, he is sitting at his desk and the killer then shoots him in the head, spreading most of his grey matter across the back wall, knocking him out of his chair.'

'Fair supposition,' Hall said.

Henry tried to imagine the scene, which wasn't too difficult. He took a few seconds to take it in, measuring the angles, working out what might have happened.

'OK, got that,' he said and was about to move past the door and sidle around the edge of the room to come in to see the victim from the opposite direction when the noise of footsteps on the stairs made him pause and look back down the hallway. 'I said no one else should come up here,' he shouted. His mouth was still open with the last word when the paper-suited figure of the deputy chief constable appeared on the landing. 'Ma'am,' he added.

'Oh, sorry, am I not allowed up here?'

'Everybody but the deputy chief constable,' Henry said. 'I didn't expect you.'

She walked towards him, paper suit billowing out, far, far too big for her, giving the impression of a Teletubby bearing down on him. 'I'm hands-on as you know,' she said, reaching him, then looking beyond into the room and seeing the wall of blood. 'Jesus,' she gasped, recovered and said, 'What've we got, Henry?'

He detailed where he was up to, the deputy nodding and listening carefully.

'. . . so we're just going to have a look at the guy's face.'

'And we don't yet know who he is?' Cranlow asked. She saw Henry and DC Hall exchange a glance.

'Not yet formally identified, ma'am,' Henry said, turning and walking around the outside of the room with Hall in tow. Two and a half walls later, Henry's knees cracked as he bent down and examined the man's face, amazed by the smallness of the entry hole just above the bridge of the nose, in contrast to the size of the exit wound.

The dead man's cheek was resting on the thin carpet. His mouth slopped open, drooling thick globs of blood. One eye was fully open, the other half closed, as if he was trying to wink, and his features had been horribly distorted by the impact of the bullet, reminding Henry of the way that G-forces work on a person's face.

He could not see the face clearly. The light was poor and the body was lying in the shadow cast by the desk and he didn't want to touch or move it. A lot of work had yet to be done and he didn't want to spoil anything.

Henry twisted his head and shoulders, trying to get a better view without getting any closer than necessary.

He glanced around at the two people behind him, both attempting to do the same thing, neither seemingly affected by the sight of such a violent death. The three stooges came to mind and he wondered how long it would be before they all fell over or started poking each other in the eye. He knew he should have had the courage to tell Cranlow to leave, then there would have only been a comedy double act.

A penlight torch appeared in the deputy's hand, which she offered to Henry.

'This help?'

'Cheers.' He twisted it on and shone the beam into the dead man's face.

The light did help.

'Bloody hell!' he said sharply.

'See, I knew you'd know,' Hall said.

'Who is it, Henry?' Cranlow asked.

Henry said nothing, but shone the torch into the face again and peered as closely as he dared.

Despite the way in which the features had been misshapen, despite the back third of the head being missing, Henry recognized the man on the floor. He glanced quickly at Hall, who gave him a knowing wink.

'You were right, I do know him.'

'Henry!' Cranlow said, almost stamping her feet in annoyance. 'Will you please let me in on this little secret?'

'This guy is an ex-Lancashire detective who was basically drummed out of the force maybe twelve years ago, and I'll bet this is the perfect example of that old saying relevant to a murder inquiry – find out how they lived, find out why they died.' He stood up. 'This is the body of Eddie Daley.'

Seven

'He was a sleazeball cop,' Henry explained, 'and I've no doubt he was a sleazeball ex-cop too, and because of that I'm pretty sure this won't take long to bottom,' he finished confidently.

'You sound quite heated about him,' Angela Cranlow said.

They had driven – separately – from the crime scene down to the new police station in the Whitebirk area of Blackburn and were walking from their parked cars to the police staff entrance. They had divested their paper suits, handing them to a Crime Scene Investigator to be bagged and tagged. Trevor Hall had remained at the scene to await the arrival of the pathologist, then to accompany the body to the mortuary in order to maintain the chain of evidence.

Cranlow slid her swipe card down the slot, the door buzzed and they entered the station, which was all white walls, glass and modernity; a complete contrast to the Victorian monstrosity that had been left behind in Blackburn town centre which, for some bizarre reason, Henry preferred. Maybe it was its sense of history he missed, because this new place, flanked by car dealerships and DIY stores, had no character to it. It was just another fancy office complex that just happened to house the police.

'I am,' he said, but did not expand. It was quite obvious to Cranlow that something about Eddie Daley had touched a raw nerve in Henry. She didn't pursue him, just yet, but her curiosity was well-whetted, and she surreptitiously watched him as they strode down the corridor to a witness interview room near to the custody complex. 'She's down here somewhere, ma'am,' Henry said, referring to Jackie Kippax, who they had come to see.

As they turned into the custody area, an interview room door opened and a crime scene investigator emerged carrying her bag of tricks and a cluster of paper and clear plastic evidence bags. Henry knew the CSI and that she had been dealing with Kippax.

'Sir,' she said on seeing Henry.

'Hi, Alex – is Ms Kippax in there?'

'Yes . . . very, very distraught.'

'I can imagine. You got all you need from her?'

'Yeah – all her clothing – she's got a change, swabs, DNA, you name it. She's been very compliant even though she's so upset.'

'Think she did it, from what she's said?'

'No.' She shook her head without hesitation. 'Not for me to say, but no.'

'Does she know who did it?'

'I think she has a pretty good idea.'

'Thanks for that.'

'Good luck boss. Ma'am.' The CSI moved away, nodding at Cranlow.

'You coming in?' Henry asked the deputy.

'If it won't cramp your style.'

'If only I had a style,' he sighed and opened the door.

Jackie Kippax was seated at the table, her head hanging downwards. A young female constable sat opposite, with her outstretched hands holding Kippax's for support. The officer looked at Henry, a haggard, emotional expression on her inexperienced face. It looked as though having to deal with Kippax had all but drained her.

Henry acknowledged her with a wan 'well done' smile. With a gesture of his hand he indicated she could leave. The officer flooded with relief and almost ran from the room, but Henry caught her before she could scarper and gave her his best little boy look (designed, he hoped, to get just what he wanted) and whispered, 'Three coffees, white, with some sachets of sugar. Can you manage that?' then released her.

He eased himself into the vacant chair, still warm. Cranlow seated herself on a chair in the corner of the room.

Jackie Kippax did not move, her head hanging loosely down. Her breathing was laboured.

'Jackie,' Henry said softly. 'Jackie.'

She did not respond.

'Jackie, we need to talk. I know it's tough, but we need to

have a chat, urgently.' He reached across and touched her hand. 'Jackie, it's me, Henry Christie.'

The words, together with the touch, acted like a charged cattle prod. Kippax's head shot up, eyes wide. She sat bolt upright and looked at Henry as though he was the devil. Their eyes clashed – hers on fire with rage, her face twisted with anger.

'That's all I fucking need,' she snarled. 'You! A cunt like you!'

'I hated you with a vengeance and now you're the one investigating his murder.' Kippax and Henry were standing outside the police station on the paved area by the front entrance. A cigarette dangled from the fingers of her right hand, a coffee in the other. 'Can't no one else do it?'

Henry shook his head as he took a mouthful of his coffee.

Angela Cranlow stood several feet away, lounging against the station wall, sipping her coffee, listening to the dialogue, watching the interaction with interest.

'What happened between us twelve years ago has no bearing on this case, Jackie,' he told her, now very definitely remembering who she was and the fun time he'd had with her and Eddie Daley a dozen years before.

'You tell that to Eddie.'

'Look, the past is gone—' he started to say.

'You!' She pointed her cigarette-bearing, nicotine-stained first and second fingers at him. 'You lost him his job.'

'No, you're wrong . . . Eddie lost his job for himself. He was corrupt and he could not stay a cop, Jackie. I did my job, that's all.'

Her head jerked as though she had some sort of nervous tic, her face scowling, and her furious eyes blazed at Henry. Finally, she could look at him no longer and turned sharply away, starting to sob. 'I loved him,' she said jerkily. 'I stood by him. We had a life, not much of one, but we did OK. We were good for each other and I don't know what I'm going to do now. He was everything to me. He looked after me.'

Henry took a tentative step closer to her. 'And I'll catch whoever did this and that's a promise. Doesn't matter what he felt about me, or what you feel, I'll do my job.'

Jackie Kippax turned slowly. 'That's you all over, isn't it, Henry? No matter what, you do your job, don't you? Eddie was your friend and yet you still did your job on him, didn't you?' she said bitterly.

'Jackie, we can let this hinder us or we can bin it and solve his murder, which I'm assuming is what you want?' He held out a hand, a gesture which said many things. Her hard features softened. Her nostrils flared and she regarded him, her eyes roving up and down him. She nodded almost imperceptibly.

'He wouldn't be dead if you hadn't hounded him out. He wouldn't have had to make a living doing shitty things.' She took a long drag of her cigarette, dropped it, ground it out. She coughed deep from within her chest.

'I'm not sure those things are related.'

'Think what you want.' She shrugged.

'So what happened tonight, Jackie? Are you going to come in and sit down and tell us? Then maybe we can make an arrest.'

Back in the interview room, another fresh coffee in hand, they were talking. Henry was making notes as he listened and chatted, but he had also switched on the tape recorder. Angela Cranlow had joined him at the table, introducing herself by name only, omitting the rank.

'Tell me about Eddie,' Henry had prompted.

Jackie Kippax gave a snort and started counting on her fingers. 'Failed cop, failed insurance agent, failed legal rep, failed solicitor's clerk, failed private investigator . . . but not a failed man. He'd had bad experiences with women in the past, but he'd made bad choices. But me an' him were made for each other and he really looked after me.'

Henry smiled sadly. He could see how much she loved him, which was good, but he wanted to get beyond the touchy-feely and get some details to start the investigation. He knew it was like playing a fish, though. It needed a bit of give and take, because if he leapt in and rode roughshod over her emotions, she would withdraw into herself.

'How long has he been a PI?' Angela asked.

'Two – no, three years,' Kippax calculated.

'And what sort of work has he been involved in?' she enquired.

'Mainly divorce stuff, serving papers on people, that sorta crap.'

'Not the kind of work to win friends with?' Angela ventured.

'It paid the bills, mostly.'

'And what do you do now?' Henry asked.

'I clean, down at the Park Private Hospital, thirty hours a week. Steady, unspectacular, but OK.'

Henry nodded.

'Eddie couldn't draw his police pension for another two years, so we needed all the money we could find. He could've got a steady job fillin' shelves at ASDA, I suppose, but that wasn't his scene. He liked doin' stuff that wasn't a million miles away from copperin'. It was the way he was, I guess.'

'Did he make some enemies?' Angela asked.

'When you find people shaggin' people other than those they should be shaggin', you don't exactly make bosom buddies.'

'What was he working on at the moment?' Henry asked.

Kippax shrugged. 'Coupla things . . . a divorce surveillance which was ongoing and he hadn't got very far with, and something involving embezzlement down at the Class Act . . . you know the Class Act?'

'I know the Class Act,' Henry said dubiously. It was one of Blackburn's most infamous nightclubs, one of those places that was always changing hands, but never for the better. It was run by crims for crims and the only surprise was that it was still going, hadn't been shut down. 'Somebody was embezzling from the Class Act?' he asked incredulously. 'I thought they taught embezzlement there.'

Kippax sneered at him, no time for his quips. 'I don't exactly know the ins and outs of it, OK, but I think the manager was diddling the owner and Eddie got called in to make some discreet inquiries, do a bit of digging.' She sniffed and stared up at the ceiling for a moment, blinking back tears.

'Did he find anything?'

Her eyes lowered and stared at Henry. 'I think he did – I know he did – but he never got into real detail with me, just said the whole thing was a bit hairy.'

'What did that mean?'

'I think he'd been threatened by the guy he was investigating. He didn't really say, but I think that's what happened.'

'Where did Eddie keep his records?' Henry asked.

She tapped her temple. 'In here.'

'In his head?' Angela asked for confirmation.

'He hates . . . *hated* paper,' she corrected herself, choking back a sob. 'He was good on the computer, though, but as for records . . .' She shrugged helplessly, then suddenly folded her arms. 'Look, how much more of this is there? I'm feeling a bit gutted, y'know? I want to go home, I want to hit the bottle and I want to cry. I know you think I'm a hard bitch, and to protect me and my own, yes I am . . . but me and Eddie . . .' Her bottom lip started to tremble. 'I don't know what I'm going to do now. Who's going to look after me now?'

Henry sensed she wanted to reveal something, but she clammed up. 'OK, I'll arrange for you to be taken home' – Henry knew she lived in a council flat on Fishmoor – 'and for a family liaison officer to get in touch. We will need to come and see you again and we may have to ask you to identify Eddie formally.'

'What?' she almost shrieked.

Henry made a pacifying gesture with his hands. 'Unless the coroner will accept my ID of him, and I'll try and push that.'

'It's the least you can do.'

Their eyes locked again. A frisson of hatred crossed from her pupils to his.

'I'll do my best, Jackie . . . just, very, very quickly, though – tell me what happened tonight.'

She released some tension inside her with a noisy exhalation of breath. 'Er, nowt really. Just a boring night in front of the telly. We'd had a curry for tea and we just sat and watched the box, boozing, and suddenly he said he needed to go into the office for something and wouldn't be long. That's the last I saw of him, until . . .'

'What time did he go?'

'Just after ten. The news had just started.'

'Did he say anything else?'

'No – just went' – here she rubbed her thumb and first finger together, in the well-known sign indicating 'cash' – 'then he said "Quid's in" and went.'

'Did he say what he meant by that?' She shook her head. 'Did he drive to the office?'

'No – it's just around the corner, as you know.'

'And he didn't come back?'

'Obviously not.'

'So what did you do?'

'Called him on his mobile – didn't answer.' That answered one thing for Henry. Daley had been in possession of his mobile phone, but it wasn't at the scene of his death. Whoever had killed him must have taken it. Kippax went on, 'I called the office – no reply. Then I went round, thinking he'd snuck off to the pub.' She winced and clutched her stomach.

'Jackie, are you all right?' Angela asked.

'Yeah, yeah . . . God, I wish he had gone to the pub.'

'What time did you go round to check on him?' Henry asked.

'It was after midnight, that's all I know.'

Angela Cranlow smiled and said, 'Wow.'

Henry eyed her. 'Wow – exactly.'

'You seem to have rattled her cage.'

'With good reason.'

'So what's the Eddie Daley story? Fill me in,' she said excitedly.

She and Henry were sitting in the front seat of her Mercedes. Henry himself had driven Kippax back to her flat on Fishmoor, ensuring he gave her his card, then met Cranlow back at the scene of the murder to check on progress, which was good. Everyone who should have been there was, and the well-oiled machine chugged merrily away. The only person who had not yet materialized was a Home Office pathologist, who was due at any time. Whilst Henry checked on everything, Cranlow had remained in her car writing up notes and generally being efficient.

Henry had tapped on the window and she motioned him to get in beside her.

'So, how am I performing?' he'd asked as he settled in.

'If you think I turned up here to check on you, think again, Henry. As I said, you're paranoid. No, the reason I'm here is because it's fun and interesting and it's my responsibility – and yes, actually you're performing OK, which is what I expected.'

'Thank you.'

'No problem.'

He gave her a sly look and, not for the first time, realized he liked what he saw – a very attractive, well-groomed woman in her mid-forties, on top of which she was a high ranking police officer who seemed friendly and approachable and, yes, unless he was mistaken, unless his ridiculous male ego was playing its usual tricks on him, there was something of a spark between them, but he wasn't going to be foolish enough to stick his match anywhere near it.

'I'm going to follow this one through as best I can,' she told Henry. 'See how this force compares to my last on murders.'

'I think it'll be favourable.'

'I'm sure it will,' she said, smiling . . . then added, 'Wow!'

'Mm, Eddie Daley,' Henry said ruminatively in answer to her question about the Eddie Daley story, which sounded like the title of some fifties bio-pic. 'Not that much to tell, really. Just before I went on Regional Crime Squad, as it was, in about 94, I did a short spell as a DS in Blackburn, just filling in really, kicking my heels until my transfer came through.

'I ended up working on Eddie Daley's team. He was a DI based in the old nick in town. We were pretty good mates, actually, had a ball. He was seeing Kippax following his two failed marriages, but the thing about her is that she's related, somewhere down the line, to a big-time Blackburn crim whose name escapes me . . .' He thought for a moment, then it came. 'Terry Burrows, who incidentally used to co-own the Class Act, spookily enough. It was called something different back then.' Henry paused, arranging his thoughts. 'Burrows was being investigated by RCS for drug-dealing and importation and I literally stumbled on Eddie passing intelligence to him about police operations. He got suspended, it went to trial, but a witness came to a sticky end and the whole thing fell apart.'

'You mean murdered?'

Henry nodded.

'Did you suspect Daley of the murder?'

Henry exhaled a long sigh. 'No,' he said eventually, 'but I think Burrows had a hand in it, but you know, shit sticks. The trial might've collapsed, but Eddie was tarred for life and he had to go. Internal discipline got him for all sorts, from checking PNC and passing details on, to getting free curries. In fact I found out he was leaning on local curry houses and Asian taxi drivers, running a sort of protection racket. Needless to say, I featured heavily in the trial and the internal discipline hearings.' He looked at Cranlow. 'It was hard, believe me. I'm no snitch and I'm no angel, but Eddie was rotten to his core and he had to go, mate or no mate. Hence Jackie's reaction to me. Me and the wife had been out with them a few times. Burrows got his further down the line in a drive-by shooting in Nottingham.'

'A complex web. Wow,' she said again.

'Aye, so it doesn't surprise me Eddie's fallen foul of the underworld.'

'You reckon the Class Act is involved in this?'

'It's a bloody good starting point.'

'Don't get blinkered.'

'Would I?'

They smiled at each other.

'So,' Cranlow said hesitantly, 'what's the Henry Christie story?'

'Something along the lines of the decline and fall of the Roman Empire, just on a smaller scale: sex, debauchery, adultery – rock 'n' roll, even.'

Cranlow chuckled and his eyes met hers at the complete opposite of the spectrum to when they had met Jackie Kippax's.

'I'm looking at a 1 p.m. briefing for this,' he said quickly. 'We'll use the MIR at Blackburn nick. I'll arrange for personnel to be drafted in and hopefully we'll be knocking on doors by three. How does that sound?'

'Good,' Cranlow said coolly, recognizing when she had been cut dead and obviously feeling a little embarrassed by it.

A car drew in behind them, headlights reflecting in the rear-view mirror. The occupant climbed out and Henry recognized who it was.

'Pathologist's here,' he said, opening the door of the Mercedes. 'Just one thing, boss,' he added. 'When I dropped Jackie off, she told me something . . . she's just been diagnosed with stomach cancer.'

'I never thought I'd see you again,' Keira O'Connell, the Home Office pathologist said as she carefully removed what was left

of Eddie Daley's brain from its cranium and carried it with
equal care over to the stainless steel dissecting tray on which
she laid it. Henry Christie followed her, standing just by her
right shoulder like a henchman. They were in the mortuary
at Blackburn Royal Infirmary and O'Connell was about an
hour into the post-mortem. 'You'd been given the boot.'

She was clearly referring to the time Henry had been ousted
from the murder of the female who had just been featured on
Crimewatch, when Dave Anger had ignominiously tossed him
off the case and replaced him with DI Carradine.

'It was a pretty public sacking,' O'Connell said, looking
over her shoulder at him. 'So how come you're on this one?'

He gave her a stupid grin. 'They needed me more than I
needed them, only they just didn't realize it.'

O'Connell wiped her blood-streaked, latex-gloved hands on
a paper towel and picked up a digital camera, taking a few
choice shots of the damaged brain.

'Did you catch *Crimewatch* last night?' O'Connell asked.

'Hm,' Henry affirmed.

'They phoned me yesterday to ask if there was anything
more from my point of view they should say on the
programme.'

'Who phoned? Dave Anger?'

'Yeah.' She turned away from the workbench and returned
to Daley's body on the mortuary slab. He was now naked, his
clothing having been removed and bagged for forensic examination. His body was overweight and pathetic and sad, and
the blood that remained in him had settled although he had
lost a lot from the head wound and bled profusely on to the
floor of his office. She dropped on to her haunches and peered
into Daley's scooped out cranium.

Henry hovered. 'Did Mr Anger say anything about the
progress of that investigation to you?' he asked speculatively,
trying not to seem too interested.

'Not much. A bit.' She poked her finger about and moved
Daley's head.

'Did he say anything about the necklace that turned up?'

'Er, yeah, apparently, the guy who found the body came
forward with it.' She stood upright. 'He'd found it when he
tripped over the body and helped himself to it, then at some
stage his conscience kicked in . . . now then . . .' She returned

to the dissecting table and picked up a hand-held tape recorder and started to speak into it.

Henry stifled a yawn. It was 11.30 a.m. The coroner, whose office did not open until 9 a.m., had been personally contacted by Henry and had allowed Henry's identification of Daley's body, though he required it to be backed up by Jackie Kippax's identification of Daley's personal effects. This had been a relief to Henry because an ID at any time was stressful and emotional, even more so when the loved one has a bullet hole in the head. He especially didn't want to put Jackie through that, bearing in mind her mental state and the revelation that she was suffering from cancer. Her future looked bleak enough without the addition of having to see Eddie on a slab.

It was also a relief because the pathologist was ready to roll on the nod of the coroner and Henry knew the value of getting an early PM done. What better than to have the preliminary results ready for the murder squad briefing?

He watched O'Connell working skilfully away at her job, impressed. She did everything meticulously from all the preliminary stuff at the scene, then in the mortuary, all the way through to the point she had just reached, the examination of the remnants of the brain. Henry did miss his old friend Professor Baines who was the Home Office pathologist for this area, but he was away on another conference and Keira O'Connell was a more than able substitute, and much prettier. He doubted whether she would want to go for another drink with him though, after boring the life out of her last time.

She clicked off the tape recorder and walked back to the brain, selecting a brain knife – a straight, finely honed, twelve-inch bladed knife which was used to make long, clean cuts through the brain tissue. She held it up to the light and inspected its sharpness, then turned to Henry. 'Do you know,' she said, 'you missed a very good opportunity when we went for a drink six months ago . . . unfortunately I'm now in a relationship.' She gave him a sad look and twizzed the knife around. She turned her attention back to the brain. 'Shall we?'

Henry raced across the outer rim of Blackburn to make it to the police station for 1 p.m., the time of the first briefing. He

had delegated the job of pulling together some staff to get the
investigation rolling to an increasingly sleepy and tetchy DC
Hall, who had responded to the request with all the enthusiasm of a death row prisoner being asked to take a seat on
the electric chair. He was tired, needed his sleep and would
have to be back on duty that evening at six whatever, he
whined. Henry just told him to get on with it, whilst he
attended the autopsy.

There was no way he was expecting a full squad on day
one, but he would be happy so long as there were enough
bodies to put together a Major Incident Room, get a few roles
allocated and get actions underway.

The car park was chocka and Henry eventually abandoned
his car, knowing he was blocking someone in. It was par for
the course in police station car parks these days not to find a
parking spot, so before entering the building proper, he left
his mobile number at the front desk so he could be contacted
if the 'blockee' wanted to get out.

As he pushed the door open into the innards of the station,
he immediately spotted Trevor Hall walking towards him, with
an anxious expression, which gave Henry instant cause for
concern.

'It's not my fault, boss,' were the first words Hall uttered.

'What isn't?' Henry asked darkly.

'I did my best, honest.'

'What the hell are you talking about, Trevor?'

'The murder squad.'

'What about the murder squad?' Henry's words were slow
and deliberate.

Hall's worried eyes rose past Henry's shoulder whilst at the
same time his head seemed to shrink into his shoulders.

'We need to speak.'

Henry spun round. Angela Cranlow, looking a little shame-
faced, had appeared behind him and from the look on her
face, Henry knew something wasn't quite right.

Angela dragged Henry out of the station, bundled him into
her car and drove him the short distance to the nearby
McDonald's just off Whitebirk roundabout where they could
have a more discreet chat.

She brought him a coffee and sat him down by a window,

plonked herself opposite. 'I'm sorry about this,' she said quietly.

Henry decided to let her fill in the silence. Inside he was churning as he wondered what could possibly be so bad.

'I've had my knuckles rapped.' Instinctively they both looked down at her hands, which were laid flat on the Formica tabletop. She gave a short laugh. 'Metaphorically speaking.'

'Why?' he asked, suddenly knowing the answer, but did not want to hear it.

'Not following procedure.'

'Oh.'

'By deciding to allocate Eddie Daley's murder to you.'

He nodded, understanding, an empty feeling overcoming him. His mouth twisted acerbically. He was going to have this one snatched from him, too, he thought. Another kick in the . . . 'Bollocks,' he said, without vehemence. He scratched his head in a gesture of despair. 'I thought it was too good to be true. But there's not many people in this organization who can rap your knuckles, ma'am.'

'It was FB . . . under immediate pressure from Dave Anger . . . he was on the phone from London first thing this morning, obviously been briefed by someone.' She sounded heartily hacked off by the whole affair. 'Apparently I should have turned out the on-call FMIT DCI who was on cover . . . I know that,' she said, wringing her hands. 'Still, serves me right. Always been my problem, that.'

'What has?'

'I hate following procedure, 'specially when it's all cock. It's obvious to anyone with a pair of eyes and an arsehole you should still be on FMIT. It's a bloody travesty you aren't.'

Henry managed a forced smile. 'Unfortunately you've come along in the middle of something and you've done what appears to be right on the face of it – and I thank you for trying, I really appreciate it. It was good while it lasted and I hope I've done a decent job with it.'

Angela blinked. Her eyes moistened softly as she looked at Henry. 'Anyone can see you've been crapped on from a great height. I might just have to take the bastards on.'

'Ma'am, I'm not being funny, but the ACPO team are all blokes and every chief super is, too . . .'

'I know what you're saying, but I'm the dep,' she said

grimly. 'Paid good money to do a tough job, which I fully intend to do.'

'Well, I wish you luck,' Henry said with a trace of resignation. As of that moment, he fully expected that the climax of his career would be spent behind a desk, pushing paper nobody wanted to see, teamed up with a bunch of misfits. 'So who gets it?'

'Gets what?'

'Eddie Daley.'

'Oh, sorry, you do – for the time being.'

Henry pulled a face. 'What?'

'Well, I did make a bit of pitch for you. I said you'd uncovered some good leads and said it was only fair that you had a stab at it. And because nearly everybody in the world is involved with the visit of the American Secretary of State later this week – me being the exception because I'm looking after everything else – you've got until next Monday. If you haven't got a result by then, you hand it all over with pink ribbons to FMIT. How does that sound?'

Henry's head bobbed unsurely. 'And the murder squad consists of?'

'Ah, well, that's something else. You haven't really got one. You can have some Support Unit officers to do some searching and stuff, but that's about it. Better than nothing.'

'So, me, basically?'

'Yep.'

His mind swam, floundered actually. 'Hell's teeth!'

'And me,' she said brightly. 'I'll give you a chuck up as best I can.'

'That's very kind, ma'am.'

'You're not impressed.'

'It's just that . . . it's a hell of a task . . . daunting. The Class Act is just a possibility, not a certainty.' He stared out at the traffic rushing by.

'Do you want me to tell Dave Anger he can have it back now, then?'

'Oh, no . . . that's just what he'd love to hear. No, let's see what we can pull out of the bag.'

'That's the spirit.'

'And in terms of a squad, I have a bit of an idea on that score – that's if you agree.'

Eight

Maybe it wasn't such a good idea after all. Henry gazed across at the shocked faces in front of him and almost wanted to turn and run out of the office. It was as though he had just declared that a nuclear warhead was en route and they had four minutes to live. He glanced quickly at Angela Cranlow, who had approved his plan, and she grimaced back as if in severe pain.

'So what do you reckon, guys, gals?' Henry asked, trying to whip up some enthusiasm. The Special Projects team, his mad idea of a murder squad, looked at him aghast and in stunned silence. 'Look, this'll be good,' he said positively, guessing this was what it was like swimming in treacle. 'Just imagine,' he said, looking beyond them to the wall and seeing an imaginary banner, 'the Special Projects Murder Squad. What d'you think?'

They were in their nice, warm, open-plan office on the top floor at headquarters, having all dragged their chairs from behind their desks, and formed a U-shape around Henry in one corner. His eyes moved from individual to individual.

'It's been approved by DCC Cranlow' – he gestured to her with a shift of his shoulders – 'and it'll do you all the world of good.'

'Speak for yourself,' someone unidentified, but suspected, muttered.

'Right,' he began, and perched himself on the edge of a desk, about to launch into his reasoning behind the idea. Before he could speak, a sergeant piped up.

'Henry, the truth is, that's real pressure. We don't do real stress or pressure in here, that's why we're in here. We're the land of misfit cops – and that includes the support staff in here, too.'

There was a general murmur of agreement and nodding of heads.

'It sounds like you're proud of it.'

'No, not proud – we just are who we are.'

Henry gathered his thoughts. 'This office,' he declared, 'is full of people who have got skills, knowledge and experience. Why you've all ended up here is not the issue, but the fact is that you are all here and I'll lay it on the line: I believe that in reality, none of you truly wants to be here, do you? You've all got talents and the truth of the matter is,' he said, using a pointing finger, 'I've got the chance to investigate a murder until next Monday, a chance given to me by Ms Cranlow, and I desperately don't want to blow it. I need your help and I know you can do this, be part of a team catching a murderer instead of just pushing paper around that no one reads, if truth be known.'

He picked up a thick manila file.

'In here I've got printouts from the HR system of all your careers to date. I know from looking at it that we have the combined ability to run an MIR – which is a Murder Incident Room, for those of you who don't know.' Henry opened the folder and looked at the person sitting nearest him. He was a constable nearing retirement, well overweight to the point of morbid obesity, but who had once been a detective locally and regionally. He had worked on numerous inquiries, but had snapped when the force refused to let him stay on NCIS when his three-year contract expired.

'Graeme – you can be my intel cell. What d'you reckon?' The PC – Graeme Walling – shrugged, but could not hide a small smile. 'I know you can interrogate all the computer systems and analyze stuff. It's what you've been doing in Special Projects for months anyway. How about it?'

The PC inclined his head in agreement, not the most loquacious of individuals.

Henry looked along at another PC, this time a female, whose attitude problems had caused her and everyone else around her severe problems, ensuring she was passed from department to department like a hot spud. No one ever got a real grip of her because she always threatened discrimination or harassment, making managers afraid of managing. She had become one of the most disaffected and bitter people Henry had ever met.

'Jenny – you've been a HOLMES indexer.'

'Years ago.'

'I'd like you to do it again – only this time you'd be all things combined: manager, inputter, quality control . . . yeah? I'll have a machine installed within the hour.'

She pulled a face. Apart from her attitude, Henry also found her to be extremely lazy, but once set off on a task, she usually got it done in her own sweet time, but to a high standard.

'OK,' she relented after consideration. Nothing like a volunteer, Henry thought.

He took a breath. This was going to be real graft, he thought, recalling the film *The Dirty Dozen*, who had nothing on this lot.

By 6 p.m., Henry and Angela Cranlow had managed to convince the Special Projects Team that they were the ideal fodder for a Murder Incident Room. Henry had laboriously worked his way from person to person, glancing at the HR file, extolling their virtues and skills, building them up in an effort to convince them they could do it.

In some cases the argument was pretty thin and he had to use poetic licence.

One of the women, who did word processing, had taken a lot of convincing. She was very old school and had joined the constabulary as a typist even before Henry, and it had taken over ten years to wean her off the Remington, via an electric typewriter, finally on to a computer. This had resulted in her struggling desperately, and because she could not keep up with new technology, no department had any use for her, however nice she was. The constabulary, in time-honoured fashion, did not give her the boot as it should have done, but shuffled her around and around until she ended up on Henry's scrapheap. She was good at making tea, filing, running errands, manual paperwork and providing emotional support for others.

Mrs Delia Wantage, thirty-three years' service, all in headquarters departments, therefore became the Murder Incident Room manager.

In front of all the others, tears rolled down her face and she could not control herself. She rushed from her seat and embraced Henry, crushing him to her ample chest and saying he was the best boss in the world. Whilst embarrassed, Henry enjoyed the moment, but only for the wrong reasons. The close proximity of a big-chested woman, even one ten years his senior, did that sort of thing to him.

Delia then went and made tea for everyone.

At 6 p.m. Henry had done his job well, he thought. The department was now buzzing with a childlike delight he had never witnessed in a group of adults before. A warm glow flushed through him, not least at the memory of Delia Wantage and her bosom.

With the best will in the world, Henry was exhausted. He had been on the go since yesterday morning and in another hour he would have been up for thirty-six hours without a break. His brain had gone fuzzy and weariness was invading his body like the slow march of a disease. He could not sustain it any longer and knew that nothing more would be achieved. He decided to call it a day, telling everyone to be ready for a 9 a.m. briefing next morning. He watched his team as they collected their personal belongings and left, still chattering excitedly about the prospect of being a murder squad. He had sold it to them well.

With the last one gone, he said, 'Shit,' and walked across to his office in the corner of the room and slumped behind his desk, rubbing his eyes and yawning. Before he left he was going to root out the Standardized MIR operating procedures and Murder Investigation manuals. The MIR manual listed roles and responsibilities and Henry intended that each of his team would know exactly what they were supposed to be doing next day.

Following this he was going to touch base with the CSI people, the pathologist and the forensic lab in order to get as much stuff processed as soon as possible. He knew that unless he struck very lucky, very quickly, he would be fortunate to crack the case of the murder of Eddie Daley with the time and resources available to him. His intention for the days ahead would be to ensure that all the policy and procedural stuff was done correctly; that all intelligence available was accessed and some inquiries surrounding the Class Act were undertaken. When he handed the whole shebang back to Dave Anger, he wanted everything to be spot on.

He opened the murder policy book – the book in which the SIO records all actions taken and decisions made – and began to jot down a few things under headings such as Crime Scene

Assessment (location, victim, offender, scene forensics, post-mortem), Evidence and Facts, Mental Reconstruction, Hypotheses, and Lines of Inquiry.

There was not much detail in his notes yet, just a few lines or words, which would be expanded when he came back tomorrow.

At 7 p.m. he closed the book and left the office, wandering through the eerily empty corridors of HQ. As he walked down the steps, his mobile rang.

'Henry, it's me, Angela.'

He had to think for just a moment: Angela? Then the penny dropped. It was the deputy chief constable. His backer.

'Ma'am?'

She had left Henry with his team a couple of hours earlier to catch up on her own work. He hadn't seen her since and assumed she had headed home, wherever that was.

'What's your location?' He told her. 'My office – come straight in.'

The first-floor corridor was particularly quiet and dark. Henry walked through the double doors halfway along, then turned right into the outer office, which he expected to be empty. On reflection he shouldn't have been surprised to see his best friend, Chief Inspector Laker still at his desk, tapping away on his keyboard, impressing everyone by working late. The door to FB's office was open and it was clearly empty.

Laker looked at him, puzzled. Henry thumbed towards the dep's door to his right. 'Ms Cranlow's expecting me.' Laker's eyebrows shot up. 'Honest.' Henry winked at him, gave one rap on the door and entered. The office was almost as big as the chief's and easily housed a large desk, a conference table, coffee table and sofa. Cranlow was sitting cross-legged on the sofa, surrounded by a sea of papers which also covered the coffee table.

She had changed her clothes, having divested the uniform in favour of a T-shirt and tracksuit bottoms with running shoes. Her hair had been pulled back into a short ponytail, revealing the true shape of her face. Which was a pleasing oval. She had no make-up on and it was obvious she had recently showered.

'Sit down, be with you in a second.' She patted the sofa

and Henry eased himself on to it, very aware he now sported a thirty-six-hour shadow and desperately needed a long, hot shower, a shave, and something proper to eat, followed by a JD on the rocks – then bed.

Cranlow scanned a few sheets of a very important looking document, then straightened the whole lot into a neat pile. She turned to Henry. 'Performance figures . . . do you know we're the top performing force in the country?'

'I've heard FB spout it a few times, bit like a cockerel crowing.'

'He's very proud of the force.'

'I know.'

'So, Henry,' she said, shuffling herself more comfortable, 'another big wow from me.'

'Why?'

'Special Projects, Mr Motivator. I half expected them to be fighting on the beaches.'

'They'll be back to normal next week. Happy, smiling, hard working – not!'

'And this week they'll work like demons, I bet. You did a good job with them.'

'Ta.'

She tilted her head slightly. 'I don't usually do this, but do you fancy a drink? It's been one hell of a day.'

'I was on my way home.'

'To your ex-wife?'

'Yeah.' The word sounded almost apologetic.

'Make it a quick one, over at the Anchor? You can tell me your plans for tomorrow.'

'Sounds good.'

'I'll see you over there.'

The Anchor Inn, situated a short distance from police headquarters, is just off a roundabout on the A59 which, in its time, had claimed the lives of several police officers, as Henry was explaining to Cranlow.

'This place used to be crawling with cops on courses at headquarters. A lot of drinking and driving went on, but less so now. A few still come in, but way back when, Tuesday and Thursday nights used to be heaving in here before everyone headed for town. Not much studying got done on courses the day after. Tuesday used to be grab-a-granny night, if I recall correctly.' He smiled at a hazy memory.

'I'm nearly a granny,' Angela revealed.

They had taken their drinks into the conservatory. Henry had gone for his usual, Stella; Angela, a red wine.

He almost choked on his. 'What?' he asked incredulously.

'My daughter's pregnant.'

'Well, ma'am, I'm sorry – but you don't look anything like a granny.'

She smiled at the compliment.

After a slight pause, he asked, 'So, what's your story?'

She considered the question. 'OK – whirlwind tour of life: preggers at sixteen to a bastard who did a runner. Gave birth to a daughter, who I adore; joined West Yorkshire Police at nineteen; did an OU degree in my spare time – and that was tough – then worked my way up through the ranks. Hard graft, but my parents were – are – brill and now it's kind of worked out, with one exception. The guy I married, also a cop, couldn't handle me. He upped and left, quite a while back now,' she said wistfully. 'No one of any note since.'

Henry sipped his lager, which, after the day he'd had, tasted amazing.

'You still live over the Pennines?'

'With Mum and Dad, yeah . . . but when I got this job, the constabulary paid for a rental house just around the corner. Twelve months, so I've still a bit of time to get sorted. Rent? Buy? Not sure yet, see how it pans out.' She shrugged. 'We'll see, but I'm actually looking forward to being a gran, all things considered.'

'Well, you get a wow from me.' Henry held up his pint and she chinked her wine glass against it.

'And I'm looking forward to the week ahead. Should be. interesting.'

'What do you see yourself doing?'

'Helping you out. Going out, making some inquiries, maybe arresting someone? That'd be great. It's a long time since I've been involved in anything like this and I'm going to play – especially as I don't have anything to do with Condoleezza Rice's visit to Blackburn this week. That's the chief's baby – and ACC Ops.' The visit had nothing to do with Henry either, for which he was pleased. Such events were a pain and best avoided. He and his Special Projects team had quality assured the operational order for the event, but that was as far as his involvement went. 'And if it wasn't for her, you wouldn't be investigating Eddie Daley.'

'I realize that. I take it you approve of me just keeping a lid on the investigation – dot the i's, cross the t's?'

'Well, yeah,' she admitted with a twitch of her nose which Henry found quite appealing. 'But an arrest would be a bonus.'

'I shall do my best.' He took another sip of his beer, aware it was going down on a very empty stomach. Angela watched him carefully.

'FB really likes you, y'know?'

'He's got a funny way of showing it.'

'I think his heart is in the right place. He's got a lot of plates spinning.'

'I didn't know he had a heart.'

She watched him take another drink. She sipped her wine, then licked her lips. 'How would you feel if an ACPO officer made a pass at you?'

Henry considered the question carefully. 'I suppose it would depend on whether or not I fancied him.'

She giggled girlishly. Henry grinned. 'What if it was a female ACPO officer, to be more precise? One living alone in a big rented house not two minutes' drive from here?' Henry's pulse quickened. He took a longer swig of his drink. 'One, say, on the verge of becoming a grandmother at the ripe old age of forty-four and one who would offer no strings attached, because she needed discretion and could not afford any sort of scandal?'

He drained his glass. 'I need another. You?' She swallowed the last mouthful of red wine and held out the glass.

'A large one,' she ordered. 'Think about it while you go to the bar. I'm going to the loo.'

Henry's weak legs just about managed to carry him as far as the bar, where with a husky voice he ordered and bought the drinks, returning to the seats in the conservatory to find Angela had also returned and let her hair down from her ponytail.

'Er, lost for words, a bit. I mean, I know it's all hypothetical and sounds a wonderful set of circumstances and my response would be that I would have to think about that sort of thing very carefully.' He spoke as if he was responding to a business proposition. 'In my experience, nothing ever comes without strings attached and I've got a very poor track record when dealing with females of the opposite sex. The older I get, the less I get them.'

'This one's simple, though. I might be an ACPO officer, but I still have pretty basic urges.' She leaned forward. 'This one is desperate for a fuck and nothing else. This one will use you and abuse you and toss you by the wayside after literally sucking you dry.' She licked her lips and looked seductively at him. 'And she wants to fuck you.'

Despite his good intentions towards Kate, there was a strong stirring in him which equated with weakness of the flesh.

'I would have to enter such a' – here, he shook his head, trying to find the right words – 'relationship, I suppose, with eyes wide open and ground rules set.'

'That would be acceptable.'

'Although I do find it amazing that an officer of ACPO rank could even contemplate such a thing.'

'Let me tell you, Henry, they're at it like knives the country over.'

'It's a bit like imagining your parents having sex.' He screwed up his face.

'Even ACPO officers are flesh and blood.' Then she added provocatively, 'All I could think of during last week's debrief was me and you, at it like knives.'

'I won't push it, Henry,' Angela said, 'and I won't hold it against you if you're not interested, but there is one thing I'd like you to think about . . .'

It was 8.30 p.m., way past Henry's bedtime. He and Angela had finished their drinks and were on the car park to the side of the Anchor, standing by the open driver's door of her Mercedes. She turned to him, standing only inches away, face turned up, and he didn't have to be told that this was the point where they kissed.

'Tonight probably isn't appropriate,' she said. 'We're both exhausted and we need clear heads for tomorrow, which'll probably be an equally busy day, but . . .' She didn't need to say another word, because they instinctively came together and kissed. Their lips mashed together, their tongues sliding into each other's mouths. Henry could feel her body through her T-shirt and his immediate hardness pressed against her. They broke apart, gasping for air, looking longingly at one another, Angela's eyes moist with passion. 'Just a taster,' she said, 'and believe me, I taste good.'

With that she pushed him gently away and slid into her car, closing the door and driving away, leaving him, as planned, wanting more.

He stood there until his manhood subsided, drawing a strange look from a couple walking towards the pub. The blood took for ever to drain away.

He sat in his car with the engine idling for a while. On the passenger seat was a slip of paper Angela had pushed into his hand which bore her address, mobile and home phone numbers. There was a big 'X' underneath. He picked it up and read it. He knew the road she lived on, just a matter of half a mile away. But he blew out his cheeks and dropped the paper on to the seat and set off down the dual carriageway towards Preston and, ultimately, home.

Henry knew his weakness and had major problems controlling it. And it was particularly tempting to be offered no strings attached sex by a woman who could not afford to get caught out because of her high-profile career.

God, why can't I change my spots? he agonized internally. He was seriously working out whether he could juggle it when his brain suddenly cleared and remembered how recently it was that he and Kate had made fantastic love and he had said all those things to her and here he was, considering embarking on an affair, or at least a one-night stand, with another woman. Which then spun his thoughts into those dangerous areas of justification . . . Well, I'm not married, I'm not engaged, so technically I'm a free man; Angela's free, too, so on the face of it I could screw her without any feelings of guilt . . . Except nothing was ever so easy . . . and he knew he had caused so much grief to Kate and the girls over the years and yet they still loved him . . . and what if Angela turned out to be a less stable character than she appeared?

He headed down Penwortham Hill and bore left over the flyover which spanned the River Ribble to the south of Preston. Then he drove down by the docks and picked up the Blackpool Road.

When his heartbeat settled back to normal, he slotted a

Stones CD into the player, one he had burned himself, and relaxed as the opening chords of 'Streets of Love' filled the air and Jagger began to croon about unrequited love. The dual carriageway out of Preston continued past the docks and inclined upwards through Lea. Henry was not in a rush, his main aim being to stay awake and make it home in one piece. He stuck to the speed limit as he passed the Lea Gate pub on his right and approached the traffic lights at Three Nooks, intending to go straight on.

He attempted to erase the memory of the kiss, not entirely successfully, and thought fleetingly about the last woman he'd almost had a fling with. He recalled how he had got her so drunk that she wasn't physically capable of sleeping with him. That action itself was a turn up for the books, a turning point in his life maybe. The 'new' and faithful Henry Christie. Or possibly the 'old and getting past it' Henry. The Henry who only wanted a plasma-screen TV and a quiet life. He had actually ordered the plasma and maybe the same was true of his life: it was on order, expected to be delivered at any time, but meanwhile he had to make do with what he had.

The lights were on red. He stretched, yawned and skipped the next two tracks on the CD and found, 'Tell Me', one of the first songs the Stones had ever written and recorded. He always thought it was a lovely song, written when Jagger and Richards were just testing their wings.

As the amber lights appeared, he moved off reasonably slowly, now thinking about Eddie Daley and the fact that Eddie's mobile phone had not been found. He'd taken it out with him when he'd gone to the office, so it stood to reason that the killer had stolen it. And was there anything else missing that should have been there? Something continued to bang away at Henry's brain.

His mobile phone rang. 'Yeah?'

'Henry, it's me, Angela.'

'Deputy Chief Constable Angela?'

'How many Angelas do you know?'

'You'd be surprised.'

He was driving with his mobile cradled to his ear by his right shoulder. Totally illegal, but still with both hands on the wheel.

'The kiss was nice.'

Henry almost growled. 'Yes, it was,' he agreed reluctantly.
'No pressure, honestly.'
'Cheers, goodnight, boss . . . see you tomorrow.'
'Yeah, bye,' she said throatily.

Henry tossed the mobile phone on to the passenger seat and, not for the first time, cursed the device. How did life go on before they existed? Sometimes that more simple life was hard to bring back to mind.

A few minutes later he drew up on the drive outside his house in Blackpool. He climbed jadedly out of the car and walked to the front door and stepped inside to the warmth and welcome. He relaxed as Kate appeared in the hall, already in her dressing gown, looking ravishing and more beautiful than ever.

'Long time, no see,' she said with a grin. She gave him a tender hug, then pushed him away, screwing up her nose. 'This is nothing personal, darling, but I think you need a bath.'

'Uh-huh.'

'Then some decent food, a bit of a chill and a good night's sleep. Again, nothing personal, but you looked wrecked and uptight.'

'Spot on.'

'You do the bath side of things and I'll put something together for you and bring up a glass of JD for the bath. How does that sound?'

'Sounds good. Are the girls in?'

'Yeah – in their rooms. Dying to see you.'

The tension drained from him as he exhaled. 'It's been a helluva day.'

He placed one foot on the first stair tread, the bath beckoning him with the prospect of hot water, Radox bubbles and wrinkly skin. He never got to the second step because the blight of his life intruded once more. The mobile phone which, even with its 'Jumpin' Jack Flash' ring tone, pissed him off severely, blaring from out of his jacket pocket.

He wished he'd left it in the car.

He fished it out, was relieved to see it wasn't the deputy chief calling – unless she had withheld her number. He answered it.

'Henry—' he started to say, but before he could utter 'Christie', a woman's voice cut in coolly.

'It's me, Jackie Kippax . . .' He opened his mouth to say something, but she continued, 'I've caught Eddie's murderer for you.'

'What?'

He heard her take a breath. 'He's right here in front of me . . .'

Henry heard a male voice say, 'You got it wrong, lady.'

Jackie said, 'Shut it, you fucker . . . Henry, I'm sat right opposite him now and I'm going to do exactly what he did to Eddie.' She screamed out the last few words, '*And blow his fuckin' brains out!*'

There was the sound of scuffling. Then a clatter, a scream and a loud gunshot – and suddenly the phone went dead in his hand.

Nine

Contacting the police these days could be a nightmare. Henry had heard some real horror stories about members of the public trying to phone in and either just never getting an answer or being passed from pillar to post with no one willing to take responsibility. One story, which might have been exaggerated over time, was that of an old-aged pensioner wanting to report a burglary at her house in Blackburn. Instead of phoning treble-nine – because she didn't want to cause any bother – she phoned the number of her local nick. The phone rang and she waited for a reply. And waited. Ten minutes later, still no reply. She hung up and patiently tried again . . . and waited . . . then was relieved when a recorded message cut in and told her no one was available, but that her call was being forwarded and she was very important. The phone continued to ring out until another recorded message forwarded her on again . . . and again . . . until one hour later, the phone was answered – by a gruff, no-nonsense detective in Skelmersdale who told her she had the wrong number, try again, and hung up. She got through six days after the burglary, by which time she'd been done again.

Fortunately for Henry Christie, he could cut through all that crap. Even he, as a fully paid up member of the constabulary, often had problems making contact with people because no one seemed to want to answer their phones, preferring the non-confrontation of voicemail which meant that the recipient could decide when and if they should respond, and always did so at their leisure. Henry almost hated voicemail as much as mobile phones.

He had the direct, emergency number of the force incident manager, who was basically the boss of the Control Room at headquarters – and that night he used it, but even then it was not easy to get his message across.

'No, I don't know where she was calling from,' Henry jabbered down his mobile whilst reversing out of the drive. With a squeal of tyres and a quick wave to Kate on the doorstep, he accelerated off the estate.

'So, er, what exactly do you want me to do?'

'Get someone round to her address for a start?' he suggested.

'In Blackburn?'

'Yes, in Blackburn.'

'What was the address again?'

'Jesus – don't you listen?'

'I don't think there's any need to take that sort of tone with me, sir,' the affronted FIM said. He was an inspector Henry did not know and guessed was fairly new to the job.

'Look – sorry, OK . . . but there's a pretty serious incident happening somewhere and I know this is all pretty vague, but we need to get patrols to her flat and for others to be made aware that something's going down . . . the ARV crew need to be put on alert, too . . . authorize them to arm, please.'

'On the strength of an iffy phone call?'

'Just do it, OK? It's a precautionary measure.'

'Your name's on the log.'

'Whatever.' Fucking jobsworth, Henry thought as he sped towards the motorway junction at Marton Circle. He was travelling through a forty zone and as he passed a speed camera he was doing sixty – and it flashed. The least of his problems, he thought, knowing he could get it written off under the circumstances.

'Have you got your PR with you?' the FIM asked.

'Yeah.'

'Tune into Blackburn's channel, will you?'

'Will do.'

Henry hit the motorway at ninety whilst at the same time reaching across to the glove compartment to fish out his PR, which had been stuffed in there, hardly used since his transfer to a desk job. Somehow, he didn't seem to need it all that often in the office. He switched it on, praying there was some charge left in the battery. There was, and as he reached a hundred, he was fumbling with the channel selector to find Blackburn's wavelength. Once he'd done this, he helped himself to one of the cheese, ham and piccalilli sandwiches Kate had rustled up for him and stuffed into his sweaty mits as he ran out of the house, still unwashed. He devoured the food and felt an immediate benefit to his system.

As he drove, he listened to the deployments initiated by the FIM though actually carried out by a radio operator from Blackburn comms. Two patrols were sent up to the Kippax address, blue lighting it. Other patrols were asked to make to the area in readiness for something untoward happening and the ARV crew covering the division were given the authority to covertly arm. It is a fairly widely held belief that mobile firearms officers patrol with their weapons on their persons. In fact, their guns are secured in a safe in their vehicle, which they can only unlock in certain tightly controlled and author-ized circumstances.

Henry's mobile rang.

'What's going on?' It was Angela Cranlow. He was going to ring her personally once he'd finished his snack, but the FIM had beaten him to it. With a mouthful of sandwich, which he tried to swallow as he talked, Henry briefed her.

'And that's it? Not much to go on.'

'I agree.'

'Could it be a wind up? Just to annoy you?'

'She sounded genuine enough . . . definitely needs bottoming, though. Even if she's just pissed up and drowning her sorrows and maybe got hold of a gun.'

'Yeah, you're right. I take it you're on the way?'

'Yep. Are you turning out?' Henry asked.

'Would you like me too?'

'That's not the issue.'

'In that case, no . . . keep me updated and it might be that you have to personally debrief me after.'

Henry's heart sank. How the hell did he get himself into such predicaments? He shocked and amazed himself sometimes . . . most times. His phone beeped, indicating there was another incoming call.

'Speak soon, boss, got another call.' He thumbed to it and saw it was from a withheld number. 'Hello, Henry Christie . . .' There was nothing, just a rustling sound as though the other phone was in someone's pocket. 'Hello?' he said hopefully. Still nothing. He glowered at his phone as though it was offending him, then put it back to his ear and lodged it on to his right shoulder, realizing he should have plugged it into the hands-free. At one hundred miles per hour, that would have been the safer option. Then the phone went dead. He looked at it again, this time in frustration, then concentrated on the transmissions from his PR.

'Echo Romeo Seven, just arrived at the address.' That, Henry knew from the call sign, meant that the ARV had arrived at Jackie Kippax's flat, the first patrol to get there. The comms operator acknowledged him and Henry waited impatiently, nervously, for any developments, although he doubted whether Jackie would be there.

'Echo Romeo Seven to Blackburn,' the ARV chirped up after a few minutes.

'Go ahead.'

'No reply at the flat and it's all in darkness. Any further instructions?'

'Standby . . . DCI Christie, are you receiving?'

'Receiving,' Henry said.

'Did you hear Echo Romeo Seven's transmission?'

'Yes.'

'Anything further for him?'

Henry cogitated for a moment. 'Just tell him to hang fire there, will you – or at least in the vicinity of the flat. I'm, about fifteen minutes away, just on the M65 now.'

'Echo Romeo Seven, I received that.'

'Blackburn to DCI Christie – what about the other patrols? Can I stand them down? I've got a lot of jobs outstanding which need to be allocated.'

'Yeah, carry on,' Henry said, feeling a little foolish he'd got so many people rushing round. He slowed as he reached junction 4 of the motorway and turned on to the A666 whilst continually looking at his phone, willing it to ring again. 'C'mon Jackie,' he urged. He would only be happy when he had seen her face to face and assured himself she hadn't actually blown someone's head off.

He drove past Ewood Park, retracing the journey he'd made when he had turned out for Eddie Daley's death. He dropped the phone and picked up his PR as an idea struck him.

'DCI Christie to Echo Romeo Seven.'

'Go ahead, boss.'

Henry thought he recognized the voice. 'Is that you, Bill?'

'Certainly is – doing my duty on division.'

It was Henry's old friend, Bill Robbins, the firearms trainer who he'd bumped into at the training centre a while back and who'd given Henry a blast down the firing range with a .44 Magnum. Henry remembered him moaning about having to turn out for regular operational duty as well as doing his 'day job'.

'I'm sure everyone in Blackburn will sleep safer in their beds knowing that,' Henry said. 'However – you're certain there's no one in at Jackie Kippax's flat?'

'Affirmative.'

'Do you know where the Class Act is?'

'Yeah, Mincing Lane?'

'Meet me there in a few minutes. I've an idea where this woman might be.'

The A666 squeezed into Blackburn town centre, morphing into Great Bolton Street under the massive railway bridge at Lower Audley, then for a short stretch became Darwen Street before the one-way system kicked in and Henry was obliged to bear left into Mincing Lane. It was an area he knew well, mainly because this was the section of town, including Clayton Street, where most of Blackburn's on-street sex trade was plied.

At 10.30 p.m., Mincing Lane was quite busy traffic- and pedestrian-wise as there are a number of pubs in that area. The figures of the prostitutes were easy to spot; usually alone, sometimes in pairs, hanging around on the corners of their patches dressed in tight-fitting mini skirts and blouses. Henry had once dealt with the murder of one several years before.

As he drove slowly up Mincing Lane he wound his window down, allowing the symphony of the street to assault his eardrums. Music blared from quickly opened and shut pub doors; groups of youths moved around, shouting. There was a siren in the distance. And the smells, too, invaded his nostrils: chips, burgers, curry, the odd, strange waft of cheap perfume and above all, the aroma of hops from the beer being brewed by the giant brewery on the other side of town.

The Class Act, a name which belied the reality, was situated exactly where it should have been to attract the trade it did: just on the edge of the town centre and the cusp of the sleazy district of the sex trade, catering for the people who often crossed that line.

The place had been in existence for as long as Henry could remember, its reputation well known to most members of the constabulary. The name had changed a few times, but its nature, as in the spots of a leopard, had not. Even though Henry had never had any direct dealings with the place, he could recount numerous incidents off the top of his head which had taken place there, the most notorious ones being a double murder in the late 80s and a serious assault in which a man had had his left leg sawn off in the 90s. The Class Act frequently featured in the chief constable's daily bulletin of news from around the county, but despite numerous efforts by the police to close it down, it remained stubbornly open.

And to be honest, Henry loved this sort of place.

It said so much about the town itself.

But it wasn't open that night.

The Ford Galaxy with smoked out windows, which was the Armed Response Vehicle, was parked with two wheels on the kerb ahead of him on the opposite side of the road to the club, hazard lights flashing.

Henry drew his Rover in behind it, clicked on his hazards and looked across to the club, which was in darkness. The building stood alone, its front entrance opening directly on to the pavement, but the double wooden doors were firmly closed. Dark alleyways ran down either side of it, places where many people had been assaulted over the years.

Henry got out and was approached by Bill and his ARV

partner, a female officer Henry did not know. They wore reflec-
tive jackets over their body armour and Henry could just see
their holsters poking out below the hems of their jackets –
including the muzzles of their pistols. They were both still
tooled up and Henry realized that the authorization had not
been revoked. Both were sipping coffee from polystyrene cups
with lids on. Bill handed an extra one to Henry.

'Hope you don't mind, boss,' he said. 'We did a quick drive
through on the way down from Fishmoor. Thought you'd
appreciate one, too.'

'No probs.' Henry gratefully accepted the drink. He knew
it all looked pretty slack, drinking like this in the eye of the
public, but he was gagging after his sandwich and his adren-
aline-fuelled dash across the county which had dried him up
like a kipper. He broke back the seal on the lid and took a
gulp, burning his mouth.

'So, no sign of life up at the flat?'

'Nothing, boss.'

'Isn't this place usually open by now?' He pointed at the
Class Act.

'Too early,' the WPC said. She was a local officer and Bill
had been teamed up with her for the night. 'Doesn't usually
open until eleven thirty-ish.'

'Oh, yeah,' Henry said, realizing. 'Of course, silly me.'

'You think this Kippax woman might be in here?' Bill asked.

Henry shrugged. He had some more coffee, which tasted
amazingly good. 'It's something we were going to look into
tomorrow as there might be some connection with the people
who run this place and Eddie Daley's murder . . . his girl-
friend, Jackie Kippax, thought they might have some grudge
against him, but we haven't had the chance to make that inquiry
yet.'

'I take it you know who owns the place now?' the WPC
asked rhetorically.

'I take it you do.'

'Johnny Strongitharm.'

'Really!' Henry knew Strongitharm by reputation, though
he'd never had any dealings with the guy. Strongitharm, an
appropriately named crim from Blackburn, was one of a dying
breed of violent armed robbers who specialized in money on
the move. Security vans, in other words. It was estimated he

had made millions from highway robbery over the years and Henry recalled several unsuccessful crime squad operations against him. He was finally convicted of a very brutal robbery-gone-wrong about ten years before at a Royal Mail sorting office when a security guard was maimed when a shotgun blew off part of his leg. A big NCIS investigation had finally nailed Johnny, but not the money, some £600,000. 'I thought he was still inside,' Henry said.

'Released last year and bunked off to Spain, but not before buying this shit-hole for some reason,' the WPC said.

'A bolt hole,' Henry suggested. 'Allows him to keep tabs on comings and goings in town.'

'Maybe . . . anyway, he owns it, but someone else manages it.'

'That someone is?'

'Guy called Darren Langmead.'

'Dear me, bad to worse,' Henry exclaimed. He also knew of Langmead, a vicious low-life enforcer and tax collector who revelled in breaking people's fingers.

'The licence is in someone else's name, of course,' she explained. 'Some clean-sheeted guy called Jones, who is never there. Way of the world,' she shrugged. 'That's how they keep the licence.'

'Right, OK,' Henry breathed, taking in these facts and not being surprised that Langmead could well have been embezzling from a boss who lived two thousand miles away, whatever his ruthless rep might be. He looked across at the club. 'Let's check it out.'

The three of them crossed Mincing Lane and spent some time at the front door, getting no response from inside and finding the door well secured, so they entered the narrow, cobbled alley running down the right side of the club. They were hit by the immediate stench of rotting food from several overfilled wheelie bins and plastic bin bags which had burst, their contents scattered by the indigenous wildlife – cats, dogs, rats and tramps. It wasn't easy to tell what was being stepped on and Henry tried not to think about it as he dropped his coffee cup on to a pile of trash.

They reached a door in a wall surrounding the rear yard of the club. Henry tried the handle, but it was locked.

'I have an idea,' the WPC announced, looking fairly repulsed by her present situation. 'Why don't I go and ring the bell again? And I'll see if comms can get hold of a key holder. You boys have fun.' She didn't wait for an answer, just turned on her heels and picked her way carefully back down the alley.

'She should be a sergeant,' Henry sniffed.

'She will be,' Bill sniffed, too.

Henry tried the handle once more, confirming it was indeed locked. He put his shoulder to it, but it didn't budge. Taking a step back he surveyed the height of the wall and wondered if he was capable of scaling all seven feet of it. He thought he could, but what bothered him was what might be on top of it, such as glass shards embedded in concrete or razor wire, and what might be lurking on the other side, such as something with sharp fangs, a bad attitude and hunger pangs.

He and Bill exchanged glances in the dark.

'Is there anything to say she's actually in there?' Bill asked hopefully.

'Nothing, a hunch, could be a million miles off the mark . . . but it needs to be checked out. Once we've eliminated this, we'll try elsewhere.'

'Better get over, then.'

'It's what we like doing best.'

Henry jumped at the wall, his fingers gripping the top of it, and found a purchase for his left foot on the door handle and, shakily, eased himself up so his elbows were on top of the wall and his head high enough to peer over.

'No broken glass, anyway . . . doesn't seem to be any wildlife in the yard, just junk and barrels.'

He scrambled on to the wall and perched there, one leg on either side, letting his eyes adjust themselves to the shadows beyond. He could see the backdoor of the Class Act reached by half a dozen steps. It looked like a reasonably easy door to break down, if necessary. He swung his legs over and dropped clumsily into the yard, jarring his knees, causing his right one to give unexpectedly, though he managed to remain upright, stumbling slightly.

Bill was with him moments later, landing heavily with all his kit on.

The yard was quite large and, as Henry had seen, full of discarded waste, wheelie bins, barrels and crates, all pretty typical of the back of a poorly managed licensed premises.

They walked towards the backdoor, stepping in and out of the mess, until they reached the foot of the steps – when Henry noticed something to his left, pushed up against the wall. As he realized what it was, he gulped and tapped Bill and at the same time thought he heard something behind which could've been a low, guttural growl.

He froze. 'That's a kennel,' he hissed.

'Yep,' said Bill, also having seen it.

'Did you hear what I heard?'

'Yep.' Bill was never the most chatty of people.

They rotated slowly and in the shadow between two wheelie bins stood a beast which had cunningly allowed them into its lair, stalked and trapped them. It stepped forwards, revealing itself, its powerful head and shoulders protruding from the darkness.

'Shit.' Henry swallowed, experiencing fear like nothing before. A kind of desolate emptiness, a panic of epic proportions.

'Pit bull,' breathed Bill quietly. His right hand moved slowly to his holster.

'If you shoot it, it'll get mad,' Henry said seriously.

'It already looks pretty mad.'

The dog took a few more steps and became clearly visible to the two officers. It was a magnificent creature, even Henry had to grudgingly admit, scared as he was and ambivalent towards canines in general. Basically they did nothing for him. He could see no further than eating, shitting and biting and costing money, which is why he had always declined his daughters' pleas for one.

This animal looked the business. A good twenty-two inches high, probably weighing in about fifty-five pounds, all of it rippling muscle, under a thick, short coat of shiny hair, the colour of which could not be made out in the light available, but was probably a light brown. On top of that, there must also have been a brain inside its thick skull which was intelligent enough to allow two idiots to climb into its den without letting them know it was waiting with bared teeth.

Its ears lay back, its hackles up, head thrust forward, lips drawn back revealing a set of dentures that would do a good job of tearing these intruders apart.

'Bugger,' Henry said weakly, already imagining his face being ripped away.

The dog took a few more steps in their direction, moving more like a leopard than a canine.

Henry swallowed. Bill slowly withdrew his Glock, his hand shaking, desperate not to make a sudden move.

'Think it'll let us go back the way we came?'

'Only minus our balls,' Bill said.

His dithering hand came out with the gun.

Henry laid a hand on his forearm. 'Back up slowly to the door,' he said. 'It might be open. One step at a time.'

As they stepped back one, the dog stepped forwards one. It was like some ritualistic dance of death. They dog knew it had them, had all the time in the world. Henry could see its eyes as it looked from one, then to the other human, deciding which to savage first.

Henry caught his heel and nearly tumbled over on to his arse, but steadied himself, knowing that a quick movement could precipitate a charge.

Bill had slowly raised the Glock, easing his left hand under his right to support the weapon, aiming at the dog's head, somewhere at a point where a cross drawn between the eyes and ears met – centre skull.

About ten feet separated them from the animal. If it leapt towards them now, it would be on them in a flash.

Each man stepped carefully back, tension coursing through them.

'It's fuckin' playing with us,' Henry said, his terror growing. Why couldn't a back yard be guarded by some knife-wielding maniac, or someone with a machine gun? Both would have been preferable to this.

The dog growled again, a primeval sound expertly designed to turn would-be prey into immoveable lumps. It worked.

Then Henry heard something from behind, inside the Class Act. The sliding of a bolt. Yes, he almost jumped for joy; the WPC had obviously managed to get inside. She had made her way through to the back of the premises to let them in.

There was further noise from inside. Keys being turned. More bolts sliding.

Bill removed his left hand, the supporting hand, from underneath the gun and it went to his PR transmitter button and mike affixed to the outside of his jacket on his left shoulder.

'Get the door open, Carly,' he said urgently, without preamble. 'Get it open now.'

'Why?'

'Because we're about to be attacked by a pit bull.'

There was more noise behind the door, something being dragged away, a scraping. 'It's stuck,' she said. 'This bolt is stuck.'

Henry could sense the dog was about to launch itself. It quivered, collecting itself, bracing itself and then it happened and it was hurtling towards Henry.

He saw it rise up into the air, ears pinned back, teeth bared, like a beast from hell. He found himself rooted to the spot, unable to move a muscle. The height it reached was incredible and it could easily have latched its jaws on to Henry's face, but at the last moment, when Henry believed he could smell its deathly breath, his survival instinct cut in and made him move. He twisted desperately away, raised his forearm in self-defence and at the same time, Bill lashed out and kicked the animal in the stomach with his steel toe-capped boots, sending it sprawling across the yard.

But this was no lapdog, which would go away cowering and whining.

As it landed on the concrete, it immediately regained its feet and launched itself back at the cops, its claws scratching the floor for leverage.

In that moment, the WPC wrenched back the sticking bolt and yanked open the door.

Bill scrambled in, leaving Henry still outside to face the oncoming savagery of the dog, which had now got ten degrees madder.

Henry's instinct for self-preservation took over. A slight slip of the pit bull as it clawed its way to him gave him an instant to do something. Stacked up next to him in a precarious pile were a dozen plastic beer crates. He grabbed them and toppled them into the gap between himself and the pooch, pushing them over the dog as they fell. In terms of hurting the dog, they were ineffective, but they impeded its charge and gave Henry that extra moment to turn and throw himself through the open door, which was slammed shut behind him by the WPC.

Henry dropped his hands to his knees, gasping for air, almost retching. Bill had adopted much the same position. They traded glances, blowing out their cheeks, a connection between them having just avoided a mauling. Outside, the dog howled in frustration and clawed at the door like a monster from a horror movie.

Henry stood up.

Bill holstered the Glock. 'That was fuckin' close.'

Everything on Henry was shaking. He took several deep breaths.

Eventually both got their breath back, and their manhood.

'Thanks,' Henry said to the female officer. 'Carly, isn't it?'

'Yeah – no probs,' she said – but the expression on her face told a different story.

'How did you manage to get in?'

'Member of staff turning up for work,' she said, unsteadily.

'Hey – it's all right,' Henry said, picking up on her voice. 'We're OK.'

'I'm not bothered about you,' she said. 'Back there.' She pointed down the corridor into the building. 'Blood every-where.'

'Bodies?' Henry asked.

She shook her head. 'I haven't seen anyone, but it's a blood bath.'

'Let's go see.'

Carly led them through to the main body of the Class Act by way of a storeroom, through another door and they emerged into the main bar room, coming in behind the bar itself, which was long and wide. The lights had been turned on and Henry could see the place was an unkempt dive. It reeked of stale beer and cigarette smoke, which was only to be expected, perhaps; but it was also a dirty mess with hundreds of uncol-lected glasses on the bar top and tables, all the ashtrays full to overflowing. There was a small dance floor to one side, next to which was a raised circular stage from which a pole rose to the ceiling. Henry could visualize the customer base immediately: the best of Blackburn.

A thin blonde woman sat at one of the tables, smoking, looking at them nervously.

'That the staff member?' Henry asked.

'Yeah, she's the pole dancer. I told her to stay put.'
'Where's the blood?'

Carly showed the way across the bar, weaving through tables over sticky carpets, crunching with broken glass and savoury snacks, through another door leading to the tiled entrance foyer behind the front doors. Henry could hear the traffic passing on Mincing Lane. Carly held out an arm to stop them going any further. 'Here,' she said. Bill peered over her shoulder. Henry was by her side, maybe half a step behind her, her raised arm preventing him from going any further. His jaw literally dropped. Blood was everywhere inside the foyer. All over the floor, up the walls, runny and congealing. 'I came in, slithered a bit, saw what I'd been standing in and after I'd dumped the dancer in the bar, I ran through to the back door. I know my way round the place,' she explained. 'Been to a few jobs here in my time.'

There were two more doors off the foyer. One, closed, had the word 'Private' stamped on it and another, slightly ajar, had a sign with the word 'Snug' on it.

'That's the posh bar in there, I take it?' Henry said.

'And kitchen,' Carly said, missing Henry's stab at irony.

Henry took a few seconds to look at the blood. Something major had taken place here and he would have bet his underwear it was connected to the phone call from Jackie Kippax.

'Looks like someone's been dragged through there,' Bill said, pointing to the 'snug' bar. There was a smeared trail of blood leading towards the door.

'Yeah,' Henry agreed. 'Let's take a look and do your best to keep your feet out of the blood if at all possible.'

Henry moved in front of Carly and tiptoed across the foyer, trying his best to place his toes in spaces where the blood hadn't splashed, which was incredibly difficult. The two firearms officers followed with equal care.

He stopped on the threshold of the snug and, using the knuckle of his right forefinger, pushed the door fully open, revealing a small bar, but no more appetizing than the larger one on the other side. It was smelly and unappealing. The blood smear continued across the carpet, making Henry wonder who was dragging who. He thought it unlikely to be female dragging male. The trail went through a double swinging door at the back of the room marked 'Kitchen'.

'What do you think, Henry?' Bill asked in his ear.

'Keep your hand on your weapon and don't shoot me in the back.' He moved off, walking alongside the trail as it snaked its way across the carpet to the kitchen door. He held his breath as he pushed open the left side of the swinging door, then stepped in, just knowing this was as far as it went. Here would be answers, he thought – and more questions.

'Hell,' he said dully at the sight that greeted his eyes.

Behind him, Bill pushed to get a look. Henry heard the breath gush out of his colleague's lungs. He turned when he heard a further groan to see Carly, whose knees had buckled under her, pirouette away in a faint. Henry lunged for her and managed to get his hands under her arms and ease her to the floor, ensuring she didn't smack her head on the descent. He left her in a swoon and regarded the tableau in front of him.

A terrible scene. Two people lay sprawled on the floor in a kitchen aisle between a sink unit and a large fridge-freezer. A single-barrelled sawn-off shotgun was discarded next to them and it was that weapon that had caused the damage.

Henry approached carefully, thinking 'evidence' all the time, and even though he knew instinctively that this was a tragedy that would go no further than a coroner's court, it still had to be dealt with as though it were a murder, which in part it probably was.

The first body he came to was that of a male, maybe forty years old, dressed in what had once been a white T-shirt and jeans. There was a massive shotgun wound to his neck, a whole chunk of it as big as an apple having been blown out; there was another horrific wound to his lower abdomen, just above the groin area.

He swallowed and glanced at Bill, who rose from attending the woozy Carly.

'I don't know this man,' Henry said. 'Could turn out to be Darren Langmead, maybe?'

'I think Carly knows him.'

Henry stepped carefully past the dead male. 'I do know this one, though.'

'Jackie Kippax?'

Henry nodded, a bitter taste in his mouth.

She was a mess, and on the face of it, it was obvious what had happened to her: she had committed suicide.

There was a perfect hole in the soft, fleshy part underneath her chin. Henry knew it would be the exact size of the barrel of the shotgun, which had been held there before being discharged. The shot had entered her at a slight angle, leaving her face virtually intact, or as intact as it could be when the back half of the head had been blown off and was stuck on the ceiling as though a pan of Bolognese had exploded. Henry looked at it and sighed.

More awake than he should have been, Henry sat opposite Angela Cranlow in the deserted canteen at Blackburn police station and handed her a black coffee from the machine. He had worked out that coffee to him was like blood to a vampire – the only thing that kept him going. Their kiss, only a few short hours earlier, was a distant memory, one he was trying to forget completely, pretend it hadn't happened. Unfortunately, he had to admit that despite her tired eyes and hair scraped dramatically back off her face, his boss looked pretty damned good – even at two in the morning. As though she'd just rolled out of bed, which she had.

He reckoned what she was seeing wasn't quite so alluring, though.

'Thanks, Henry. Reckon you'll ever get to bed again?'

'I think I'm capable of living without sleep from now on. Sleep's just a bad habit. All you need is a bit of willpower . . . and amphets, obviously.' He swigged his own coffee and winced. 'Just kidding.'

'Where are we up to, then?'

Henry took it to mean the investigation into Eddie Daley's death and the subsequent double deaths of Jackie Kippax and Darren Langmead, erstwhile manager of the Class Act, now closed down for the foreseeable future. He hoped she did not mean him and her.

'Seems that Jackie believed Langmead was Eddie's killer and she's taken the law into her own hands, gone out to challenge him about it before we got the chance to do it properly. A quick PNC inquiry showed that Eddie was the holder of a shotgun certificate, which accounts for her access to the weapon, though I doubt it should have been a sawn-off one.'

He paused. 'Trying to put it all together isn't easy, but looking at the scene, it seems she's gone to see Langmead at the Class Act, they've had a discussion which has obviously gone pear-shaped. I'm guessing he probably denied killing Eddie, she disagreed and produced the shotgun and blasted him in the gut. They were upstairs in the living quarters at this point. Probably mortally wounded even at that point, Langmead has managed to do a runner and she's gone after him and pumped another into his neck in the foyer, which killed him outright. Somehow and, for the moment, for reasons unexplained, she has managed to drag his body all the way into the kitchen then topped herself. How she had the strength and why she dragged him I don't know. A tragedy on top of a tragedy. But she had nothing to lose, I suppose. She said she was dying of cancer, Eddie had gone and she had nothing left to live for. I'm guessing . . .' Henry shrugged uncertainly.

'All supposition at this stage?'

'It's called hypothesis in the world of investigation, ma'am.'

'Guessing, you mean?'

'Absolutely. She didn't trust me to bring in Eddie's killer, so she did the job herself.'

'What about the phone call?'

'Er, well, perhaps she had him bang to rights, admitting everything under the duress of a shotgun, then he went for her, although I did hear a man in the background say "You got it wrong" when she phoned me . . .'

'Do you think Langmead killed Eddie?'

Henry leaned back and gazed at the high roof above. 'I don't know. I'm not convinced, but it's something I need to follow up.'

'You've still got a few days left before it all gets handed back to Anger. Use the time constructively.'

'I will, boss.'

She yawned, covering her mouth and saying, 'Sorry,' in a girlish way. 'I need to get some sleep . . . got meetings all day from eight . . . no rest for the wicked . . . no chance to be wicked, actually.' She grinned. 'I'm off. Night.'

She left and Henry was still buzzing. He toyed with his plastic cup, knowing that the journey home would give him time to wind down, but something still nagged at the back of his mind.

He picked up his PR and called Bill Robbins, asking him
to ring back on the mobile phone facility on the PR, which
he did.

'Bill, thanks for tonight.'

'No probs, boss,' he said laconically.

'How's Carly?'

'Shaken, but OK. Gone home.'

'Did you fix up the RSPCA for the Hound of the
Baskervilles?'

'Done.'

'What time're you finishing?'

'Round about now . . . why?' he enquired cautiously.

'Fancy a quick peek round at Jackie Kippax's flat?'

There was a pregnant pause. Then, 'You authorizing the
overtime?'

'Yeah, why not. See you at the back door of the nick
in ten.'

Henry entered the flat using the key found on Jackie's body.
It was a typical council flat, plain, functional, not modern, but
quite well looked after by Jackie and Eddie. They seemed to
have had everything they needed and although not luxurious,
there was a nice suite, TV, DVD and video player/recorder, a
computer, a decent CD player and lots of discs. The kitchen
was basic and clean. Henry imagined they rubbed along all
right, despite the fact he had allegedly ruined their lives all those
years before.

Henry let his eyes wander as Bill drifted through the flat,
but not touching anything. Later in the morning the CSI team
would be in doing a full job on it.

'Owt in particular?' Bill asked.

'Dunno.' Henry scratched his head, aware that he did that
far too often. He flattened his short hair down and wandered
around the flat, feeling that the visit was probably useless.
The he went round it again, that 'something' nagging at his
mind.

On the third sweep, he had a Eureka moment, one of those
moments that can affect the whole direction of a murder investigation when there is a realization that the most simple thing
has been missed. Henry gave himself a contemptuous mental
kick up the arse.

Ten

Henry was hard pressed to recall a time when he had been more exhausted, but the regular slush of adrenaline and/or caffeine pumping into his system kept him going through the night and into the morning, right up to the briefing with his Special Projects Murder Squad, now the 'SPMS' to the people in the know. It reminded Henry of something vaguely Roman.

Although his mind was a mush, he forced himself to present the bright-eyed bunch with the developments that had taken place overnight.

'. . . but despite all that, this investigation continues until we ascertain whether or not Darren Langmead is Eddie Daley's killer. Once we have done that, then, yeah, it's over bar the paperwork, but we need to keep an open mind about it. Just because Jackie Kippax thought he killed Eddie doesn't mean to say he actually did and we need to keep all lines of inquiry open.'

At first, the news of the shooting incident at the Class Act had deflated the team, but Henry's belief that Eddie's killer could still be at large reinstated their enthusiasm. There was something to aim for, not just a lot of paper sifting, which they did anyway.

Henry had managed to snaffle two cars from the HQ transport by sneaking into the office in the garage, purloining two sets of keys and then driving the cars to distant points of the car park so they would not be found that easily. He knew he could get into trouble for it, but he was past caring. The newly formed SPMS needed transport because he was intending to send them out to Blackburn to do some knocking on doors and digging around and there was no other alternative than to steal vehicles. He knew that the lack of staff numbers was a big drawback to the investigation, but he intended to achieve as much as possible in the short time he had left, by targeting them at a few important facets as he saw fit.

He dispatched two pairs and handed them car keys, sending them wide-eyed into the big, nasty world, and hoping they wouldn't get into too much trouble. He deliberately held back the ex-detective Graeme Walling and the WPC with attitude, Jenny Fisher, to task separately. As they then departed, leaving Henry alone in the office, Detective Chief Superintendent Dave Anger entered, smirking.

Henry, lounging back in an office chair, purposely swung his feet up on to the desk and remained lounging. Anger saun- tered over and balanced on the corner of the desk and adjusted his Gestapo-style spectacles.

'The sick, lame and lazy murder squad, I understand,' he said. Henry chose not to respond. 'A bunch of seasoned incom- petents, led by a major incompetent.'

'*Captain* incompetent, if you don't mind,' Henry said, fancying a verbal joust. He was determined to stay calm.

'Sounds like the job's solved itself, which is a good thing. At least it means you won't have egg all over your mush when you hand it over to a real murder squad after Friday – a team which, by the way, I'm starting to pull together now. As soon as the lovely Condoleezza Rice has gone, we'll take over and start tying it up.'

'Fine by me.'

'Just make sure it's all settled paperwork-wise, etcetera, etcetera . . . otherwise I'll continue to humiliate you, even if you think you have Angela Cranlow's ear.'

They glared at each other like a couple of savage dogs, each wanting to rip out the other's throat.

Anger eased himself to his feet. 'Good progress on your last case, by the way,' he said, trying to rub a bit of salt in.

'The TV appearance on *Crimewatch*?' Henry chuckled. 'You go on that programme when a job's gone tits up, don't you? And by the way, you look even porkier on the box.'

Anger chortled. 'That could've been you,' he taunted.

'Nah . . . I would've solved it long ago.'

Anger breathed in unsteadily and Henry wondered if they would ever come to serious blows. He relished the thought of pounding Anger to a pulp, but knew it would never happen. And, regardless of his desire to stay cool, he was finding himself becoming more and more worked up by Anger's presence and could not resist saying, though he knew it was childish, 'In case it's eating away at you, your missus does give good head.' He immediately regretted it, particularly as Anger rushed him, grabbed his legs and with a remarkable burst of strength, tipped Henry backwards off the chair into the wall. He toppled off, catching his head on the rim of a metal wastebasket, caught napping by Anger's speed.

Henry was quickly on his feet, ready to go for it, but Anger had already reached the door where he turned and growled, 'You need to watch your balance, mate.' Then he was gone.

Henry rubbed the side of his head, feeling ashamed of himself at falling to Anger's primeval level. Not good.

Shaking his head in disbelief, he walked across to his office in the corner and sat behind his desk, determined to do some brainwork. Suddenly, though, his thinking became blurred with fatigue.

It was just after 10 a.m., so he swooped down to the canteen, constructed a crispy bacon sandwich from the self-service counter, washed it down with tea for a change, then felt himself begin to chill. He had about four hours before any of his team were due to report back and the post-mortems of Kippax and Langmead weren't due to take place until after 5 p.m.

In the meantime, Henry knew exactly what he was going to do.

It was slightly strange and a little bit decadent to be easing himself into bed at ten thirty in the morning, but also fantastic. He had managed to appropriate one of the newly refurbished rooms in the student accommodation at the training centre, which even had an en-suite toilet and shower, a kettle and a TV. Truly luxurious in comparison to how the rooms were years before, when he came on courses. Then they were basic and uncomfortable and after a night on the razz the choice was either to pee in the sink in your room, or traipse all the way to the cold, tiled-floored toilets at the end of the corridor, then back again, shivering, possibly to find that the room door had mysteriously locked behind you. Henry had peed in many sinks in his younger days.

The sheets were crisp and cool and as he pulled the duvet

over his head to muffle the sounds of the centre, he was soon asleep.

The reconstructed face of the murdered and horrendously burned female featured in Henry's bleak dreams. He talked to her and she replied with tears in her eyes. The words were indistinct, but Henry could see the woman was happy, but worried at the same time. Then the torture came – the drowning, the strangulation, the beating, the flames and out of the fires emerged Dave Anger like a deranged phoenix who leapt into a Rover 75 and drove it at Henry, jarring him into reluctant wakefulness . . . but only for a moment before he slid back to sleep and the dream evaporated . . . until he found himself walking down a cell corridor, responding to the soft knocking of a prisoner in a cell. He opened the door, but the cell was empty . . . yet the knocking continued . . . until he realized it was not a dream and the tapping was coming from the other side of his own door.

He twisted, picked up his watch from the bedside cabinet and squinted at it. He had set the alarm for 1 p.m. . . . it was 12.45 p.m. He sighed – he could have had fifteen minutes more – and with a curse he rolled out of bed, putting his eye to the peephole in the door.

'One second,' he called. He massaged his face quickly, grabbed his trousers and dragged them on before opening the door to the deputy chief constable.

Underneath her trench coat, which she quickly removed, she was in full regalia, with all the 'bird shit' emblems associated with her rank on the epaulettes on her narrow shoulders and lapels, which seemed to weigh her down. She looked bright and fully awake, very well turned out and sweet smelling. Her eyes did a quick once-over of Henry's bare stomach and chest, making him inhale quickly, suddenly devastatingly aware he had far too much loose skin and flab hanging around. Her eyes rose.

'I thought I'd see how things were progressing,' she explained. 'I've got a short break before my next meeting.'

'Oh, OK,' Henry said, holding his left arm across his chest, feeling vulnerable. 'It's going all right,' he began.

'I know it is,' she said throatily, her eyes sparkling with lust. She eased herself past Henry, her soft hands touching his arms as she moved him gently aside. He watched her as she switched on the TV, turning the volume up slightly, then turned back to face him. It was only a small room and there was very little distance between them. 'Unfinished business,' she said.

Her right hand went to the back of his neck, pulling him down to her and forcing her lips on to his. At first he resisted – slightly – but she tasted and smelled delicious and he couldn't hold himself back. His arms encircled her and she crushed against him, her hands running up and down his naked spine, sending shocks through his nerve endings, making him shiver. Finally they broke apart, Henry almost bursting out of his trousers.

'This is so dangerous,' he said.

'I laugh in the face of danger,' she said mockingly, throwing back her head, exposing her neck. 'And in case you hadn't worked it out, I get what I want. My looks deceive people.'

She bit Henry's left nipple, making him utter a tiny squeal like a kettle, then she divested herself of her uniform in what seemed to be a well practised manoeuvre. In a moment she was standing there in a functional white bra, frilly knickers and – completely amazing Henry – stockings and suspenders.

'Dear God,' he slavered.

She unhooked her bra and tossed it aside, then slid her hands into the waistband of his pants and drew him towards her, unzipped him and eased them down his legs, kneeling in front of him.

Not completely sure it hadn't all been a dream, Henry grabbed a prawn mayo sandwich and coffee-to-go at the training centre canteen. He guessed there was a Race and Diversity course running because he recognized a transvestite and transsexual sitting together at one of the tables, then hurried back to headquarters. He was still wearing the clothes he'd had on for the last two days, but at least he'd had a shower and had quickly ironed everything in the laundry room before putting it all back on, hoping the steam would force a bit of freshness back into his gear. He had plans to dash home and get changed before this afternoon's post-mortems.

Two members of the SPMS were waiting for him when he bustled, red faced, back into the Special Projects office. Graeme

Walling and Jenny Fisher sat there patiently and he knew they knew. Everybody knew. He had just had amazing sex with the deputy chief constable in one of the rooms in student accommodation at the training centre. It was bound to be common knowledge. Not that it was unusual for cops to have sex in those rooms – they even sold condoms in the training centre shop, for God's sake – but it was usually confined to young, horny probationers going wild or macho detectives on their initial CID course proving how manly they were. Not two high-ranking, experienced officers and in the middle of the day.

'Hi guys,' he said, flushed. 'What news?' Each waited for the other, until Henry said, 'Jenny?'

Her task had been to liaise with the Telephone Unit to get details of the phone bills from Eddie Daley's office. Simple enough on the face of it, and something the police did in a lot of cases, but it was usually a slow, bureaucratic process. Getting it done quickly was hard.

She held up a few sheets of paper. 'Success,' she said, smiling.

'Oh, well done,' Henry said genuinely. He saw her blush with pleasure and he guessed she probably hadn't had many pats on the back before, that very simple motivational tool, rarely used by managers.

'Eddie had a BT account from that office . . . and you were right,' she said. Henry crossed to her and looked over her shoulder. Her finger pointed to a frequently dialled '0845' number. 'That's the number for Orange pay as you go internet service. It used to be Freeserve.'

'So he did have a computer in that office?'

'Looks like it.'

Which confirmed Henry's brainwave he'd had whilst looking through Jackie Kippax's flat in the early hours. He noticed Jackie had a computer and it had suddenly clicked with him that a computer wasn't something he had seen in Eddie's office, yet he recalled Jackie telling him how much Eddie used one. It stood to reason, therefore, that someone carrying on the dubious profession of a gumshoe would have one in his office. Who the hell didn't these days?

Henry had seized Jackie's computer and then, with Bill, had driven the short distance to Eddie's office over the shop and entered what was still a crime scene.

No computer.

But Eddie, being such a slob, never dusted and it did not take a mastermind to look at his desk and see the faint outline in the dust of a circular stand on which the monitor had rested. But there was no monitor, no keyboard, no computer, no wires and no printer.

Hindsight, being such a powerful tool, made Henry wish he had spotted this gap before; made him wish he had asked different questions of Jackie; made him realize, or at least guess in an educated way, that whoever had killed Eddie had also stolen his computer. Which begged the question, why? What was on the computer that was so precious? Was it something that pointed to the killer? And this was why he had tasked two of his team to find out if Darren Langmead had a computer, or if he had got Eddie's computer stashed away somewhere.

Henry looked at Graeme Walling. He knew that Walling was a bit of a computer nerd and had given him Jackie's computer and asked him to go plug it in somewhere and see what was on it. After all, it wasn't such a long shot to imagine that Eddie also used Jackie's computer. 'What've you got?'

Before he could answer, the office door opened and Angela Cranlow came in, slid into a seat at an unused desk. She smiled encouragingly at everyone. 'Don't mind me.'

Her hair had been pulled back into a ponytail because she'd been unable to tame it back into a smooth bob after Henry had finished with her. She still looked the business, he thought.

'I've been through her computer, as you asked.' Walling indicated the computer on the desk at which he sat. 'There's some interesting stuff on it. Lots of visits to porn sites, some white supremacist stuff, BNP.' Walling's face creased with distaste. He beckoned Henry to stand behind him. He, Jenny and Angela took up a position behind him and Henry twitched as Angela tweaked his rear. 'Let me just log in . . . there's no security on this, by the way, no passwords, nothing . . . but that's pretty usual for home computers.'

The computer was already switched on. Walling selected an icon from the desktop and double-clicked the mouse. The Orange Internet screen came up and he pressed 'Connect'. The computer began to make the horrible screechy connection noises as the modem found the server and the Orange

homepage appeared. Walling then went to the Google homepage and clicked the history button and allowed the cursor to
hover over a website address.

'Google is the main search engine used,' Walling said.
'Obviously it's impossible to tell whether these searches were
done by Jackie or Eddie,' he explained. 'I trawled through
loads of stuff to see what had been visited and one thing sort
of stood out. I mean, it was mostly rubbish, but when I started
looking at the history pages I saw there had been a series of
searches for doctors' surgeries and health centres in London,
which I found interesting.'

'Why interesting?' Angela asked.

Walling shrugged. 'Anything a bit odd interests me,' he said.
Henry glanced at him and thought, A jack speaking, and knew
that Walling should have been better looked after, should still
have been a detective somewhere. Henry waited. Although
curious, he knew there was nothing more annoying for a cop
than to be interrupted in full flow, especially when the cop
thought he was going to reveal something vital. Walling was
on a little stage, the centre of attention, and needed his few
moments of fame.

'I went into every site visited and then dug into the sites
as well. Just curiosity, really, but, like I said, it just struck me
as odd and I assumed this was because of something maybe
Eddie had been investigating. These searches, by the way, are
about six months old. The history pages have never been
wiped, so there was a lot of crap on it, if you'll pardon my
French. Most of the recent stuff doesn't have any sort of
pattern to it. People look at such rubbish.'

A yawn tried to break from Henry's mouth. He held it back,
his face rippling with the effort. He caught Angela's eyes and
she opened them wider, seductively. A quick memory of her
straddling him on the single bed flitted in and out, her lovely
boobs hanging just above his face. Hell, a deputy chief
constable. What a coup! Not that there were many like Angela
Cranlow. Mostly they were gnarled, angry looking blokes and
the idea of sex with them, even from a female or gay perspec-
tive, was pretty bleak.

'. . . So, I went on every site visited,' Walling said, and in
true dramatic fashion, revealed the best last, 'and this is the
one that's the key.'

He clicked on it. The computer thought for a moment and then the connection was made, revealing the site of the Empress Medical Centre, Earl's Court, London. The homepage showed a photograph of a newly built, single storey building which could have been any health centre anywhere in the country.

There was a menu on the right side of the page: general practitioners, the practice team; how to use the surgery: repeat prescriptions; services available to patients; well baby clinic; zero tolerance – violent patients; self treatment of common illnesses; useful telephone numbers; locums.

He moved the cursor over each one and most of them expanded into a sub-menu.

'Mostly uninteresting stuff until we get to this one,' Walling said. He clicked on the 'locums' icon. This produced a further list of names and he clicked on one, which opened into a photograph of an Asian woman by the name of Dr Sabera Ismat. 'Ring any bells?'

All three observers peered closely at the photo.

Henry's brow creased. The woman looked familiar and somewhere deep in his subconscious he believed he should know why, but he could not drag it up. She was a very attractive woman with sparkling eyes and an infectious smile, useful qualities for a doctor.

'No.' Henry looked at the other two. They shook their heads.

'OK,' Walling said, clearly relishing this. 'What about this then?'

He clicked on the 'minimize screen' button and the photograph disappeared and the blue background of the desktop reappeared. He clicked through a number of programmes. 'This is a programme that is used to download digital photos from a camera on to a computer to store them, view them, mess around with them, print them off – whatever. The photos I'm about to show you were put on about six months ago, according to the properties.'

'I've got one on my computer I use for my holiday piccies,' Jenny chirped up.

'Yeah, they're pretty common. There's a lot of photos in this file, mainly of Eddie Daley and Jackie Kippax on holiday, by the looks of them. But this is the interesting one, filed under "Work".' He clicked on a file icon and a series of small photographs unfolded which focused in on a woman sitting

at a table outside a restaurant, with some other people. Walling
selected one and expanded it to full screen size. In it, the
woman was laughing at something, her head thrown back,
revealing her long, slender, dark neck. An Asian man was
sitting next to her, smiling.

Henry's mouth opened slowly.

It was a photograph of the woman doctor, Sabera Ismat.

But there was something on the photograph that had caught
his eye, which made him go quite weak.

'There's about ten photos in this file,' Walling said, 'mainly
of this woman sitting having a meal.' He minimized the photo
and clicked on a few more of them to prove his point. 'It's
the locum.' Walling did a bit of rearranging of the size of
the frames and put two photos side by side, one from the
health centre website and one of the digital photos. 'Dr Sabera
Ismat.'

He fiddled about a bit more and then worked his way back
through the health centre website and clicked open the list of
GPs, clicked on a name and opened one of the files. 'Dr Sanjay
Khan. Dr Ismat was sitting with this guy at the restaurant.'
He again minimized the screen and went back to the file with
the downloaded digital photographs, picked one and enlarged
it. It was a fairly grainy image of two people embracing. 'The
two doctors, I'd say.'

'I don't understand,' Angela Cranlow said, quickly checking
her watch. She was obviously short of time. 'Why are you
showing us these?' She looked at Henry, puzzled.

Henry already knew why, but he still let Walling have the
floor.

'Aha,' Walling said, sounding like a second-rate magician.
He tabbed back to a better photograph of the couple at the
restaurant. In the background was another pretty Asian lady.
'One of Eddie Daley's locate/trace jobs, don't you think?'

'What has this to do with Darren Langmead?' Angela asked.
'Like you said, these are six months old?'

'Nothing at all, I'd say,' Walling said. 'Just hang on . . .'
Using the zoom tool on the programme, he focused in on the
Ismat woman, bringing her closer and closer, moving down
away from her face to her neck. 'Now what do you see?'

Henry kept quiet.

Jenny said, 'A necklace.'

'Yep.' Walling glanced over his shoulder, smiling at his audience. He reached for a piece of paper on the desk and flipped it over. It was a copy of Lancashire Constabulary's latest intelligence bulletin, solely devoted to an update of the murder of the female found six months earlier near Blackpool, her body having been burned to a crisp. There was a photograph of the facial reconstruction and also of the unusual necklace, believed to have been worn by the woman, which had turned up when the conscience of the man who had found the body got the better of him.

The two women gasped.

Henry had already done his gasping internally.

The necklace on the bulletin was exactly the same one as around the neck of the woman in the photograph, an image, Henry assumed, that had been taken by Eddie Daley. Henry picked up the bulletin and held it alongside the computer screen, comparing the facial reconstruction to the actual face of the woman in the photo.

'Pretty bloody good match,' Walling said. He raised his eyebrows.

The implications of this sank in immediately. Henry placed a hand on Walling's bulky shoulder, realizing that if he could get him a job as an operational detective again, he would have to lose some weight.

'Brilliant,' he said.

'My office, now, Henry,' Angela Cranlow said.

'What've we got then?' She was sitting on the business side of her wide desk, dwarfed by its size. Her back was to the window, which overlooked the playing fields at the front of HQ.

'You know as much as I do,' Henry pointed out. 'Photos on a computer of a woman wearing a necklace similar to one found on the body of a woman who was murdered. I'm sure there's more than one woman with a necklace like that.'

'I don't believe in coincidence, Henry.'

'Me neither. And the necklace is supposed to be unique.'

'So go on, hypothesize – or guess.'

He had been standing by the window, watching the rain that had started to lash mercilessly down. He moved to sit on the public side of the desk.

'First assumption is that they are photos Eddie took and downloaded and that they were from a job he was working on.'

'And the woman was subsequently murdered?'

Before following Angela to her office, Henry had taken a minute to jot down the dates on the computer. 'According to the details on the PC, the website of the health centre was initially accessed three days before the dates the digital photos were taken – bearing in mind the dates on the photos could be manipulated.' Angela nodded. 'And the date that the body was discovered was one day after those photos were taken.' Angela gave a twitchy gesture of her shoulders and hands, urging him to carry on. 'So, if we suppose those computer dates are right, then it looks like Eddie may have had something to do with, or knew something about, her murder.'

'Aren't we jumping ahead of ourselves, slightly?'

'What do you mean?'

'We don't yet know if the woman in the photo is one and the same as the dead woman.'

'True, and that needs to be established first, I'd say.'

'How do you propose to do that?'

'The Smoke.'

'When?'

'Tonight.'

'Wouldn't a phone call suffice?'

'I like the personal touch.'

'Damn!'

'What?'

'I can't go – Police Authority meeting. Can't get out of it.'

'I'll go alone,' he said, never having even considered that she would have gone down to London with him. 'I'll get Graeme to cover the post-mortems of Jackie and Langmead. He'll be fine with that.'

'You think this could be connected with Eddie's death?'

'Who knows? What I need to do is capture all this and start making some policy decisions . . . the first one being to establish whether or not this Dr Ismat is alive and kicking. If she is, then it's going nowhere and it all means nothing and everything swivels back to Darren Langmead, I guess.'

Angela leaned her chin on a hand and gazed at Henry. 'You're the first man I've been with since my divorce . . . it was lovely, and risky. Hell of a combination.'

She leaned back, reverting to business, not giving Henry a chance to respond. 'If this woman in the photos turns out to be the dead one, Dave Anger will have to be informed, you know.'

'Let's establish facts, first. It would be quite nice to hand it on a platter to him.'

'Last laugh?'

'I'm morally above that sort of thing.'

'But morally bankrupt in all other areas?'

'Probably,' he said dubiously, and the thought rocked him.

6.15 p.m.: Preston railway station, about halfway down the west coast line between Glasgow and London Euston. A bitter wind blew down the tracks and swept along platform 4, making Henry shudder. He checked his watch, then the departure screen – his train was due to leave at 6.45 p.m. and was expected to be on time – then looked towards the station entrance.

'Come on, love,' he urged. 'Ahh!'

He had spotted Kate hurrying across the footbridge spanning the platforms at the northern side of the station. He dashed up the pedestrian incline to greet her. She was loaded down with luggage. He pecked her cheek.

Over her left arm she had a zip-up suit carrier and she was pulling along a wheeled holdall, which Henry recognized as belonging to his youngest daughter, Leanne. Perched on top of the holdall, resting against the retractable handle, was a plastic carrier bag.

'Hiya, sweetheart. Traffic was horrendous,' Kate said, clearly flustered. She had been put under pressure by Henry's request to get him some gear together and get across from Blackpool to Preston in time for his train. She took a deep breath and handed him the suit carrier. 'Fresh suit, shirt and tie.'

'Thanks.'

He took it and the holdall.

'In there is a change of clothes for now – or whenever: jeans, T-shirt, socks, trainers and undies. Obviously I had difficulty packing the undies cos they're so huge.' She laughed and then gave him the carrier bag. 'In here is your leather jacket, wash bag and the book you've been reading, which I thought you might want for the train.'

'Great,' he said, swallowing back a bitter taste of guilt.

'I've only got twenty mins on the car park for free,' she told him.

'In that case, I'll get changed on the train. Fancy a quick coffee?'

He was travelling business class at the expense of the firm, guaranteeing him a decent seat, waiter service and a bit of comfort as the Pendolino train whistled through the country-side, leaning on the curves. He sat back and tried to enjoy the journey, but his mind was awash with thoughts and feel-ings.

His stupid escapade with Angela Cranlow was high on the agenda. Then the barefaced cheek at having phoned Kate to ask her to rush and bring his stuff over to Preston and real-izing that she did it without a moment of hesitation, murmur of dissent or a moan. She just did it because she loved him and nothing was too much trouble. She would have travelled to the ends of the earth for him. Just because she loved him.

He tried to get his head into the book she had thoughtfully brought along for him, a Simon Clark novel, but he couldn't hold his mind to it.

It might not have been one of the world's greatest partings, but he was unable to snap the picture out of his mind of Kate waving from the platform as he boarded the train and leaned out of the window as it drew out of the station.

'Bastard,' he said to himself, knowing for certain that the liaison between him and Angela had gone as far as it was going. His problem was he always went back for more, always fell in love. This time had to be different.

He ordered another free scotch and lemonade from a passing steward. He had declined the meal, which had not sounded appetizing, but had decided to avail himself of the free alcohol instead.

By Crewe he was on his third whisky, feeling warm and comfortable.

He would find somewhere to eat in London. Maybe even get room service at the hotel he'd been booked into by Angela's secretary. He closed the book, then closed his eyes, knowing that if he fell asleep it would be impossible to miss his station, which was at the end of the line.

* * *

The hotel, often used by cops visiting London on business and one which Henry had stayed at a few times before, was the Jolly St Ermin on Caxton Street, around the corner from New Scotland Yard. It was a big, old, comfortable place, now owned by an Italian chain but nonetheless good, though not particularly cheap.

By the time the taxi dropped him off, he was wide awake again. After registering and then dropping his luggage off in his room and getting changed, it was just after ten and although his appetite had now deserted him, his desire for drink had not; he decided on a short walk to a half-decent pub.

He left the hotel and sauntered up to Victoria Street, strolling along until he found something that took his fancy. He rolled into a pub called the Bag o' Nails about ten minutes later and went straight for a pint of London Pride, which hardly touched the sides.

In a seat by the window he watched a bit of London life go by, which wasn't all that much different to Blackpool life, he guessed. After another pint and a bag of crisps, he stepped out to find that the bad weather from the north had tracked him.

Hunching down into his leather jacket he hurried back along Victoria Street, the rain increasing from a heavy downpour to a torrential tropical storm, completely drenching him within seconds. It hammered down like rods of steel, even hurt his head, and he knew he was in for a first-class soaking.

After a hundred metres he'd had enough. He ducked into a shopping precinct for cover whilst he waited for some abatement. He stood looking out, hands thrust deep into his pockets, his face a picture of pure misery. The weather seemed set for the night and he knew he would have to brave it sooner or later.

Behind him, in the shopping centre, came the sound of chatter, laughter and cutlery and the great whiff of garlic. He glanced over his shoulder and saw a restaurant with a paved area, many people chomping merrily away. His brow furrowed as he turned slowly, his eyes taking in what he was seeing. He walked into the centre and saw it was a Spanish restaurant. He stood and inspected it, a strange, unworldly sensation overcoming him. To his right was an Italian restaurant across the concourse, again with outdoor seating, albeit protected by the fact it was inside the shopping centre.

His head flicked back to the Spanish restaurant.

'Well, well, well,' he said out loud, and, '*Una Cerveza por favor*,' the only Spanish phrase he knew by heart.

Eleven

Henry woke at 6 a.m., feeling refreshed after six hours' uninterrupted sleep, batteries recharged. He had a long, medium-hot shower, then dressed in the suit that Kate had packed for him. He wandered down for an early, leisurely breakfast, which he scoffed with the delight of a man not picking up the tab.

He spent the next hour sitting in the huge reception area, his ear affixed to his mobile phone, talking tactics with Angela Cranlow, who remained curiously professionally detached, which puzzled him but at the same time pleased him; maybe she was backing off. He also spoke to some members of the SPMS.

Graeme Walling, the ex-NCIS detective now floundering in the wasteland of Special Projects, had thoroughly enjoyed himself dealing with two grisly post-mortems. He thanked Henry profusely for the opportunity and reported that the PMs didn't tell them anything they hadn't already surmised, but did confirm that Jackie Kippax had an advanced form of cancer of the stomach which would have given her only a few months to live. That would answer the question as to why she turned the shotgun on herself, but they would never know what was said between her and Darren Langmead, a dialogue that had died with the both of them. Walling would be spending the day doing follow-up inquiries for an inquest scheduled early next week, just for the purpose of identification. The full inquest would take place way in the future.

'The pathologist sends you her regards, by the way,' Walling said.

'Professor O'Connell?'

'That's the one. She also said to tell you she's sorry you missed your chance, whatever that means, but there could be an opportunity to try again due to a vacancy if you wanted. Does that make sense to you?'

'Yep – perfect,' Henry said.

He next spoke to one of the people he'd sent to Blackburn to do some digging into Darren Langmead to see if there was any truth in Kippax's assertion that he had threatened Eddie Daley over Daley's investigation into the alleged embezzlement from the Class Act. Nothing had come to light; neither had Eddie Daley's computer turned up. Henry gave instructions to trace Johnny Strongitharm, the club's owner, to find out if he had contracted Eddie to investigate Langmead.

Lots of things were going on. His team were buzzing in a way they had never done before.

It was amazing what a sense of purpose and a pat on the back could do.

After the phone calls, Henry spoke to Kate, who sounded bubbly and full of life and plans. He felt dreadful as he ended the call.

'So bleedin' weak,' he chided himself.

He'd brought a soft leather business case with him into which he'd packed printouts of the digital photographs from Jackie Kippax's computer, all blown up to A4 size. He fished them out and had a good long look at them. They had lost none of their sharpness on enlargement, not even the one that had zoomed in on the necklace around the woman's neck.

It was a very unusual pendant on the chain, he had to admit, though he didn't know too much about this sort of thing. It had an oriental look about it, two serpents wrapped around an orchid, quite understated and expensive.

He examined the photographs closely.

She was definitely a beautiful woman. He had compared them to the photos of the facial reconstruction and there was a very strong likeness.

So was she the burned corpse?

Was she called Sabera Ismat?

Or was this woman still alive and was he barking up the wrong tree?

But more importantly, was there a chance of him getting

one over on Dave Anger? Whilst he did not really want this
woman to be dead, part of him hoped she was.

His mobile rang.

'Henry, it's Jenny Fisher at the office.'

Jenny with the attitude. 'Hi, Jen, what can I do for you?'

'Just an update for you . . . you asked me to make some
inquiries about the medical qualifications of this Ismat
woman?' Henry told her to go on, which she did, telling Henry
where and when Sabera got her degree, did her medical
training. 'But, guess what? She's a Blackburn lass according
to university records.'

'Which fits in with the geological profile of the dead
woman,' Henry said.

'Certainly does.'

'Jenny, you're a star.'

He almost heard her purr down the line.

The photographs were spread across the coffee table in front
of him. He pulled them together with the best one on top, one
just of the woman with the pretty young Asian lady in the
background.

'Hello, Sabera,' he said, now feeling very confident that
this trip south was worthwhile. 'What's your story?' He knew
there and then that she was dead. Just for good measure Henry
gave a one finger salute to his mental picture of Dave Anger.
'Swivel, you git,' he said, picked everything up and went
across to the doorman to arrange for his luggage to be stored
and to get him to wave down a taxi.

As slow as it was in the monumental traffic, travelling by cab
across London was definitely great fun. Henry did not often
get to London, so he looked upon it as a treat and loved seeing
the sights, travelling down roads and streets he'd only ever
heard of in films, TV or whilst playing Monopoly.

As the cab turned out of Caxton Street, he caught sight of
New Scotland Yard and the spinning, triangular sign which
always looked bigger and far more impressive on TV. In real
life it was a disappointment, as was Scotland Yard itself. Just
a dull office building, squeezed in tight amongst others, with
no atmosphere about it at all. Very uninspiring.

He was driven firstly around Buckingham Palace, then
generally in a south-westerly direction across the city. The

next sign he recognized was Sloane Square, was amazed to
see a Lamborghini dealership, then on to King's Road and
right up Sloane Avenue, cutting across Fulham Road, then
across on to Old Brompton Road and he knew he wasn't far
away from Earl's Court then. The taxi passed Brompton
Cemetery, then on his right he caught sight of the towering
Empress Building which he knew the Metropolitan police now
leased, a far more impressive building than Scotland Yard.

'Here we go,' the cabbie said, pulling into the side of the
road. 'Empress Medical Centre.' Henry peered through the
window and saw the centre looking, as expected, exactly
the same as on the website.

He paid and took a receipt before stepping out of the cab,
and watched a low-flying jumbo jet passing overhead on its
descent into Heathrow to the west.

He breathed in the London air, then looked at his target.
He loved going unannounced into places, to take his chances
with jobs like these, just to gauge the reactions of people not
prepared for the cop-knock on their door. It was like being a
cat amongst pigeons, sometimes, watching them scatter in
fear.

Or, as he said out loud to no one in particular, 'Pig in the
city.'

The health centre was much like thousands the country over.
He walked through an automatic sliding door, across a plant-
adorned foyer and into the reception area, joining a short
queue at the desk. The place was busy and the waiting area
quite full of miserable looking people.

As he reached the front of the queue, he wasn't even sure
what he was going to say. As usual, he was going to wing it.
He produced his warrant card for the receptionist and introduced himself. 'Detective Chief Inspector Henry Christie from
Lancashire Constabulary . . . I wonder if I could have a word
with your practice manager, please.'

'Could I say what about?'

He pushed his card into his top pocket. 'Not really,' he said
painfully. 'A delicate matter, police business.'

'OK.' She picked up a phone and punched in a number.
'Helen? It's Rachel on reception . . . there's a police officer
here wishing to see you . . . no, he didn't say . . . OK.' She

hung up. 'She'll be along in a couple of minutes. Would you like to take a seat?'

Henry stood browsing the notice boards, fearing for his very existence if he didn't eat five portions of fruit and veg per day, didn't exercise for twenty minutes, three times a week, and had erection problems. Sometimes he wished he did have the latter. An erect penis had put him in so many hairy situations.

A pleasant looking middle-aged lady appeared by his side, smelling strongly of smoke. 'Hello. I'm Helen Baxter, the practice manager. I hope I haven't done anything wrong, but if I have, I don't mind being handcuffed.'

It was an admission that stumped Henry for a moment.

'Just kidding,' she said and tapped him on the arm.

'Ha ha.'

'So what can I do for you, DCI Christie, is it?'

'Yes, it was an odd thing,' Mrs Baxter – 'call me Helen' – was saying as she looked at the photograph Henry produced from his case. It was a close-up of the woman's face with no one else in it. 'She just upped and went.'

'So this is definitely Sabera Ismat?'

They had retreated to Mrs Baxter's small office in the far reaches of the health centre and were awaiting tea. She was being helpful in a playful sort of way.

'Oh yes, that's definitely her. She came as a locum and then started running a sort of clinic/self-help group for Asian women who'd been abused. It was very popular and she was doing some good work. But to be fair, I can't say I knew her all that well.'

There was a knock on the door and an Asian lady came in bearing a tray of tea and biscuits.

'Excuse me,' she said politely.

'That's OK, Aysha – just put the tray down here.' She pointed to a coffee table by the desk. Henry glanced at the woman and his glance turned to a squint as he recognized her as the Asian woman positioned behind Sabera Ismat in one of the photographs. She began laying out the cups and saucers.

'So she just disappeared?' Henry said, slowly taking back the photograph from Mrs Baxter.

There was a clatter and a crash as a cup dropped on to the

tray. It did not break. The tea-bearing lady said sorry and stood the cup upright on a saucer.

'You can let us do the mothering,' Mrs Baxter said.

The young woman turned to leave and Henry watched her go, fleetingly catching her eye, seeing a troubled look on her face.

He did the honours and poured the tea. 'What do you know about her, then?'

'Not a lot, really,' Mrs Baxter said thoughtfully. 'Look, what is this about?'

'I just need to find her and speak to her about something. Beyond that, I can't really tell you a lot. You understand?'

Mrs Baxter tapped her nose. 'Police business?'

'Exactly.'

'Mm, OK, let me think . . . she sort of came from nowhere, I suppose. Dr Khan took her on. He wanted her to start immediately as a locum, even without interview, but that's not too unusual. Dr Khan's one of the practice partners and what he says goes, I suppose.'

Henry nodded. 'Does he know what happened to her?'

'He told me she'd had to deal with a family emergency. I asked him if she'd be coming back and he said he doubted it.'

Henry nodded. 'I need to speak to him, then, I suppose.' He paused. 'Do you have any employment records for her, just out of interest?'

'I do.' Mrs Baxter rose and crossed the office to a filing cabinet. She slid open the top drawer and riffled through the suspension files with her fingertips. She got to the end, then worked her way back, muttering, then started her search again. 'Odd,' she said, this time going slowly through the files, peering carefully at the tabs. 'Strange . . . her file isn't here . . . and I know I haven't archived it.'

They were words which sent a suspicious tingle down Henry's spine. As ever, when he became excited by the prospect of prey, his bum twitched with anticipation. 'Is Dr Khan in today?' he asked calmly.

'I haven't actually seen him, to be honest,' Mrs Baxter said, her face still down looking for the missing file. 'He is in, though, because he had an early surgery, although . . .' She raised her head and looked at the wall clock. 'He could well be out on home visits now.'

She slammed the filing cabinet drawer shut. 'Not here,' she pouted, 'definitely not here.' Back at her desk she picked up the phone and dialled an extension at which there was obviously no response. She redialled. 'Oh, hello Aysha, it's Helen . . . has Dr Khan gone out on home visits? Yes? Right, OK, thanks for that.' She hung up and said, 'About half an hour ago.'

'Right.'

'He's usually out all morning, but he has another surgery at two. Why don't you call back about one thirty? He should be in by then, and available.'

'I might just do that.'

'Can I ask you something?'

'Fire away.'

'Is Sabera in trouble?'

Henry got a brief mental glimpse of a pathetic, charred corpse. 'Like I said,' he grimaced in a way which suggested he really would like to tell her something, 'I can't really say.'

'I understand,' she said with disappointment. 'Ooh, I know! She was quite friendly with Aysha, the lady who came in here with the tea? She's a receptionist. I think her and Sabera were pretty pally. It might be worth having a chat with her.'

'Sounds good.'

'Come on.' Mrs Baxter stood up and led Henry back through the complex. 'You've come a long way,' she commented. Henry nodded. 'Sabera was from up north, I'm pretty sure. Blackburn, I think.' She led Henry to a door at the back of the reception desk. 'Rachel?' she called to the girl who had greeted Henry earlier. 'Is Aysha about?'

Rachel, sitting at the counter behind the Plexiglass screen, turned with a harassed expression. There was a queue of patients and two phones were ringing. She was the only one there. She glared at Mrs Baxter. 'No, she just put her coat on and dashed out, leaving me to sort all this.' She held up her hands to indicate her world of chaos.

'Where has she gone?'

'How would I know? Just ran out.' Rachel forced a smile at one of the people in front of her and said, 'Just one moment,' then picked up a phone and said a curt, 'Yes?'

Mrs Baxter turned to Henry. 'Strange.'

'Lots of strange things going on, but no matter,' he said.

'I'll pop back and see Dr Khan later . . . and thanks for your assistance . . . Helen . . .' He shook her hand quickly and headed at a pace for the exit on the off chance he might be able to catch up with the receptionist who had gone AWOL.

The pavements were still wet from the overnight downpour, but the rain had ceased and the clouds were dispersing. Henry rushed out of the health centre clutching his briefcase under his arm and dashed on to Old. Brompton Road, scanning as he went.

The young woman could not have gone far, but as Henry knew, people could disappear within the blink of an eye. He had no way of knowing in which direction she had legged it, so he took a fifty/fifty chance, followed his instinct and hurried towards the West Brompton tube station on the District Line and caught sight of her standing on the road bridge opposite Earl's Court Exhibition Centre spanning the underground line. She was talking into her mobile phone, constantly looking around as she did, as though the cops might be after her. Henry ducked into a doorway, keeping her in sight, his arse doing some real twitching now.

Was it coincidence she had done a runner from work on the very morning he'd turned up asking a few questions and showing photographs?

Naah.

Although he was not close enough to hear her, he could tell she was screaming down the phone, gesticulating as she spoke, until the call ended. She looked at it with frustration, as though she was going to lob it over the bridge, shaking it angrily. Spinning on her heels, she crossed over the bridge, staying on the same side of the road, and scuttled away.

Henry stepped out from cover, began to follow.

He stayed about fifty metres behind her as she rushed past the entrance to Brompton Cemetery. Henry glanced to his right and caught sight of Stamford Bridge football ground, home of Chelsea FC, giving an involuntary shiver at the thought of all the money that had been ploughed into it.

Aysha walked across the junction with Finborough Road, then Redcliffe Gardens, pushing in a north-easterly direction towards South Kensington.

It was easy to tail her using buildings and other people for

cover, and because she did not once look back over her
shoulder.

Suddenly she turned into a Starbucks and went out of view.

Henry stopped, again relying on his instincts and what little
he knew of the woman. She was a health centre receptionist,
seemed to be in a panic, wasn't likely to be versed in street-
craft, so he guessed it would be unlikely she had spotted him
and gone straight through Starbucks and out the back. He
needed to get in a position from where he could monitor the
front door. There was a Costa Coffee shop diagonally opposite on the other side of the road. He crossed quickly, took the
chance to buy a coffee and wedged himself into a window
seat, placed his briefcase on the window ledge, settled down
and waited whilst churning the morning's events and discov-
eries through his brain.

If Sabera was the burned-out corpse, then he believed he
had just unearthed a very good suspect for her murder in Dr
Khan – someone who at the very least had some hard questions to answer – and possibly an accomplice, too, in the form
of Aysha.

Henry was having great fun. And the coffee tasted great.

He did not have to hang around long.

Ten minutes later, a man he instantly recognized walked
hastily past his window, a matter of only three feet away, then
crossed the road and entered Starbucks.

He waited a few moments. Let him settle. Let him get a
brew.

A smile came to Henry's face, the kind of smile a cat gives
when it's been amongst the pigeons and is now about to lick
the cream.

The couple were sitting at one of the tables in Starbucks, in
deep but agitated conversation. They didn't even see Henry
enter the café, didn't even look up as he wove his way between
tables, chairs and other customers.

It took a couple of seconds before they even registered he
was standing behind them, rather like the spectre of their
consciences.

They turned slowly, theatrically, faces horror-struck, plas-
tered with guilt.

The kind of expressions Henry enjoyed seeing.

'Mornin',' he said, grinning.

Unfortunately, his ebullient approach to the situation meant that he dropped his guard and unexpectedly, the man who he knew to be Dr Khan, twisted round hard and drove his elbow into Henry's groin with all the force he could muster.

Aysha stood up and screamed.

Henry doubled over, dropping his briefcase, both hands instinctively covering his testicles, whilst he blew out like a whale.

Khan shot to his feet and pushed him over backwards, again with force, knocking him over a chair and sending him sprawling into another table at which two young mothers were sitting gabbing with their offspring in prams next to them. Henry's right knee gave way at that moment and he fell between them, sending their hot frothy drinks everywhere. He just caught a glimpse of Khan's feet running past him.

He reached out to grab, but the doctor sidestepped neatly and was gone.

There was no time to apologize. He heaved himself up using a table, rising wet from the spilled coffee, aware of the stunned faces of the customers and shouts of dismay and anger.

Henry had a decision to make: should he bag Aysha or go for the doctor?

He somehow knew that the doctor was the one he needed most.

He jabbed his finger at Aysha and slavered, 'You get back to work and stay there,' with spittle coming out of his mouth.

He flung his briefcase over the serving counter, shouting, 'Look after that,' to staff and, leaping over the table he'd upended, he gave chase, chunnering the word 'Bastard!' between his teeth as he flung open the door and skidded comically out on to Old Brompton Road, seeing Khan running in the direction he'd come from, towards the tube station.

Seething, Henry clenched his jaw and set off, attracting worried looks from all other pedestrians. He got going like a lumbering steam train, arms pounding like engine cylinders, glad of the time he'd spent in Special Projects because one of his own special projects had been to get fit again and being dumped in headquarters had given him that chance by way of extended lunchtimes and three-mile daily runs. In fact, he didn't consider himself a steam train. By dropping more than a stone in weight, he'd become a whippet, all six-two and thirteen stones of him.

Unfortunately, Khan also looked like he could run. He was small and wiry and had no trouble skipping round people, but his lack of experience in running away from the police showed. Anyone who had experience of having to outrun the fuzz would have known to cross the road and dive into the busy area outside Earl's Court, using the cover provided by others. Instead he chose to do a left into Brompton Cemetery through the north gate and run down the central avenue of the huge, almost deserted cemetery in the direction of the chapel at the far end.

Henry powered after him, also aware that most doctors don't practise what they preach: health and fitness. At least, Henry's own whisky-swilling GP didn't.

Khan began to flag after another hundred metres. Henry started to gain, although he was tiring and regretting his overindulgence at breakfast.

But Khan had nowhere to go. He eventually sagged down on to his knees, as though his batteries were running out, then slumped on to all fours and puked.

Henry skittered up behind him in the gravel, panting, 'You . . . are . . . under . . . arrest . . . onsuspicionofmurder.' He emitted the last four words as one.

Even though the complication of Henry being a detective from Lancashire operating without the knowledge or blessing of the locals was quickly dealt with, his prisoner was not. After pinning Khan down and dragging him back to the north gate, Henry had called 999 on his mobile and waited patiently for the promised response, which took about twenty minutes.

The circumstances took another ten minutes to explain to the two PCs who arrived in a Transit van and then conveyed him to the police station on Fulham Road, via Starbucks where he collected his briefcase and made his apologies. Unsurprisingly, Aysha had disappeared.

Booking the prisoner in took an interminable length of time.

Southwest London must have had a busy morning. Henry was told he had to remain with his prisoner until the booking-in was done. He wasn't required to remain physically by the side of Khan, but was instructed to stay in the custody area.

Khan was put into a holding cage with six other prisoners who all looked like serious armed robbers.

Henry paced the cell corridor, straightening his thoughts, wondering what the best course of action would be.

As ever, he decided to wing it.

'DCI Henry Christie, Lancashire Constabulary,' he introduced himself to the Met custody sergeant. He pushed Khan up to the desk, caused the sergeant to look at him, then at Henry, then back to Khan.

'Hello, Dr Khan.'

Khan nodded miserably.

'Do you know this person,' the sergeant said to Henry, 'is one of our police surgeons?'

Henry gave him a pained look. 'How would I know that?'

'You wouldn't.' He smiled thinly at Henry. 'What's this about?'

'I've arrested him on suspicion of murder.'

Once again the sergeant glanced from one person to the other. 'Murder?' he said in disbelief.

'Murder,' Henry confirmed.

'Which murder?'

'That of a woman called Sabera Ismat, whose body was found in Lancashire about six months ago. I was the SIO,' he concluded.

'Do you have anything to say, Dr Khan?'

Khan shook his head, but he was clearly affected by what Henry had just said. The sergeant again gave Henry a stare which said it all, and with a heavy sigh began the process of detaining Khan under the Police and Criminal Evidence Act, not impressed.

It was four miserable hours before a duty solicitor became free and the time was approaching 3 p.m. Henry had expected to be on his way back to Lancashire by now.

His newly formulated plan was to have a quick interview with Khan and then arrange for him to be transported up north where he could be dealt with properly.

They were in a grotty interview room with peeling paint on the walls and a strange smell of sewers. Henry had the tape on and had cautioned Khan.

'I'm investigating the murder of Sabera Ismat whose body was found six months ago in a field in Lancashire,' he began. It was the first time Henry had actually been face to face with Khan properly. He was a good-looking Asian man around about the thirty mark. As he spoke the words, the colour of Khan's skin faded to a grey. He looked as though he was about to say something, but nothing came out.

'You knew her, didn't you?'

'That doesn't make my client a murderer,' the weasley-faced brief interjected. 'I already have the feeling that this is a purely speculative arrest.'

Henry ignored him. 'Please answer the question. Did you know her?'

'I knew her. She used to be a locum for the practice.'

'How well did you know her?'

Khan rubbed his head. 'Not that well.'

'How well would you say on a scale of one to ten?'

Khan thought. 'Four, maybe.'

Henry gave him a withering look.

'I'd met her back in med school, but then I didn't see her again until a few months ago when she came asking about a job.'

'Which you got her?'

'I did.'

'Without even a formal interview.'

Khan's face turned stonily towards Henry. 'It was based on her references, qualifications and my personal knowledge.'

'Yet you say you didn't know her that well?' Henry paused. He liked waiting. It made people feel uncomfortable and often they had the urge to fill in the gaps. If used well, silence could be a deadly trap, a void into which the unwitting could tumble. Khan, though, just looked down at his hands as his fingers intertwined in anguish. His chin shook.

'Where are her employment records?'

'What do you mean?'

'I mean, they seem to have disappeared from the filing cabinet in which all the health centre employment records are kept.'

'No idea.' His eyes closed and opened slowly as he said the two words.

'How come you haven't asked me more about the fate of

one of your employees? Someone you knew from university, someone you gave a job to, someone who then suddenly disappeared? Aren't you curious about what happened to her? Or is it that you already know?' Henry was still aware that he did not have a hundred per cent proof that the dead woman was Sabera Ismat and that Khan could feasibly tell him where she was, alive and kicking . . . although his marked reluctance to say anything convinced Henry he was on the right track.

The woman in the photos was Sabera Ismat and Dr Khan, renowned police surgeon, damn well knew something about her.

And yet, there was something about this man that made Henry doubt he could have killed her . . . but he'd been wrong about killers before. Everyone – *everyone* – was capable.

Khan remained silent. He was sweating and Henry almost believed he could hear the man's heart beating against his rib cage.

'Dr Khan, you have a lot of questions to answer. I'm going to arrange for you to be conveyed to Lancashire for further questioning. You are a very good suspect for her murder. You knew her, you employed her, and I'll prove you pulled her records when she mysteriously disappeared. And while I'm waiting for transport from Lancashire, I'll be going to arrest your receptionist too. She can have a trip up north, because you're obviously both in this together—'

'No!' Khan erupted. 'Neither of us hardly knew her! Aysha . . .' His voice tapered out.

Henry reached down for his briefcase at his feet under the interview table. He laid it on his lap, opened it and pulled out two sheets of paper, which he positioned face down in front of Khan.

'For the benefit of the tape I am showing Dr Khan two photographs. The first shows him sitting at a restaurant with the victim, Sabera Ismat.' Henry slowly turned the photograph over and slid it across to Khan so it was right under his nose. Henry's eyes remained firmly fixed on Khan's reactions. 'The second is a photograph of Khan embracing the victim, as though they were lovers.' He did the same with this one, the photograph taken of Khan and Sabera holding each other on a bridge. Khan's face was a picture to behold. 'So, Dr Khan, just run that past me again, will you? How well do you know Sabera Ismat?'

The next problem was arranging transport from Lancashire to come down to London and pick up the prisoner. Not the easiest thing to arrange because it meant two uniformed bobbies coming down from Blackpool, as that was the division in which the body was discovered, who had to be released from other duties to tear down south.

Henry wrestled with it, working it all through his head; how long it would take to get them down to London, how long back, how it would all impact on the time factor in relation to the prisoner. He was sitting in the police surgeon's room, weighing up the factors, hand on the phone, when the custody sergeant came in.

'Guv,' he said, 'Dr Khan wants to see you. Says he's got something to tell you.'

Henry jumped up and hurried through to an interview room to await the arrival of Khan and his solicitor. He was surprised when only Khan was escorted through by a gaoler. He sat down opposite Henry, clearly crushed and worried.

'Where's your brief?'

'Sacked him.'

'Is that wise?'

'I don't think he was very wise.'

'What do you want to tell me?' Henry unwrapped a double-pack of cassette tapes and dropped them into the machine.

Khan took a deep, unsteady breath.

Twelve

Not even 125 mph was fast enough for Henry Christie. As the early morning Virgin Express Pendolino service left the environs of London and scythed north-west towards Rugby, even his full English breakfast, as good as it was, hardly tickled his taste buds. Once again he read through the twelve-page statement he had painstakingly extracted from Dr Sanjay Khan, the man he had suspected of murdering Sabera Ismat – or, as Khan had corrected him, Sabera Rashid.

On the previous evening Henry had listened with fascination, and then with a chilled heart, as Khan spilled the truth and recounted the story of a beautiful young woman whose hopes of freedom and a decent life had been cruelly terminated.

It took him half an hour to haltingly tell the tale the first time round, after which Henry took him from the suspect interview room and found a more comfortable room in the police station in which he could get Khan to relax and expand on everything whilst Henry recorded the statement on paper.

It was clear that Khan was a man who, underneath his veneer of being a normal GP and police surgeon on the side, lived in fear. He looked desolate, afraid.

'Yes, we fell in love,' he said painfully, tears welling in his eyes. 'It was wrong, but it was also very, very right.'

Henry made a guggling sound to encourage him.

'All she wanted was freedom, the right to be her own person, to follow her vocation, but that was denied her by a tyrant of a husband who beat and raped her most horribly . . . we met at university and we were just good friends, though there was a spark.' He looked desperately at Henry. 'We knew she would return to get married and that was accepted between us, so nothing happened in those days . . .' His story was all over the place at first, but Henry allowed him his ramble before putting structure to it. 'Then she came back to me out of the blue . . . I'd never married . . . and she told me she had left her husband and wanted a new life. God, it was so hard for her . . . so much pressure on her from inside and outside, but she knew that when she had made that step, returning was out of the question . . . those photographs you showed me . . . taken by a private investigator?'

'I think so.'

'So she was tracked down, got careless I suppose. Her husband had that sort of money, though. He is quite wealthy, I believe.' Khan paused. 'That night, the night of the photographs, was the last night I ever saw her . . .'

Henry was running these words through his mind when the

train began to slow down, then stop . . . in the middle of
nowhere. South of Milton Keynes, he guessed. The regretful
announcement was that there would be a short delay whilst
a broken down train ahead of them was removed from the
lines. Henry cursed, but smiled when the pretty stewardess
appeared by his side offering more coffee. There was nothing
he could do about any delays. Not as though he could get out
and kick the wheels, call the AA or remonstrate with anyone.
If a train ain't going nowhere, it ain't going nowhere. He held
up his cup. The coffee was good.

Dressed in jeans, trainers and leather jacket, he relaxed in
the business-class seat. He was at an individual table so he
stretched out and thought back to the evening.

'What happened that night?' he had asked Khan.

Khan snorted, shaking his head sadly. 'She had been in
London for about six months. She was working hard, doing
well, and we were falling in love slowly, at arm's length,
yeah? To leave her husband was one thing for a Muslim girl;
to start seeing another man whilst still married, that's a whole
new ball game. Very big stuff for a Muslim female.
Monumental, in fact. But it started to happen and the irony
was that it happened on that night of all nights.'

'Meaning?'

Khan sat back, remembering. 'Romantic meal, romantic
stroll across the river, back to my flat where' – he hesitated
with an embarrassed cough – 'we made love.'

Henry nodded, feeling very sorry for this man. Not that he
was going to let him off the hook, though. He'd been spun
many a lying sob story by murderers trying to get sympathy
and walk free. 'And after that, you never saw her again?'

Khan nodded.

'Meaning you killed her? Isn't that right?'

'No! Never!' he protested.

Henry gave him a look of disbelief. 'Keep talking.'

'She stayed the night at my flat . . . and at about four in the
morning, something like that, the door was kicked in—'
He stopped abruptly at that point and dropped his head into
his hands, beginning to sob. Henry let him get it out of his
system.

Finally, when it looked as though he had finished his snivelling, Henry said, 'The husband?'

'Him and three other guys. They came in hard and fast and I didn't do a damn thing to protect her. They put tape over her face, tied her up and rolled her into my duvet and carried her out. And I just watched. I was shitting myself.'

'You just watched?'

'Yeah – with one guy holding a knife to my throat.' He raised his chin and pointed to a small, silvery scar by his windpipe.

'Ahh,' said Henry, understanding.

'Then I was warned off, I guess by Sabera's husband, although he didn't introduce himself.'

'That was it? They warned you off?' Henry said incredulously.

'They beat me with canes, just on my body and legs, so no one could see.'

'Any marks to prove this?'

'They're still there.'

Henry sat back. 'I'm still not sure whether I believe you.'

'It's the truth.'

'When did you next hear from her?'

'Never.'

'Did you try to contact her?'

'I didn't dare . . . I was under threat.'

'Didn't you wonder what had happened to her? I mean, it all seems a bit thin to me.'

Khan suddenly stood up, knocking his chair over backwards, and leaned on the table, looking down at Henry with something burning in his eyes. 'I have lived a nightmare every day, Mr Christie.' His jaw rotated as he spoke. 'I have not slept a full night's sleep for six months. I am screwed up with guilt and shame, but at the same time I made myself believe Sabera was OK. Not happy, but OK. Alive and back living the miserable existence she had tried to flee.' He stood up and stalked across the room, pacing. 'I am torn up I did nothing on that night, nor have I done anything since because I prove to myself every single day that I am a coward. The fear of her husband has kept me from doing what anyone who's half a man should have done . . . but my fear is real, not imaginary.'

With that, he turned to Henry and tore off his shirt.

* * *

The train began to move at last.

It was 8 a.m. and Henry had been on the tracks for an hour and a quarter. He should have been much further than this.

He visualized Khan's back, bearing injuries which were tantamount to torture. He had been beaten like a prisoner in a concentration camp and the marks were still there, alive and glowing like living things.

'I give myself strong painkillers just to get through the day.' He pulled the shirt back on and sat down, slowly buttoning it up, not looking at Henry now, a faraway something in his eyes. 'Don't think I didn't want to call the police, I did,' he said defensively.

'Didn't you think it odd that she didn't try to contact you in any way?' Henry had been shocked by Khan's injuries, but not so much that he was going to be deflected from getting to the truth. It could all still have been a big lie.

'Not really. She would've been kept like a prisoner, everything taken away from her, maybe even guarded.'

'Let me get this straight: she was dragged away in the middle of the night, you were beaten senseless and you thought she'd still be OK? Call me a cynic, but . . .' Henry shrugged and gestured with his hands as his voice trailed off, lost for words.

'As I said, I was under threat.'

'And the threat was?'

'Death.'

'Carry on . . . convince me.'

'I was told that any attempt by me to contact her, or to tell the police, would result in my death . . . and I believed that.'

'And if you'd phoned the police on the night she was kidnapped, she might still be alive now.' Henry sighed, looking at him with undisguised disgust.

The train moved a good quarter of a mile. Then stopped. Henry gazed out at the countryside, sipping his fourth coffee of the morning and wondering when the caffeine overdose would kick in. He had watched Khan from across the table with little sympathy as the doctor cried uncontrollably. He let him cry himself out, not interrupting, just letting him outpour his grief and personal shame. The photographs Eddie Daley had taken were on the table between them, almost taunting Khan. In them Henry saw a couple very much in love.

Then he started to imagine what sort of life they would have had.

It would have been hard to the point of impossible, Henry thought. The husband would have always been there, his spectre always at their shoulders.

'Where does the receptionist, Aysha, fit into all this?' Henry inquired, looking at the photo with her in the background.

'She became a friend to Sabera. I introduced them and Aysha took her in. She's the only one who knew about me and Sabera, and the only one who knew what happened that night.'

Henry had reached the stage where he believed Khan and needed to get a statement down.

Khan raised his bloodshot eyes. 'Mr Christie? How did she die?'

'I'm not sure you really want to know that.'

'Oh yes, I do.'

Against his better judgement, Henry told him, but not in gory detail. Even so, it had the effect of destroying Khan and as Henry took the statement he guessed that the doctor would be in for a worse time emotionally than he was already experiencing.

When Henry had finished taking the statement, he then released Khan on police bail – Henry wanted to keep some hold on him – to return to the police station in two weeks' time.

'What happens now?' Khan asked as Henry led him to the custody office door.

'The investigation continues. I'll let you know what you need to know.'

'Thank you – and sorry for hitting you and running away. It's something I've been doing for six months and I'm glad you caught up with me, in a strange sort of way.'

Henry shrugged. 'Whatever.'

'There is one more thing. Could I have a copy of the photographs?' It sounded a helpless request. 'It was a tragic night, but before the tragedy it was magical. I'd like to hold on to that.'

Henry handed them over and Khan looked at them with dewy eyes. 'That necklace was the first thing, the only thing, I ever gave her,' he said, pointing at the close-up of Sabera's face and neck. 'I bought it when I was in India a few weeks before. That night seemed the right night to give it to her.'

At 11.15 p.m., the worn-out Lancashire detective had jumped into a cab and headed back to the Jolly St Ermin, where he had left his luggage and where he hoped to be able to get another room for the night. He was fortunate and after a bar snack and two pints of Stella, followed by a quick call to Kate, he had hit the bed and crashed out.

. . . And the Virgin Express started to move and tear through the countryside again.

'Thank fuck for that,' Henry breathed and held out a dithering hand with an empty cup and almost pleaded for another shot of coffee from the stewardess.

He took out his note pad and jotted a few things down to collect his thoughts.

> *Sabera Ismat? Rashid – abducted/murdered*
> *Eddie Daley – shot thru head/ murdered*
> *Sanjay Khan – lover boy*
> *Mansur Rashid – husband/killer – Eddie's killer? Eddie's*
> * employer?*
> *Sabera's family – accomplices? Knowledge*
> *Honour killing – as per PM*
> *Is Eddie's death connected to Sabera?*
> *Darren Langmead & Johnny Strongitharm? Class Act?*
> *Is Eddie's death linked to them, not Rashid?*
> *Connection?*
> *Coincidence? Don't like 'em*

He read through what he'd written several times, trying to get a handle on it all, scratching his head.

Eddie Daley traced people. It was a big part of his job, probably something he was very good at. Sabera had done a runner from her husband and it looked as though the red-faced Mr Rashid had hired Eddie to find her.

So good, so far.

Eddie did the job.

But how far did it go? Did Eddie play a part in Sabera's abduction that night? Henry doubted it. Not his scene. He was more likely to be the one who guided the husband in once he'd located her, a bit like an army recon squad. Henry knew that Eddie was not great at the physical stuff. He packed a good punch, but that was as far as it went. Henry had no reason to believe things had changed, especially when he recalled Eddie's massively overweight corpse on the mortuary slab. Not the sort of physique associated with bursting into a house and kidnapping someone. Once he'd pointed out where Sabera could be found, Eddie would back off.

Milton Keynes whooshed by.

Then there was the Langmead/ Strongitharm case Eddie was working on. This was the one Jackie believed to be the key – hence her tragic confrontation with Langmead. Henry pinched the bridge of his nose, then smiled as his mind span off at a tangent: maybe he could get a trip to Spain out of this? A jolly to visit Johnny Strongitharm on the Costa del whatever?

Not a chance in hell, he thought, and returned to his notes.

The word 'coincidence' jumped out at him.

The night of Eddie's murder.

Was it a coincidence that it occurred on the same night as the *Crimewatch* appeal? The appeal in which – and it stuck in Henry's craw a little – Dave Anger had revealed some top-class information which could lead to a positive ID of the unidentified murder victim?

The facial reconstruction

The geological origin of the deceased

The necklace

Had Eddie Daley put all these things together? From everything that Daley would have known about the deceased, he could easily have added up the sums and worked out that the woman he had located was now dead and that there could easily have been something monetarily in it for him.

Henry knew that whilst Eddie wasn't good at the physical side of things, he didn't hesitate to put the squeeze on people. Had he leaned on Mansur Rashid? Was that why he had hurriedly left Jackie Kippax alone that night? To call on his ex-client and say, 'Remember me?' And was that why he was killed? He'd chosen the wrong person to lean on. Which, Henry thought back to a conversation he'd had with Jackie Kippax, would explain why Eddie had made the international

sign for cash – rubbing his finger and thumb together – when
he left her that night, just as the news was starting – *just after*
Crimewatch *had ended.* And if Rashid knew that Eddie had
used his computer to assist the search for his missing wife,
that would explain why it was missing from the office, together
with Eddie's mobile phone, which could well have revealed
a number which could have linked him to Rashid.

Making Rashid a cold, calculating and very dangerous man
to know.

A surge of excitement made Henry's arse twitch and brought
a smile to his face as he thought, When some great detectives
have their epiphany, they get a moody, all-knowing look about
them, a certain smugness. I, on the other hand, get a contrac-
tion of the arse. And therein lies the difference between a
great detective and a jack like me – a ring piece.

His amusing contemplation was disturbed by the ringing
of his mobile phone. He automatically checked his watch
before answering: 8.30 a.m.

'Henry, what the hell's going on? This is the deputy chief
constable here, by the way, in case you hadn't worked it out!'

'Morning ma'am,' he almost genuflected. 'I was about to
call,' he said truthfully, 'but the signal on the train comes and
goes.'

'On the bloody train? What're you doing on the train?
You should've been back by now – last night in fact. Your
staff are all waiting for you upstairs like a bunch of stuffed
dummies . . . what's going on? What's happening?'

'Didn't get finished until late last night,' he explained, 'and
I was going to ring on the way back. You beat me to it . . .
and I did expect to be back in Preston by ten-ish, but the
train's delayed.'

The words seemed to pacify her. 'Right,' she said, climbing
down from the walls, 'any joy?'

'A lot of joy, actually – a lot of things to tell you.' Henry
spent quite a few minutes doing exactly that.

'Where do we go from here then?' Angela asked. 'Your
team are bouncing. They need something to do.'

'Well, we need to check out Mansur Rashid PDQ.'

'Shouldn't that be passed to Dave Anger?'

Henry made a long creaking noise down the phone. 'I
suppose he needs to be brought into the loop, but if we go at

it from the angle of Eddie's death, then we could get away with it – at least until Rashid has been questioned about his murder. Just a suggestion.'

'I'll buy that . . . and it's not as though Dave will be wanting any distractions today, anyway.'

'Why not . . . oh, Condoleezza Rice is in town today, isn't she?'

'Yeah, and just about the whole of the force is tied up doing security for the visit.'

'In that case,' Henry ruminated, checking his watch again and then seeing the signs for Rugby railway station whiz by, 'why don't you see if you can get Rashid's address from somewhere – it's one of the things I don't have – and get, say, Graeme Walling and someone else from Special Projects to go and grab him? Lock him up on sus of killing Eddie Daley and he can be arrested later for Sabera's murder . . .'

The line went dead as the train picked up speed, leaving Rugby behind, and plunged into a deep cutting, severing all links with the civilized world. Henry looked accusingly at the phone, seeing no signal bars on it.

He sat back and gave up on the phone, opened the *Daily Express* he'd bought on his dash through Euston and tried to do the Sudoku on the inner page, which quickly left him floundering.

As the train approached Crewe, its first scheduled stop of the journey, he received a text message: 'Have found Rashid's address in B/burn. Will arrest this morning. He'll be waiting 4U when U get bak – so will I. Ang.'

An uneasy feeling made Henry reply: 'Bcareful.'

Thirteen

And then there was the next agonizing delay between Leyland and Preston when a points failure halted the train perhaps two miles short of his destination for almost thirty minutes, making Henry want to scream. He could almost see Preston railway station and it felt like it would have been quicker to jump off and walk.

When it eventually slid into platform 3, Henry was ready and waiting at the door with his luggage gripped under his arms, leaping out on to the platform and racing to the car park pay station, which also seemed intent on delaying him as he attempted to feed it a £20 note.

Frustration boiling over, he found his car on the car park, threw his gear on to the back seat and dropped behind the wheel. Before setting off he rang Angela's mobile from his. The phone went straight on to answerphone, which he found peculiar. Shrugging his shoulders, he headed the four miles south to police headquarters at Hutton.

The Special Projects office was empty apart from one person, Jenny 'Attitude' Fisher. He nodded at her, went into his own office and picked up his PR, then came back into the open plan area. 'Can you give me an update?'

Jenny was on the phone, but put her hand over the mouthpiece. 'The dep and Graeme have gone to look for Mansur Rashid.'

'I know that!' he almost squeaked. 'What time did they go?'

'About nine.'

Henry's eyes rose to the wall clock, doing a few quick calculations. Half an hour to Blackburn, ten to fifteen minutes finding the address, say . . . if Rashid was there, arrest him, then down to the cells by 10.30 a.m., he guesstimated. If things went according to plan.

'Have you heard from them since?'

Jenny shook her head and pouted, then concentrated on what was being said to her down the phone and said, 'Thanks for that.' She scribbled something on a notepad and hung up.

'Boss . . . just been on to Orange – oh, you won't know, will you?' she said, seeing Henry's puzzled expression. She stood up and crossed to him. 'During a search of Jackie Kippax's flat, we found phone bills relating to Eddie Daley's Orange mobile account.' Henry was suddenly interested. 'The latest bill wasn't there, but I've been on to Orange today and they're going to fax it to me . . . but in the meantime – voila!' She showed Henry her pad. 'This is the last number he phoned from his mobile – at 10.05 p.m. on the night he was murdered. It was to an O$_2$ number and I'm going to try to get the name of the subscriber without all the bureaucracy if I can.'

'Well done, Jenny,' he said. 'Keep at it.' He ducked back into his office where he dialled the extension for Blackburn custody office. It rang . . . rang . . . and rang . . . and was then answered by a harassed sounding gaoler. 'Custody.'

'DCI Christie here . . . is the deputy chief constable there? Or has she been there?'

'No to both.'

'Is there a guy called Mansur Rashid in custody?'

No hesitation. 'Nope.'

'You've been exceedingly helpful.'

'Ta.' The phone slammed down, leaving Henry holding a dead handset. He dialled Angela Cranlow's mobile again. But got the same response as previously, the answerphone. 'Jenny?' he yelled through his door. 'Have you got Graeme's mobile number?'

'No.'

'Has anyone?'

'Don't think so.'

Henry replaced his phone, which he'd been holding in readiness to use. He hurried out of the door, down one flight of stairs and along the corridor. He didn't knock, but just turned into the anteroom that housed the bag carriers and secretaries. Only the deputy's secretary was at her desk, no one else in.

'I need to make contact with the dep,' Henry told her breathlessly.

'You and me both. I can't get hold of her.'

'Has she got her PR?'

'Yeah – no reply on that, either.'

'Did she say where she was going?'

'To make an arrest in Blackburn,' the secretary said sourly. 'DCCs should not be doing things like that.'

'Any address?' The secretary shook her head. Henry said, 'Thanks,' and scurried back to Special Projects, a scary feeling in the pit of his stomach. He did not like it when cops could not be contacted. He went to Jenny's desk. 'Did they tell you Rashid's address?'

'No . . . something wrong?'

'Bloody hope not.' Henry gestured to the office. 'Where's everyone else?'

'Out doing jobs . . . on Eddie Daley's murder, yeah?'

'Right.' Henry stomped back to his office, cursing today's reliance on communications. If you couldn't get hold of someone these days it was always a problem. In the old days, if you couldn't make contact you lived with it. Maybe he was being a bit too nervous, but Mansur Rashid, whether he had killed his wife or not, was a violent man, as evidenced by Dr Khan's injuries. If Angela Cranlow and Graeme Walling had gone in a bit gung-ho, they might have bitten off more than they could chew.

He tried her mobile again and got the same response, then sat at his desk deep in thought, tapping his chin with his knuckles before rising and walking into the outer office and going to the desk of the woman who'd been given the job of Murder Incident Room manager when the Special Projects team was turned into SPMS.

'Where's Delia?' he asked Jenny.

'Gone sick.'

'What a surprise,' he muttered, shaking his head. He picked up a sheaf of actions. The top one of the pile gave him what he was looking for. It was handwritten by Angela Cranlow and simply said, 'From info received, arrest Mansur Rashid on sus of murder.' There was nothing else. He took the sheet and went to Jenny's desk. 'Mansur Rashid,' he said, placing it in front of her. 'See if you can find out his address for me, somewhere in Blackburn. Interrogate all the intel systems if you have to . . . then call me on my mobile and let me know it. The dep and Graeme have found it somehow and they should've written it on here, but they haven't.' He leaned to her. 'This is urgent.'

Henry hurried out to his car.

His radio was already tuned into Blackburn's frequency. As he drove out of HQ he turned up the volume to listen.

Airwave traffic was busy, a lot going on, much of it generated by the visit later that day of Condoleezza Rice, even though the operation actually dedicated to it had its own specified channel and was running separately to the day-to-day policing of the town. It would have been impossible for such a large-scale operation not to have some overlap. Cops from all over the county had been drafted in for the day. Search teams and sniffer dogs were scouring the venues she was due to visit and the routes she would use were being constantly patrolled by armed officers. It seemed to Henry that a visit instigated at the whim of a politician was causing uproar – and not just within the police. The public, particularly the Asian community, were not exactly welcoming her to town and some demonstrations had been planned.

But that was not his problem.

He drove hard and fast through the country roads behind HQ before joining the motorway and heading towards Blackburn for what seemed the millionth time in just a few short days. Throughout the journey he continually called Angela's mobile but got no answer, which increased his agitation and concern.

He hated it when officers went to a job and then you didn't hear from them.

Ninety-nine per cent of the time it was for a legitimate reason and sooner or later they came back on the radar.

It was that last percentage point that bothered him today. He wondered if Cranlow, in her eagerness to be hands-on, had been a bit reckless and not obeyed the golden rule of telling someone where you were, what you were doing and that you were OK when you'd done it.

Henry grimaced.

Even the most experienced made mistakes. The unfortunate thing was that sometimes those mistakes became banner headlines.

Or was he overreacting?

During the course of his journey he picked out the voice of Bill Robbins on the radio, his old friend he had faced the pit bull with. It seemed he was not working the Condoleezza Rice operation, but doing a general ARV patrol – much to his chagrin, Henry suspected.

Henry tapped Bill's collar number into his PR and called him up, using the mobile phone facility.

'Bill, Henry Christie . . . are you available to give me a chuck-up?'

'Is there a dog involved?'

'Hope not.'

'In that case I'm free.'

Henry suggested an RV point at Blackburn police station in ten minutes. As his conversation with Bill ended, his own mobile rang.

'Henry, it's Jenny . . . got that address for you. Took a bit of doing, though. It's only on the Special Branch system.'

Major relief flooded through Henry's system.

Fifteen minutes later Bill Robbins and his partner for the day, the policewoman called Carly, were travelling behind Henry's car towards Whalley Range, an area in Blackburn which is predominantly Asian. Henry had been there many times over the years, particularly in the late 1970s just after he had joined the force, when there had been a great deal of racial unrest caused by the activities of the extreme right-wing political party, the National Front.

As he turned on to Whalley Range, a long, narrow road, sided by terraced houses and various Asian shops just off Blackburn town centre, he noticed a lot of street activity, more than was usual. No doubt generated by the arrival in town later that day of the American Secretary of State. From the snippets he'd heard, Henry knew there was to be a protest at the town hall by the Muslim community later that day, and maybe the bustle on the street was connected to this. A visit to a local mosque had been called off because of fears that protesters would invade. There was a distinct buzz of tension and he saw many people stop and coldly watch the liveried ARV behind him.

Henry drove on, feeling the hairs on the back of his neck begin to prickle. He wasn't a cat amongst the pigeons any more; he was a cat tiptoeing through a dog pound.

The street he was searching for was just off Whalley Range, one of the myriad of tight terraces clinging to the steep hill-side north of the town centre: Balaclava Street, a name to conjure with, one which gave a good idea of the time when it was built. They were all pretty standard, two-up, two-down, many now extended at the rear for a kitchen, and almost all the outside privvies demolished and the toilets now indoors, although some outside loos still did exist. The street reminded Henry of the one in Accrington into which he had led a PSU on a dawn raid that seemed an eon ago. A stroke of luck had saved him that day. He hoped he wouldn't need such fortune again.

Still the questions lingered. Where was the dep? Where was Graeme? Henry had asked Blackburn comms to try and contact them, but there had been no reply. And still no reply from the dep's mobile phone.

Henry pulled in on Randal Street, just before the junction with Balaclava Street, the ARV Ford Galaxy drawing up behind. He jumped out with the intention of speaking to Bill and Carly. Before he could open his mouth, all their personal radios interrupted.

'Chief Constable to DCI Christie, receiving?' FB's gruff tones demanded over the airwaves.

Henry rolled his eyes. He knew that FB was at the helm of Condoleezza Rice's visit today, that he was to be found at Blackburn nick, kicking everyone's arses. 'Go ahead, sir.'

'I've been made aware of the situation, Henry . . . any developments?'

'I'm just about to knock on a door.' Henry gave FB the address.

'Is there any reason why we should be concerned?'

'Only in as much as communication has broken down and we can't contact two officers.'

'OK – do what you have to do . . . oh, have you got back-up?'

'Yes – an ARV crew have joined me.'

'Keep me informed.'

'Roger.' He regarded the two firearms officers. 'I'm just going to go and knock on the door, just like I'm a cop knocking on a door. Can't see any reason to do it any other way, except if you've got a spare ballistic vest in the back, I'd appreciate it.'

They did and he put it on. It was a new style vest, very light and flexible, giving just as much protection as the older, heavier vests; however, it didn't stop a bullet to the head or the groin. He put his leather jacket over it.

'If I've worked this out right, it's up on the right. I'll walk to it and you just stay here ready to rumble and I'll see how the land lies. If I suspect anything's amiss, I'll yell. I don't want to spook anybody unnecessarily.'

'OK, Henry. What about tooling up?' Bill asked.

'Based on what?' Henry replied. Bill shrugged, under-standing that so far there was nothing to suggest that firearms were likely to be encountered – that anything was likely to be encountered, actually. He and Carly climbed out of the Galaxy and lounged against it, arms folded. Henry set off around the corner and up Balaclava Street, out of their sight.

The house looked no different than any of the others – and why should it? A front door, opening directly on to the foot-path, with a living room window next to it, two windows above on the first floor. The curtains were all drawn. But nothing outwardly untoward.

Henry paused outside the door, holding his PR in his left hand and warrant card in his right. He banged firmly, using the bottom edge of his radio, waited. There was no response, so he banged again – harder. Still no response. As he was about to turn away and make to the back, there was a noise from inside and the sound of footsteps approaching the door.

His cop instincts, honed over many years of knocking on doors, tingled and told him to beware. Two experienced cops didn't go missing for nothing. It was always the 'routine' jobs that took everyone by surprise.

There was someone behind the door. He could hear them. Then it opened an inch to reveal the eye of a man peering out across a security chain.

'Hello,' Henry smiled. 'I'm DCI Christie from Lancashire Constabulary . . . I wonder if I could have a word, please?' He held up his warrant card.

'About what?' Through the gap, Henry could make out the guy was of Asian background and appeared to be quite big.

'I'd like to speak to Mansur Rashid, if he's at home.'

The man shook his head. 'Don't know him.'

Henry's guts did one of those sick-inducing somersaults. He swallowed as he identified the first lie.

'I'd still like a word.' He moved slightly closer to the door and gave the eye he could see the evil eye from himself. 'I won't be going away,' he added.

The man nodded. 'I have to close the door to unlock the chain.'

'Please make sure you reopen it.' Henry saw the man smile.

The door closed. The chain slid back. The man opened up

and stood on the threshold, one step above Henry on the pavement. He had to look up to the man and did not like what he saw – an unusually tall and wide Asian man with yellows for his eyes, rather than whites, and a scar on his face running from his upper lip to just below his right eye. He was probably in his mid-thirties and looked mean. He smelled clean and wore a crisp white shirt and pressed jeans, as though he had just got showered and dressed. His thick black hair was slicked back, and wet. Henry noticed his hands and wrists were thick. They looked capable of strangulation.

'May I come in?'

The man smiled again, stepped down off the threshold and looked both ways up and down the street before standing aside to allow Henry to brush past him into the hallway. The man came in behind, making Henry realize that, because there was a Yale lock on the door, it was now locked from the outside.

Henry hesitated but the man gestured, saying, 'Go through, please . . . the door at the end is the kitchen . . . we can talk in there . . . I'll make tea.'

'Thanks,' Henry said, lulled by this. He set off down the hallway, horribly aware of his vulnerability, but at the same time chiding himself for being so cynical as to tar everyone he came across as a potential psycho. There could be the simplest explanation for two cops being out of contact. Maybe they'd just gone for a brew somewhere, switched everything off. Cops had been known to do stupid things like that, difficult as it was to believe.

Four steps down the hall and Henry knew he was in real trouble.

What gave the game away was the blood on the floor and the walls.

His eyes firstly saw a blood spurt on the wall, level with his shoulder.

Since blood gets pumped by the heart around the body under great pressure, when a major artery or vein is severed there is a forceful gush of blood – and what Henry saw was a textbook example of such a spurt.

He had seen enough bloodstains in his life to know when he was looking at one caused by such an injury. Even as he was registering this, and seeing the rest of the blood splattered around the walls and floor, his body was reacting by spinning around to face the man behind him – and seeing the

knife in the man's right hand already on its downward tra-
jectory as he tried to stab Henry in the back.

It was a hell of a knife too, ten inches of honed steel blade,
and even then, part of Henry's mind tried to work out where
it could have been concealed – but that was an academic muse
in that split second of time. The fact was, he had hidden it
and now he was using it.

Henry twisted away with a grunt and the knife slashed
harmlessly through the air, narrowly missing him. He heard
it whoosh by.

Now standing at ninety degrees to the man, Henry brought
up his elbow and rammed it ferociously into the man's face
before the knife could come back up. He caught him a hard
blow just on the nose, knocking him staggering backwards.
But the blow did not connect with the accuracy or force Henry
would have truly wished, and instantly, despite the blood flow
from his smashed nose, the Asian guy found his balance and
charged back at him, with a howl on his contorted lips, the
knife coming upwards towards Henry's solar plexus.

There was hardly room to manoeuvre in the three-foot-wide
hallway, but as the knife curved upwards, Henry jumped back
like a scalded cat, knocking the knife out of the way and feeling
it slice across the soft, fleshy part of his left hand below his
little finger, making him drop his radio. Still the man came at
him, yelling, 'You should not have come!' and trying to slash
Henry, who found himself stumbling backwards in an effort
to keep clear of the attack, his forearms raised defensively. He
felt the material in the sleeves of his leather jacket slice open,
but offer more protection than a normal suit jacket.

The man was moving quickly at him.

Henry's back slammed against the kitchen door, trapping
him, making him an easy victim.

But then the attack stopped, but only because the man realized that he now had Henry just where he wanted him. He
readjusted his grip on the knife, wiped the blood from his
face, smiled and lunged again, intent on murder.

Which gave Henry no choice in the matter.

Either he stayed where he was and tried to fend off the
attack, which he knew would end in a messy, sliced-up death;
or he got in close and personal and fought dirtier than he'd
ever done in his life.

The knife arced towards him, its silver blade flashing.

Henry knocked it away with a sweep of his hand, making the man's right arm flick briefly sideways and thereby giving Henry an 'in' into his body which he knew he would not have again.

He flung himself low and mightily into the man, twisting and driving his shoulder into the man's chest, expelling all the air out of him as his shoulder connected with his breastbone. Henry did not stop, did not allow the impact to break his momentum, but continued to power back down the hall, wrapping his arms around the man, pushing him relentlessly back, keeping him off balance, all the way to the front door, crashing against it with a massive whack. Henry kept himself crushed tight into the man, body to body, and began pummelling him as the man struggled to climb away from Henry's onslaught and get himself into a position to drive the knife over Henry's shoulder into his back.

Henry managed to deliver a powerful body punch, making the man drop the knife. The man gasped, hurt, but immediately smashed his forehead into Henry's face, catching him below his right eye.

The blow stunned him. Stars and lightning rushed past Henry's eyes. Instinctively his hands went to his face, even though he knew he should not let it affect him.

He took a blow to the groin as the man tried to ram a knee into Henry's testicles. It was a weak blow, not serious or painful, but it made Henry respond by grabbing the man's throat and whacking his head against the front door, twice.

Suddenly the man got a surge of energy and power from deep within.

With an inhuman cry he managed to wrestle Henry's hands from his throat and bend back Henry's fingers, forcing him on to his knees as he attempted to break his fingers.

Meanwhile, Henry's own strength had evaporated and he found himself being overpowered by a big, fit man. He stared into the man's wild eyes, the eyes of the man who was going to murder him.

Simultaneous thoughts skittered through Henry's mind as he sank to his knees: I haven't called Kate this morning; why did I screw Angela Cranlow? I don't want to die here.

Then he deliberately fell backwards, catching the attacker

by surprise, upending him so that he would lose balance, let go of Henry's fingers and fall on top of him. Suddenly they were face to face, rolling from side to side across the narrow hall, each trying desperately to be the one who got on top, get the advantage. They punched, kicked, scratched.

As they smacked against the skirting board, they were cheek to cheek. Henry opened his mouth, bared his teeth, then sank them into the man's ear lobe and bit hard, worrying the ear like a dog on a rabbit, drawing blood which he tasted. The man howled in excruciating pain, spurring him on with a resurgence of effort.

The man's face reared back and he spat a mouthful of blood into Henry's eyes and for the next few moments Henry had to fight blind, until suddenly the man got in a punch, connecting with the side of Henry's head, jarring his brain. He went limp and disorientated, let go of the man, who scrambled away from him and crawled down the hall.

Henry's senses flooded back. He wiped his face and rolled on to his stomach, realizing that the man was trying to reach the knife. Henry grabbed the man's left ankle and yanked him backwards and tried to crawl up him as though he was climbing a rope. The man kicked out and caught Henry in the face, just on the spot where he had previously head-butted him under the right eye. Something cracked, sending a nauseous feeling through him, but he held on, grimly determined that he would not lose this one. The man continually kicked back, but Henry wrapped his arms round his legs, preventing him from reaching the knife.

Henry saw that his radio, dropped when he was initially attacked, was in easy reach. The man pulled and kicked and fought, but Henry held on for death, wondering if he could keep him secure whilst getting the radio and screaming for help.

The man twisted so he was on his back, Henry holding on, his face now level with the man's knees. The man managed to sit up and reached out, pounding Henry's head with his fists. Henry tucked his face between the man's shins, riding the blows, which hurt badly.

Then, with a great heave of strength, he broke one leg free of Henry's grasp, flat-footed Henry on the shoulder and managed to yank his other leg away, then lunged for the knife.

Henry grabbed the radio and teetered unsteadily to his feet, backing breathlessly towards the front door, whilst at the other end of the hall, the Asian guy was in a leopard's crouch, having retrieved the knife.

Both men panted heavily, eyeing each other warily.

'You put up a good fight, infidel,' the man said through the blood streaming down his nose. He wiped his face with his forearm. To Henry, he looked terrifying, waiting to pounce, blood soaking him. He spun the knife in his hand and Henry imagined it plunging into his neck.

Henry raised the radio to his lips. He had to get the call out. He had twelve feet in which to do it, in the time it would take for the man to reach him. Maybe a second and a half.

The man rose, pushing himself up as though he was a sprinter, except he held a knife, not a baton.

Henry was about to shriek something into the radio, along the lines of, 'Fuckin' help me!'

Two things did not happen.

The man did not reach Henry.

Henry did not manage to utter any words.

There was a massive, all encompassing 'boom' from somewhere behind the man and his right shoulder seemed to explode into bloody fragments. His arms shot up and he crashed down on to his knees, dropping the knife, then falling on to the floor, moaning and writhing in agony.

Henry's mouth clamped shut and he lowered the PR.

A man in a ski mask and dark clothing stood at the now open kitchen door. A big man, his wide frame and height almost filling the gap. In his right hand he held a smoking pistol, which he lowered slowly. With his left hand, he pinched the top of his ski mask and slowly pulled it up off his head, revealing his features. Then he stepped forward and stood with his big feet straddling the knife man. There was a big grin on his face.

Henry was speechless, but the guy with the gun wasn't.

In an American accent, he drawled, 'Well, Henry, the cavalry's come to bail you out again, I reckon. What you say to that, pal? Nothin'? Cat got it?'

Then Henry found the power of speech and said simply, 'Thanks, pal . . . what the hell're you doing here?'

Fourteen

He put his hand on the doorknob and slowly turned it. He was trembling, hurting, and he didn't want to do this, but he knew he had to. It was his responsibility. He glanced at the people behind him in the hallway, then at the walls splattered with blood, the floors also, and pushed the front room door open.

His mouth closed tightly as his eyes took in what was beyond, then his lips popped open when the enormity of it hit him. 'Oh God,' he groaned.

They had died horrendous deaths, their bodies splayed out on the floor of the empty room, their throats severed from ear to ear, their heads almost hacked off.

The room from hell.

Henry stood immobile, unable to move, as he computed how it had happened.

They had knocked on the front door, been invited in – just as he had – and in the hall, they had been savagely attacked.

They'd probably gone for Graeme first, the big guy. Someone had taken him from behind and sliced his throat open, hence the blood spurts on the wall from the thick arteries in his neck. Then Angela had been overpowered, suffering the same fate, and their bodies had been dragged into the front room where it looked like the attack had continued frenziedly, and they had been butchered, almost beheaded.

Henry shuddered. His nostrils flared.

He had seen many awful things in his life. Most had no effect on him. But this horror was something he was having big problems with already. It was one of the most barbaric scenes he had ever witnessed, like something from the Dark Ages.

Their faces were twisted in his direction, both clearly identifiable. Graeme Walling had one eye closed, the other half open; Angela Cranlow's were both wide open, staring accusingly at him, her tongue lolling in the blood which had gushed from her mouth.

Henry was short of breath. His heart started to pound fast. Suddenly it was hard to inhale.

A hand clamped down on his shoulder and the big American looked over his shoulder.

'Hell,' he said. 'C'mon, Henry, close the door . . . step back, let the CSI guys have this.'

The hand steered Henry away from the room, through the kitchen and into the backyard, where he was forced to sit down on the edge of a metal dustbin.

'Deep breath, pal.'

Henry complied, his hands on his knees, his arms locked at the elbows.

'Let's have a look at you.' The American settled on his muscular haunches and held Henry's face, tilting it to the light. 'That's a hell of a shiner,' he said, inspecting Henry's right cheek.

'Think my cheekbone's bust.'

'Let's look at the hand.'

Henry held out his right hand, slashed by the knife. He'd wrapped kitchen towel round it but the bleeding had continued, soaking the paper. The American slowly unravelled the paper, making Henry wince. His hand dithered. 'Needs stitching, I reckon.'

'You still haven't said what you're doing here,' Henry said dreamily.

'And I haven't got time to explain just yet. We need to do some pretty fast manoeuvring here first.'

Henry shook his head and forced himself to return to the world. He looked directly into the American's eyes. 'What the hell's going on?'

'Critical threat,' he said.

His name was Karl Donaldson.

A bemused Henry Christie, still on the edge of a dustbin in the backyard of a terraced house in the predominantly Asian area of Blackburn, watched the activity in a haze. His face hurt and was swelling by the second and the rest of the injuries and knocks he had taken whilst fighting for his life were starting to have some effect. He compared it to being dragged under a truck.

Suddenly the backdoor of the house opened and the two firearms officers stumbled out, Bill almost dragging Carly, who immediately spewed her guts up over the back wall, retching with a disgusting sound. Bill shot Henry a look of horror. Henry nodded, still not quite with it, but realizing they had just seen the crime scene.

Karl Donaldson came out behind the two officers and pulled Bill to one side. He spoke urgently in his ear. 'Get her home, get her out of the way and get her to keep quiet, OK, pal?'

Bill turned to Henry for guidance.

'Do as he says, Bill.' Bill's facial response did not look positive. 'Trust me,' Henry assured him.

Bill gave him another look, one of incomprehension and fear.

'You heard, Bill – trust him,' Donaldson said. 'Get her home, and if you want to go home too, then that's fine.'

Henry nodded. 'Do it.'

'You're the boss,' he said, sounding aggrieved.

Carly vomited again, narrowly missing Henry's feet with the remainder of her breakfast. She was completely out of it, overwhelmed by shock. Bill led her out of the yard and down the alley. She did not resist.

'They're good people,' Donaldson said.

Henry regarded his old friend, but then his attention was redirected when he heard the warning beep-beep of a vehicle reversing up the back alley. It was an ambulance.

'For me?' Henry asked, squinting through his one good eye.

'No, for the guy I shot.'

'I assumed he was dead.'

'He's not well, but he's conscious and we need to have speaks with him urgently.'

Two paramedics in green overalls dropped out of the ambulance and armed with their kits and a fold-away stretcher, they dashed into the house. It wasn't long before they reappeared with a body on the stretcher, completely covered as though it was a corpse. They rushed past Henry and Donaldson and slid the stretcher into the ambulance. One jumped in with it, the other clambered back behind the wheel.

'Should I get in?' Henry asked.

'Nah – you come with me . . . you're in this up to your neck and I think we can use you.'

Henry sat dumbly in the passenger seat of his Rover 75 whilst Karl Donaldson drove through the crowded streets of Blackburn. Henry's face was scrunched up in an expression of unhappiness, the posture of his body matching it.

'Where are we going?'

'You'll see.'

Henry had known Karl Donaldson for about ten years. They had first encountered each other when Donaldson, then an FBI field agent, had been investigating US-related mob activity in the north-west of England. That initial link-up had resulted in their paths crossing several times more over the next few years, both professionally and personally, and they became good friends. Donaldson even married an ex-Lancashire police-woman and settled just outside London, enabling him to commute into the city where he'd landed a job as an FBI legal attaché based in the American embassy. His role entailed a lot of liaison work with police forces across Europe.

Over the years, Henry had glimpsed a different side of Donaldson. He came across as a big, handsome, friendly guy who could charm his way into a mother superior's panties if he so wished, but underneath that veneer Henry had seen a band of ruthlessness a mile wide.

His appearance today, whilst welcome under the circumstances, was also a shock and Henry was somewhat mystified . . . but hoped for some answers soon.

Donaldson handled Henry's car easily. He had driven his own Jeep on British roads for over ten years and was comfort-able with traffic. He had ordered Henry to get into the passenger seat, continually reassuring him about the crime scene and that it would be looked after and that it would all be taken care of, and after taking his keys, had settled behind the wheel and set off with a squeal of rubber. He headed swiftly back down Whalley Range out of town, anxiously checking the rear-view mirror until, at last, a smile crossed his face and he relaxed.

Curious, Henry glanced down at his door mirror and, with some shock, saw that the ambulance that had set off a couple of minutes before them was behind, no lights flashing.

Henry uttered, perplexed, 'Is that the same ambulance?'

'You'll see . . . now just relax, H, I'll explain soon.'

'Am I being abducted?'

Donaldson laughed. 'So I could have my wicked way with you? Don't kid yourself.'

As Henry adjusted his position to get more comfortable, he grunted in pain. He put a finger in his mouth and touched a tooth, which waggled loosely. Then he groaned again for good measure.

Donaldson accelerated through an amber light, straight across from Whalley Range into Plane Street, then Plane Tree Road and sharp right on to Robinson Street.

'How the hell d'you know your way around Blackburn?'

'Sat nav.'

'And why is that ambulance still behind us? Why hasn't it gone to the hospital?'

'Trust me, I'm an FBI agent.'

Henry waggled his tooth again. It sent a shock of exquisite pain through his face.

Donaldson dropped down on to Philips Road and turned left into an area that was mainly industrial estates within easy reach of the M65. They were not far from Blackburn police station and Henry assumed this was their destination.

Assumed wrong.

There were lights at the junction of Philips Road and Whitebirk Drive – a dual carriageway, also known as the arterial road which curved around the north-west perimeter of Blackburn, hence the name. To reach the police station, Donaldson should have turned right. Instead, he drove straight across the lights on to Whitebirk industrial estate, a sprawling conglomeration of business units of all shapes and sizes, which seemed to expand continually into the hillside beyond. Henry had always known it to be there. It was probably one of Blackburn's oldest industrial estates, post-cotton.

Henry could still see the ambulance in the wing mirror, following them.

Donaldson muttered something. Henry turned to him to ask, 'What?' but realized the American was talking into a tiny radio mike. To Henry, he said, 'Nearly there, pal.'

'Nearly where?'

'There,' he said mysteriously. 'Actually, I could get into

deep shit for bringing you here and letting you see where
"there" is. But because I trust you, I'm willing to take a
chance . . .'

'Eh?' Obviously Henry's brain had been addled from the
beating he'd just taken, compounded by the horrendous blood-
bath. He thought he might have damaged something up there,
because this was making no sense to him.

Donaldson drove to the far reaches of the industrial estate,
which got grottier and grottier the further they went. He steered
down a cul-de-sac and then turned in through some high steel
gates, topped with barbed wire, and drove through an open
shutter door into a cavernous industrial unit which was
surrounded by a ten-foot-high steel mesh fence. The ambulance tailgated them in and the shutter door started to close
as soon as the vehicles stopped moving.

The unit was similar to thousands of others: breeze-block
built up to about ten feet, then the remainder constructed of
corrugated steel walls and roof. There were no windows and
illumination was provided by banks of strip-lighting hanging
from the roof.

The floor was made of poured concrete and on it were
parked many vehicles. Henry recognized Donaldson's Jeep
and amongst the others was a Royal Mail van, a United Utilities
transit van and a Tesco home delivery box van; there were
also several non-descript cars of a variety of makes and a
liveried Lancashire Constabulary traffic car.

And the ambulance.

Donaldson eased his big frame out of Henry's car and leaned
on the roof, looking across at his bemused friend, who had
also got out and was staring around the unit with a little-boy-
lost expression.

'Welcome to Homeland Security, Blackburn Branch,'
Donaldson said, with a wide sweep of his arms.

Henry nodded, still unable to take it in, but slowly beginning to slot things together.

He watched the paramedics pull the stretchered casualty
out of the ambulance and carry him across to a door in one
corner of the unit. With a bit of contortion, they managed to
manoeuvre through without tipping him off.

'That's Bob and Bob,' Donaldson explained for Henry's
benefit. 'American Special Forces, both highly trained medics.'

'Of course they are,' Henry said, as if seeing two Delta
Force soldiers dressed up as Lancashire Ambulance Service
paramedics, carrying a man who had been shot on a stretcher
between them, across the floor of an industrial unit on the
edge of Blackburn, was the most normal thing in the world.

Henry's legs went weak.

Donaldson saw him sag. He rushed round to him, held him
up under the armpit and led him across the unit. 'There won't
be too much time for explanation,' he said. 'I'll just get you
cleaned up, get some painkillers down you and then we'll try
to keep the American Secretary of State alive . . . how does
that sound?'

'Just doody,' Henry said, using an expression bandied about
by his youngest daughter Leanne, which seemed entirely
appropriate for the situation.

Fifteen

Donaldson steered Henry diagonally across the floor of the
unit, through the doors the paramedics/soldiers had gone
with the injured man. This led into a narrow corridor off which
were a number of half-glass doors on the left. Henry presumed
that there were offices behind them. There was a wooden staircase at the far end, leading up to the first floor.

Donaldson took him to a door marked 'toilet' and said, 'Get
in there, wash yourself off, and I'll be back in a few minutes
with some new clothing for you.'

Henry complied and found himself in a tiled loo with a
couple of wash basins and mirrors. He leaned on a basin and
stared at his reflection. His eyes were sunken, his whole visage
a scarred, swollen mess. His cheek was swollen and purple
and he thought he could see it throbbing.

There was blood streaked all over him.

He slid his leather jacket off and had a look at the slashed
arm, grateful that Kate had brought it for him when he'd set

off for London. Its thickness had probably saved him from being seriously wounded. Four hundred quid to replace, he thought sourly, pulled his shirt off and tossed it on the floor. It needed to be incinerated. Then he got to work, washing himself down, aware that his jeans were a mess.

The water did little for him, other than to clean off the excess blood and make him look a little more presentable.

Donaldson reappeared bearing a change of clothing over his arm.

'These should all fit you,' he said and handed it all over – jeans, T-shirt, boxer shorts, socks. Henry stripped in front of him and stepped into the fresh, clean clothes, which fitted him snugly. 'Sorry, but I ain't got any trainers for you. You'll have to stick with the ones you've got.'

'No worries,' Henry said.

The toilet door opened and a pretty, white-coated black woman in her late twenties entered, a stethoscope dangling around her neck and a notepad in one hand.

'Walking wounded,' Donaldson said, nodding at Henry, who managed a pathetic smile. 'This is Dr Arlene Chambers, Henry. She'll give you a quick once-over, see if your brain has been permanently damaged or not.'

'Hi,' she said brightly. 'What happened to you?'

'Er . . . been in a fight, was well on the way to losing it, got slashed by a knife.' He held up his left hand, which he had washed and was bleeding again. 'And got whacked in the face.'

'OK – let's have a look at you.' She turned to Donaldson. 'Karl, a bit of privacy, please.'

'Ma'am,' he said, and Henry saw the doctor quiver with pleasure and flutter her eyelashes. He reversed out and left them alone. Dr Chambers began a fairly thorough inspection, concluding with taping up the cut on Henry's hand.

'That cheekbone is undoubtedly broken. An X-ray will confirm it, but that's one thing we don't have here. Your hand could do with stitching, but those strips will hold it together for the time being . . . I know you're not going to have time to go to hospital just yet.'

'I'm not?' Henry exclaimed.

'The rest is just bruising, soreness and swelling – all the usual things you get when you fight. These will help with the pain.' She handed him two tablets as big as pebbles. 'Army issue – very effective.'

'If you can swallow them.'

The door opened and Donaldson came back in. 'Finished?'

'He's all yours,' the doctor said, smiled at Henry, looked up gooey-eyed at Donaldson, and left them.

'OK?'

'Never better.' Henry put his mouth to a tap, filled it with water, then swallowed the tablets with a bit of difficulty.

'I think you're only supposed to have one,' Donaldson said.

Henry shrugged.

'Follow me.' Donaldson led him back out into the corridor and in through a door which had 'The Swamp' scribbled on it. Beyond was a large office with a big window, blinds drawn. A roomy old settee dominated one wall and three easy-looking armchairs and two plastic chairs made up the rest of the seating. A microwave, oven, kettle, coffee-maker, toaster, fridge and an array of loaves of bread, packets of bagels, jam, marmalade, peanut butter, tea, coffee and milk cartons covered a worktop next to the sink. This was obviously a chill-out room.

'Take a seat,' Donaldson said, and Henry lowered himself gratefully into one of the armchairs as the American boiled the kettle and made two mugs of instant coffee, handing one to Henry.

'Fuck, I'm sore,' Henry said, adjusting his position.

'You look it . . . but Arlene's magic medicine will work wonders in no time, especially a double dose of it.'

Henry raised his eyebrows. Chit-chat time was over.

'OK – quick story from me,' Donaldson said.

'I'm all ears.'

'The American Secretary of State is visiting the north of England at the request of your Foreign Secretary, who is also your local Member of Parliament.'

'That much I know.'

'She's due to reach Lancashire this afternoon after visiting Liverpool,' Donaldson said. He settled his big frame into the seat next to Henry, crossed his long, muscular legs. 'As you can imagine, the security arrangements are way up there.' His index finger pointed skywards.

'I QA-d the Operational Order,' Henry said.

'That only tells half the story . . . no doubt you are aware that your English cops and security services have been in constant contact with their American counterparts?' His voice rose at the end of the sentence with that curious American inflection that seemed to make every statement a question. 'Even if the world wasn't in the state it is, the security arrangements for the visit would still be massive and as it is, they're well beyond that.'

'But there's more?' Henry prompted.

'Much more,' Donaldson said gravely. 'Think you can stand up?'

They were in a darkened room, two rows of chairs, five in each row, facing the front where there was a brightly lit, but blank, projector screen. Henry sat in the middle of the front row, the only member of the audience. Donaldson stood at the front of the room to one side of the screen, bending to look at the keys of a laptop computer, hooked up to a data projector, which was throwing bright light on to the screen.

Donaldson spoke as he faffed around with the computer, occasionally muttering something about 'hi-tech shit' under his breath. 'This will have to be quick, Henry, and I make no apologies for that . . . shit! . . . computers!' he tapped a few keys, then said, 'Ahh, here we are . . . found it.' He picked up a remote mouse and sat next to Henry. 'Since your Foreign Secretary visited Condoleezza Rice in her hometown of Birmingham, Alabama last year, we've known she was invited back by him to visit this backwater . . . so far, so OK. Our security service, your security service, start to get heads together with the politicos to arrange the visit. High profile, lots of cops, lots of spooks. However, a seed of information came to light, then blossomed into a flower, if you will.' He cleared his throat, uncomfortable with the metaphor. 'An arrest was made in Spain . . . do you recall the Madrid train bombing?'

'Who could forget that?' The carnage wrought on a morning commuter train into that city, bombs exploded by Islamic extremists, killing and maiming many.

'To this day suspects are being pulled in. Two months ago Spanish police arrested a guy suspected of involvement and interrogated him—'

'Interrogated?'

'OK, tortured him,' Donaldson said flippantly. 'Turns out he was very peripheral to the actual bombings.'

'Because torture always elicits the truth?'

Donaldson gave him a cold look. 'Don't get all moral high ground with me, pal,' he warned Henry, who shuddered. It was a definite shot across the bows. 'We don't have time for any of that.'

'OK.' Henry shrugged, chastened, but experiencing something very nasty crawling through his lower intestine.

'This guy dropped some names, one of which was this fella.' Donaldson pointed the mouse at the computer. A face appeared on the screen. It was a grainy, black and white headshot of a bearded man of Middle-Eastern origin. The sort of photo Henry had seen hundreds of times in the media over the last few years, particularly after 9/11. Dark-haired, bearded, staring, deadly eyes peering out accusingly.

Clicking the mouse again, a caption slid across the screen accompanied by a sound effect: a machine gun firing. It made Henry jump.

'Mohammed Ibrahim Akbar,' Donaldson said. 'That's only one of his names, by the way – he's got dozens of others. And just so you know where I'm coming from, I've been hunting this son of a bitch down ever since he was involved in the bombing of the Nairobi embassy in '98 . . . as well as doing my day job. Two of my closest friends died that day.'

'I never knew,' Henry said simply.

'You didn't have to.'

Something else. Another hidden facet to Karl Donaldson which slightly scared Henry.

'Anyway, he's been on the FBI most wanted list for maybe eight years now. He's an Al-Qaeda enforcer, very, very skilled at brainwashing, explosives, firearms, torture, a superb marksman and good at killing people at close quarter . . . connected to many atrocities around the world, both as a planner and executioner, if you will. Extremely good at his job. And one of Osama Bin Laden's top travelling men.' The words were tinged with a grudging respect. 'But if I didn't have a day job, and I'd been given the permission, I'd've tracked the bastard down by now single-handed,' Donaldson said bitterly, with no bravado. 'Do you recall the American journalist kidnapped in Pakistan last year, guy called Lonsdale, a Reuters man?'

Henry shook his head. There were so many, a new kidnapping hardly even registered with him now.

'He was beheaded. It was shown on the Internet.' Donaldson clicked the mouse and a fuzzy video clip began to run on the screen. This showed a dishevelled man sitting tied to a chair, his face a terrible mess of cuts, bruises and swellings. His head lolled loosely.

A figure appeared behind the man dressed in loose white overalls. He took up a position to one side of the hostage.

'Guy on the chair is Lonsdale. Guy behind is Akbar.'

Suddenly Akbar grabbed Lonsdale's hair and yanked his head back, exposing the throat. In his free hand he held a large, curved knife, which he placed against Lonsdale's throat.

'You're not going to show me what I think you're going to show me?' Henry asked with dread.

Akbar tipped Lonsdale's head forward so he was looking directly at the camera recording this terrible event. His eyes were wide, bulging with fear. The knife was still at his throat.

'Know why he did that?' Donaldson asked.

'Did what?'

'Pushed his head forwards again?'

Henry shook his head.

'Because if his head is back, it's kind of counterproductive,' he said, matter-of-fact, his eyes staring emotionless at the screen. 'It allows the main arteries to slip back and be protected by the windpipe. And I'll bet you thought the guillotine was bad. That's a walk in the park in comparison to this.'

With one smooth, practised, hard stroke, Akbar slit Lonsdale's throat.

Henry recoiled in horror, turning his head away. 'Jesus!' he croaked.

'*Allah*,' Donaldson corrected him cynically. 'He then proceeds to hack his head off . . .'

'Turn it off,' Henry said disgustedly. 'Point made – whatever the point was.' He was appalled by the spectacle.

Stone-faced and silent, Donaldson clicked the mouse and the picture dissolved into white screen.

'He used that knife and a tenon saw. Fortunately we believe Lonsdale was drugged up to the eyeballs, if that's any comfort . . . his body hasn't yet been found, nor his head.'

'OK, where is this leading?' Henry demanded. This whole

thing had started off as a killing of a squalid private eye, leading to a domestic murder and now here he was, head reeling, plunged into a world of terrorism. He could hardly believe what was happening.

'Our friend in Spain had come across Akbar as the Madrid bombings were being planned and a couple of times since,' Donaldson said, going back to his original story. 'Akbar does a lot of work brainwashing young, gullible Muslims who then merrily strap explosives on to themselves and walk into a crowded market to kill a hundred people and then they go to their vision of heaven. The suspect blabbed that he'd heard Akbar was operating in Britain, masterminding a series of bombings which were to culminate in the assassination of Condoleezza Rice on her visit to your good country – a coup that, Akbar claims, will be his crowning glory, one he would gladly die doing, apparently.'

'Ahh,' Henry said.

'Consequently, all our efforts have been concentrated on that little gem of gen . . . and incidentally, the guy in Spain was released without charge. He was found murdered two days later, having been subjected to real torture.'

'Hence the Blackburn Field Office of the FBI.'

'We set up here six weeks ago. Only your chief constable and a few people higher up the ladder know about us and we've been pulling our guts out trying to track Akbar down. It's a joint task force – FBI, CIA, Secret Service, the military . . . there's a helluva lot of territory arguments.'

'Is he definitely in this country?'

'Intelligence says yes . . . and intelligence brought us to East Lancashire last week in a hastily prepared series of raids, carried out by you guys – remember?'

'So I was right to whinge that the whole thing was poorly set up.'

'Not only that, pal – you missed Akbar. You!' Donaldson pointed at him, then smiled and patted him on the knee. 'Not your fault.' He winked. 'But he was there, DNA at the scene proved it.'

'He was getting those two young lads to do his dirty work?'

'In one! The intelligence was that he was spending time with young rebels and was about to push them out and cause merry mayhem on the streets of your cotton towns. Until you knocked

on the door and spooked him . . . that's the way it goes, sometimes.' Donaldson took a breath. 'But earlier today one of our
surveillance teams slotted in behind a guy in London called Fazul
Ali, a known associate of Akbar. They tracked him all the way
to Lancashire – to Blackburn, actually. Ali is Akbar's right-hand
man . . . and if you'd had the stomach to watch the video you'd'a
seen him help his mate to decapitate Lonsdale . . . Anyway,
we follow Ali to Blackburn, then we lose him.'

'Brilliant,' Henry said sardonically.

'These things happen, as you well know . . . but the interesting thing for me is, Henry, how did you end up knocking
on that door this morning?'

'It's a long story.'

'Shorten it,' Donaldson said, checking his watch. 'We've
got two hours before the lovely Condoleezza Rice sets foot
in this county.'

Henry related his story quickly, feeling as though he was
telling a sordid tale of everyday life, grubby murder, sleazy
passion and cultural issues which had no relation whatever to
the world of terrorism. He had been dealing with the sad story
of a woman who thought she could break free of a life that
was strangling her and of an ex-cop who was trying to make
a quick buck by leaning on somebody. What both had done
was to underestimate the person they were dealing with. Just
another tale of everyday folk caught in a vortex of mixed
circumstances . . . but the sad reality was that terrorism now
often overlapped into day-to-day life. It wasn't something that
happened on the other side of the world anymore; it happened
on the doorstep, as evidenced by the 7/7 London bombers,
boys who lived next door.

'Mansur Rashid? I wonder what we've got on him . . .
Name doesn't ring any bells,' Donaldson said as Henry
finished.

'I haven't had the chance to do any digging yet, either.'

Donaldson stood up and switched on the lights. 'Next door,'
he said. 'Think you can stand up?'

The pain relief administered by Dr Chambers had actually
kicked in, numbing down Henry's injuries. 'I might need a
Zimmer frame,' he joked.

Donaldson took him next door. Four people sat at computers,

tapping busily away. No one looked round. Donaldson approached the nearest operator and laid his hands on the guy's shoulders, making him jerk out of his concentration on the screen.

'Mansur Rashid,' he said simply. With a nod, the man began to interrogate his PC. 'Access to thousands of databases,' Donaldson said to Henry, 'including every single thing Lancashire Constabulary has on computer record – and every other force in the country.' He wasn't bragging, just being matter-of-fact. Henry didn't even raise an eyebrow. Nothing surprised him anymore.

Ten seconds later, the man said, 'Mansur Rashid.' He leaned back to allow Donaldson and Henry to look at the screen. 'This is from Special Branch files in Lancashire.'

The two officers looked at the computer.

Donaldson read out, 'Mansur Rashid, date of birth 22/10/64 in Pakistan . . . address on Balaclava Street, Blackburn . . . attends a local mosque . . . and that's about it, a one-line entry . . . very thorough, you lot,' he said critically, then more magnanimously, 'Though to be fair, there's a hundred thousand entries like this the world over, one-liners about people who might be of interest.'

The computer guy scrolled down the screen and said, 'This file has been looked at twice today, by the way.'

Angela Cranlow and Graeme Walling, Henry guessed. That's how they discovered his address. And Jenny Fisher accessing it for the same reason following Henry's instructions: to find Rashid's address.

'No trace on any other database,' the guy said.

'Anyway, Karl,' Henry said, 'you haven't told me how you magically appeared on Balaclava Street and saved my life.'

'Eavesdropping,' he admitted. 'Our surveillance team lost Fazul Ali, then not long after I hear the chatter on the local radio channel that we are monitoring. I recognized your voice and picked up that a couple of your officers have gone missing in the same vicinity as Ali was mislaid, and you were investigating. I just decided to take a look . . . and in case you haven't worked it out, pal, this is the second time that you've missed Akbar because I'm pretty sure that he was in the house when your people knocked . . . and how do I know that? The dead cops, for one thing, and for another, the guy who wanted to slice you up.'

'Is Fazul Ali?' said Henry, deadpan, suddenly realizing he'd been in hand-to-hand combat with one of the world's most dangerous men.

'Fazul Ali,' Donaldson confirmed.

'And you shot him.'

'Winged him, actually,' Donaldson said with a grin. 'Now let's go and torture him.'

Sixteen

Henry's disbelief diminished as Karl Donaldson took him along the ground-floor corridor, up the set of wooden steps and on to the first-floor corridor, which virtually replicated the one below. 'The far offices have been turned into sleeping quarters,' Donaldson said with an airy wave of the hand, 'and this is the interrogation suite.' He opened the door of the first office and stepped through, Henry behind him like an obedient puppy.

They entered a dimly lit room. It took a moment for Henry's eyes to make the adjustment and to his amazement he saw that there was a large two-way mirror in one wall, on the other side of which there was a very bare looking room. In the centre of that room was a chair and, tied to it and slumped forward, was the naked form of Fazul Ali, his head lolling drunkenly to one side, eyes glaring sullenly towards what must have been a very large mirror to him. He must have realized what it was and that he was being observed from the other side of it. The chair was screwed to the floor and Ali's feet were shackled by thin chains to bolts fixed in the floor, his wrists cuffed to the back legs of the chair.

His right shoulder was bandaged, blood flowering slowly through the gauze from the gunshot wound underneath. Henry had a flashback of Ali being shot by Donaldson, recalling how the shoulder had seemed to explode. It was a bad wound, one which required hospital treatment.

There were two people in the observation room – Dr Chambers and a man in his late thirties who wasn't even introduced to Henry. They were sitting on chairs, looking through the mirror at Ali. A door adjacent gave access to the interrogation room beyond. The two looked up at Henry and Donaldson as they came into the room, nodding, then, as if on cue, all three Americans put their right forefingers into their ears and their brows furrowed. Henry realized they were all listening to tiny earpieces.

Donaldson said, 'Roger.' They all removed their fingers. He looked at Henry. 'The Secretary of State is due to leave Merseyside, nothing of interest to report. Estimated she'll be crossing into Lancashire in twenty minutes. They hand over to your escort at Switch Island and then she'll be brought into Lancashire.'

Henry knew that Switch Island was the complex round-about to the north of Liverpool at junction 7 of the M57 where it joined the A59 and where the M58 started.

'Which way will she come up into Lancs?'

'M58, M6, M65 then off at junction 4,' Donaldson reeled off from memory.

Working that out, Henry guessed that it would be less than an hour before Rice actually set foot on Lancashire soil once she actually got on the road. Security escorts stop for neither man nor beast.

'What's her itinerary?' Henry asked. He'd seen it, but couldn't recall it.

'First stop is a school in Pleckgate, then she's due to visit Ewood Park after that, home of that soccer team, Blackburn Rovers, which doesn't give us much time.'

'To do what, exactly?'

'Find out exactly how Akbar intends to kill her, otherwise it'll just be pot luck – and I don't like pot luck.'

'So what's your plan?'

Donaldson ignored the question and turned to the mystery man and Dr Chambers. 'How is he?'

'Alive and likely to remain so, but doped up with a few choice drugs,' she said.

'Has he said anything?'

'Said I should fuck off back to Satan.'

'Nice,' said Donaldson. To Henry, he said, 'Shall we?'

*   *   *

Feeling – *knowing* – he was being dragged into something better avoided, Henry followed Donaldson from the observation room into the interrogation room. The words of his dear old mum rang clear in his ears, often shouted at him when he was a youngster in trouble: 'You're easily led, you!' and he knew she was right.

The two men walked across the vinyl-covered floor and stood in front of Ali, whose black-ringed eyes watched with a simmering hatred. He might have been shot, might have been drugged up, but Henry could tell he knew exactly what was going on.

'How are you, Fazul Ali?'

'I need to go to hospital,' his reply came, the words slightly slurred through cracked, dry lips.

'All in good time.'

Ali's eyes settled on Henry. A reluctant grin came to his lips. 'You fought well.'

Henry chose not to respond. Inside he was being torn apart, drawn into a situation completely alien to him. A wounded prisoner, shackled and naked in an interrogation room. Interrogation wasn't a word ever used in police circles. It represented everything bad about how the police used to obtain confessions in the very bad old days. Now they 'interviewed', sought the truth using approved methods. Interrogation was totally negative and had links with corrupt and murderous regimes. And torture.

Not that Henry would ever class himself as a saint and maybe he was being two-faced about this. He had hit prisoners before, he'd bent the rules, but he'd always known the boundaries and deep down had always felt uncomfortable when he did such things . . . but those methods had never approached anything as brutal and lawless as this.

There would be outrage if it was discovered that such things were taking place on British soil.

'I'll come straight to the point, my friend,' Donaldson said to the prisoner. 'Mohammed Ibrahim Akbar.' There was not even a flicker from Ali's sullen eyes. 'How does he plan to murder the Condoleezza Rice? It's a simple question, the answer to which will see you receiving the best medical treatment money can buy.'

Ali stared at the floor. 'So I have to bargain for my basic human rights?' He cackled.

Henry looked at him, his hairy body, genitals hanging loosely, thick-muscled legs, trying to convince himself that, even though nothing had yet happened to him and this man was probably responsible for butchering two of his colleagues, this was completely wrong and went a hundred per cent against his beliefs. And yet, did he deserve to be treated this way?

'You have no human rights, Ali. Just like those two innocent people you murdered today. What happened to their rights?'

A sneer morphed on to his lips. 'I demand to be taken to hospital.' He glowered defiantly at Donaldson. 'I demand the rights of any prisoner held in Britain.'

Donaldson gave a short laugh. 'Bad news, old buddy . . . because you ain't in Britain anymore . . . right here, right now, just think of this place as a little piece of America – like Guantanamo Bay – and those rights you're bleating about just don't exist.'

For the first time, Henry saw a glint of doubt and fear in Ali's eyes.

'What do you mean?'

'I mean, that as if by magic carpet, you've been transported to hell and yes, you're looking right into Satan's eyes.' Donaldson pointed the first two fingers of his right hand towards his own eyes, then pointed the same two at Ali. The words in themselves were comical but the way and the context in which they were said were terrifying, even to Henry who was now seeing a dark side of Donaldson that, yes, he'd suspected existed, but deep down in his soul he'd wished didn't.

Ali squirmed uncomfortably against his shackles, then farted and excreted a vile, almost green-coloured shit, the stench of which immediately filled the room. Then he urinated a stream of thick yellow piss in an arc into this awful mess underneath him.

'That's the drugs and fear combined,' Donaldson said brutally. 'And we haven't even started yet.'

Henry shot a worried glance at the two-way mirror, but all he saw was a reflection of himself, beaten and bruised.

'Like I said, simple question,' Donaldson continued. The pool of shit and urine had collected underneath Ali's chair and his bare feet slithered in it. 'What are Akbar's plans for today and also, how is Mansur Rashid involved?'

'I don't know what you're talking about.'

'You are Akbar's right-hand man.'

'I don't know him. Never heard of him.'

Donaldson smiled. 'OK, Fazul, those were the denials. Those were the formalities. We ask, you deny . . . you now have no need to keep this up . . . we'll let it be known that you did your best before crumbling . . . your bravery will filter through the grapevine – and unless you do wish to suffer further, please tell me what I want to know . . . next step, electrodes to testicles.'

Ali winced as a surge of terrible pain arced through his shattered shoulder.

'Karl, that's enough,' Henry whispered behind Donaldson, who did not even acknowledge him as he eased on a pair of latex gloves from out of his pocket and made a show of pulling them on to his hands with a snap.

'I have no time for subtlety, Fazul,' the American said. He walked behind the prisoner, ensuring he did not step in the mess. 'That takes far too long.' He came up behind Ali and peeled off the blood soaked bandage that had been applied to his shoulder, tossing it on to the floor where it landed with a wet slap.

As Henry suspected, the wound was awful. The bullet had entered the shoulder blade, then deflected upwards into the shoulder joint, destroying it before exiting and making a huge, shredded hole, in which Henry could see splintered bone and gristle, blood oozing.

Donaldson squeezed Ali's shoulder between his fingers and thumb.

Ali screamed.

Henry cowered back.

Donaldson leaned in close to Ali's right ear. 'Tell me. Stop this pain.'

'Fuck you,' he uttered with a gasp, spittle flecking out of his lips. A torrent of sweat poured from his hairline. His eyelids fluttered and his head rolled as he slid towards a merciful unconsciousness in default to the pain.

Henry now saw his friend clearly. Donaldson's face was showing no emotion as though he was totally untroubled by what he was doing. He wasn't even breathing heavily. If Henry had to make a guess, he'd say that Donaldson was actually enjoying himself in some perverted way.

Then, Henry noticed something in Donaldson's right hand and wasn't sure where it had come from.

'Oh no you don't,' Donaldson said to Ali, tapping him on the cheek, bringing him back from the edge of oblivion. Ali looked desperately up at him, then at Henry with eyes that pleaded for help.

'Karl,' Henry said warningly.

Donaldson sniggered. To Ali he said, pointing at himself, 'Bad cop' – then, indicating Henry – 'good cop. A winning combination.'

'Karl, this has to stop,' Henry said.

But the big American did not seem to hear Henry, as once again, he walked behind Ali and raised his right hand, gripping the instrument Henry had noticed him holding: an expanding baton, which he wrist-flicked to shoot it out to its full length, then smashed it down on to Ali's shoulder.

It was like hitting a tomato. Blood flicked everywhere.

And Ali's scream of agony rent through the fetid air.

'There's no one to hear you,' Donaldson said when the sound had died down and Ali sat there sobbing and moaning, rolling his head and eyes, his face contorted with sheer agony. 'So tell me – *now!*' It was the first time Donaldson had raised his voice.

He laid the baton gently across the wound so that Ali could see it from the corner of his eye.

Then he raised his hand once more – at which point Henry could not stand it any more. Ashamed he had let it go so far, he moved and took hold of Donaldson's forearm.

'No,' he said through a short breath. His head shook as he stared into Donaldson's blazing eyes. 'No,' he said again.

'Good cop, eh?' Donaldson sneered.

Clearly the American was on another level of consciousness. The red mist had truly descended to cloud whatever judgement he had. Henry had experienced something like this on many occasions when he wanted that result, or was under real pressure, but never to this intensity.

'Time for you to speak to him,' Donaldson said.

'What?' Henry said, realizing that Donaldson believed Henry was about to play his part in this scenario. 'No – I mean it, Karl. This whole thing has to stop. Can't you see how wrong it is?'

Donaldson shook himself free from Henry's grip and raised the baton.

Henry pushed him away and stepped between him and the prisoner. The two men stood like statues for several beats until Donaldson growled, 'You'd better get out of here, Henry.'

Henry regarded him for another brief moment of contempt, then strutted out of the interrogation room.

He needed air, to escape the reek of the room. He clattered down the wooden steps to the ground-floor corridor and stumbled to a fire exit, ignoring the fact that a notice on it declared 'This door is alarmed'.

Not as much as me, Henry thought as he crashed through it and found himself in a high-fenced courtyard somewhere down the side of the industrial unit. He fell against the fence and listened to the high-pitched alarm he'd just activated.

No doubt a soldier would come out and shoot him now. It would be a blessed relief, he thought.

The air tasted sweet. Beyond the tightly meshed fence was an expanse of wild moorland which Henry could smell.

He took in deep breaths, trying to slow his body down. His head ticked nervously and his heart pounded.

A man with a gun drawn did appear at the door. One of the 'Bobs': the soldiers-cum-pseudo-paramedics.

Henry raised his hands defensively. 'It's OK – I needed air, fast.'

'OK, pal.' The soldier muttered something into a discreet radio mike secreted somewhere on him and the alarm came to a sudden halt, its echo lingering. He looked curiously at Henry, then withdrew, leaving him alone.

Henry turned to face the fence, hardly able to see anything through the tight steel mesh, and laid his forehead on the criss-cross strands, standing there until he became aware of a presence behind him. Without looking, he knew it would be Donaldson.

'I thought you'd be up for this, Henry,' Donaldson said. 'That's why I brought you here and trusted you,' he said accusingly, hurt.

Henry could not bring himself to turn because he knew that something very fundamental had changed in the relationship between him and the Yank. There was now no more burying his head in the sand. He had seen up close and personal just what sort of a man Donaldson was, or had become. Now there was no going back. He either had to accept it, or not. Henry was lost for words as he choked something back in his throat.

'That guy and his pals are out to kill the Secretary of State today, and I will do anything within my power to prevent that happening. This is a war, Henry. You know that.'

Henry's nostrils flared as rage boiled inside him.

Donaldson went on. 'We are dealing with mass murderers, people who want not only to destroy our way of life, but us too,' he said reasonably. 'He would have killed you today. He's already had a hand in murdering two of your colleagues. I saved your life today.'

'And for that I'm eternally grateful,' Henry said truthfully. He now turned to look upon his friend, tears beginning to well.

'And they are planning to kill Ms Rice today. Just for your information, maps, itineraries, photos and descriptions of venues have been found in that house this morning . . . and also the clothes Ali was wearing when our surveillance team latched on to him early this morning – covered in the blood of your colleagues, who stumbled on him, Akbar and Rashid, and maybe others, planning an assassination.'

Henry recalled how Ali had been dressed when he'd answered the door, how he had smelled. Clean, fresh, as though he'd just had a shower.

And to confirm his thoughts, Donaldson said, 'The shower upstairs is clogged with blood.'

'How do you know Akbar was there?'

'We've had a forensic and CSI team at the scene who specialize in dealing with scenes like these. They've got fast-track DNA equipment in their vehicles and Akbar's DNA has been found in several locations in the house already . . . simple.' He shrugged. 'He's on the loose and the Secretary of State's life is on the line.'

'Cancel the visit, then,' Henry suggested.

'Can't be done . . . she's a politician and she won't be seen to bow down to the threat of terrorism. It's our job to make sure the hit doesn't happen.'

'More fool her.'

'It's a principle, Henry. The world is at war, and we have to do anything we can to win, don't you see?'

'You sound as brainwashed as them,' Henry said. 'Another side of the same coin.'

Donaldson stared at him.

'I know that guy tried to kill me and I know I've got a lot to thank you for over the years and today, but you need to know one thing about me . . .'

'What's that?' Donaldson asked, a sneer on his lips.

'I believe in the rule of law, ultimately, and human rights and that the end does not justify the means and all that shit. I know all that stuff trips us up, makes it almost impossible to operate and I know that if I'd had to kill Ali this morning to stay alive myself, I would've done . . . but he's alive, I'm alive, and now the process of law should take over, not the rule of the fuckin' jungle—'

'You're in a dream world, Henry . . . I brought you here today because I thought you were in and understood what was going on. Obviously I was wrong and I've compromised myself because of it.'

'Has Ali told you anything?' Henry asked.

Donaldson looked involuntarily at the floor and scuffed his foot. 'No,' he admitted, 'but he will.'

'In that case, you'd better get back up there, hadn't you? Put a dog collar round his neck, maybe that'll help.'

Without warning Donaldson leapt at Henry, went for his throat and pinned him against the metal fence with a crash. His face, red, furious, dangerous, was nose-to-nose with Henry's, who gagged for breath and tried unsuccessfully to prize the American's big fingers from his windpipe. Then, just as he was about to say something, Donaldson seemed to realize what he was doing. He relaxed his grip and let Henry go, who fell to his haunches, choking and massaging his throat.

Donaldson spun on his heels and stalked back inside, leaving Henry alone in the courtyard, gulping for air, aware that in the space of just over an hour, his friendship with Karl Donaldson had ended more dramatically than he could ever have imagined and that his whole day had been turned on its head.

Seventeen

A huge area surrounding the house on Balaclava Street had been cordoned off. Traffic diversions were in place and the police were out in numbers to keep onlookers from pouring in and trampling any evidence there might be.

Henry stood just inside one of the stretched police tapes at the junction of Randal Street and Limbrick, speaking to a bleak faced chief constable and Detective Chief Superintendent Dave Anger.

'This is completely horrendous,' FB was saying. He was more affected than Henry had ever seen.

'Incredible,' Anger said, shaking his head in disbelief.

Their eyes were on Henry, but not in a critical way for once. They knew the full story leading up to why Angela Cranlow and Graeme Walling had knocked on the door in Balaclava Street and understood that no one could have suspected that the officers were stepping from a routine inquiry, albeit concerning a murder, into the world of international terrorism. FB seemed to have been hit particularly hard and was struggling to take in the enormity of the event . . . as was Henry.

He fished out a pack of Nurofen tablets he'd bought from a nearby chemist and thumbed a couple out of the blister pack, tipped his head back, filled his mouth with saliva and tossed them into the back of his throat, swallowing them with ease.

'Two cops dead, terrorists on the loose intent on murdering the American Secretary of State who, despite the warning, is determined to visit the town and mingle . . . shit!'

'Why can't you pull the plug on the visit?' Henry said plaintively.

'Because politicians don't have the sense they were born with,' FB commented dryly, 'and because we are expected to protect her.'

And because your own job would be in question if you took the unpopular step of cancelling it, Henry thought, but didn't say anything.

'Fortunately she's been delayed in Liverpool, which has given us a bit of time to draft in virtually every remaining bobby from around the county who isn't involved in the visit. There'll be more cops than crowds.'

'Let's hope nothing happens anywhere else for a few hours,' FB said grimly. 'If the nuclear reactor blows in Heysham, it'll just have to burn and destroy the known world.'

'And nothing's come from this Ali guy?' Anger asked Henry, who shook his head and bit his tongue . . . but only for a moment.

'How the hell is it going to be explained that the Americans are torturing people in Blackburn?' he demanded.

FB gave him a stern look. 'Shut it, Henry,' he said. 'What people don't know won't hurt them, got that? Blab one word, and you'll regret it for the rest of your life.'

Henry could hardly believe his ears, but yet he wasn't surprised to discover that the people 'up there' were colluding in such unlawful acts. After all, it's a war, he thought resentfully. 'We've totally lost this if we can't do things by lawful means,' he bellyached.

'Fine words, Henry. Admirable sentiments. You're getting very highly principled in your old age and it's very commendable . . .'

'Don't patronize me, Bob.'

'I'm not. I'm just saying, let's get real here and stop blubbering, which you seem to be doing an awful lot of recently.' His eyes slid sideways for a quick glance at Anger. 'The here and now is what's important. There's a killer on the loose and one way or another, we have to neutralize him, or the threat, either by catching the bastard or by putting him off by the massive police presence. I'm all for prevention, and at least everyone on duty in the town now has a recent picture of Akbar,' FB concluded.

Henry wished his painkillers would just numb everything.

'Why don't you go home, pal?' FB laid a gentle hand on Henry's shoulder. 'Maybe via a quiet A&E department? Everything round here's being taken care of.'

'I couldn't,' Henry admitted.

'I know you couldn't.'

He was thinking now, working things out. Everything had been screwed up by the morning's events but yet somewhere, he knew, *somewhere* amongst this awful mess was the key to nailing Akbar and Rashid, maybe. He turned away from FB and Dave Anger and walked back to his car he'd had to park over a quarter of a mile away.

He had things to do. Such as track down Mansur Rashid.

He sat back in the leather upholstery in the most comfortable car he had ever owned. So what did it matter if there was no warranty with it? That the manufacturers had gone bust? It was a bloody good motor . . . if a little staid.

Reaching up, he tilted the rear-view mirror to an angle so he could look at himself.

'Jeez,' he grunted and shook his head, but not too severely because it made his face hurt, like there was something loose in it. He leaned back and thought ahead, not back. It was the immediate future that was important now.

Could he do anything?

Firstly, Condoleezza Rice.

For some reason she had been delayed in Merseyside, for her sins, but would only be stuck for another hour or so before she hit the road. Then she would be travelling in a very skilled, highly-trained convoy concocted of police motorcycle outriders, police cars and armed cops in high-powered vehicles. She herself would be in a vehicle that could probably withstand an RPG or a roadside bomb, so the chances of her being hit whilst in motion were slim.

If Akbar had not been put off by now – because he would no doubt know about the detention of his 2i/c, Ali – then the strike against Rice would probably take place at one of the venues she was visiting, either the school in the Pleckgate area, or at Ewood Park, the football ground.

Akbar, according to Karl Donaldson, had allegedly been heard to say that killing Rice would be his crowning glory and he would achieve this even if he lost his own life doing so.

Did that smack of a suicide bomb?

But from what little Henry knew of Akbar, this wasn't his personal style of killing. He got others to do that – such as the impressionable youths he'd supposedly been working with in Accrington.

And he would see it as a personal victory if some poor, brainwashed kid managed to penetrate the security and blow up Rice and a hundred other innocent people. Akbar would take the glory in this life, whilst putting others en route to paradise to meet twenty-four virgins, or whatever the promise was in paradise.

Henry thought this could be a good option for Akbar. All the plaudits and none of the danger.

He started the car.

Akbar was an expert marksman, apparently. Maybe he intended to stake out the venues from a vantage point and take out Rice like the Jackal. One deadly shot through the head from a high-powered rifle, then filter away back to the east, again able to bask in living glory – and no doubt be presented with twenty-four real virgins.

But that option, Henry thought, was pretty unlikely. The venues would already be staked out with police rifle officers and any obvious vantage points for a sniper would be neutralized.

Another option was the stand-alone bomb, placed maybe weeks ago at one of the venues with either remote or timed detonation.

Henry thought this unlikely, too. The itinerary of the visit had been kept pretty tight – Henry hoped – and even at this late stage was being chopped and changed and rescheduled, the delay in Liverpool being an example of that. So an already hidden device would be too hit and miss. Plus Henry knew that the venues had been searched and secured by police search teams and he knew they were ultra-professional and no stone would have been unturned during that phase of the operation.

So did it all come back to a suicide bomb?

And if so, how could it be legislated for completely?

It couldn't.

The bombs were getting sleeker, slimmer and less easy to spot. They weren't as bulky as they used to be and didn't have to be hidden under heavy coats any more, or even in rucksacks. Any sort of zip-up jacket would conceal a bomb big enough to blow the visitor to smithereens on her walkabouts.

Henry thumped the steering wheel.

Then there was Mansur Rashid. Something told Henry that
the investigation into Eddie Daley's and Sabera Rashid's
murders would not reach a satisfactory conclusion. If Rashid
was ever caught, it was unlikely that Henry would ever get
within spitting distance of him now. He'd probably end up in
chains in Guantanamo Bay.

Which skipped his thoughts on to Karl Donaldson.

A bridge had been crossed in their relationship, then destroyed
by fire. Henry could now only look back across a vast chasm
and wish things were different. He hoped Donaldson's consuming
quest wouldn't be the end of him.

He swallowed, feeling ill, wondering whether he would best
be served by finding a darkened room and curling up into a
foetal ball and sucking his thumb.

Henry's radio rang out like a mobile phone. It was Bill
Robbins calling him.

'Any further instructions, boss?'

'How're you doing, firstly?'

'I'll survive, bit of a rough morning, though. Carly's as sick
as a dog. Doesn't have the stomach for the gruesome. Not
that I do, really.'

'I think I've had my fill of it, too,' Henry divulged. 'Are
you going to get some counselling?'

Bill laughed. 'I don't do navel gazing. Get back doing it,
that's my motto, and the best cure, if you ask me.'

The words struck Henry as good sense. 'You know, I think
you're right there, pal . . . how's about meeting at Blackburn
nick in ten minutes? You can take me out on patrol.'

He didn't add that something at the back of his mind was
bugging him, something within his sphere of knowledge that
had some crucial bearing on the events of the day. If only he
could unearth it from all the other dross that was swirling
around.

Sitting high in the front passenger seat of the ARV Ford Galaxy,
Bill in the driving seat, gave Henry a good view over most
other traffic.

'What's the plan, Henry?'

'Let's go and have a ride round to the venues.'

'OK – and as I drive, you can tell me what's going on.'

'I'll tell you as much as I know,' Henry agreed.

Henry's radio was now tuned into the frequency being used by the officers involved in the Rice visit. The dedicated comms operator broadcast to them that 'the package', as the American Secretary of State was referred to over the air, was about to set off from Merseyside. She was well behind schedule, but in less than an hour she would be setting foot on Lancashire soil. Henry hoped this would not be the last county she would ever visit.

Henry's thoughts turned to Fazul Ali and whether he was holding up against the sophisticated interview techniques of Karl Donaldson. In some respects, Henry hoped he would spill the beans, not least for his own well-being; in others he hoped Ali would not break, in spite of the possible consequences. It would be a minor victory to show that torturing people did not necessarily work, war or no war.

Bill drove around Blackburn, firstly past the school on Pleckgate Road which Rice would be visiting, then across town to Ewood Park. Both places were crawling with cops: cops on foot and cops with dogs, cops on horses and cops with guns. It was always going to be a massively expensive operation and now, because every other cop in the world had been drafted in, would probably double in price.

The Galaxy pulled on to the car park behind the Darwen End stand of Ewood Park, inside which the police facilities had been constructed, including cells, refs rooms and a custody office. Henry sat ruminating as he looked at the big stand, erected in the 1990s on the back of the millions of pounds provided by a local businessman. Not like the days of corrugated roofs and rotting concrete stands, it was all steel girders and seating. The River Darwen flowed – or trickled – by the north-eastern side of the ground and beyond it was a steep, grassy hill from which, in the old days, fans who could not afford to get into the ground could watch some of the action of the matches, though they could only ever see one or the other goalmouth at one time.

'Not a bad place for a sniper.' Henry pouted thoughtfully as he looked at the hill. 'Have you got a copy of the operational order?'

Bill reached into the back seat and found his dog-eared copy which detailed the visit. Henry skimmed through it. 'Blah, blah, blah . . . she's being driven from the school to the football ground . . . stopping on Nuttall Street at the front and entering through the VIP door, then she's into the ground itself. Visiting the police post, the CCTV room, the players' changing rooms, going to the shop – no doubt buy herself a Rovers' shirt – meeting the staff, then leaving as she came in . . . so, scratch the sniper on the hill theory cos he can't see Nuttall Street from there,' Henry said glumly. He turned to Bill. 'What would you do if you were a fanatical terrorist and you wanted to kill her today?'

'Well, she's pretty well protected, so it won't be easy, but I've always said that if anyone doesn't give a fuck about themselves and thinks they're going somewhere better, it becomes a hell of a lot easier. She'll be doing walkabout, touching heads, kissing babies . . . and if you're a fanatic you can definitely get close enough to her to stick a gun in her face or blow everyone in the vicinity to kingdom come. You just can, cos not everyone can be searched and no one knows what a terrorist actually looks like.'

'But they do know what this terrorist looks like, because his most recent photo's been circulated – except he doesn't do dirty work like this himself. He gets other dumb arses to do it. He's like a paedophile in some respects, preying on young, vulnerable people.' Henry paused for thought again. His brain had been so battered that he was finding it difficult to keep it concentrating. 'There's just something about Mansur Rashid that keeps eating away at me.' His face rotated slowly to Bill. 'Get me back to my car,' he said quickly. 'Something's clicked.' Henry gave Bill a quick explanation and by blue lighting it down the M65, heading north, then coming off at Whitebirk, they were back at Blackburn police station within minutes, where Henry had left his Rover.

He had been blocked in by other cars, but that did not matter. He rooted out his briefcase from the back seat and rejoined Bill, who had gravitated to the canteen to get two coffees. They sat at the only empty table – the canteen was swarming with bobbies because of the visit and they all needed food and drink at some time.

'Thanks.' Henry took a sip of the coffee, then put his briefcase on the table and delved into it. He extracted the A4 document wallet which contained the statement taken from Dr Khan the previous evening, together with all the notes he'd scribbled. He glanced through the statement, frowning because he could not see what he wanted. He knew it was there somewhere.

'I'm sure I wrote it,' he said absently.

Bill watched him intently.

'Nah, not there.' He put the statement down and browsed through the notes he had taken whilst interviewing the doctor. Not everything in the notes had gone into the statement. 'Ah ha! This is it . . . um, um, um . . . here we are . . . this girl Sabera leaves her husband. Big thing for anyone to do, let alone a Muslim girl . . . seems they're expected to hang in there whatever shit's thrown at them, which I find total bollocks . . . Anyway, she obviously misses her family and therefore succumbs to the occasional chats with them . . . natural thing to do – I'm OK, don't worry, sort of thing . . . Ow!' Henry touched his cheek, which was throbbing again. 'God, that's sore . . . Then she makes the mistake of contacting her sister and arranges to meet her on a motorway service area – but the sister turns up with the husband!' Henry said excitedly.

'Shit – bitch!' Bill said.

'Exactly . . . anyway, Sabera gets away unscathed, but that's basically the end of her relationship with sis . . . but what I'm getting at here is that if the sister was in cahoots with Rashid she must know an awful lot about him – and maybe if we can get hold of her now, she might be able to tell us something. Like where he is.'

'I suppose it's better then just bumming about hoping for the best,' Bill admitted.

'In the very near future, we are going to have to speak to Sabera's family anyway just because she's dead. What do you think?' he asked Bill, screwing his face up.

'Can't hurt. Any addresses?'

'No.' The word came out with a sigh. 'Just somewhere in Blackburn. This Khan guy couldn't remember it and he's actually destroyed her employment records which had it on, as well as anything else which related to her, he was so scared and intimidated.'

'Needle in a haystack, then?'

'Mm.' Henry tapped his fingers on the edge of the table. 'She's called Najma Ismat.'

'Voters list?' Bill suggested.

'Does it have a search facility?'

'No.'

'Do you want to go through every name? Two hundred odd thousand in Blackburn?'

'Not specially. How about PNC?'

'Worth a try, but only useful if she has a conviction, which I doubt.'

'Intel check?'

'Same applies . . . although Special Branch files might have something . . . they collect stuff just for the hell of it,' Henry said, thinking back to the entry concerning Mansur Rashid. Henry then recalled how Eddie Daley had been able to trace Sabera without too much trouble and expressed his thoughts out loud. 'Bill, we are two experienced cops and if we can't locate this girl within the next half hour, then I'm calling it quits and going home. And I have a bloody good idea how we can do it.'

Minutes later they were back in the Galaxy. 'Now then, Bill, I want you to drive me somewhere – somewhere that is very secret and, of course, you'll have to be blindfolded, and if you blab to anyone, even your missus in your sleep, I'll have to come and murder you, then kill myself.'

'What the hell are you on about?'

Henry realized he'd rambled a bit. He put it down to the pain. And the drugs. 'Just drive out of here, turn left up the arterial road, then right on to Whitebirk Industrial Estate, then I'll direct you from there.'

Bill shrugged.

Henry fished out his mobile and made a call.

'Sorry to interrupt your torture session, but I need to come and see you, Karl . . . a favour, yeah. I know it's a lot to ask, but I'm asking . . . I need a name putting through your super-duper computer.' Henry listened, then ended the call. He stared straight ahead through the windscreen, his heart thumping at the prospect of seeing Donaldson again so soon.

Henry directed Bill to the front gates of the unit now leased by the American security services, although he doubted whether that fact was actually revealed in the rental agreement. The gates were closed and did not open on their arrival.

'What goes on here?' Bill asked.

'It's been rented by the Yanks to house some of their vehicles whilst the Rice visit takes place,' he answered blandly.

Bill looked at him disbelievingly.

'OK, all right,' Henry answered with a shrug. 'Can't tell you, OK?'

'Fair enough. I know my place.'

The gates opened wide enough to allow a very tired, harassed Karl Donaldson to contort out of the gap. He approached Henry suspiciously, eyeing Bill. Henry dropped out of the Galaxy.

'So now you need us?' Donaldson said bitterly.

'I don't have a problem with you hacking into other people's computers. It's hacking into people's heads that bothers me.'

Donaldson nodded at Bill. 'You shouldn't have brought him.'

'He's OK, won't blab.'

'He stays here, then.'

'So be it.'

Donaldson inclined his head for Henry to follow. Henry mouthed and gestured for Bill to stay put and followed the American through the gate, who then ensured it was locked. He walked ahead of Henry through a normal door adjacent to the main shutter door into the unit where the array of vehicles was parked up.

As he walked, Donaldson said, 'Don't know why the hell I'm doing this,' without turning.

'Cos deep down you're an old softie?' Henry speculated, trying to lighten the atmosphere between them.

'I misjudged you, Henry.'

'No, Karl, I misjudged you,' Henry said, realizing the atmosphere was not likely to rise much.

The rest of the short walk was made in silence, through the door leading to the ground-floor corridor, then into the communications centre. Donaldson approached the same man who had done the earlier check on Mansur Rashid.

'Give him the name, tell him which database to interrogate.' Donaldson pushed out past Henry, saying, 'I trust you to make your own way out . . . and by the way, hacking into other agencies' databases is not ethical.' Then he was gone.

Henry gave the man the name and suggested some databases

to interrogate. After a few moments, he leaned back. 'There you go, pal.'

Henry squinted at the screen, memorized what he saw and rushed back out to Bill who waited patiently in the Galaxy. He gave him the address.

'I'm not even going to bother to ask how you got this.'

'What you don't know, don't get you killed,' Henry said.

It was fortunate that the liveried Ford Galaxy with a uniformed police officer lounging by the side of it was parked behind Henry in the driveway, otherwise he would have had the front door slammed in his face. Even then, it was a close-run thing. He could tell from the look of horror on the Asian woman's face when she answered the door and found herself confronted by a man who looked like he'd been dragged under a bus for a hundred metres.

He quickly presented his warrant card and the woman hesitated, still considered closing the door, then relented because of the police vehicle.

It was probably unusual to have anyone knocking at the door in this neck of the woods anyway. Henry guessed the most regular visitors would be the postman and the Sainsbury's home delivery driver.

The house was in one of the better parts of Blackburn, on Meins Road, right on the edge of town. A big detached property in its own grounds, with sweeping views behind it towards Preston and beyond to the faint shimmer of the Lancashire coast. The huge British Aerospace complex in the middle distance slightly marred the vista. It was the house of a wealthy family.

The woman was late fifties, dressed in a very western style. She was also extremely attractive and Henry could immediately see the likeness between her and the photographs taken by Eddie Daley of Sabera Rashid. He caught his breath.

'My name is Henry Christie. I'm a detective chief inspector with Lancashire Constabulary . . . please don't be alarmed by my appearance – it's been a tough day . . . I'm looking for Najma Ismat.' He tried one of his boyish smiles, but all his broken cheekbone would allow was a scary grimace.

'What is going on out here?' an Asian-accented male voice with a definite Lancashire twang demanded to know from inside the house. An old man appeared behind the lady. When he saw Henry, he said, 'You!' accusingly. It was Mr Iqbal, the old man Henry had innocently involved in a dangerous car chase whilst on the lookout for a suspect who had dropped through his ceiling and fled from the police raid Henry had led.

'Mr Iqbal!'

'Out of the way, girl,' Iqbal said and elbowed past the woman, holding out a hand for Henry to shake. 'Salma, this is the policeman I was telling you about,' he said proudly, his chest swelling as he stood next to Henry and put his arm around him. 'Henry Christie, this is my daughter, Salma Ismat. She's a doctor, you know,' he said proudly.

Henry proffered his hand hesitantly. She responded coolly, but shook his fingertips.

'I am pleased to meet you,' she bowed slightly. 'My father cannot be quiet about his exciting ride in a police car . . . it made him a happy man.'

'I thought I'd terrified you.'

'Only in a good way,' the old man said. He banged his chest with his fist. 'Got the ticker pumping . . . exciting as hell.'

'I'm pleased.'

Iqbal looked curiously at Henry. 'Have you had a car crash?'

'No . . . look, I don't want to be abrupt, but does Najma Ismat live here?'

'Najma is my daughter,' the lady said.

'Is she in?'

'No, why?'

'I need to speak to her urgently . . . I'm afraid I can't explain why. She's not in any trouble, it's just that she might know something. I'm trying to trace Mansur Rashid and I think she might know where he is.'

'That bastard!' Iqbal hacked up and spat. 'What's he done?'

'Do you know where he is?' Henry asked again. 'I need to locate him.'

'No, we don't,' the woman said. 'And we don't want to.'

Another man appeared behind her, Henry guessing this was her husband.

'What's going on?' he asked, his eyes taking in the scene.

'This policeman wants to talk to Najma,' she explained.

'Why?'

'I don't know . . . when I saw the police car, I thought they'd come about Sabera for some reason.'

'Why Najma?' the father asked.

'It's not about Najma, it's about that Mansur scum,' Iqbal blurted.

'You haven't come about Sabera?' the father said.

'No . . . look, please,' Henry said, aware this situation might well descend into farce if he wasn't careful, especially when he noticed a fourth person standing behind the father, a young lad in his early teens, bobbing about on the balls of his feet, trying to see what was going on. Henry executed a chopping motion with the edges of his hands. 'I'm trying to trace the whereabouts of Mansur Rashid, that's all. I thought Najma might know where he was. If you know, it'll save me talking to her.'

He felt a bit of a fraud not letting on about Sabera, but he didn't want to complicate matters further at that moment. Time was critical, He glanced at his watch. Condoleezza Rice should just about be arriving at her first venue.

'We don't know where Najma is,' the father said sadly. 'But she works for Rashid and spends a lot of time with him, too. She's become very influenced by him and his radical views. We're very worried about her. And we're worried about Sabera, his wife, our other daughter.'

'I know where Najma might be,' Iqbal interjected, raising a finger. He looked at Bill and the Ford Galaxy. 'If I get a ride in that, I could take you.'

Eighteen

Iqbal positioned himself like a VIP in the middle of the back seat so he could lean forwards between Henry and Bill to direct them. He was chewing that sort of unidentifiable paste again, giving his breath a sweet tang.

Both officers leaned outwards to put a bit of distance between themselves and the old man.

'Tell me about Rashid,' Henry said as they set off, leaving a total of five people now standing at the door, another two relatives having emerged from inside the house.

'He's an extremist, always winding people up against the Brits,' Iqbal said, chewing his cud. 'Go down Preston New Road towards town,' he instructed Bill.

'What does he do for a living?'

'Owns two petrol stations, two Indian restaurants, three shops, lots of property and drives fear into people's hearts. Everyone is terrified of him, but the young kids – teenagers – think he's great cos he's always on about bombing and fundamentalism and stuff. I just think he's a gangster using religion as a means to an end, but I'm an old guy, so what do I know, except I love this country. It's been good to me.'

'And he's married to your granddaughter, is that right?'

'Sabera, yeah.' He looked glum. 'It was an arranged marriage, but turned bad. He treated her horribly and eventually she did a runner, and to be honest, we didn't blame her. If only she'd talked to us, though. We would have understood. We're very liberal, you know. Haven't seen her since . . . we're very worried about her, actually. We think he may have done something to her, but we don't know for sure.'

For the moment that was a path Henry did not want to venture down. Maybe later. His priority was to find Rashid and Akbar and hopefully stop a terrorist atrocity from occurring. The murder investigation could be put on hold for a few hours.

'Has he ever been to your house in Accrington?' Henry asked.

'Oh yes, he was thinking about buying a house in the same row and had a good look around mine to see what it was like.'

'Did he go into the attic?'

'Yes – he was up there for ages, actually.'

'And did he buy a house in the row?'

'Dunno.'

Henry churned it over. That explained the escape route. And I'll bet Rashid is the owner of the house that was raided, probably through some innocent intermediary, Henry guessed. Something to follow up, if it wasn't already being done by other parties.

'So what's Rashid done?' Iqbal asked. 'Not planning to kill

Condoleezza Rice, is he?' he laughed, then stopped abruptly when he saw the expressions on the faces of the two coppers. 'He bloody is, isn't he?' the old man gasped, shocked.

'We think Rashid and another man are planning to assassinate her and I'm trying to find out where he is,' Henry admitted.

The old man had slumped back in his seat, his hands laid on his chest, a stunned expression on his face, which had seeped a pale grey colour, similar to the shade he'd gone during the car chase.

'Are you all right?' Henry asked worriedly, hoping the old guy wasn't going to expire in the back of the car.

He nodded, leaned forward again and said with urgency, 'Down here, turn right into Montague Street . . . Najma could be working in the shop at one of Rashid's petrol stations on Preston Old Road, that's what she usually does . . . if she's not there, I know where his other places of business are.' He licked his lips and said, 'Bastard,' under his sweet breath.

According to the radio, Rice, aka 'the Package', had arrived safely at the first venue.

She was still alive.

Bill drove down the steep Montague Street, then at the bottom turned right into Preston Old Road, which snaked in a westerly direction out of Blackburn. The first mile or so of it was largely car showrooms, industrial units, shops and other business premises, before it became more residential further out of town.

'Next petrol station on the left,' Iqbal said.

About two hundred metres ahead Henry could see a BP garage with a large, wide forecourt and a shop. 'What do you think?' he asked Bill.

'Pull up, go in?'

Bill drew the Galaxy on to the forecourt next to one of the pumps. Not an unusual sight as police vehicles are always filled up at local garages these days. A couple of other cars were at the pumps and there was a customer in the shop, browsing through the magazines.

A young Asian girl sat behind the counter.

'That her?' Henry asked.

Iqbal peered through the windscreen. 'My eyes aren't as good as they used to be, but yes.'

'OK. Mr Iqbal, you stay in the car. You and me go in, Bill.'

They strolled together across the forecourt and into the shop. A customer ahead of them moved away from the counter and left the shop as they stepped in. As they approached the counter, Henry saw her name badge: Najma Ismat.

A shadow crossed her face as she watched the two men come up to her, her eyes flicking from Bill's uniform to the battered face of Henry Christie.

Henry saw the family resemblance in Najma. She was less stunning than Sabera, but still very attractive, although her nose was quite hooked and her eyes were set deep and dark in her face.

Henry fished out his warrant card and leaned on the counter. 'Najma – I'm DCI Christie . . .' She immediately glanced round to the door behind her which led to a small office at the back of the shop.

'Yes?'

'Where is Mansur Rashid?'

'I don't . . . what?' she blubbered, flustered. 'Why would I know, and if I did, why should I tell you?' she barked defensively, pulling herself together quite quickly, giving Henry a haughty, arrogant look . . . because of which he decided to give it to her right between the eyes. The time for pussy-footing around had long since gone.

'Because he killed your sister, Sabera. That seems a pretty good reason to tell me.'

Najma winced as though Henry had applied an electric shock to her. She shook her head in denial. 'I don't know what you're talking about. Sabera's still alive, living down south somewhere.'

'When did you last hear from her?'

Behind the officers, another customer entered the shop. Henry spoke out of the side of his mouth to Bill, keeping his eyes on Najma. 'Get him out and lock the door.'

A car also pulled up at a pump on the forecourt and the driver unhooked the petrol nozzle. A buzzer beeped and a button started flashing on the control panel in front of Najma. She pressed it automatically and the man started filling his tank.

'A long time ago. Months,' she said.

'Does that not strike you as odd?'

'I fell out with her.' She was tight lipped.

Henry had come prepared. He took a folded, but slightly crumpled piece of paper out of his pocket, unfolded it and laid it out on the counter. It was a photograph of Sabera, showing her laughing, glowing whilst she sat in a Spanish restaurant.

'A day after this, she was dead,' he said brutally. 'That was six months ago. She's only just been identified.'

Najma's face sagged.

The customer who had filled his car up was now at the shop door. Bill, who had nudged the other customer out of the shop and locked the door, mee-mawed at him to wait. There was a bit of a queue building up.

'Mansur said he'd spoken to her recently.'

'Mansur's lying. He found her, abducted her, murdered her,' Henry said, not one bit liking what he was doing.

'No . . . you're wrong. I know he hired a private investigator to trace her, but he said he'd spoken to her and . . . and . . .' Her voice trailed off into the ether.

Najma sat back on the stool behind her, stunned.

'Where is he?' Henry said slowly. 'If you know, you must tell me, if only for your sister's sake.' He was praying that she didn't react so badly to the news that she became hysterical and impossible to handle.

Another car drew on to the forecourt. The buzzer on the control panel sounded as the driver removed the nozzle from the pump. 'Listen, we don't have a lot of time and I need to find Mansur rapidly. If you know where he is, tell me.'

'Boss,' Bill called from across the shop, 'the package is preparing to move from venue one,' he said, referring to Condoleezza Rice.

Henry nodded, but did not turn. His eyes bore into Najma.

'Boss,' Bill called again. Henry looked round this time and Bill pointed out of the shop door. He saw that Iqbal had got out of the ARV and was now at the shop door.

'Keep him out.' He twisted back to Najma. 'Where is he?'

Najma glared up at him, sheer bloody defiance in her eyes. She stood up and spat at him. 'You are lying. I need to tell you nothing.'

Henry wiped the spittle from his sore face, beginning to simmer. Not much more and he'd be at boiling point, but he kept himself under control.

'He killed your sister, strangled her, beat her, drowned her and burned her body and he's also got his hooks into you, hasn't he . . . if you need protection, then I'll give it, but tell me where he is now!'

Suddenly Iqbal emerged from the office behind the counter, having found his way into the shop via the rear door. He had overheard Henry's last few lines to Najma and his face was contorted with rage and grief.

'Granddad!' Najma exclaimed on seeing him.

'Najma – tell this man everything he needs to know, you foolish girl.'

'But he's lying . . . can't you see he's lying? They all lie. They hate us.'

Iqbal's open hand came from nowhere as he cracked her across the face and sent her crashing against the cigarette shelves next to her shoulder. 'This man does not lie,' he screamed. 'Mansur is evil. You have come under his spell. You must speak or more people will die.' He raised his hand. She cowered.

'Iqbal – no,' Henry said, leaning across the counter and gently taking the old man's arm.

'Sometimes it is the only way.'

'Maybe, maybe.' Henry looked at Najma, who was down on her haunches in the narrow space behind the counter. To her he said, 'He killed Sabera and today he's going to kill again and I want to stop him before he does.'

Najma's frightened eyes darted from Henry to Iqbal and back again. Iqbal still had his hand hovering for the follow-up slap.

'I don't know where he is,' she said simply, totally deflated as tears welled up and cascaded over her face, 'but I know what he plans to do.'

Henry turned to Bill. 'Tell them all to clear off' – he gestured with his hand at the confused customers on the forecourt – 'the garage is closed and they've just had a free fill-up.'

The office behind the counter was tiny, just big enough for a small computer workstation and a couple of chairs. Najma sat at the desk sobbing into a piece of kitchen roll. Iqbal sat on the other chair, staring angrily at her, his arms folded, whilst

Henry perched on the corner of the workstation and Bill filled the door with his bulk. The petrol pumps had been turned off from the main switch behind the counter and the shop door had been locked.

Henry was speaking softly. 'I'm sorry about Sabera. I know you were close.'

'How could you know?' she demanded through her tears.

'I'm a detective. It's my job to find out things about people.'

'He promised he would never hurt her for what she did.'

'You are a fool, child,' Iqbal sneered, still fighting back the urge to slap her again.

Henry held up a placatory hand. One slap had been quite enough, thank you. Her face was a livid red from the blow, almost glowing.

'Are you in a relationship with him?' Henry probed.

Najma's head rose, her face distorted cruelly from the anguish. 'Not one you mean,' she said disgustedly. 'I am a good Muslim girl. We don't think about sex all the time, like you westerners . . .'

'You were bloody well born in this country, you fool!' Iqbal snarled. 'Your mother was born here, too – and your father. You are a westerner.'

She regarded him coldly. 'Mansur and I are joined together in our fight against people like you – and you,' she turned to Henry. 'I have been assisting him to prepare for this day, a great day for Islam . . . but he promised me Sabera was fine.'

'How have you helped?' Henry asked urgently.

'By recruiting a martyr.' She bit her lip and held up her chin. 'Someone proud to die for Islam.'

'One God whose name is Allah,' Henry said scathingly – and Iqbal exploded and smashed her hard across the face.

And that martyr was a young man by the name of Abdul Hussein, who had been a regular attendee at the mosque frequented by Mansur, Najma went on to tell Henry. He had shown great promise and great faith, rejecting the poisoned ways of the west and declaring himself a foot soldier of Allah. There were many like him attending the mosques, but because there had been so much negative publicity about the role of mosques in brainwashing idealistic young people, the process of turning someone from a person with high ideals into a potential mass murderer had to be done with more subtlety, away from the place of worship, in the terraced houses of Blackburn or Accrington – which is where Rashid came in. He targeted promising individuals, moulded them, fired them up, ensured they were trained and ready to give their lives for the cause, ably assisted by Najma Ismat, and provided the premises which could be used for such long-term aims.

Abdul Hussein had been groomed for two years and suddenly, at the peak of his fanaticism, he had found himself in the right place at the right time, because as well as being a follower of Islam, he was also a fanatical follower of Blackburn Rovers.

During the week he worked in the souvenir shop at Ewood Park and on match days he donned a steward's hi-viz jacket so he could direct people and get paid for watching the match.

When the visit of the American Secretary of State was announced, it became common knowledge within the Rovers' camp that she would call on them together with Jack Straw, the local MP and Foreign Secretary, who was an avid Rovers fan.

And Mansur could not believe his good fortune.

He already had someone in place, someone who the police could 'vet' for ever and find nothing untoward.

With one explosion, the British Foreign Secretary and the American Secretary of State would be destroyed.

And Mohammed Ibrahim Akbar would assist with the final preparations for this triumphal event, giving it the whole-hearted blessing of the Al-Qaeda leadership.

They were in the ARV, Henry and Bill upfront, Iqbal and Najma in the back, their identities protected by the smoked glass windows.

'I don't know the details,' she screamed. 'I only know it will happen at Ewood Park.'

Bill accelerated down Preston Old Road and did a skidding left through a red light into Spring Lane, blue-lighting it through an area called Mill Hill, towards the football ground.

Henry was twisted in his seat, chucking relentless quick-fire questions at her.

'Come on, you must . . . how are they going to do it?'

'I think Rice will meet the staff and Abdul will be wearing a bomb underneath his yellow jacket. When he shakes hands with her . . .'

'How has he got the explosives into the ground?' Henry's voice went quiet at the end of the question, because he could answer it himself: Abdul Hussein worked at Ewood Park. He would have already secreted the explosives and detonator somewhere in the ground. Someone like him who had worked there for some time would know all the best hidey-holes and all he would need to do today would be to go into work as normal, go through all the police searches, kill time and at the last possible moment grab the explosives, line up, shake hands, smile, hope his courage didn't desert him – then boom!

Two dead politicians, lots of dead dignitaries, cops and colleagues. And probably a big hole in the pitch.

'How come you're not directly involved in this today?'

'I have orders just to have a normal day.'

Bill flicked on the two tones as he overtook on Hollin Bridge Street, then cut back before having a head-on with an oncoming car. He bore left into Hamilton Street, under the aqueduct, reaching the junction with Bolton Road, and Ewood Park came in sight.

He slowed and eased through the busy lights and a few moments later braked sharply on the car park behind the Darwen End stand – where he and Henry had paused earlier – near to the entrance to the police cells.

Henry organized his thoughts, remembering what he had read in the operational order. 'Right – all staff entering the ground are required to sign in, produce ID, and they all enter through the staff door on Nuttall Street round the front. Let's go and see if Hussein has landed today.'

He looked at Bill.

'You want me to drive round the front? I've just driven past that entrance.'

'Yes.'

He raised his eyebrows, did a quick spin-reverse, driving out of the car park and pulling up amongst the multitude of no-parking cones which had been placed all the way along Nuttall Street. They were immediately swooped upon by a young patrolling constable.

Bill wound his window down.

'Sorry, you can't park here, ARV or otherwise. Nothing's allowed on here today.'

Henry jumped out and flashed his ID. 'Yes we can,' he said, almost adding 'son', but refraining from being too patronizing. The constable peered at the warrant card and shrugged.

'Makes no difference, sir.'

'Makes every difference.' Henry strutted past him and went to the staff entrance, ID still in hand, where he was greeted by a uniformed private security guard in a booth by a turnstile. He was aware that behind him, the PC was having heated words with Bill in the ARV. 'You checking in staff this morning?' Henry said.

'Uh-huh.'

'Is Abdul Hussein on your list?'

He ran a thick finger down a typed list. 'Yep.'

Henry loved laconic people. 'Has he shown up for work this morning?'

'Yep.'

'How long ago?'

'Uh – ten minutes.'

'You've been a great help.'

'Ta, mate.'

He spun away from the booth and crossed back to Bill who was just staring blank-faced at the foot patrol PC, who was only doing his job by trying to get the vehicle to move on. Henry tapped him on the shoulder, smiled at him and said to Bill, 'He's in,' then to the PC said, 'Get the venue commander down here, please – now.'

Henry's heart sank to depths never before experienced when he saw the hastily summoned venue commander walking along Nuttall Street. It was often the case that headquarters wallers with career aspirations grasped at opportunities out in the real world of policing to show that they could still do the job and enhance their CVs. Henry didn't even know what a CV looked like, but he suspected that the venue commander for the day did. His name was Andy Laker and his day job was the chief constable's staff officer.

Laker's expression was one of sheer annoyance. 'This better be good, Henry. I'm expecting the Foreign Secretary and the

American Secretary of State to arrive any time now,' he said
imperiously, as though they were coming to see him.

Henry had no wish to get embroiled in any discussions with
Laker, so he got straight to the point.

'You've got a suicide bomber in the ground – how does
that grab your balls?'

The CCTV control room was situated slap-bang in the centre
of the Darwen End terrace. A huge picture window overlooked
the pitch and the three other stands and Henry took a moment
to appreciate the view. The pitch looked excellent. He knew
it was one of the best in the league.

Then he turned back to the room and the bank of monitors
along one wall hurriedly being switched on by a technician.
Coloured images came on to the screens one by one, giving
myriad views from the many cameras dotted around the
ground, inside and out.

The souvenir shop had already been checked for Hussein,
but he wasn't there and none of the other staff knew where
he'd disappeared to.

'Let's see if we can spot this guy,' Henry said. He jerked
his head to Najma, standing in one corner of the room with
Iqbal. She came to stand next to Henry, her arms folded tightly
across her chest. 'Start looking,' he said sternly to her. 'If you
spot him, yell.'

The CCTV room door burst open and FB rolled in, accompanied by Dave Anger and a harassed looking Andy Laker.

'I gather things have moved on a-pace, Henry,' FB said and
patted him on the back.

'Yeah – and I haven't had to torture anyone yet.'

Najma was sitting next to the CCTV operator, looking at the
monitors.

FB, Dave Anger and Andy Laker were silent, standing next
to Henry. Their combined tension was palpable. Iqbal sat in
a chair behind them. Bill came back into the room, having
been out to the ARV following the authorization to arm himself
overtly. He had his Glock holstered at his side and a Heckler
and Kock MP5 machine pistol slung across his chest. He
sported a chequered baseball cap. He looked pretty cool, even
though he was weighed down by all his equipment, which

also included a Taser gun, CS gas, rigid handcuffs and his expandable baton.

Henry glanced at him and nodded.

'Najma – seen him yet?' Henry asked her. She looked drawn and exhausted, her eyes red raw, face a mess. 'Is it really true about Sabera?' she whispered.

'Sorry.'

She seemed to slump inside herself for a moment. Henry thought she was going to collapse and topple off her chair and half-moved to catch her. 'I can't see him,' she said hopelessly.

Henry turned to FB. 'Cancel this part of the visit,' he said.

FB shook his head. 'She's on her way, Henry, and nothing will stop her from coming here. She's already had to do a lot of chopping and changing and she won't do any more.'

Then Najma suddenly shouted, 'That's him!'

Everyone rushed to look over her shoulder at the screen.

It showed one of the internal concourses under one of the stands, a wide concrete area on which there were toilets and on match days bars and counters selling beer and pies, the staple diet of football fans. Now the shuttered screens were locked down. And it was deserted other than for one person walking slowly along.

'That's Abdul,' she confirmed as the camera zoomed in on him. He was a small, thin youth, wearing a hi-viz steward's jacket.

'Where is that?' Henry demanded of the CCTV operator, just as Abdul stopped, looked cautiously around, then directly into the lens of the camera which he had no reason to suspect was recording his movements. He inserted a key into a door, opened it and stepped inside, out of sight. 'Where is it?'

The operator pointed down at the floor. 'Here! Right below us. It's the Darwen End concourse . . . it's a store room . . . he's right underneath us.'

'He must have hidden the explosives in there.' Henry turned urgently to FB and the two other men. 'Stay here and make sure she doesn't disappear.' He pointed at Najma. 'Bill – you up for this?'

Bill nodded and gripped the HK firmly. 'It's what I live for,' he said, tongue in cheek.

'Gimme the Glock,' Henry said. Both men looked towards

the chief constable for the nod, which he gave immediately. Bill handed Henry the pistol.

Henry tore out of the CCTV room, followed by Bill. They sprinted down the corridor, then twisted left into a stairway which doglegged down on to the concourse below. They turned left off the bottom step and ran down the deserted concourse towards the door Hussein had entered. Ten metres before they reached it, he backed out, not noticing them initially.

Henry and Bill came to a sudden halt, side by side. Bill had instantly adopted the classic firing position for the HK: butt pulled into his right shoulder, left foot forward, left knee slightly bent, his right eye sighted down the short barrel. He did not flinch.

Henry dropped into a combat stance, feet shoulder width apart, the Glock in his right hand, supported by the left, safety off, right finger tip resting on the trigger.

Both guns were aimed at Hussein's head.

He saw them, went rigid.

Henry's eyes quickly took him in and could see something between the gap in his jacket around his waist, about the size of a paperback book. Was it a belt of explosives, strapped around him?

'Abdul Hussein,' Henry said. The young man blinked on hearing his name. 'Yes, I know who you are . . . please raise your hands – slowly – or we will shoot you.'

He did as instructed. But his right hand remained clenched in a fist and Henry saw something black, like a pen, poking out from his grasp and also a thin wire running down his sleeve.

A switch connected to a detonator.

His thumb hovered over it.

All he had to do was press.

This time Henry knew it would be connected.

'It's over, Abdul,' Henry said. 'There is no need for this, no need at all.' Henry offered his left hand in a gesture to him to surrender and took a careful step towards him, but kept the Glock aimed.

'*No!*' screamed Hussein, jerking as though an electrical shock had been passed through him. His thumb quivered. 'You don't understand. I have lived my life for this day.'

'Now you cannot achieve your aim,' Henry said. Inside he

had turned to jelly, terrified of the position he was now in. 'This doesn't have to be, Abdul. You know the Quran's teaching is about the brotherhood of mankind,' he went on, desperately digging up some of the stuff he'd been taught on his wonderful Race and Diversity course, 'and you will not enter paradise if you injure your neighbour.'

'You dare preach the Quran to me?' Hussein demanded.

Henry brought his left hand back under his right. 'Abdul . . . it's over . . . if your thumb moves again, you will be shot dead . . . come on, man, this is not worth it . . . both of us will blast you.'

Hussein slowly uncurled his fingers to reveal the switch, which he allowed to fall out of his grip and hang there on the wire, and he descended slowly to his knees, with both weapons covering him all the time, ready to kill if necessary. Henry saw all the fire and determination leave the young man like a relieved ghost.

The radio blared at that moment and announced the arrival of the security escort at the front of the football ground.

The package had arrived safely.

Nineteen

He was at home now, staring blankly into space. Kate sat next to him on the settee in a silk dressing gown. The TV was on, showing the rolling news on BBC 24; images of the smiling American Secretary of State visiting Blackburn accompanied by Jack Straw, the Foreign Secretary. The sound was off. Henry's eyes focused momentarily on the screen, but then his thoughts meandered again. Confused, self-pitying, desperately blaming himself for the deaths of two innocent cops. What an absolute fool he had been, firstly to even think that members of the Special Projects team were anything like capable of being a murder squad, and secondly to allow Angela and Graeme to go and arrest Rashid. He should have insisted that they waited for him.

He groaned as he massaged his eyes tenderly. His face throbbed like a jackhammer.

Kate squeezed his leg, looking worriedly at him. He had told her all the details of the day with the exception of his visit to Karl Donaldson's torture chamber and she had listened with a growing horror and sympathy.

On his way home he had managed to call in at Blackpool Victoria Hospital's A&E department where they had confirmed his cheekbone was fractured and that nothing could be done with it, other than to allow it to heal naturally. His hand wound had been clipped and bandaged. Everything else, bar the inner emotional turmoil, was superficial.

He was on his third JD on ice within an hour.

'Henry?' Kate said apprehensively.

He looked sideways at her through his good eye. He could tell she was actually asking how he was feeling. He patted her arm. 'I'm OK,' he lied easily, picking up the JD from the coffee table and taking a sip. 'Honestly,' he assured her. He snaked his arm around her slim shoulders and pulled her close.

'Bed yet?' she asked.

His eyes flickered to the mantelpiece clock. Just gone midnight. 'Nah, couldn't sleep even if I wanted to. You go if you want.'

'I'll stay up with you, love.'

Henry gave her a peck on the cheek, then finished his drink with one big swig. He held out his empty glass. 'Smidgen more?' he pleaded.

She gave him a mock-withering look and took the glass. Before going into the kitchen, she paused directly in front of him. 'You *can* talk to me, you know?'

He nodded, aware he would never do so completely. It wasn't in his nature. She raised her eyes and shook her head, accepting that to be the case, then went out. He leaned back into the big comfortable settee and closed his eyes. He was drained, yet his mind kept revolving, constantly reviewing the day and not enjoying the experience at all, not one second of it. The late arrival back into Preston. The realization that two cops had gone missing. The desperate fight in the hallway with Ali. Karl Donaldson arriving on the scene. The dead bodies. 'Little Guantanamo Bay', as he had named Donaldson's industrial unit. Sabera's parents.

Najma and Iqbal and the race to uncover the plot to kill
Rice. Suddenly his mind jumped ahead to his retirement
day and he began loosely calculating how many working
days he had left . . .

Kate reappeared and handed him the refreshed JD, which
tinkled with ice.

'Just a little one,' she said, edging past him. She was about
to sit down when the front doorbell rang. She shot him a
puzzled look. 'Who can that be?'

He shrugged noncommittally, not in the least surprised there
was someone at his door at 12.10 a.m. Not today, anyway.

'I'll go.' He placed the JD on the coffee table and Kate
helped him creak to his feet.

FB and another man Henry did not immediately recognize
stood there in the chill morning. The three men eyed each
other, then FB banged his palms together and said, 'Are you
inviting us in? We need to talk.'

Henry stood aside to allow his late-night visitors into the
living room. Kate hovered there nervously, her dressing gown
wrapped tightly around her, looking suspiciously at the two
interlopers, even though she knew FB.

'Kate,' FB said. 'How are you?'

'Fine thanks,' she said stiffly.

Henry shuffled in behind them, slightly creased by a pain
across his back which had come from nowhere.

There was an uncomfortable silence, broken by FB. 'Like
I said, Henry, we need to talk.' He eyed Kate, hoping she took
the hint.

'We can go into the conservatory,' Henry suggested.

'No, no, you stay in here. It'll be cold in there and I was
about to go to bed anyway,' Kate said. 'But can I get you a
drink first?'

FB had noticed the whisky glass. Hopefully, he said, 'A
little tot of something like that will do nicely.'

'OK – and yourself?' she asked the other visitor.

'That would be lovely,' he said.

Kate retreated to the kitchen and poured out two generous
measures, with ice, of Sainsbury's own brand cheapo whisky
which she and Henry referred to as 'firewater'. There was no
way FB was getting any of the decent stuff. She came in and
found the men seated, Henry in the centre of the settee, the

other two in the armchairs either side. The TV was off. She
handed them their drinks and said goodnight, catching Henry's
eye with a concerned expression as she went out.

FB sipped his whisky and winced slightly, waiting for Kate's
footsteps to reach the top of the stairs before opening his
mouth.

'Henry, this is . . .' he began to introduce the man he had
brought along.

'We've met,' Henry said, having now placed him. 'Martin
Beckham, Home Office?'

The man nodded. Henry had met him briefly on the morning
he had been called into FB's office following the dawn raid
on the house in Accrington. Beckham had been the one at the
conference table Henry had stereotyped as a pinstriped
commuter. He had remained pretty silent throughout the
debrief; yet Henry had also surmised that Beckham was probably the one running the show.

Henry sat back nursing his JD, waited.

FB coughed nervously and took another sip of his drink.
'Firewater, this,' he commented, holding up the glass and
inspecting the pale, straw-coloured liquid. 'First of all, both
the Foreign Secretary and the American Secretary of State
have been apprised of the situation and the events that took
place today; they send you their heartfelt thanks for the job
you did.'

'Do I get a commendation?'

FB ignored the flippancy. 'And from me, too. Well done,
H, you did an excellent job. Bet you never thought you'd end
up confronting a terrorist when you got out of bed this
morning.'

'And from me,' Beckham said. 'Very well done.'

'OK, thanks . . . and?' he enquired suspiciously. 'It's just
that I can't even begin to imagine you've come knocking on
my door at this time of day to congratulate me . . . maybe it
was something to do with the fact I was quickly surrounded
by spooks and hustled off the job and told I wasn't needed,
keep gob shut and go and take some gardening leave . . . call
me a cynic.' His temper had started to flare.

FB acceded the points with a gracious tilt of the head.
'Whatever . . . but we do mean what we said. You did a fantastic
job today, it's just that there's some teeny-weeny details' – he

held his thumb and forefinger together to illustrate the point
– 'that we need to make clear to you.'

'Just tell me,' Henry said, his mouth turning down at the
corners with distaste.

Beckham leaned forwards, elbows on knees, glass gripped
between his palms. 'Through no fault of yours, two officers
who believed they were investigating a domestic murder, and
then you yourself, stumbled into an Islamic terrorist plot. Those
two officers paid with their lives and you almost paid with
yours, and would have done if not for the intervention of a
sharp-witted American agent who saved your life.'

'Granted,' Henry said.

'Since we last saw you, as you can imagine there have been
numerous meetings in order to decide the correct way ahead
for all concerned, and this is how it will all play out.'

'Why do I feel suddenly even more uncomfortable?'

Beckham went on, 'As regards Mansur Rashid, he will be
circulated as wanted for the murder of your two colleagues,
and on suspicion of murdering his wife and that private investigator, Daley—'

FB cut in there. 'We found Daley's computer and mobile
phone in the house in Balaclava Street and a firearm which
is currently being examined, but could well be the one Daley
was killed with. We've also started raiding his business premises and found credit-card cloning machines in them, so it
looks like he's been defrauding his customers to gather funds
for AQ. Also in one of his garages there is evidence of combus-
tion, which could be where he killed his wife. Forensics will
tell in due course. You uncovered a very bad man, Henry.'

Henry sat there, glum, feeling it was all being taken away
from him, despite the accolades.

'We are not going to make any public reference to his
involvement in the plot to kill the Secretary of State, however,'
Beckham said. Henry didn't even bother to ask why, because
he would not be told. It was just because it was the way they
wanted to run it. The Home Office man continued, 'And neither
will any reference be made to Akbar. Incidentally, there is a
treasure trove of "stuff", shall we say, in the house in Balaclava
Street which is very, very useful to the security services.'

'I'm so happy,' Henry said.

'Wind your neck in, Henry,' FB growled.

Henry gave a pissed-off shrug. 'Does it mean that Akbar escapes justice? I mean, he must've had a hand in killing Angela and Graeme, surely?'

'You're probably right, Henry: he won't be brought to justice in the way you're thinking . . . but somewhere along the line, justice will be done, if you know what I mean?'

'I'm not sure I want to know . . . anyway, at least Fazul Ali is in custody. If nothing else, he can be linked to their murders, can't he?'

The two visitors exchanged a strange glance Henry was unable to interpret.

'Actually, he's off the radar now,' Beckham said.

'You mean he's now an informant? So the torture worked?'

'If you like,' Beckham said, obviously unwilling to expand.

'Anyway, the arrest of Hussein at Ewood Park will simply be put down to good policing and will be a stand-alone thing. He will be described as a lone chancer with some vague AQ connections, but that's all.' Beckham finished, 'So that's how it stands.'

'But—' Henry started to protest.

'No buts, Henry. This is rather like one of those newspaper competitions where the editor's word is final and no correspondence will be entered into,' FB said.

'Don't tell me – we're at war.'

FB smiled triumphantly. 'By Jove, I think he's got it.'

'So are Rashid and Akbar out there together?'

'It's an assumption we can make,' Beckham said, 'but it'll be interesting to see how long Rashid will be there, because, even though he is obviously a low-level financier of terrorism, he's blown and may not be of much use to Akbar any more . . . we shall see.'

'And no doubt if he does turn up, I won't get a shout because it's the spooks who'll want him for what he knows and then they'll do a deal, and two good people will not get justice. Nor will Eddie Daley or Sabera Rashid, I suspect.' Henry reached for his JD and swigged it down. 'I need another.' He went into the kitchen and poured himself a large one.

When he returned, FB and Beckham had gone, their empty glasses the only evidence they had even been there.

Henry sat down and took a drink.

It was going to be a long night.

Twenty

Six months later

He had the look of a hunted man, even though he was the hunter. He now sported a full, unkempt beard and his eyes stared out like a beast from the jungle, for ever watching and checking. He was truly exhausted and was beginning to doubt whether he could maintain the pace, despite his innate fitness and personal determination.

Maybe it was time to give up, hand the mantle over to someone new.

Except that he wouldn't. It would be tantamount to admitting defeat and he would see this thing through to the bitter end, whatever the toll on himself. After all, he had pleaded – *begged* – for this chance and been given it and, mentally drained and exhausted as he was, it would reach its conclusion.

He rubbed his tired eyes and replaced his sunglasses, watching the hordes of people swarming by in the intense morning sunlight already baking the streets.

Hell, this place was busy. He didn't think he had seen anywhere more so; even New York paled by comparison.

Karl Donaldson, dressed in loafers, chinos and a Real Madrid soccer shirt, sat outside the Café Zurich at the top of the first part of La Rambla, possibly the best-known thoroughfare in Barcelona. He pulled the peak of his baseball cap down over his hawk-like eyes and slouched down in the metal-framed chair, wondering if today would be the one.

La Rambla stretches one mile from the Placa Catalunya, where Donaldson was sitting, down to the Rambla de Santa Monica, and is a massive tourist attraction with its souvenir shops and stalls, human statues, fortune-tellers, card sharps, puppeteers, dancers and musicians. It draws thousands of visitors each day, who pulsate up and down in a swell of humanity.

Ordinarily, Donaldson would have loved this. He had been to Barcelona a couple of times with his wife, Karen, and fallen in love with its vibrancy, its food, its wine, history and people. But this was no romantic break . . . he scowled at the thought of his wife; not at her – he loved her deeply – but because he had neglected her so much over the last six months – had not even spent two consecutive nights with her in the last three – and she was becoming edgy and worried about him and their marriage. He had made and broken several promises to her recently and their whole relationship was straining at the seams.

He resolved that if nothing came of today, he would take a week off, sweep her off her feet and get back into her good books . . . until he set off again doing something he could not even tell her about – hunting down the dangerous, elusive, Mohammed Ibrahim Akbar.

After Donaldson and everyone else had missed him in Blackburn, a special multi-agency team had been quickly assembled, dedicated to tracking down Akbar. Donaldson had almost got down on his knees to get a place on it, then had become totally obsessed with Akbar, who seemed to have a sixth sense when it came to avoiding the clutches of Donaldson's team.

Akbar's will-o'-the-wisp trail had led Donaldson and the small team to the Middle East, Africa and across all of Europe and finally, it was hoped, here to Barcelona. It was known that he had been fund-raising on behalf of AQ and the intelligence suggested he was supposed to be meeting a man in Barcelona who took a cut from the African street traders who pitched illegally on the waterfront, selling wares such as fake designer sunglasses, watches and clothing, then passed a generous percentage of that on to Al-Qaeda.

The man, of North African origin, went by the name of Suleiman, was known to the Spanish intelligence service and had been under the surveillance of Donaldson's team for six days, but Akbar had not shown. It looked increasingly likely that the intel was incorrect – what a surprise – and Donaldson would have to wait again for another snippet which would get him back on Akbar's scent.

Donaldson felt like a greyhound chasing a rabbit that was always out of his reach and was inexhaustible.

He shifted uncomfortably in the chair as a trickle of sweat rolled down his back into the crack of his backside. He took a sip of his mineral water. The ice had melted and the water was lukewarm . . . rather like Akbar's trail.

'Suleiman's on the move,' a tinny voice said and Donaldson resisted the urge to touch the minute earpiece fitted into his left ear, just in case he was being watched. One mistake followers often make, even though it is drummed into them in training, is succumbing to that instinctive desire to press their almost invisible earpieces so they can hear better, especially in a crowd. It's one of those silly mistakes that can completely wreck an operation and put individuals in unnecessary danger. The voice was from one of his fellow team members who had been sitting on Suleiman's apartment on the Calle Comtel in the Old City. 'Heading towards La Rambla,' said Jo, the only female operative on the team. She was a CIA agent. 'Looks like he's going for his usual,' she said. This meant that Suleiman was going to stroll down La Rambla as he did each morning, constantly checking to see if he was being followed, then take a seat in a pavement café near to the Maritime Museum where he drank copious amounts of coffee into which he dunked donuts. From there he would conduct his morning's business. As yet he hadn't clocked the team, which probably meant whilst he was going through anti-surveillance motions, he was getting lazy about it. The team was also very good, but not good enough, or big enough, not to get spotted eventually.

Unless Suleiman had actually seen them and was playing a game . . . always a possibility.

Donaldson settled back. His job was static observation that morning.

He ordered a *café con leche*, thinking about how he and his family had actually drank here in the past . . . then his mind flicked to Henry Christie and the reaction he'd had to the way Fazul Ali had been treated. Henry would be even more upset to learn that Ali had died whilst being interrogated and had had to be disposed of. It hadn't happened whilst Donaldson had been talking to him, but as a result of a bad reaction to some drugs that Dr Chambers was testing out which had given him a heart attack. Donaldson shrugged mentally, not even remotely moved by the thought of Ali's death, since he was just as bad as Akbar. What bothered him was his own relationship with Henry and how it might be revived – or was it just to be another casualty of this war?

'Moving down La Rambla,' Jo piped up, describing Suleiman's movements.

Perhaps he would try and speak to Henry once this Akbar thing was over . . . but he would not apologize. No way . . .

'Seems to be the same old routine,' Jo said.

Donaldson closed his eyes briefly – but not for long. His coffee came and he paid the waiter immediately, just in case he had to move quickly. There was nothing more embarrassing for someone on surveillance than being chased by a bill-wielding waiter demanding payment. It drew attention. Thinking back to Henry also made Donaldson speculate about Mansur Rashid, who in some respects was similar to Suleiman: a legit businessman on the face of it, but providing funds for AQ at the same time. Rashid had completely gone off the radar since Blackburn and rumour was that Akbar had seen him as a liability, someone who couldn't control his temper, who allowed his emotions to get the better of him – firstly by killing his wayward wife and then the private investigator he had been stupid enough to hire who then got in a position from which he could blackmail Rashid. Akbar had no place for people like that and it was believed that Rashid had been murdered somewhere in Pakistan. Whether that was true or not, no one knew, but Rashid had never appeared on the intelligence radar since that fateful day in Blackburn.

'He's taking his time today . . . a lot of a/s activity,' Jo said, meaning anti-surveillance.

Donaldson sat up. Suleiman was being extra careful today for some reason. The hairs on the back of his muscular neck prickled. No more closing of eyes, no more daydreaming, he told himself.

Jo and Jed were on Suleiman.

Terry and Marcus were somewhere behind them.

Barney, the team leader, was sitting at the café Suleiman was expected to visit.

Two others were on a free reign – Wayne and Harry.

And he was sitting here.

Maybe today, he thought.

'He's turned around, nearly made me,' Jo said shortly. 'He's on Ferran now.' For ease, the team had dispensed with using the Spanish word *calle*, meaning street. 'Travelling quite quickly, carrying a black briefcase.'

The other members of the team acknowledged this change of habit.

Despite the urge to join in, Donaldson remained at the café. His hand dithered excitedly when he drank from his coffee.

'Now left up Banys Nous,' Jo related.

The followers slotted in behind him and though he used several quick manoeuvres, they stuck with him, were not seen, following him through the narrow streets until he turned into a restaurant on Calle Montsio called Els Quatre Gats, making Donaldson raise his eyebrows. He knew the place, had been there with Karen, drawn by the fact it was once a popular hangout for artists such as Picasso. It was a beautiful old building, circa 1897, an ideal place to meet someone for a coffee.

'He's sat at a table just inside the door,' Jo said, 'and he's ordered.'

Perhaps he was just having a change of scenery, Donaldson thought, glancing across in the direction of the huge department store on the other side of the square, El Corte Ingles, then allowing his eyes to pull back, rove across the crowds, examining individual faces, then settle on the front door of the Hard Rock Café diagonally opposite to where he was positioned.

And there he was.

Emerging from the front door. Wearing a baggy Green Day T-shirt and dark glasses.

Mohammed Ibrahim Akbar. The man who had murdered hundreds of people across the globe, who had recruited young men and women to blow themselves and others to pieces, who raised and collected money for AQ . . . and who had killed two of Donaldson's closest friends amongst many other innocent people in Nairobi in 1998.

Donaldson recognized him immediately, a face etched on his mind for eternity.

Donaldson stood up as naturally as he could and walked to the pedestrian crossing which would take him across to the mouth of La Rambla, just as Akbar himself was swallowed up in the mass of bodies in that wide street.

Akbar was walking quickly, then stopped abruptly, ostensibly to admire one of the human statues dressed like a cowboy, painted silver. Donaldson swerved into a magazine stall just before Akbar's head swivelled round to check behind him. Through a gap in the side of the stall, Donaldson got a good look at him, confirming the ID and feeling his heart accelerate sickeningly.

A swell of adrenaline surged into the American's system as he said, 'I'm on Akbar,' into the minute mike fitted into the collar of his football shirt. He gave the location and described Akbar and his clothing.

'Confirm, confirm,' the voice of Barney said excitedly.

'Confirm.'

'OK – your call, Karl . . . how do you want to run it?'

He emerged from the stall as Akbar set off in the direction of the Monument a Colon at the end of La Rambla.

'He's edgy and careful . . . don't want him spooked.'

'Tell me,' Barney said.

'OK – Jo and Jed stay on Suleiman . . . Terry, Marcus to the bottom of La Rambla . . . You stay put, Barney, he's headed in your direction. Wayne, Harry to make to your location, too . . . I need to check if he's alone . . . he could have back-up.'

'You got it.' Barney asked if everyone understood.

And meantime Akbar walked down La Rambla, past the junction with Calle Ferran, the street Suleiman had walked up.

Behind him, Donaldson became acutely aware of two things . . . the Sig 9 mm pistol tucked into the waistband of his pants at his spine and the flick knife strapped to his right ankle. Both items seemed to burn holes into his bones.

Using his tradecraft, Donaldson kept both his quarry in sight and himself out of sight, constantly scanning to be certain that Akbar was alone, not being supported by a team, or being tailed by another intelligence service. He knew that Mossad were also after him.

He was pretty certain Akbar was alone. He was about to relay this information when, without warning, Akbar burst into a sprint and plunged headlong into Calle Escudellers in the Barri Gotic, Barcelona's superbly preserved medieval quarter.

'He's running, he must have made me,' Donaldson said, discarding all pretence of subtlety and racing after him.

The change in atmosphere and temperature was dramatic in the tight, shadowy streets of the gothic quarter, sending an instant chill through Donaldson.

As his big feet pounded into the ground, he was amazed that it always came down to this; despite all the technology in the world, the hunt for a fugitive always came down to a confrontation, whether it be in the mountains of Afghanistan or the backstreets of Boston; ultimately it was always a one-on-one.

Akbar skidded out of sight twenty metres ahead as he spun into Passatge Escudellers. Donaldson flung himself after him, feeling for his pistol as he ran, his fingers curling round the stock, but as he entered the passage, Akbar, wily as a fox, was already out of sight.

'Shit,' he uttered, but kept running hard, having to believe that he would catch and destroy him. There was nowhere the man could have disappeared to, must have gone down the next tight alleyway which connected to the street which ran parallel. 'Lost eyeball,' he panted down the radio.

Exclamations in several forms came back as replies.

'Still with you,' Barney said, meaning the deployment of the team was still down to Donaldson.

'Everyone keep going as instructed,' Donaldson said as he emerged on to a wide street which he powered across and into the continuation of the alley opposite, hoping he was still going in the right direction. But, running on from street to street, down likely looking alleys and losing his sense of direction, there was no sign of Akbar.

He had disappeared into the city.

Finally, Donaldson jarred to a halt and walked a few metres down another narrow alley and came into a deserted, brightly sun-lit square, not much bigger than a courtyard, which somehow seemed to have no shadow in it. His face was a contorted mask of anger and annoyance at himself. Akbar had been that far from him. Arm's length. He had nearly had him.

The disappointment was like a raging animal inside him. He stopped to catch his breath in the square, not exactly sure where he was. He squinted up at the high medieval stone walls surrounding him, narrow windows in them.

'Totally lost him,' Donaldson admitted into his radio, still gasping for air and now sweating heavily. 'He's gone, shit!' He punched the air in frustration.

'So where are you?' Barney asked into his ear.

'Where am I? Not a clue,' he said disgustedly.

'Agent Donaldson,' came a voice from behind him.

Suddenly all of the American's vital functions seemed to freeze up. He rotated slowly to see a man who had materialized from nowhere standing not ten feet away.

'Akbar,' Donaldson hissed.

He nodded, smiled.

'How the hell do you know me?' Donaldson asked.

'Know thine enemies – and their motivations,' he said. 'Though I wouldn't have known it was you except for a small mistake you made.'

'Which was?' Donaldson was judging how quickly he could cover the gap and draw his weapon.

'Who in this city pays for their drinks before they need to? A knowledge of culture is a vital tool in our armoury, wouldn't you say? Keeps us alive.'

Donaldson swallowed.

'Then I recognized you properly at the magazine stall.'

'In that case, if you know so much, you'll also know there's a team on your ass and they're all closing in now.'

'Following your directions?' Akbar smiled again, his perfect white teeth a testament to the dentistry of the western world. 'I think not. Either way, I know time is of the essence for both of us.' He raised his right hand in which was a small calibre pistol pointed easily at Donaldson's body mass. 'I'm afraid I'm a man who does not like to be pursued by fanatics and I will take every opportunity to dispose of them. You see, I know your motivation and it's best if you are dead.'

Just at that moment, from the eaves high above them, there was a loud cry and the mass beat of wings as a huge flock of pigeons took off.

Akbar's eyes glanced up for a split second.

Donaldson knew he could not make the distance between him and his prey, so he pitched himself to the side, rolling across the uneven paving, drawing the Sig from the small of his back – a manoeuvre he'd practised hundreds of times in training – and as he came up, the gun swung round and he fired twice – at exactly the instant Akbar fired at him.

The bullet from Akbar's small gun seared into Donaldson's

abdomen with a sickening jolt. A terrible pain splayed through him.

Gasping, tasting something horrendous in his mouth, he managed to clamber to his knees, woozily steeling himself to look at the wound just below the rib cage on his left side. He yanked up his blood-soaked shirt to inspect himself, but saw nothing positive. It looked bad – was bad, he knew.

Though his vision became suddenly blurred and he felt nauseous, he looked to where Akbar had been standing. Was he still there? Had Donaldson missed? Had he escaped again?

Crawling on hands and knees, leaving a trail of thick blood in his wake, Donaldson found Akbar, who had managed to stagger several feet away before falling in a crumpled heap.

Donaldson groaned in agony, coughed and spat out some blood as he tried to concentrate on looking at Akbar's body. He didn't appear to be moving, though his eyes were open and staring. His clothing was blood soaked. Donaldson had shot him twice, once in the chest, once in the neck.

But Donaldson wanted to be sure before he himself died.

Using the last ounces of his determination, fighting through the tsunami of weakness that was pervading his mind and body, he dragged himself to lie next to Akbar, placed the muzzle of the Sig, which weighed a ton, against the terrorist's temple, and pulled the trigger.

'Critical threat neutralized,' he said, before falling backwards and looking at the pigeons circling high above in the clear blue sky.